SUBMITTING TO HIM

FIRE AND ICE SERIES BOOK 1

T.L. CONRAD

To my Sir,

You are the heart behind this story. You are the breath i breathe. my yesterday, my today, and all my tomorrows. i love You.

~Your baby girl

NATALIE

I finished my last mid-term and was able to book an earlier flight back to Missouri. Spring Break is only one week, and I want to spend every second of it with Tommy. It's been hard being so far apart, but we're both living our dreams. I'm living in NYC and attending New York University, studying to become a therapist, while he's attending Mizzou on a football scholarship.

It wasn't easy getting here. My parents didn't want me to go to NYC. They felt the distance would put too much of a strain on Tommy and me, but we talk every night and see each other on our breaks. This trip home will be unforgettable. We've been dating since we were fifteen years old, and Tommy's finally hinting at proposing to me.

Between classes and working, I've never been able to see any of Tommy's games in person or visit him on campus. The plan is for him to pick me up tomorrow at the small airport in North-meadow. I can't wait to see his face when I surprise him at his dorm.

I've been so busy reading my bridal magazines I don't realize how much of the flight has passed until the fasten seat-belt light turns on and the announcement plays through the plane's overhead speakers announcing that we'll be landing shortly. I stuff the magazine into my bag and look out my window. My heart beats wildly, knowing this trip home is going to change my life. I'll be one step closer to becoming Mrs. Thomas Moore.

An hour later, I'm back on the ground and getting into the rental car. It's a short ride from the airport to Mizzou's campus.

Before too long, I'm pulling up in front of the Rotunda building. The campus is beautiful, but it's enormous. Although I know his dorm's name, I have no idea where it is, and I don't want to waste time driving around. A group of what appears to be students is walking down the sidewalk. I put the window down.

"Excuse me?"

"Do you need something?" one of the girls asks.

"Can you tell me where Center Hall is?"

She gives me directions to the far end of the campus. "You can't miss it. The big, red brick building in the middle."

"Thank you," I say and put the window back up.

I find the dorm easily and park in a visitor spot. My hands shake as I put the keys in my purse and make my way to the building.

When I get to the door, I try to pull it open, but it's locked. Putting my hand up to the glass, I can see inside. A few guys are sitting in a lounge area. I knock on the door, hoping to get their attention. It only takes a second for a big guy, no doubt a football player, to stand and come over to the door.

"You looking for someone?"

He towers over me, and I have to lift my head to see his face. "I'm looking for Tommy Moore."

"You are, are you?" He steps aside and lets me in as he yells over his shoulder. "Hey guys, she's here to see Tom."

The group laughs and whispers to each other.

"Is he here?"

"What's your name?" he asks.

"Natalie," I answer quietly, feeling a bit intimidated being the only girl here with a group of guys.

"I'm Mike. We're on the team together." He reaches out to shake my hand. "Are you his sister or something?"

"No, I'm his girlfriend."

Everyone stops what they're doing. The room goes silent. I know it's not a coed dorm, but I'm sure I'm not the first girl who's come by.

"I know his room number. Can you just point me to the steps?"

"Is he expecting you?" Mike asks.

"No." I smile. "We were supposed to meet at the airport tomorrow, but I got in early and came to surprise him."

He glances back to the group as if trying to decide what to do before turning back around and shrugging his shoulders. "Come on. I'll bring you up."

We walk down a hallway. Mike opens a door, then we enter the stairwell and begin the climb. Hearing a shuffle behind me, I look back and see the group that was sitting in the lounge is now following us up the stairs.

"Why are they coming?" I ask, motioning over my shoulder.

"Guess they want to see the big surprise too."

I was hoping this would be a private moment, but I'll go with the flow.

We arrive on the third floor and walk down a hallway. Doors are lining both sides, and bulletin boards hang on the walls announcing all the latest campus happenings. Finally, we stop outside Tommy's room. I find it odd that there's a tie draped over the doorknob.

"You sure about this?" Mike asks. "It's not too late to turn back."

The vibe I'm getting from these guys is bizarre. "I'm sure."

"Hey Scott, you have your key?"

"I don't think this is a good idea, Mike," a tall blond guy behind me says.

"Key." Mike puts out his hand.

Scott pushes his way through the group. "Move. I'll do it." He grabs the tie off the knob before he unlocks the door and pushes it open.

When I look in the room, the sight in front of me nearly brings me to my knees.

A blonde woman is on top of Tommy, urging him to fuck her harder.

"What the fuck?" Tommy yells and pushes her off him.

She turns around, not caring she's naked in front of a group of men. There's a smug smile on her face.

"Ash?" She and I just talked yesterday. She knew I was coming—knew I'd find them. "How could you?"

I spin around and see Mike and a few of the guys laughing and elbowing each other. Scott's standing in the doorway, clearly unamused by his roommate's behavior.

"I need to get out of here."

"Come on, sweetheart." Scott takes a final look in the room, throwing the tie on the floor. "You're an asshole, Moore."

He leads me back to the steps. I rush down to the main floor, needing to get as far away from Tommy as possible.

"I'm sorry you had to see that," Scott says.

The realization of what I just witnessed hits me, and tears fill my eyes. I squeeze them shut. I can't cry. Not here.

"How long have you two been dating?" Scott asks and shifts uncomfortably on his feet.

"Eight years."

"Damn." He looks shocked.

"Has she—" I stop myself for a second. Even though I already know the answer, I need to hear it anyway. "Has she been here before?"

Scott looks at me, his eyes uncertain, as if he's asking if I want him to answer. I nod my head. "Yeah, she's been coming to see him since he started here. He introduced her as—"

"Stop, please." It's too much. I can't stay and listen anymore. "I have to go." I push the door open and run to my car.

"You're in no shape to drive," Scott calls after me.

"I'll be fine." I look up and see Tommy coming out the door. I fumble through my purse, trying to find the keys.

"Natalie, wait," Tommy yells.

But I don't wait. I don't look back. I drive straight to the airport and book the next available flight back to New York City.

The flight is nothing more than a blur. It isn't until I hear the wheels screeching down on the runway that the repeating vision of Tommy with Ashlynn disappears, and I'm brought back to the present.

With the plane so full, disembarking takes forever. Then I find myself standing in the middle of JFK. People are all around, smiling and talking, going about their lives, but I'm alone— betrayed by my best friend and the man I was supposed to marry.

When I walk outside, a line of yellow taxis is waiting to transport people wherever they need to go. It will cost a small fortune, but I'm desperate to get back to my apartment.

I open the door of the nearest taxi and slide in the back seat. Immediately, I'm hit with the strong scent of incense.

The driver, an older Asian man, turns slightly in his seat. "Where do I take you, miss?"

I give him my address in the Village, and he types it into his GPS.

"You're crying. Are you okay?" His voice is kind.

"Not really." I sniffle.

The driver opens the glove compartment, grabs a small pack of tissues, and hands them to me. I guess I'm not the first passenger he's picked up in this state.

5

"My name's Shusuke," he says as he glances at me in the rear-view mirror. "I listen if you want talk."

"Thank you." I manage a small smile and wipe my eyes with a tissue.

The lights of the passing cars hypnotize me as I stare blankly out the window. After a few minutes, I pull my cell phone out of my bag and turn it on. There's a barrage of alerts from the missed calls and texts. My phone starts ringing. I see Tommy's name on the caller ID and send him to voicemail. He doesn't leave a message. The phone rings again. This time I answer.

"What do you want?"

"Please let me explain," Tommy says.

"How can you explain me finding you in bed with my best friend?"

"It was a mistake. It won't happen again."

"I know it won't happen again." I let out a sarcastic laugh. "Because we're over."

"Natalie, wait—"

I disconnect the call. The phone starts to ring again, but I'm not playing this game all night. Instead, I power off the phone and throw it back into my purse.

"That's who makes you cry?" Shusuke asks.

"Yes," I say softly. "It's my boyfriend—was my boyfriend." I take a deep breath. "I flew home early to surprise him, but instead, the surprise was on me." The fissure in my heart grows when I say the words out loud.

"You loved him. I can tell."

"We've been together for eight years. He told me he was proposing to me. I was supposed to marry him."

We ride in silence.

Shusuke's taking the Queensboro Bridges, not the typical way a cabbie would go, but I'm glad. This is my favorite way to enter the city. The view at night is something that will never grow old. As soon as we're on the other side, I feel as though we've crossed into safety and comfort—a place untainted by

Tommy. Thankfully, it's late, and there's not a lot of traffic. I just want to get home, crawl into bed, and pretend this night never happened.

The taxi pulls in front of my apartment, and I move to get out when Shusuke turns in his seat.

"Your heart is broken now. It is a blessing when the wrong person leaves your life." He gives me a kind smile. "Don't let hurt turn into anger. Tonight is start of a new journey. Now the right person can come."

"Thank you." I manage a smile in return.

I think about his words in the elevator up to my apartment. I'm sure he meant well, but I'm not taking a chance with my heart again.

NATALIE

I don't even know what time it is when I finally walk into the apartment I share with Svetlana. We met two years ago when we shared a dorm room on campus and became fast friends. When we started graduate school, her dad rented us an apartment in the Village.

The lights are off, so I try to be quiet. I don't want to wake Lana and end up explaining why I'm home early. Right now, I just want to sleep. Tomorrow will come soon enough.

Using the flashlight on my phone, I walk down the hallway to my bedroom. That's when I hear it. Lana's whimpering, begging someone to stop.

There's someone in her room, and she's in trouble. I dial 911.

"What's your emergency?" the dispatcher asks.

"There's someone in my apartment. My roommate's being attacked," I whisper into the phone and give them our address. Although they tell me to wait on the line, I disconnect the call, intending to stop the attack. I tiptoe closer to her door and take a deep breath before throwing it open.

Shining the light in the direction of her bed, I yell, "Stop! The police are on their way."

The man freezes, and Lana picks up her head. "Natalie?" she shrieks, "what are you doing home?"

The light from my cell phone isn't enough, so I flip on the overhead light. When I look over at Lana, I scream. She's naked and tied to the bed. A man I've never seen before is hurrying to pull on his pants. "You. Don't move," I yell at the man. He stops his pants at his knees and holds his hands up in surrender.

"Nat, this isn't what it looks like," she says and turns to the man. "Can you untie me?" He looks back and forth between us before quickly untying her.

Svetlana jumps out of bed. "I thought you were in Missouri," she says as she grabs her robe and puts it on. She walks over to me. "What are you doing back so soon?"

"Are you okay? Did he hurt you?" I look over Lana for injuries before glaring over her shoulder at the man who's now pulled his pants up.

There's pounding on the door. "NYPD, open up."

"Oh my God, you really called them." Lana's voice is panicked.

"Of course, I called them."

The police pound on the door again. "NYPD, open the door."

"Come with me." Lana grabs my arm. "We need to fix this."

She pulls me out of her room and into the living room. Lana makes quick work of the locks before opening the door.

"Good evening, officers," she says. "Please come in."

"We received a call of an assault in progress." The officer looks past me. "You, put your hands up and stay right where you are."

I turn, and it's only now I get a good look at the man. He's tall and very well-built. It's clear he spends a lot of time working out. His skin is creamy brown, but it's the color of his eyes that makes me pause. They're a deep gray like clouds before a storm, and right now, they're open wide from fear.

My body falls onto the couch from a mixture of exhaustion and confusion.

Lana and the officers are by the door talking. I can hear her voice, but I can't make out what she's saying. She turns and motions to the man, who cautiously makes his way across the room. Their conversation continues for a few minutes longer.

"Thank you and sorry for the confusion," Lana says and shakes the officers' hands before they turn and leave the apartment.

"Do you want me to stay?" the man asks Lana quietly. "I can help you explain."

"I don't think that's a good idea." She looks at me, concern on her face. "I'll call you in the morning."

"Okay, I'm going to call Alex, see if he's free to meet for a few drinks," he says and kisses her forehead before walking out the door.

Lana locks up and comes over to the couch, and sits next to me. "I don't know where to start," she says. When she turns to face me, the expression on her face changes. "You've been crying."

I'm overwhelmed, there are so many questions running through my head right now, but I manage a nod.

"What's wrong?" she asks. "Why are you home?"

"Tommy," I say. "What was going on back there?"

She looks down the hall before responding. "It wasn't what it looked like."

"Did he hurt you?"

"No," she says. "Not any more than I asked for." She giggles.

"What?" I'm so confused right now.

"I'm going to grab us a glass of wine. I think we're going to need it," Lana says before standing and going into the kitchen. "What happened with Tommy?" she asks as she gets the wine out and pours us each a glass.

I sit back on the couch. "I got to his dorm and found him in bed with Ashlynn."

She hands me a glass of red wine. "Ashlynn, as in your best friend?"

"The one and only." I take a big drink.

Lana sits down. "Wow."

"Right now, I'm more concerned about what was going on here." I motion around the room.

"I wasn't expecting you to be home." Lana takes a drink of her wine before setting it down on the table next to the couch. "What you saw wasn't what you thought. I mean, it was, but not like you think."

"You were tied up and begging him to stop." I pause for a second. "It looked like he was hurting you."

She puts her head back on one of the cushions and laughs. "Oh boy, I don't know where to start?"

"How about the beginning?"

"Have you ever heard of BDSM?" She blurts out the question, and I nearly choke on my wine.

"I've read about it in some romance novels. It's all that kinky sex and stuff." Once the words leave my mouth, the realization hits me. "Is that what was going on back there?" I set my wine glass down before I drop it.

"Yes," Lana says and slowly nods her head. "I grew up in the lifestyle. My father's a Dominant, and my mother is his submissive."

I don't know what I was expecting her to say, but that wasn't it. "You mean to tell me your dad goes all *Christian Grey* and ties your mom up in the bedroom?" It's a lame joke, but it's all I can manage at the moment.

"Ha, ha. You're so funny." She shakes her head and laughs. "That's not exactly how it is in real life. My father adores my mother and she him. Their relationship has always been an example of what I hope to find someday." She beams as she talks about them.

This is all a bit TMI. "Why would you want to know what your parents get up to in their bedroom?"

"Eww." Svetlana pretends to gag. "We didn't talk about any of *that* stuff. BDSM is about so much more than just kinky sex." Lana explains BDSM is lived outside the bedroom as well. The submissive, man or woman, takes care of the daily needs of their Dominant.

I've been to Russia with her to meet her family. I remember thinking their relationship seemed a bit old-fashioned, even more old-fashioned than my parents. Every day Mrs. Solonik wore a dress and heels, her hair and make-up always perfect. She spent every minute doting on her husband, making sure he had everything he needed—before he even asked for it. I found myself exhausted just watching her. But I'll never forget the expression in Mr. Solonik's eyes when he looked at his wife— pure adoration. What really made an impression on me was his openness with showing Mrs. Solonik affection. He was generous with his kisses, caressing touches, and loving pet names. At the time, I remember wishing Tommy was half as loving with me. I couldn't even get him to hold my hand in public.

"What you walked in on tonight." She hesitates. "That was a scene Brandon and I'd been planning for a while. You were supposed to be gone."

"Wait a minute. You do this BDSM thing too?"

She nods. "I'm a submissive."

"How were we roommates for two years, and I never knew?"

"It's not a topic that's easy to bring up," Lana chuckles. "Hi, I'm your new dorm mate. I like to get tied up and whipped."

We both laugh.

Lana explains to me how she first got into the lifestyle. She was eighteen when she went to her father and expressed an interest. They had some serious conversations regarding sex and what being in the lifestyle meant.

"I already knew I was a submissive, but Mom and Dad both stressed the importance of my being mature enough to put my needs second to the needs of someone else daily," she explains. "It isn't as easy as it sounds."

She talks about her relationship with her parents so casually it makes my heart ache. I could never talk to my parents the way she does hers. My parents' view on sex is it is something you do after you're married—period, end of story. If they knew I wasn't a virgin, they'd go crazy.

"Mom gave me some books to read and introduced me to a trusted friend who was an experienced submissive. She trained me for two years before I submitted to a Dominant for the first time."

I'm stunned by my friend's confession but also curious. "Do you still happen to have the books she gave you?"

Lana raises her eyebrow. "Why?"

"I figure reading them might come in handy for when I graduate." I shrug my shoulders.

"I've been to Northmeadow." She sits back on the couch and crosses her arms. "I don't think your teen clients are going to be into BDSM."

When I go back home, I'll be working as a school therapist, but she's right. "Maybe, I'm curious." I shrug my shoulders, trying to make light of it.

"I'll be right back." She walks down the hall and disappears into her bedroom. When she comes back, she's holding an e-reader. "They're loaded on here." She passes me the electronic device. "Now tell me exactly what happened when you got to Mizzou."

The level of betrayal I feel toward Tommy and Ashlynn is indescribable. Maybe my parents were right when they said I shouldn't go to New York City, but would that have changed anything? Were they seeing each other even while I was in Northmeadow? The thought makes me sick.

"Now I have to come up with an excuse to tell my parents," I say through a yawn. "There's no way I'm going back there right now."

Lana stands up and grabs our empty wine glasses, and brings them to the kitchen. "Why don't you sleep on it first. We can come up with something later."

The sun is beginning to rise, and we haven't slept at all. Between being up all night and the wine, my head is spinning.

"You have to promise to tell me more about you being tied up by that hot guy." I grin.

"I just hope he's still interested." She links her arm in mine, and we walk to our rooms. "Someone scared the shit out of him by calling the police." We both share a laugh as we go our separate ways. I need to sleep off the worst night of my life.

NATALIE

The next morning, I call my parents and tell them the counseling center I'm interning for asked me to fill in for someone last minute, and I couldn't tell them no. They were disappointed that I wasn't coming home, but they seemed to understand. I need some distance from Northmeadow until I figure everything out.

Tommy calls and texts me every day, begging for forgiveness and making every excuse possible for his *indiscretion*. When the tone of the messages shifts to blaming me for coming to New York, I decide to change my phone number. Funny though, Ashlynn hasn't bothered to call. We've been friends since we were born, we've done everything together, been through everything together, and this is all I have to show for it. That pain hurts almost worse than Tommy cheating on me.

All of this has forced me to open my eyes to everything that's in front of me. I've kept one foot in Northmeadow, afraid to let go of everything familiar. I pick up the picture of my brother Michael and his boyfriend Evan that sits on my dresser. I miss them so much. I can't believe they've been gone seven years. Sitting down on my bed, I'm transported back to my junior year in high school. The day Michael told me about Evan.

"Nat, do you have a few minutes?" Michael asked from my doorway.

I looked up and smiled. Even though he was only a year older than me, he was my hero. I would do anything for him. "I always have a few minutes for you." Closing my math textbook, I jumped up and followed Michael outside.

"Let's go for a walk," he said.

He was nervous. He wouldn't look at me, and his hands were shaking. I followed him out the door and down the path that led into the woods behind our house. We walked in silence for what seemed like forever until we came to the clearing we always played in when we were kids. When we got there, Evan was waiting for us.

"I thought you'd never get here," Evan said, a smile on his face.

Michael finally looked at me. "I have—we have something to tell you." Evan moved to stand next to Michael.

"Okay." I looked back and forth between them.

"I don't know how to tell her," he said and looked to Evan.

"I'll do it." He grabbed Michael's hand and looked at me. "Natalie, your brother and I are together. I'm in love with him."

I wasn't surprised by this revelation.

Michael and I grew up with Evan; his family lived on a farm across town. We played together as children, but as we've grown up, I've seen how they look at each other—it's different from just friends. Michael doesn't know that I know, but I've watched him sneak out his bedroom window late at night to meet Evan. I've seen them embrace and kiss. I didn't say anything, though. This was Michael's to tell me when he was ready.

"I know," I said with a big smile. "And I'm so happy you guys finally told me."

Michael stood there, his mouth hanging open.

"You know?" Evan asked.

"I've seen you two together," I said and looked at Michael, who had turned pale.

"Do mom and dad know?"

"I doubt it; they sleep like the dead."

We all shared a laugh.

"Are you going to tell them?"

"Yes." Michael shuffled his foot nervously. "We're telling all of them tonight. We wanted you to know first because things probably won't go well after that."

"I'm so glad you told me." I reached out and gave them both a hug. "I'm so happy for you both."

I run my finger across Michael's face. He was right. After they told our parents, nothing was the same.

My mother cried hysterically. You would have sworn someone had died. Dad yelled so loud the dishes in the china closet rattled. Evan's dad had passed away when he was young, so it was just his mom. I'll never forget her reaction. She was silent for a long time, watching the spectacle my parents were making. When his mom finally spoke up, she told the boys she loved them both and was proud of them. My parents kicked Michael out that night. Thankfully they were able to live with Evan's mom.

They were seniors that year. After coming out, they continued to go to school. But they didn't expect the hate that came their way.

My eyes fill with tears as I remember the hell they were put through.

They were called fags and fairies by kids in the hallway. Messages of hate were posted on their social media accounts. It seemed the entire school turned on them.

Looking back, I think the breaking point for Evan was seeing his mom's car parked in their driveway. Written in soap on the windshield was a message telling him and Michael to kill themselves.

One month to the day after they came out, he took his daddy's gun and went out into the field and shot himself. Michael wasn't the same after that.

The only time I was able to see Michael was at school. I wasn't allowed to go to Evan's house, so it wasn't until later I found out that he lived in a tent in the woods.

It was graduation night when I realized something was wrong. My parents refused to go to the ceremony, so I went on my own. Michael never showed up, and I called the police. Because he was over 18 and not *officially* missing, they couldn't file a report but said they'd keep an eye out for him. The next day an officer knocked on our door. Before he spoke, I already knew. He told my parents they found Michael's body near a tent in the woods, not far from Evan's house. They found a note addressed to me.

I open the picture frame and carefully take out the worn piece of paper.

Natalie,

I hope one day you can forgive me for leaving you. The pain is too much. I can't do it anymore. I'm going to find Evan—going to find our happily ever after. Don't be sad for me. I want you to find someone truly worthy of all the love you have to give. Get out of Northmeadow, live your life to the fullest. I expect you to make your mark on the world.

I will always love you and will be watching over you.

Love, Michael.

I sit quietly as the tears continue to fall. I wish my big brother were here right now. After reading his note one more time, I take a deep breath and carefully fold it back up and tuck it safely behind the picture.

"I'm going to make you proud of me, Michael," I say aloud to my brother, hoping he can hear me.

My past hasn't changed, I still have to go back to Northmeadow after I graduate, but right now, I'm living in one of the biggest cities in the world. It's time I embrace everything it has to offer.

I've been reading the books Lana gave me about BDSM. At first, I was so horrified I turned off the e-reader and almost gave it back to her. I put it on my desk, where it sat for a few days taunting me until curiosity got the better of me. The other night I turned it back on, determined to keep an open mind, and started reading. The more I read, the more intrigued I became. The ideas about sex are different from anything I've ever known, but the basic principles of a relationship and respect between two people are exactly how I was raised.

I finish the last book and walk down the hall. Lana's in the kitchen cooking when I come out of my room. I sit on one of the stools at the counter and tap my fingers nervously.

She turns around, spatula in hand. "You're driving me crazy with the nervous tapping," she says and laughs. "What's up?"

I'm not used to talking openly about sex, so I take a minute to muster up the courage before I answer her. "I was wondering if I could ask you some more questions? You know, about the books I'm reading."

"Sure," she answers without hesitation before turning her attention back to whatever she's cooking, which smells delicious.

"What're you making?"

"Piroshki. It's kinda my mom's recipe, except I cheated and bought the dough." She laughs. "But I don't think that's what you wanted to ask. Dinner's ready. We can eat and talk." She grabs two plates out of the cupboard and dishes out the food. I get the forks and glasses, pouring us each a generous portion of wine, before joining Lana at our small dining table.

I love when she makes one of her mom's dishes. I dig right in. "Oh my god, Lana. This is amazing."

"Thanks, but you're avoiding."

"I want to learn more," I say quickly and take another bite.

Lana laughs. "That's what you were so nervous to say." I shrug my shoulders. She grabs my phone and unlocks the screen. "Here's the club I go to. It's called Fire and Ice." She hands me the phone with a web page pulled up. "They have classes for people who think they might be interested. You should take one."

"I don't know," I say. "Isn't there anything else I can read?"

She sets her fork down. "There are tons of books, but you'll learn more by taking the class and talking to real people."

"I'll think about it." I bookmark the site and go back to eating. I'm not sure I'm quite ready to take that big of a step.

NATALIE

*I*t's mid-morning on Saturday. I'm sitting cross-legged on the sofa, my face buried in my textbook. Looks like another weekend that I won't be going out. Although I made up my mind to embrace city life, I have to maintain my grades to keep my scholarship.

"Are you still studying?" Svetlana grabs my textbook out of my hand and reads the title aloud, "Love and Attachment: Adult Relationships." She laughs. "You need to get out of this apartment."

"I have to study." I jump up and take a swipe at the book, but she's taller than me and holds it out of my reach.

"You can study tomorrow. I want you to come out with me tonight."

"But—"

"Come on, Nat." She hands back my book; her glacier blue eyes plead with me.

I resume my sitting position on the sofa and open the book to find my place. "I'll go out next weekend, I promise."

"I need you to come out tonight." Lana flops down next to me.

"Why is tonight such a big deal?"

"Well, you remember Brandon, the guy you called the cops on?"

My cheeks heat from embarrassment. "How could I forget."

"Thankfully, you didn't scare him away."

"That's good because he sure is hot."

She pulls a throw pillow out from behind her and hits me in the arm. "He is, isn't he," she says with a huge smile on her face. "I've agreed to be his submissive." She pauses, allowing me a minute to digest this new information. "We're doing a scene at the club tonight, and I really want you there."

I close my books and set them next to me so I can give Lana my full attention.

"You're doing a scene? Like getting naked in front of an audience?"

She nods her head up and down slowly as if she's measuring my response.

"This is what you want?" I ask, making sure she is a totally willing participant.

"I'm so excited about it, but I need my best friend there, please." She bats her eyes at me.

"I wouldn't miss it for the world."

She pulls me in for a tight hug. "I'm so glad you said yes. You're going to have a great time."

I'm not sure I'll have a great time, it all seems a bit overwhelming, but I think tonight will satisfy a lot of my curiosity. I plan to go, sit in a quiet corner, watch Lana do her thing, and apologize to Brandon for the huge misunderstanding a few weeks ago. Then I can move on.

The rest of the afternoon is spent getting ready for our night out. We give each other manicures before I help Lana fix her long brown hair in an updo. She says it's important her hair be up and out of the way.

"There, all done," I say after I put in the last bobby pin. "I need to go jump in the shower quick and find something to wear."

"Thanks, I love it," Lana says as she checks out her hair in the mirror.

I make my way to my bedroom and head straight to my closet. I've upgraded my wardrobe over the past few years, but I'm not sure I have anything appropriate. Actually, I have no idea what one wears to a sex club. I close the closet door and go back to Lana's room.

"I have no idea what to wear tonight." I lean against her doorway.

"I was hoping you'd say that. I have the perfect outfit for you." She hurries into her walk-in closet and comes out holding a hanger with a tiny black scrap of material on it. A huge smile is on her face.

"You're kidding, right?" I say in disbelief. Lana's stunning. She's tall and fit, with curves in all the right places. Everything she wears looks fantastic on her. I'm five-two, and although I work-out, my body looks nothing like hers. There's no way I can wear that dress.

"Nat, you have a fabulous body." She pushes the hanger into my hands. "You're going to turn heads tonight."

"Do I want to turn heads tonight?"

"You never know who you might meet," she says as she points me to my room, giving me a nudge forward. "Go shower and get dressed. Now."

"Are you sure you're not a Domme? You're awfully bossy," I call as I head down the hall.

My statement is met with Lana's laughter.

When I get to my room, I hold up the hanger and take a good look at the dress—if that's what you can call it. It's black and made of a spandex material. There's a crisscross cutout that will leave my midsection exposed. Two straps hold up the top section that wraps around the neck and crisscross in the back.

Peeking my head out, I yell down the hall. "How do I wear a bra with this thing?"

"You don't," she answers.

Rolling my eyes, I go back into my room, shutting the door behind me, and toss the dress onto my bed. I head into my bathroom and shed my sweatpants and t-shirt to take a shower. My hands shake as I shave my legs. I'm surprised I don't cut myself. I stand under the hot water, letting it wash over me, hoping it helps calm my nerves.

When I'm done, I wrap a fluffy towel around my body and stand in front of the bathroom mirror to apply my make-up and dry my hair. I'm wearing it down tonight, letting my blonde curls fall softly down my back.

I turn my attention back to my bedroom, where the dress lies on my bed. I walk across the plush carpet on my bedroom floor to grab a pair of panties and a black strapless bra from my drawer. There's no way I'm going sans bra. I smile as I pull on the sexy thong.

Tommy was a fan of sensible cotton bras and panties. As soon as I got back to my apartment after discovering he was cheating, I emptied them all into the garbage. Lana took me shopping for some adult lingerie. It started as an act of defiance, but I've grown to love wearing something sexy under my clothes. It gives me a sense of confidence I didn't realize I'd been missing.

With my bra and panties on, it's time for the dress. You can do this, Natalie. I step into the black fabric and slide it up my body. The material clings to my curves, leaving little to the imagination. Grabbing a pair of black heels from my closet, I put them on and slowly turn to face the full-length mirror in my bedroom.

Svetlana appears behind me in the mirror. "I knew it! You look amazing!" She hugs me tightly.

I've never worn anything like this, but I like what I see.

"What should I expect tonight?" Suddenly this all seems too real.

"The car's here," Svetlana says. "I'll tell you on the way."

"The car?"

"Brandon sent a car to pick us up." She smiles. "You ready?"

"Yep. Don't want to keep your man waiting."

ALEX

*I*t's late, and I'm still at my office trying to finish up some work when my phone rings.

"Hello?"

"Hey man," Brandon says. "Where are you?"

"At the office."

"You're the only person I know who's at his office on Friday night."

"I thought you were with Lana?" I ask. "Why are you calling me?"

"It's a long story," he says. "Can you meet me for a few drinks?"

I've been here all day and I'm exhausted, but it sounds like Brandon needs to talk. "Text me where and I'll be there."

I walk into the bar, and even at this late hour, it's still hopping. I'm only a few steps in when a group of girls approaches me.

"Hey, handsome," the brunette says and wraps her hands around my arm. "You here alone?"

"I'm meeting someone." I brush her hand off.

Brandon sees me and waves me over.

"Excuse me, ladies," I say and head to Brandon.

"He's gay," one of the girls says.

"All the gorgeous ones are," another says.

I laugh at their assessment of me, but I don't care. I'm not here to find a date.

There's a beer waiting for me when I sit next to Brandon at the bar.

"Why are you here drinking with me instead of with Lana?"

Brandon tells me about his evening—how he and Lana were in the middle of their scene when her roommate came in.

"She called the cops?" I almost spit my beer out from laughing so hard.

"Yeah," Brandon says and shakes his head. "I thought I'd be calling you to bail me out."

"And you wonder why I'm not with anyone."

"Lana and I are doing a scene at the club next weekend," Brandon tells me. "It's our first public scene. I'd like you to be there."

"Wouldn't miss it." I slap my friend on the back.

The week passes by like all the rest. Wake up. Work. Sleep. Repeat.

It's finally Saturday, and I'm out for a run when I get a text from Brandon.

(Brandon) Lana's roommate is coming to the club tonight. I need a favor.

(Me) Don't say it.

(Brandon) She needs an escort.

(Me) The same girl who called the cops?

(Brandon) Yeah.

(Me) And you want me to babysit her?

(Brandon) Come on, bro.

Why me? Just what I want to do with my Saturday night. Babysit a college girl who's going to be scared out of her mind.

(Brandon) You know I'd do it for you.
(Me) I'm not feeling well. I'm not sure I'm going to make it.
(Brandon) The fuck you aren't. You're out running right now. Tell me I'm wrong.

Am I that predictable? This is the last thing I want to do tonight.

(Me) Fine. But you owe me.
(Brandon) Thanks, man.

I slip my phone back into my pocket and finish my run. I can't believe I just agreed to babysit tonight.

NATALIE

$\mathcal{T}$he car drops us off in front of the club. Fire and Ice is an exclusive club in Chelsea, nestled among traditional businesses. I'm surprised when Lana pulls the door open. I've walked by here many times and never realized what it was.

Just inside the door, we're standing in a foyer area that's pretty non-descript. It could pass for the entrance area to any office. A stunning woman wearing a black latex one-piece that hugs her perfect body stands behind a counter, checking in the people who are waiting to be granted admittance.

Feeling insecure, I tug at my dress, trying to give it length that isn't there.

"Stop fidgeting," Lana scolds me while trying to hold back a smile.

"I'm so nervous, but I'm also kinda excited. Is that normal?"

Lana grabs my hand. "It's perfectly normal. Don't worry; we're going to have a great time tonight."

Trying to distract myself, I shift my focus to the oversized dark wood doors that grant entrance to the club. They look like something from medieval times with their ornate hinges. In the center of each door is an iron door knocker with the BDSM triskelion forged in the center; I recognize it from pictures in the books. It represents the three divisions of the lifestyle: bondage and discipline, dominance and submission, sadism and masochism. It also represents the motto of *safe, sane, and consensual.* Although simple in its design, the triskelion holds deep meaning for those in the lifestyle.

"When we get to the desk, you'll be checked in as my guest." Lana motions to the woman behind the counter, "Mistress Star will give you a colored wrist band."

"What's that for?"

"Each color represents a person's status." She motions to a sign on the wall.

On it is the colors of the rainbow, each representing a guest's position, whether they are a Dominant or submissive, with a partner or alone, just watching or looking to play.

"You'll get a purple band," Lana says. "It means you are a guest being sponsored by a Dominant. No one can approach you without asking the Dominant's permission first."

Although I don't know Brandon, Lana trusts him. I like knowing that I have some sort of a safety net tonight.

"Good evening, Lana," the woman at the desk greets my friend.

"Good evening. Mistress, this is my friend, Natalie," Lana says. "She'll be our guest this evening."

"Yes, Brandon gave me her information." Mistress Star turns to me. "Has Lana explained our color system?"

"Yes, she has."

"Do you have any questions?" she asks?

"No."

"May I have your right arm so I can put the bracelet on?"

I lift my arm, and Mistress Star snaps on a purple band.

"You understand you'll have a Dominant responsible for your comfort and safety tonight?" she asks me.

"I do."

"And you are comfortable with this decision?"

"Yes, ma'am." They take informed consent seriously.

"You ladies are clear to go in. Lana, Brandon is waiting for you by stage three," Mistress Star says. "Natalie, I hope you have a great evening. I'll be walking around the club all night if you have any questions or concerns."

Her confident demeanor puts me at ease. "Thank you."

Lana grabs my arm. "Come on. I'm so excited for you to meet Brandon officially."

It's our turn to walk through the wooden doors. As I take my first steps into the club, I'm surprised by what I see. I had imagined a seedy nightclub, but it's nothing like that. The main room is quite expansive and has a modern, industrial vibe. It's brightly lit from overhead, and there's soft instrumental music playing in the background. I expect to find people naked and engaging in sex acts, but right now, the people here are in casual clothes and appear to be putting the final touches on the setup.

"Things don't start for a few hours," Lana says. "That's when the real fun happens." She waggles her eyebrows, making me laugh.

We continue our trek across the room to where a man is standing, his back to us. He's giving directions to the people setting up the stage. He must hear us behind him and turns to greet us.

"Natalie," Lana touches my shoulder to get my attention. "I'd like you to meet my Dominant, Brandon."

Turning my head, I'm met with those same gray eyes, but this time they're less frightened. "It's nice to meet you," Brandon says and reaches his hand out to shake mine.

I find myself embarrassed, struggling to meet his gaze. "It's nice to meet you too." I shake his hand. "I'm so sorry for calling the police on you."

"Already forgiven." He smiles. "It's good to know Lana has someone looking out for her."

Movement on the stage behind Brandon catches my attention. Two big men are pushing a giant wooden X onto the stage. There are cuffs hanging from the tops and bottoms. "What's that thing? It looks like a torture device."

Brandon laughs. "That's a Saint Andrew's Cross. I'll be securing Lana to it and using my whip to bring her pleasure."

"Your whip?" I ask. "Won't that hurt her?" Gruesome visions of my best friend being tied up, her body being torn to shreds, run through my mind. I'm ready to grab Lana and get the heck out of here.

"I won't hurt her—much." He winks.

I look at Lana, but she shows no hint of fear.

"It's okay," Brandon says, "Lana likes pain, and I know how to give her what she craves without hurting her."

"It's okay, Nat," Lana reassures me. "Brandon and I have already talked about everything we're going to do tonight. This is something I want."

"You're sure?" I'm not sold on the idea.

"Positive," she says and offers a smile meant to be reassuring.

I know Lana knows what she's doing, so I guess I shouldn't freak out yet.

Brandon looks over my shoulder; his smile widens. I turn around to see what he's looking at and am captivated by the sight. Just inside the doors stands a tall, well-groomed man. He's running his hand through his dark hair as he looks around the room. When he looks in our direction, he nods and begins to walk, exuding confidence with each step. Women and men smile and whisper to each other as he passes by, but he pays them no attention. I'm unable to take my eyes off him as he approaches.

"Glad you made it," Brandon says as he shakes the man's hand.

"I wouldn't miss this for the world," he says and then turns to Lana. "How are you tonight?"

"I'm fine, thank you," Lana answers, keeping her gaze cast downward.

I've never seen my best friend act so demure. It's an odd contradiction to the self-assured, outspoken girl I know. It leaves me wondering how she manages to separate these two opposite parts of herself.

"Natalie," Brandon motions to the man standing next to him. "This is my best friend, Alex."

Our gazes meet, and I'm drawn into the depths of his brown eyes.

"Alex is also a Dominant here. I've asked him to be your escort in my absence tonight."

"Oh, I thought I'd be staying with you and Lana?" I look to Lana, who's wearing a mischievous grin. She shrugs her shoulders.

"Lana and I won't be available at all time. Because you're a first-time guest, you can't be alone in the club," Brandon explains. "I assure you that you're in good hands with Alex."

"Um, okay." I have a feeling Lana knows more about this than she's letting on. She and I will be having a chat later.

"I've heard a lot about you," Alex says with a grin.

"You have?" I question and look to Lana, who's now hiding behind Brandon.

"Yep. You're the girl who called the police on my friend here." He slaps Brandon on the back.

My face heats with embarrassment. "Oh my God. I can't believe you guys told anyone about that." I know I promised Lana I'd be here tonight, but I want to find the nearest exit and run right now.

"There's no reason to be embarrassed," Alex says. "It's good to know Lana has someone looking out for her. Not everyone here can say the same."

"Lana and I have to finish setting up our stage," Brandon says and takes Lana by the hand. "We'll see you two later."

Lana waves goodbye before she walks away, leaving me standing awkwardly with Alex.

"How about I show you around before things get started?" he asks and offers me his arm.

"Okay," I answer and hesitantly link my arm in his. When I do, I swear I feel a current of electricity run up my arm. Did he feel the same thing? I chance a glance up to his face. He's focused on the direction we're walking; his expression gives nothing away.

NATALIE

"We'll start here," says Alex. "As you can see, all three stages will be used for scenes tonight."

The stages aren't anything extravagant. Just simple areas set a step above the main floor. Alex and I watch as Brandon walks up to the cross, checking the cuffs before picking up his whip, giving it a few practice swings. A loud crack fills the room.

"I'm assuming Lana told you what their scene entails?"

"We talked about it," I say. "But I still don't understand why anyone would volunteer to be whipped. Seems more like torture than pleasure."

"People find pleasure from many different activities. What one sees as torture, others see as the ultimate pleasure."

"If you say so." I shrug.

"Come, there's more to see," Alex says before leading me to the next stage.

Stage two looks much less threatening. A black metal bed sits in the center of the stage. Beside the bed is a matching table. A short, older man with a dark complexion is standing, his back to us, carefully arranging candles into color groups. A second man with shoulder-length blond hair and crystal blue eyes smiles at us as he walks by and steps onto the stage. So, this is where all the good-looking guys hang out. I almost laugh out loud at my wayward thoughts. He approaches the older man, who points to the table and appears to give him directions. The blond man looks our way before whispering something in the other man's ear. He nods before turning and coming over to us.

"Alexander Montgomery," the man says. "It's great to see you."

"Good to see you, Anthony." Alex shakes the man's hand. While they talk, I watch the stage.

The blond man fits the mattress with a black rubber sheet and finishes setting up the candles before joining us. He stands next to Anthony, his hands at his sides and head bowed slightly. I stare shamelessly at the two men.

Alex places his hand on my arm. "Natalie, I'd like to introduce you to Anthony and his submissive, Leopold. Tonight, Anthony will be demonstrating his skill with hot wax on Leo here."

I look between the men, my interest piqued. "It's very nice to meet you both."

"I didn't realize you took a new submissive," Anthony says.

"I'm not—"

Alex interrupts. "Natalie's a guest of Brandon and Lana."

Anthony smiles. "Well then, I hope you enjoy yourself tonight."

"I'm excited to see everything," I say.

"We'll let these two get back to work."

Alex places his hand on my back. His touch feels natural and familiar like we've been together much longer than a few minutes.

As we turn to walk away, a group of women approaches Alex, smiling and giggling.

"Hello, Sir," a pretty brunette bats her eyes at Alex.

I inch closer, feeling a hint of jealousy.

"Ladies," Alex says as he leads me away, paying them no attention.

Looking over my shoulder, the girls glare at me. Alex laughs softly as he tightens his arm around my body. His territorial action causes my heart to race.

The final stage area is sectioned off by red ropes and has chairs set up in front. The stage holds nothing more than a few piles of rope neatly laid out on bamboo mats. In the far corner, a man sits on the floor cross-legged with his eyes closed—Alex motions to the man. "Master Kiyoshi is a guest at the club tonight. He'll be closing the evening with a Shibari demonstration."

"I've seen pictures of that online."

"You have?" Alex seems surprised.

"The designs they're able to make with rope are beautiful." I debate whether telling him I like it so much I have a secret board for it on Pinterest but decide against it.

"I took the liberty of reserving us two seats." Alex's gaze meets mine once again. "Let's continue the tour before everything gets started."

We make our way toward a dining area. It's set apart from the rest of the club by a half wall.

"This is the Fire and Ice Café," he says. "The restaurant is for club members only." Employees are finishing putting linens on and setting the tables.

As we continue the tour, I notice more people have filled the room. I can't help but see the different ways the men and women present themselves. Some are dressed in nearly formal attire. Others, some of whom I recognize from earlier that were in casual outfits, are barely dressed.

One couple walks by us, the man, who's holding a leash, nods to Alex. On the end of the leash is a man on his hands and knees. He's wearing a collar and a hood that make him look like a dog. I watch them walk by and notice whenever the man stops walking, his pet kneels at his side, waiting patiently. Pet play, I remember reading something about it in one of the books. It's not something that appeals to me, but they appear happy.

Body shape and size doesn't seem to be a concern. Not everyone here has a model's figure, yet they still wear revealing outfits, if they're wearing clothes at all. No one appears self-conscious. No one is pointing or judging appearances. It's a foreign concept to me. When I look in the mirror, all I see are my flaws—I'm envious of the body positivity portrayed around me.

We turn a corner, Alex leads me down a hall away from the activity and noise. Pointing to the doors in front of us, he says. "These rooms are available by reservation for anyone who wants to do a private scene and for aftercare time."

"May I see inside one?"

"Sure." Alex goes to the first door that doesn't have a reserved sign on it. He pulls a card from his pocket and inserts it into the reader on the handle. After the lock clicks, he pushes the door open, moving aside so I can enter first.

I take a few tentative steps into the room and pause, allowing my imagination and reality to catch up with one another. I was expecting to see something resembling a cheap motel-like room, but instead, I'm standing in a high-class suite. One of the first things I notice is there are no windows. A beautiful crystal chandelier hangs from the ceiling casting a soft glow, creating an almost romantic atmosphere. The walls are painted light grey, adding to the calm atmosphere in the room. My heels click on the black tile floor as I make my way to another door, which is slightly ajar. When I peek inside, I find an en suite bathroom with a large soaking tub.

In the center of the main room, sitting on a dark grey area rug, is a four-poster bed made of thick carved wood. Moving closer, I see a red plush blanket folded along the bottom of the mattress. I run my hands up the silky black sheets stopping at the pillows that have been arranged neatly at the top of the bed. Next to the bed is a table with a dozen fresh red roses in a vase. Someone thought of everything.

"This room is incredible." I turn to face Alex, who's leaning in the doorway, hands in his pockets.

"It is." The lustful tone in his voice makes me think he isn't only referring to the room.

I continue my exploration. The wall to the right has downlights that showcase various leather instruments hanging neatly from a wooden shelf. I walk closer to them. "What are these?"

"Floggers," Alex says.

Running my fingers along the leather tails sends a trail of goosebumps up my arm. "What do they feel like?"

"Floggers can offer a sting or a sensual caress, depending on how they're used."

"Will you show me?" Part of me can't believe I'm asking this man, who I've only just met, to use a flogger on me. What's wrong with you tonight, Natalie?

He pauses and inhales deeply. "You want me to show you how a flogger feels?"

I nod my head. There's something about this man that's doing strange things to me. Lana wouldn't have let me go with him if he wasn't safe, right? Maybe it's that knowledge that tells me I can trust him with my body.

A silent minute passes before he pushes off the door frame, standing to his full height. He hits a button that shows the room as occupied before he closes the door. I hear a lock click.

"They lock automatically from the outside," he says. "All you have to do is turn the inside handle, and it will open."

"That's good to know," I reply.

His dominant presence fills the room as he strides toward me. Moving aside, I watch as he reaches up, his muscles straining the fabric of his black button-down shirt, and removes a flogger from the wall. He runs the purple tails over his palm. His eyes never leaving mine.

"You need to have safe words. We'll use yellow and red." His tone is serious. "Yellow means you're reaching your limit. Red means stop immediately. Do you understand?"

I nod my head.

"I need a verbal answer, Natalie." His voice leaves no room for argument.

"Yes, I understand." My heart's racing. While part of me thinks I've lost my mind, the other part of me feels as though my whole life has been building toward this moment.

"I'll be gentle because you have no experience." Alex closes the gap between us and runs his knuckles gently down my cheek. "You're a courageous young woman."

I can't help the soft gasp that escapes my lips.

He takes my hand and leads me to the edge of the bed. "I need you to bend over. Place your hands over your head."

Without hesitation, I do as I'm instructed.

"Good girl." Alex praises me.

Those two words, although they seem simple, make my insides quiver. Why does knowing I've pleased him matter so much?

"May I pull your dress up?"

Bearing myself to a man who is little more than a stranger should scare me, but instead, I'm dripping with arousal. "Yes," I answer.

Alex's hands gently brush the back of my thighs until they find the bottom of my dress. Slowly he pulls it up to my waist, exposing my black lace panties; I hear his breath catch.

"You have a beautiful body."

That statement catches me off guard. I've always been insecure about the way my body looks. Tommy played on that by pointing out my flaws. But when I look over my shoulder, I see Alex's eyes are sincere.

"You need to keep your hands above your head and stay still. Don't be afraid to use your safe words," Alex says. "I'm going to start now."

I hear the soft swoosh of the tails in the air a second before I feel the sting across the back of my thighs.

"How did that feel?" Alex asks quietly.

"It stung, but it felt good," I answer right away.

"Do you want me to do it again?"

"Yes." The words leave my lips, and immediately, the sound of the flogger fills the room.

Alex continues his strikes, alternating where the tails of the flogger land. Each time the tails make contact with my skin, nerve endings come alive, but at the same time, my body relaxes. It's a paradox of feelings that are as confusing as they are arousing.

"We're done," Alex says, and he slides my dress back into place.

I'm so caught up trying to process what is happening that I don't realize right away that Alex has stopped.

"Are you okay?" he asks as he places his hand on my lower back.

His touch grounds me, and I slowly stand and turn, finding myself in his arms.

"That was amazing."

Alex gives me a dazzling smile. "I'm glad you enjoyed it, but I think it's time we head back out."

I remember the reason I'm at the club. "I hope we didn't miss Lana's scene.

ALEX

$\mathcal{I}$ return the flogger to its place on the wall, allowing myself a few minutes to figure out what I just did.

Brandon called a few weeks ago and told me he was doing a scene with Svetlana tonight. He wanted me to come to watch them. I was prepared to be here and observe, but then, at the last minute, he asked me to escort his submissive's roommate—the same girl who called the cops on him. I envisioned having to spend the evening calming a frantic girl who was scared by everything she saw. That thought was enough for me almost not to show up. Not ever for a second did I imagine spending the evening with this beautiful young woman who is not only unafraid, she's curious and interested in trying things.

As I struck her with the flogger, her black lace underwear grew wet with her arousal. I busy myself, pretending to straighten out the floggers to give my own arousal time to calm down before turning back to Natalie. She readily takes my hand and allows me to lead her back to the club's main area.

Lana's scene has already started. She's naked and restrained to the St. Andrews Cross, her back to the small group of people gathered to watch. We haven't missed much. Brandon's still warming Lana up.

A few submissives toward the front notice me approaching and move aside to allow me space at the front. Not wanting to interrupt the scene, I raise my hand to stop them. Natalie and I have a good view from where we stand. I appreciate the respect they've shown and make a mental note to compliment the submissives later.

Brandon pauses, the overhead lights in the club go dim, leaving only the stage illuminated. The room is silent as everyone waits for Brandon's next move. He cracks his whip loudly, his signature move before he increases the intensity of his strikes.

Lana's skin quickly turns a beautiful shade of red; her cries a mixture of pain and pleasure. Over and over, the whoosh of the leather fills the room before the tails connect with her body. Brandon creates an intricate crisscross pattern on his willing sub's body.

He stops swinging and lays his whip on the table. Moving to the back of the cross, he leans in close to Svetlana.

"What's he doing?" Natalie whispers.

"He's checking on her, probably asking her color."

Natalie studies their interactions. She's most likely trying to make the connection of how the man who was just leaving welts on his submissive is now feathering kisses on her face and stroking her hair gently. They may be in a room full of people, but right now, they're only aware of each other's presence. Watching their tender interaction spurs a longing I haven't felt in over three years.

Although I come to the club, I usually just observe. I've had offers, sure, but I've turned them all down. I hadn't had a desire for a sub until moments ago. Natalie's only here to watch her friend, but this woman standing next to me makes me question my past decisions. I wonder if she'd be interested in getting to know each other more. That's if I ever see her again.

Natalie's soft voice pulls me from my thoughts. "She looks so peaceful."

I shift my attention back to the stage where the action has resumed. Lana's body is now relaxed in the restraints. Her earlier cries now only whimpers. "It looks like she's starting to experience subspace."

"Subspace?" Natalie asks. "What's that?"

"When a submissive experiences extreme pain, it causes their endorphin level to climb. When that happens, the person feels a sense of euphoria. In her daily life, Svetlana tends to be a take-charge kinda person," I say, causing Natalie to giggle quietly. "This scene, her submission in general, allows her the freedom to give up that control and to simply feel."

"The intense pain becomes her release," Natalie whispers.

She's already figured out part of the intricacy of the plea-sure/pain response. That's an uncommon observation from someone inexperienced.

"Being in subspace makes Lana vulnerable, though," I add.

"How so?"

"Her ability to gauge her pain level may be compromised. Brandon's experienced and recognizes this," I explain. "He's decreasing the intensity of the lashes. They'll be done soon."

Natalie doesn't take her eyes off the stage as Brandon delivers the final strikes and drops his whip. He moves closer to his submissive and runs his fingers over his creation before leaning close and whispering in Svetlana's ear. He then makes quick work of uncuffing her ankles and wrists, lifting her into his arms.

Lana curls into him, resting her head on his chest. It's an inti-mate moment we're all privileged to witness—the intense bond shared between a Dominant and their submissive. People move aside, allowing Brandon passage through the club.

"Where are they going?" Natalie asks.

"He's taking her for aftercare," I say. "As her Dominant, his job doesn't end after the scene. It's his responsibility to care for his sub while she comes out of subspace."

"I thought this was all about sex." Natalie quickly puts her hand over her mouth.

Her embarrassment at letting her unfiltered thoughts slip is adorable. "Sex is a part of it, but this world is about so much more."

"I'm beginning to see that."

What else are you beginning to see? I study her face looking for any clue as to what she's thinking.

NATALIE

*A*fter Lana's scene ends, the lights in the club come up. We stand off to the side while the audience begins to break up.

"Excuse me, ladies and gentlemen." Alex gets the attention of a small group of people moving past us.

They stop in front of him, heads bowed.

"I appreciate the respect you showed in your willingness to give up your spots for me," he says. "Your actions did not go unnoticed."

I'm quietly impressed that Alex took the time to compliment these individuals for their actions earlier. It speaks to his character.

"Thank you, Sir," each one says before walking away.

"The next scene will start in a few minutes," Alex tells me. "Shall we head over to get a spot near the stage?"

"I'd like that." I've never seen wax play, but I'm very curious.

Alex leads the way to stage two, where a small group is already forming. We take our place near the front of the crowd. Anthony and Leopold are already on the stage. Leopold is wearing a black silk robe and is kneeling at Anthony's feet.

Anthony's speaking quietly to him. I wish I could hear what he's saying.

Leopold finally stands and unties his robe. It falls to the floor at his feet. My mouth falls open as I take in the tattooed perfection standing completely naked and unashamed on the stage. Anthony looks over his submissive appreciatively before kicking the robe out of the way.

"Lie down," Anthony instructs.

Leopold climbs onto the table and lays on his back. This time the lights stay on, and New Age music plays through the club's sound system. Anthony begins to light the candles he has prearranged on the table. With the precision of a skilled practitioner, he picks up the candles and drizzles the hot wax on Leopold's chest. Anthony gazes lovingly at his submissive, offering caresses and kisses in between his movements. Leopold looks almost like he's sleeping. His eyes are closed, and his hands rest at his sides.

"I never realized wax could do such amazing things," I say, not taking my eyes off the men.

"There are many things we use in ways you've never imagined," Alex whispers in my ear.

I look at Alex and realize a part of me longs to experience all of it with him.

Over the next half hour, Anthony drizzles pink, purple, orange, and yellow wax across his willing canvas. The design is beginning to come together; it's a stunning depiction of a summer sunset. When he's finished, Anthony kisses Leopold and starts stroking him, causing him to become aroused. Leopold moans in ecstasy as his Dominant brings him to orgasm.

Their sexual display is erotic, and I find myself aroused watching them. I chance a glance at Alex and find him staring at me, his eyes filled with desire. Our gaze stays locked until the applause from the audience ends the moment.

"We should head over to Master Kiyoshi's stage and get

settled. He'll be starting in a few minutes." Alex's voice is deep, only adding to the arousal I'm experiencing. Is he feeling what I'm feeling?

"Umm, okay." I struggle to put my thoughts into words. "That sounds like a good plan."

Alex offers me his hand. I slip mine into his, loving the feel of his strong hand enveloping mine.

The area around stage one has been sectioned off. Mistress Star stands at the entrance.

"Are you enjoying your evening, Natalie?" Mistress Star asks.

"Very much." I smile.

"I'm glad to hear that," she says before directing us to our seats.

"Master Kiyoshi chose one of our female submissives to participate in his demonstration tonight," Alex says as he motions to the stage where Master Kiyoshi and a woman are kneeling facing each other.

"Wow, she's a lucky girl," I say. "She must be excited."

"I'm sure she is. Master Kiyoshi is well-known for his Shibari skills. To be chosen by him is an honor."

The lights in the club dim, the muffled tones of conversation fade, and the soft sounds of a bamboo flute fill the room. Master Kiyoshi rises and offers his hand to the submissive, who then stands. He removes her kimono, and I'm expecting her to be naked, but instead, she's wearing a white body suit with a sheer flowing skirt; she looks like a ballerina.

Alex must notice my surprise because he leans in and whispers, "Not everyone has to be unclothed to do a scene." He gives me a big smile, and I can't help but return it with one of my own.

The woman is led to the middle of the stage. The lights in the club turn off, and a soft spotlight illuminates her figure. Master Kiyoshi moves gracefully, wrapping her body in colorful ropes, all to the flow of music.

I've read accounts from those who've experienced Shibari.

They describe the sensation of the ropes being wrapped around their body and the knots' tightness allowing them to slow their breathing; to relax into the bondage. Many times, the knots are placed on erogenous zones or pressure points, further amplifying the extreme sensations. The rope allows them to experience a deep, almost meditative, relaxation.

The submissive's body is being manipulated into challenging positions and bound by the rope. I can see her body physically relaxing as Master Kiyoshi nears the end of his design.

With the last tie of a knot, he stands back looking over his artwork. Then he walks to the side of the stage. He takes a rope that's attached to the submissive and begins to pull it. The woman's body leaves the ground. The arabesque position she's been bound in takes shape as she's suspended in mid-air. The sheer skirt blows gently, adding to her seemingly weightless form held only by the rope's intricate weaves. It's a breathtaking site.

After allowing her to fly for a few minutes, he gently lowers her and begins the process of untying her. Rather than it being a hurried process, she's released with great care and grace.

While he works, his eye never breaks the connection he has with his submissive; it's incredible seeing how choreographed it seems when they've just met. It speaks to his level of mastery.

Alex places his hand on my shoulder. "How about we grab a table and get a bite to eat?"

I didn't realize how hungry I'd gotten over the last few hours. "That'd be great."

We head over to the restaurant and are seated at an empty table. A male server dressed in black pants and a white button-down shirt brings us waters and menus.

"What did you think about tonight?" Alex asks.

I take a sip of water and think about everything I've experienced this evening.

"Watching Lana get whipped, I know I should've been scared, but I wasn't." I pause.

"All the rest of this..." I gesture around the room, "I was expecting to feel uncomfortable, and maybe I'm crazy, but everything feels right. I'm surprised by my thoughts."

"Surprised? How so?" Alex asks.

"This is all foreign to me. If you knew how I was raised, you'd understand just how much. When I walked in on Lana that night—" I feel my face redden, and Alex chuckles. "I read all the books she gave me, but I still had a very different picture in my mind." I stop and shake my head. "Being here tonight, it's nothing at all like I imagined. Each pair we watched shared a connection. There was nothing wrong about—"

No sooner have the words left my mouth than I feel a pair of arms wrap around my neck, causing me to nearly fall off the chair.

"Scared ya." Lana's excitement pulses through her body. "I'm so glad you liked it."

"Great scene tonight." Alex stands, shaking hands with Brandon. "Grab some chairs and join us."

Brandon finds two empty chairs and brings them to our table, gesturing for Lana to sit.

"Are you enjoying your evening?" Brandon asks.

"Yes." I glance at Alex, and my stomach does flip flops. This man is incredibly gorgeous, and I've been the lucky recipient of his attention all night. "I think I'd like to learn more."

"We offer intro classes during the week. You should sign up," Brandon says.

Lana has told me about the classes. Before tonight I didn't think there was any way I'd feel comfortable enough to sign up, but now, I can't imagine just walking away.

ALEX

The four of us spend the next few hours talking and laughing. I catch myself staring at Natalie far too often. I didn't think I'd want a submissive ever again, but if she expressed an interest, I'd jump at the chance.

"Oh, wow, it's almost 2 a.m.," Lana announces. "I promised Cinderella here I'd have her home early." She pats Natalie's shoulder. Turning to Brandon, she asks, "Sir, do I have permission to leave?"

"You've pleased me greatly tonight." Brandon runs his knuckles lightly down Lana's cheek. "Go, get your roommate home."

"Thank you for the tour, Alex."

I stand and place a kiss on her cheek. "It was my pleasure."

The girls turn and head to the door. My feet remain bolted to the floor, watching Natalie walk away.

"Go after her, man," Brandon says as he nudges me forward. "Don't let her go."

I don't need to be told again. Hurrying my pace, I catch up with the girls as they're signing out with Star.

"Natalie," I call from behind her.

"Alex."

The sound of my name on her lips makes me feel like a schoolboy with his first crush.

"I'm hoping." I fumble for the words. "Can I give you my number? Maybe, we could get together again?"

Star chuckles behind the desk, obviously amused with my awkwardness.

"I guess that would be okay." She takes her cell out of her purse.

Sensing some hesitation, I ask, "May I?"

She looks to Lana, who nods in approval before she unlocks the phone and hands it to me. I open her contacts and enter my name and number. Then, I shoot myself a quick text, ensuring I have her number, too.

"Done." I hand the phone back.

She gives me an awkward smile and slips the phone back into her purse. I'm confused by her reactions. She seemed so receptive until now. Did I do something to offend her?

"Thanks," she says. "I guess I'll talk to you soon."

"Yes, you will."

With that, the girls walk out the door.

I turn to Star. "That girl is going to be mine."

NATALIE

*A*lex calls me the next day and tells me he had a great time. Honestly, I didn't think I'd hear from him, but I'm glad he called.

"Have you given any more thought to taking the intro session?" Alex asks.

"Yes," I answer. "I'm going to call tomorrow and sign up for the next start date."

"I can't wait to hear what you think about everything when you're done." His voice holds a hopeful tone.

"I'll be sure to tell you everything."

On Monday, I call Fire and Ice and register for the six-week intro course. My time in NYC is winding down, so I'm taking this opportunity while I still can.

The classes start the next night. Our group is small, just five of us; a mix of men and women. Mistress Star and Master Owen, who both own the club, lead the first few classes.

In our first class, we talk about the different places a person can fit in the lifestyle. I thought the only options were Dominant or submissive, but I was wrong. A person can be a switch or just a top or bottom. With so many options; there's a place for everyone.

We're now in week four of class, and all of us have a good feel for where we might fit in the lifestyle. This week we're being paired one on one with other club members for some more personalized instruction. I've been given my room assignment and am off to see who I'll be working with.

When I open the door, I'm shocked at who I find waiting for me. "Leopold." I smile. "I'm so excited to get to work with you." I was impressed by his wax scene, and he's easy on the eyes too.

"Leo, please," he says and pulls me in for a big hug. "Let's sit and make a list of your questions, so I know where we need to start."

It's easy to talk to him. He's a sweet, genuine man who's very knowledgeable about the lifestyle. He's been a submissive for over ten years. Five of those years have been spent with Anthony.

Leo reminds me of my brother, probably why we connected so quickly. It feels like I've known him forever.

The last two weeks of the class go by quickly. I'm now armed with information.

Tonight, we're meeting for drinks to celebrate the end of the classes. I know Leo's going to want to know more about what direction I'm headed with Alex. Problem is, I don't have the answer to that.

"Have you talked to Alex lately?" Leo asks as we drink our margaritas.

"We talk once a week and text almost every day."

"So, things are going well?"

"I think so." I look down, fiddling with my hands.

"For a girl who says things are going well, your face tells another story," Leo says. "Start talking."

"Alex asked if I'd be interested in discussing a Dom/sub relationship."

"The problem with that?" He motions for me to keep talking.

"I'm going back to Northmeadow next summer. I don't want to start something and then have to walk away."

"When you start vetting, you can ask to specify a time limit for your contract. This way, there are no unrealistic expectations," he explains.

"That's an option, I guess." I play with the straw in my drink to avoid making eye contact with Leo.

"Wait a minute." Leo claps his hands together. "The problem is you like the guy, and you don't want it to end in a year."

"Maybe." I shrug my shoulders. "Doesn't matter, though. I'm pretty sure he isn't interested in me as anything more than a submissive, and I can't stay here anyway. I don't see any use in starting anything."

"Have you ever heard of a plane?" Leo asks with a wink.

"If it were only that easy."

Leo rolls his eyes, "Girl, if that man were interested in me, I'd scoop him up and never look back."

"I bet Anthony would love to hear that," I say, laughing.

"My Master knows I'm completely faithful to him and him only. But he also knows a sexy man when he sees one, and Alex is *all* that. Don't let him get away."

Leo's words play over and over in my head the rest of the evening.

At the end of this school year, NYC will become a part of my past. Alex has asked me a few times about discussing a potential contract—I keep putting him off. I haven't told Alex about my deal or having to go back to Northmeadow yet. I'm sure when I do, it'll change everything.

NATALIE

*A*lex and I haven't talked much the past week. I had so much work to do studying for midterms. Thankfully, they're over, and now I have some time to breathe. I'm lying on my bed when my cell pings with a text.

(Alex) Do you have plans tonight?
(Me) I'm staying home tonight. About to order a pizza.
(Alex) Let me take you to dinner. We can celebrate the end of your semester.

I want to go out with him, any sane woman would. But I can't get involved with someone right now.

(Me) I don't know.
(Alex) Can I pick you up at 6?

I should say no. Just say no, Natalie.

(Me) Sure. I'll see you then.

I set the phone down and rest my head in my hands. I can't

believe I'm going on a date with Alex tonight. I know he's going to ask if I've given any thought to his question about us.

The problem is, I haven't stopped thinking about it. I think we'd be good together, and I'd love to explore the lifestyle with him, but I can't risk getting my heart involved in something that can never be.

Checking the time, there's two hours until he picks me up. I hurry to take a shower and then try on every outfit in my closet and finally settle on an ankle-length soft pink dress with open shoulders and a pair of sandals. I pin my hair up, leaving only a few loose curls that fall softly around my face.

The doorbell rings as I'm putting on my lipstick. Since the night at the club, I haven't seen Alex in person, that's almost two months ago. My stomach does flip flops as I pad through the living room and open the door.

Alex stands on the other side in black dress pants and a light gray button-down shirt. His dark hair has grown since I last saw him. He's even more handsome than I remember. In his hands is a bouquet of red roses.

"These are for you." He hands me the flowers. "You look gorgeous," he says, his eyes taking in every inch of my body.

"Thank you." I move aside, giving him room to enter the apartment. "Come in. I just need a minute to put these in water."

"Sure."

He follows me into the kitchen while I grab a vase. I can feel his eyes tracking my every movement.

Once the flowers are neatly arranged, I set them on the kitchen island.

Offering me his hand, he asks, "Ready to go?"

I thread my fingers in his as we walk to the door.

"It's a beautiful night, and the restaurant is only a few blocks away," he says once we're outside. "Do you mind walking?"

"I don't mind at all." I find myself enjoying the envious glances of the women we pass on the busy New York streets.

Sorry ladies, he's taken. Where did that come from? Just because we're going out tonight doesn't mean he's mine.

We walk past Washington Square Park over to MacDougal St. When we reach Italiano Desiderio, we stop. "I hope you like Italian."

"I've been dying to come here, but they're booked solid. How did you get a table?"

"I know the owner," he says with a wink and then opens the door. "After you."

When I step inside, the street noise disappears. The restaurant looks like a scene straight from Italy. The room is long and has a series of arches with ivy growing up the columns. Small lanterns hang from the branches providing soft lighting to the room. Instrumental music is playing quietly. If we hadn't just walked through NYC, I'd think we were in Venice.

We wait for the hostess, whose back is turned while she's talking to a server. She spins around and sees Alex; her eyes light up.

"Mr. Montgomery, so nice to see you tonight," she says, batting her eyes at *my* date.

I don't know what it is that is making me feel so territorial over him.

"Thank you," Alex says, not paying attention to her flirting. "Is our table ready?"

The hostess glances my way, her saccharine smile faltering. "Right this way."

We follow her through the restaurant, past the diners already seated, eating their meals.

I swear she's swaying her hips just a little extra as she leads us through the restaurant and out the back door. It's as if we've stepped through a magical portal from the city into a lush garden, the smell of lavender permeates the air. We continue down a softly lit path until we reach a small table set for two.

Alex pulls my chair out, and I sit before he moves around the table and takes his seat.

The hostess hands each of us a menu. "Is there anything else you need?" she asks, placing her hand on Alex's arm.

He stiffens. "No."

She seems annoyed by his abrupt answer and quickly removes her hand. "Your server will be with you shortly," she says before turning and walking away.

"This place is amazing," I say, trying to ease the tension.

"It is. Tony and Leo have done a great job with it."

"Tony and Leo?" I ask. "As in Anthony and Leo from the club?"

I hear a man's deep laugh coming from behind me. "The one and only."

"Tony, great to see you." Alex shakes his hand. "You remember Natalie?"

"How could I forget a girl as beautiful as her?" He leans down and wraps me in a hug. I giggle and look to Alex, who's shooting a death glare in Tony's direction, which only makes Tony laugh. Alex shakes his head before joining in the laughter. "I'm glad you two could make it tonight. If you'll allow me, I'd like to offer you a bottle of our finest champagne, on the house."

"Thank you," Alex responds.

Tony motions to a nearby server, who hurries over and pours us both a glass of the bubbly drink.

"Enjoy your meal," says Tony, "I'll be back to check on you later."

We're left alone to look over the menu.

"Would you be okay if I ordered for you?" Alex asks.

I lower my menu and look at him. I'm not entirely surprised by his question. This is something Leo and I talked about—ways a Dominant can take charge. He's asking me first, which is appropriate because he isn't my Dominant. I take a quick mental inventory and realize I'm not bothered by his request. I'm curious to see how this will work.

"Yes," I say and close my menu. "I think I'd like that."

"Thank you." Alex smiles and returns to looking over the menu.

The server returns a few minutes later and takes our order. I'm impressed with the food choices Alex makes for us. I also notice the server doesn't seem at all thrown off by Alex's ordering for both of us. I wonder how often he sees something like this.

When he turns to walk away, the garden transforms once again. Soft violin music begins playing through what must be hidden speakers, and fairy lights appear, twinkling from trees. We're the only two people enjoying this private serenade in a magical garden. It makes me feel like I'm in a fairy tale.

"May I offer a toast?" Alex asks. "Congratulations on being one step closer to completing your education."

I'm not entirely sure if he's referring to discovering my submission or completing my midterms or a combination of both.

We raise our glasses, clinking the crystal together before bringing the flute to my lips. I take a sip and savor the sweet effervescence of the exquisite champagne.

"Have you given my proposition any thought?"

"I have." I set my glass down. "And although I can see myself in this lifestyle, I don't know if the timing is right."

"You could?" Alex seems intrigued. "Why isn't the timing right?"

I've practiced this conversation for weeks, knowing it was something we were going to have to discuss. Now that the moment is here, I seem to have forgotten everything I'd prac-ticed and find myself struggling to stay on script.

Without much thought, I lift my hand and start biting my fingernails. How do I tell him I'm not staying in New York permanently? And that as much as I want to try this, I can't ask him to put an expiration date on a relationship, even if it is a relationship bound by a contract?

Thankfully, our server arrives with our appetizers, a beautiful

Caprese salad. I've been granted a reprieve, at least for a short while.

I pick up my fork and cut a piece of the tomato and cheese. Alex's eyes follow my movements as I lift the food to my lips and take a bite. The fresh cheese coupled with the tomatoes' sweetness and the acidity from the balsamic vinegar explode in my mouth. I close my eyes and moan in delight. "This is one of my favorite dishes."

"I'm glad to hear that," Alex says before taking his bite. "But you didn't answer my question."

He doesn't miss a beat. "In a perfect world, I'd like to give the lifestyle, give us a try, but—"

Alex interrupts, "What's holding you back?"

"I'm not sure it fits with my other obligations." I take another bite before attempting to change the subject. "Tell me more about how you became so successful in marketing." Although we've talked a few times since we met, Alex hasn't told me much about his company.

For the moment, he lets that line of questioning go as he tells me how he opened his firm five years ago with only a few small accounts.

"I struggled for the first few years." Alex sets his fork down. "I was at the point I thought I'd have to close until the right client walked in. I was incredibly lucky."

With how persistent he's been in getting me to go out with him, something tells me luck is only a small part of the reason for his success.

Our meal is served at a leisurely pace, one decadent dish after another being brought to our table. "I've never been to Italy, but this is how I imagine the food to be, fresh and rustic," I say as I take a bite of manicotti with truffle shavings.

"That's because it is," Alex says. "Behind where we're sitting is Tony's vegetable garden. He grows as many ingredients as possible, and he makes all the pasta fresh."

"No wonder it's impossible to get a reservation here," I say and take another bite of my food.

We're served the last course, espresso, and cannoli.

The dessert looks fantastic, but after everything I've eaten, I can't eat this too.

"Don't you like cannoli?" Alex asks.

"I do, very much," I say.

"Then why haven't you touched it?"

"I already overate." I look down and fold my hands, trying hard not to bite my nails. "With the way I look, I can't eat stuff like this."

"The way you look?" Alex's eyes narrow. "What's that supposed to mean?"

"My weight. I need to watch everything—"

"Stop." He puts his hands flat on the table. "I will not have you talking about yourself that way. You're beautiful. Your body is beautiful."

My eyes are locked on his, ready to challenge him when a man clears his throat.

"I'm sorry for interrupting," Tony says. "I can come back in a few minutes."

"No need," Alex says without taking his eyes off me.

"How was your meal?" Tony asks cautiously.

"It was incredible," I say. "I'm so full I can't manage to eat my dessert. Can I have it wrapped?" I glance in Alex's direction.

"Absolutely." Tony smiles, clearly relieved that the tense moment has passed.

"Thank you, Tony," Alex says. "Everything was perfect."

"Anytime, man." Tony slaps Alex's shoulder. "Natalie, I hope I see you again soon."

"I'd like that very much."

"Alex will give you my number," says Tony. "Call me anytime you want to come by."

"Thank you." I can see why Leo is head over heels for this man.

Tony leaves the table, our server taking his place to wrap my dessert. Alex settles our check before standing. "There's a back exit we can take."

He offers me his hand, the tension from before melts away slightly as we exit the restaurant.

We walk in silence, enjoying the warm Autumn evening until we come back to Washington Square.

"Can we sit and talk?" Alex asks.

"Sure."

He leads me into the park to a bench facing the illuminated fountain. We sit together and spend a long moment watching the people milling about before Alex breaks our silence.

"You said you're interested in the lifestyle, but it doesn't fit with your *obligations*." He pauses and searches my face. "Can you tell me what that means?"

I take a deep breath before I say, "I'm only in NYC to go to school. When I graduate in the spring, I have to go back home. The scholarship I have requires me to work in Northmeadow for five years."

Alex stares at the fountain for a minute before turning back to me. "We still have plenty of time to try it out." He reaches out and takes my hands in his. "Before it's time for you to leave, we can talk and decide if we want to continue our arrangement or walk away."

"You'd be okay with a time limit on this?"

"Yes," he says. "I'll take any opportunity to explore us as a Dom/sub couple. We can work on the details after you say yes." His smile reaches his beautiful brown eyes.

"Okay," I say, returning his smile with one of my own.

"Is that a yes?" he asks.

"Yes, Sir," I say, a giggle escapes my lips.

Alex sits up straighter. "Let the negotiations begin."

NATALIE

"*L*ast night was like a fairy tale," I tell Lana as we sit at the table drinking coffee. "Alex is amazing."

Lana smiles proudly. "I knew you two would get along."

"How long have you known Alex?"

"A little while," she says.

"How long's a little while?" I have a feeling there's more to this story that she's not telling me, but our conversation is interrupted by the doorbell.

Lana jumps up. "I'll get it."

"Saved by the bell," I call. "But this conversation isn't over."

"Alex," Lana says after she opens the door. "I didn't know you were coming over."

"Is Natalie here?" he asks.

Yes, I'm here, but I'm not letting Alex see me like this. I'm wearing the sweatpants and T-shirt I slept in last night. My hair's thrown up in a messy bun, and I haven't even brushed my teeth yet.

"You bet," Lana says. "She's in the kitchen."

I make a move to get up from the table, hoping to sprint to

my room and get dressed, but Alex's voice stops me before I can even stand up.

"Good afternoon, Natalie."

"Good afternoon," I reply. "Can you excuse me for a minute? I need to get changed."

"You're perfectly fine as you are." He smiles.

I lift my head and raise an eyebrow.

"I'm going to go take a shower and get some studying done," Lana chirps. "I'll leave you two alone." Her pace is fast as she walks down the hallway into her bedroom.

"I wasn't expecting you." My heart is beating rapidly. "Can I get you some coffee?"

"I'd like that," he says. "I brought a contract with me. I thought we might go over it together."

I almost drop the mug I just took out of the cupboard. "You have a contract ready already?"

"I have a standard contract that I made some adjustments to," Alex says. "Since this is your first time as a sub, I made it very basic."

My fluffy socks cushion my steps as I walk across the kitchen and place the coffee on the table. "Do you take cream or sugar?"

"No, this is perfect." He looks up at me, his brown eyes dancing with excitement. "Thank you, baby girl."

Baby girl? Those words sound so intimate coming from him. I melt as I sit in my chair.

He slides a copy of the contract across the table to me and keeps a copy for himself. "We don't need to make final decisions on anything today," he reassures me. "I thought we could read it through together, in case you have any questions right away."

This is all new to me, but his statement puts me at ease. I lift the papers and sit back in my chair as I begin to skim through them.

Mistress Star showed us examples of contracts during class, so I have some idea what to expect. I look up and find Alex watching me intently, his hands folded on the table in front of him. I imagine this is what he looks like when he's at work conducting a meeting with a client. I give him a small smile and go back to perusing the document.

Although the contract reflects my newness to the lifestyle, Alex seems to have covered everything. The contract details how he, as my Dominant, will treat me with respect and be responsible for my safety. As his submissive, I will also treat him with respect and conduct myself appropriately, as I am a reflection of my Dominant. Although we won't be together twenty-four hours a day, the contract specifies things such as daily check-ins and obligations, including exercise and a healthy diet. Another section details rules and the consequences for breaking them. Some of the things I won't be allowed to do are drinking to intoxication, disrespecting my Dominant, and orgasming without his consent.

"No biting my nails?" I look up at him.

"I'd like to keep that in the contract," he says. "We can discuss other, less destructive ways for you to deal with anxiety."

Wow. His reasoning isn't what I thought it would be. "I'm open to that."

"On page three, you can see I included a list of things I'd like to do sexually." He flips the pages in his hand. "Can we discuss your experience level first and then go over the list?" he asks. "We can address your limits and remove whatever is necessary."

I flip to page three. Blindfolds, crops, floggers, bondage, anal trainers, and gags are some things on the list. Talking openly about sex is still a new concept for me.

"I'm not a virgin," I say quickly. "But I've only been with one person, and it was all very plain."

Alex laughs. "Plain?"

"Yeah, vanilla, I guess you'd call it." I pause. "Tommy, my ex-boyfriend, did his thing and never, well, never made sure I got anything out of it." I can feel the heat from embarrassment creeping up my cheeks.

"He never gave you an orgasm?" Alex leans forward.

I shake my head back and forth slowly. "No."

"Baby girl," Alex says. "That will not happen between us. Part of my job is to give you pleasure."

His words cause me to squirm in my seat. I've already had a small taste of how my body responds to Alex's touch from the night at the club. I can't imagine how much more exciting it will be as his submissive.

"I have a question."

"You can ask anything you want." His voice is calm and steady.

"Anal trainers?" I ask. "What's that?"

"I'm assuming anal sex is new to you?" he asks.

I nod my head in agreement.

"They're a series of butt plugs designed to stretch you so I can enter you without causing any physical damage." He pauses. "If that's not something you're open to right now, we can take that off the list. I want to help you grow but not push you too far."

Anal sex is something I've always been curious about, but when I tried to bring it up to Tommy, he shut me down. "We can leave it on there, as long as we go slow."

"Deal." Alex smiles.

His smile, the way his face lights up, is a sight I don't think I'll ever grow tired of.

We spend the next hour talking about everything in the contract. The longer we speak, the more comfortable I become. Alex doesn't pressure me or have expectations I feel are unreasonable.

"The contract will expire seven months from now, in time for your graduation," Alex says. "We can reevaluate things if we want, or we can choose to part ways."

The thought of parting ways already makes me feel sad. It's something I'll have to get used to though, I have to go back to Northmeadow in June whether I want to or not. I take a deep breath and remind myself, it's only November. We have plenty of time to spend with each other.

Alex looks at his watch. "I need to get going. I have to be in the office for a meeting."

"On a Saturday?"

"I try not to, but this is an important client, so I make myself available whenever he needs." Alex stands. "Take some time with the contract. If you have any more questions or changes, let me know, and we'll take care of it."

I stand and walk with him to the door. "Is there a deadline on when you need it back?"

"No." He chuckles. "There's no rush. I want you to make a fully informed decision before we continue."

"Okay, that sounds good."

Alex leans in and places a kiss on my cheek. "But I do hope I hear from you soon."

I smile as I watch him walk down the hall. The past few months, my life has changed dramatically. When I went to the club with Lana, I wasn't looking to meet anyone, and I certainly had no intention of becoming a submissive. After reading the books and taking the classes, pieces of me that I didn't even know were missing, start falling into place. Now, here I am considering signing a contract to be a submissive to a kind and thoughtful, not to mention an extremely gorgeous, man. Closing the door, I drop my forehead against it and blow out a breath.

"Is he gone?" Lana peeks out from the hallway.

"Yes, he just left. He had to work."

"And?" she asks as she walks into the living room and flops herself onto the sofa.

"He brought a contract," I say and sit next to her. "Will you look it over with me?"

"I'd love to," Lana says with a satisfied grin.

ALEX

It's over a week before I hear from Natalie. I've picked up my phone to call her almost every night but stopped myself. As much as I want her to sign the contract, the decision isn't mine to make. It may be the hardest thing I've ever done, but I need to give her the time and space she needs to make the right decision for her.

I'm in my office going over some files from Maxim Solonik, Svetlana's father and my biggest client. I owe him everything. If it weren't for him, I probably would've had to shut my firm down years ago. I certainly wouldn't be as successful as I am today.

Opening the security software, I click the button to encrypt the information before saving it. Taking this account was risky yet lucrative. While the files are saving, I recline in my black leather chair. My mind drifts back to my first meeting with Maxim.

Early in my college career, I decided on a double major in Marketing and Bioethics. Climate change and ecofriendly business practices were beginning to grow in popularity, and I intended to take full advantage. Fresh out of school, I said goodbye to my life in Seattle, searching for fame and fortune in

New York City. I planned to take the city by storm rebranding businesses, highlighting their eco-friendly efforts.

I'd been left some money when my grandfather passed away. Dad helped me invest it wisely, so I had a small nest egg. Deciding that office space was more important than living space, I used most of the money to secure a prime location. I rented a cheap room in a hostel, sure it would only be a temporary stop, and I'd have a steady cash flow for an apartment soon.

Finding clients wasn't as easy as I'd expected. Not many people wanted to take a chance on the new kid in town. I'd been able to sign a few small clients, but they weren't bringing in enough to pay the bills. My ego had taken a hit, and I was quickly running out of money. My father knew I was in trouble and offered to help me out, but I was too stubborn to accept it. He was still recovering from the loss of my mother. I didn't want to take anything else from him.

One night I stayed late, trying to figure out how I could afford the rent for the business and my room. I was considering just living in my office. I must've forgotten to lock the door. The jingle of the bells startled me. A man in an expensive tailored suit entered my office and was walking directly toward me. He hadn't yet spoken, but something about the way he carried himself made me sit up and take notice.

I stood to greet the man. "Can I help you with something?"

With a strong Russian accent, he introduced himself as Maxim Solonik. As if he owned the place, he took a seat and began telling me about his company.

He was in Russian oil and sought to expand his operations into the US by getting involved in the natural-gas pipeline network. His company held technology that would be useful with advancing the cleaner energy source. He had my full attention as we discussed his unique needs at great lengths.

As the hour had grown later, Maxim proposed we continue our meeting over food and drink. That night he made a strong case for why I should take him on as a client. We shook hands and have been working together ever since.

Being young and naïve, I didn't ask many questions. I only saw the chance to save my failing business. I didn't know why he chose me or that our partnership would go far beyond environmental technology. Meeting him not only ensured my business became more lucrative than I ever dreamed, but it also led me to the best thing in my life.

When Maxim and I started working together, we spent a great deal of time together, both here in the states and at his home in Russia. Besides partnering in business, we became friends. One of his trips to New York happened to be on the first anniversary of my mother's death.

I'd always admired my parents' relationship, both as a typical married couple and as a Master/slave. When I was twenty, I entered the lifestyle, hoping to find what they had until I witnessed my dad lose everything that mattered to him. In a reckless move, I left the lifestyle behind. I walked away from my submissive without so much as an explanation. It hurt her, something I've made amends for. My mother's death had wrecked me and left me stumbling blindly through life. I refused to be involved with anyone and risk falling in love.

That night, after I hadn't answered any of his calls, Maxim came to my apartment. I was drunk, trying to numb the pain and loss. He stayed with me that night as I told him everything.

He didn't know my history with BDSM, or so I thought. The next night he invited me to Fire and Ice and introduced me to a submissive I was able to play with—no strings attached.

Eventually, he told me why he chose me. Years ago, my parents were in Russia. The two couples met at a dungeon. My dad was interested in learning how to use a bullwhip, and Maxim was an expert. They spent a lot of time together, Maxim teaching Dad everything he knew. The two couples never lost touch.

He mentored me as I cautiously started practicing the lifestyle again. It was because of his intervention that night that I not only found myself but eventually, I found Natalie. I owe that man more than I can ever repay.

With the encryption done, I shut my laptop off and push myself to a standing position. My muscles are tight and sore from sitting in one spot for so long. Before heading out, I check my phone one last time and finally see a text from Natalie.

(Natalie) I've gone over the contract and have one request.
(Me) What's the request?
(Natalie) I'd like to add rope bondage. You know, like Shibari.

Her request makes me smile. She sure is adventurous. One big problem, I don't know much about it. But for her, I'll learn.

(Me) Done. Is there anything else you want to add?
(Natalie) No, that's everything. I'm ready to sign.

I'm ready to sign. I read those words over and over, making sure they're real. Sure enough, the words are still on the screen. Having a submissive is a big responsibility, one I've screwed up in the past. I hope you have your shit together, Alex, because you can't mess this up. Natalie deserves only the best.

(Me) Do you have plans tonight?
(Natalie) Nope. I was planning on making popcorn and watching a Christmas movie.
(Me) How about I pick you up. We can grab some dinner and watch a movie at my place?
(Natalie) I'd like that.
(Me) I'm getting ready to leave the office now. I'll be at your place in about 20.
(Natalie) I'll be ready.

I shutdown and slide the phone into my pocket before

locking up and walking to my car. My driver, Viktor, is standing outside the passenger door of my black Model 3 Tesla.

"Where to boss?" Viktor asks.

He wasn't with me when I picked Natalie up last time, so I give him the address before I get in.

It's a typical Friday evening in NYC, traffic is terrible, and we take longer than my anticipated twenty minutes. When we finally arrive at her building, Viktor waits in the car while I go in to collect my new submissive.

NATALIE

Twenty minutes to get out of my cozy jammies and get ready to see Alex. You've got this, Nat. I rush around my room, looking for something comfortable yet sexy. Tonight's a big night. We'll be signing the contract, officially starting our Dom/sub relationship. My hands shake as I put on my light pink strapless bra. I slide on my cream, off the shoulder sweater and then step into my favorite pair of jeans. I had my hair pulled up in two little buns, it's going to have to stay that way, or else my curls will be a frizzy mess. There's just enough time for me to put on mascara and lip gloss before my doorbell rings.

Standing back, I take a look at myself in the mirror, knowing this is a defining moment in my life. For the next several months, I won't be living for myself. Alex will come first in everything I do. My words and actions will not represent just me but will now also represent my Dominant. It's a huge responsibility, but one that I'm ready to take. With one final breath, I walk to the door and open it. Alex stands on the other side wearing a black suit, his red tie loose around his neck.

"Hi," I manage to say.

"Hi," Alex responds. "You look beautiful."

I lower my gaze, unable to meet his. He puts his finger under my chin and lifts my face so I can't avoid his eyes.

"Don't look away when I compliment you," he says in a stern yet calm tone. "Let's try this again. You look beautiful, baby girl."

"Thank you, Sir." I smile shyly, not used to accepting a compliment.

"Are you ready to go?"

"Let me just grab my coat," I answer and pull it off the rack.

Like a true gentleman he helps be into my coat before offering me his arm. Together we make our way out into the cold December air.

He leads me to a high-end luxury car with a driver, poised and waiting for us.

"This is yours?" I try not to let my mouth hang open.

"Yes," he answers proudly, "I'd like to introduce you to Viktor."

"Nice to meet you."

Viktor nods and opens the back door, allowing me to get into the car. The seats are soft black leather and are heated, a nice addition given how chilly it is outside. Alex slides in next to me; our legs brush up against each other. A sizzle of electricity runs through my body.

Christmastime in the city is a special time. The usual excitement turned up a notch by all the tourists who've come to see the decorations. Even though I've lived here for several years, I still feel like a child when I walk past the Rockefeller Center Tree or the oversized decorations scattered throughout the city. It's something I'm really going to miss when I go back home.

Inside, the car is silent. I steal a glance at Alex; his posture is tense. Could he be nervous too?

My thoughts are interrupted when Viktor turns the car into an underground parking garage. He pulls into a reserved parking spot, turning the car off before we get out. Alex leads me to the waiting elevator. We step inside, and he punches in a code before pressing the penthouse button. When the elevator arrives, it opens directly into his apartment.

Alex gets out first. "Make yourself at home. Can I get you something to drink?"

"May I have a water, please?" I say without looking at him. Instead, my gaze is focused on the floor to ceiling windows lining two walls. One overlooks his Upper West Side neighborhood, the other a spectacular view over the Hudson River. "The view is stunning."

"The view *is* stunning," Alex says before going to his kitchen to get our drinks. "Come sit on the sofa," he says. "We need to talk."

His apartment is magnificent. The ceilings are easily ten feet tall. The rooms open into each other with a clean, modern feel. The sofa is a large dark grey sectional situated by a fireplace, which adds warmth to the room. I sit down as Alex comes over and hands me a glass of ice water. I take a sip before setting it down on the glass end table next to the sofa. Alex sets his glass down as well.

I fidget with my fingers, bringing one to my mouth, biting my nail. Alex reaches out and takes my hand, placing it in my lap. "Relax, baby girl. There's no reason to be nervous." His voice is like a calming balm to my nerves.

"Where do we go from here?" I ask.

"Before we move any further, we need to go over the contract one more time. If you are sure you're ready, we'll both sign it."

"I forgot to bring my copy."

"I have one in my office," he says. "Wait here."

Alex stands up and walks down a hallway. His shoes make a loud clicking sound that seems to echo in the large space.

I silently chastise myself for forgetting something so important.

It only takes a minute before he's back with papers and a pen in his hand.

"Here's a copy for you." He hands me the contract. "I made the requested changes."

We take the next few minutes to go through everything, making sure it's written exactly as we both want it.

"It looks good," I say and offer him a nervous smile.

"Are you ready to sign?"

Am I ready to sign? This is my chance to try something new and exciting—to live on my terms. "Yes, Sir."

The smile he gives me in return lights up his face, making my insides quiver.

Alex hands me a pen, and I sign my name on both copies. When I finish, I pass him the pen, and he does the same. He takes our papers and the pen and sets them down on the table.

The energy in the room suddenly shifts, sexual tension fills the room. Every time we're together, there's a chemistry between us, but we couldn't act on it during our negotiations. The first rule Mistress Star drilled into each of us was not to get physically involved with anyone we were vetting because it would cloud our judgment. But now, the vetting is over, we're officially Dom/sub and can finally act on the feelings we have.

Alex brushes a strand of hair from my face and tucks it behind my ear. The small amount of contact sends chills down my spine. He leans in and brushes his lips against mine in a slow, gentle kiss. His tongue explores my lips before I open, allowing him access to my mouth. When I do, it's as if a dam has opened. The connection we've shared explodes. Our kiss turns desperate, primal. He lifts me, so I'm straddling his lap as we continue to kiss.

"Do you feel this between us?" he asks breathlessly. "Do you want me as much as I want you?"

I nod my head in response.

"I need a verbal answer, Natalie."

"Yes, Sir. I want you."

The words have no sooner left my mouth before his lips are back on mine. He stands, lifting me with him.

"Wrap your legs around me." I obey immediately, and he begins walking down the hall toward his bedroom. He sets me on his bed before he steps back and starts unbuttoning his shirt, throwing it over a nearby chair.

Following his lead, I pull my sweater off and drop it on floor.

"You. Are. Beautiful," Alex says. He makes quick work of his button and zipper before pulling his pants and boxers off. The size of his erection causes me to gasp. When he hears my reaction, he holds his arms open. "This is all for you, baby girl."

With quick strides, he closes the gap between us, his body pushing mine back on the bed as he begins kissing me once again. His hands reach around my back, unhooking my bra. He tosses it to the side. His mouth is on one breast, sucking and nipping before switching to the other one, paying it the same attention. Sliding his body down mine, he kisses a trail between my breasts, down to my abdomen.

"I need to taste you," he says before unbuttoning my jeans and sliding them off. Slowly and carefully, he removes my lacey panties, feathering kisses along my leg as he does.

He spreads my legs and gives an appreciative groan when he sees I'm waxed and smooth, just as he specified in the contract.

"You're so wet for me already," he says before kissing my inner thigh, moving higher and higher. When he reaches my center, his tongue teases my clit, tracing light circles around it.

My hips move of their own accord, and he pulls back. "Stay still."

"Yes, Sir," I answer.

His tongue returns to work, and he adds two fingers, sliding them in and out of me, matching the rhythm of his tongue. I've never had a man's mouth on me before, the feeling is exquisite, and I struggle to remain still. It doesn't take long before an orgasm washes over me, and I'm yelling his name. He continues to lick and suck until the waves of my orgasm subside, then he crawls up my body.

"You taste even better than I imagined," he says before he

kisses me deeply, allowing me to taste myself on him. It's subtle and tangy, like nothing I've tasted before.

"Sir, I need you inside me." My voice is breathy.

He sits back on his knees. "You need to learn some patience." I watch as his hand strokes his length, up and down. "Is this what you want?"

"Yes, please."

He leans in and drags his cock over my sensitive clit, teasing me before he lines himself up with my opening and slides in ever so slowly.

Once he's fully sheathed inside me, he pauses, closing his eyes. "Fuck, you feel so good." He begins to move slowly, not rushing our first time together.

I reach up and run my fingers through his dark hair before lifting my head and kissing him. Although this is only supposed to be a contractual relationship, I can already feel my heart softening toward him.

Our bodies move together in a passionate rhythm. Alex's hands slide up my stomach to my breasts. He holds them in his hands, rolling my nipples before giving them a hard squeeze, eliciting a gasp from me. "Did you like that?"

"Yes." My words are barely a whisper.

"These will look beautiful with clamps on them."

His words only heighten my quickly building arousal. "I'm so close."

"Do not come yet," he orders as he increases his pace. "Open your eyes. I want you to look at me when you come—to remember who you belong to."

Our eyes remain locked on each other as Alex thrusts harder and faster.

"Come now," he orders.

An orgasm sweeps through my body. With one more thrust, Alex is coming inside me. He kisses me deeply as we ride out the pleasure together.

He drops his forehead to mine. The only sound in the room is our mingled breaths. "We're so good together, baby girl. I'm glad you decided to give us a chance."

"Me too." His words fill my heart with hope for the future.

Alex rolls onto his back and pulls my body into his. I lay wrapped in his arms, my head on his chest, until I drift off to sleep.

ALEX

J've been in back-to-back video conferences all day. My company is picking up some big clients. Over the years, I've assembled teams of very talented individuals who design successful campaigns. Because of this, I've built one of the most sought-after marketing companies on the east coast.

I'm sitting in my fourth meeting of the day when an email notification pops up on my phone. A quick swipe of the screen shows it's from Maxim. The subject line reads *New Client Coming Onboard*. This gets my attention, and I sit up straighter. Another client? I'm eager to open the email and read more about it.

"Mr. Montgomery, your thoughts on the new campaign slogan?" My team leader interrupts my reading.

"Everything looks good here." I gather the papers in front of me before pushing my chair back and stand. "If you'll excuse me, I just received an email that needs an immediate response. I trust you have this under control." Without waiting for his response, I walk out of the meeting room and head straight to my office.

At my desk, I type in my password to unlock my screen and open the email.

Alexander,

A colleague of mine, Mr. Nicholai Federov, requires your services. He has technology that will be of interest to alternative energy companies. I'd like to arrange a meeting with the three of us to discuss how we wish to proceed. This client will require a great deal of time but will be mutually beneficial to us both. Attached you will find a proposal. Take your time reviewing it. We will make a time to speak next week.

Maxim.

Opening the proposal, I get started reading it right away. Nicholai is involved with a company studying Neutrinovoltaic Energy, the latest in renewable energy resources. That's the official work. When Maxim and I on talk on the phone next week, he'll fill me in on how Nicholai fits into the more sensitive aspects of his business.

When I look up, I see the sun has long since set. I got so involved in reading the proposal I didn't realize how time got away from me. Grabbing my phone off the desk, I text Viktor telling him I'll be out shortly. Then I send a reply to Maxim, letting him know I got his email and that I'll be in touch.

My house is quiet and lonely when I return after a long day at the office. Natalie and I lived in our little bubble over the holidays. I convinced her to stay at my place since she didn't have school. It was something I've never done before—never shared my apartment with a submissive. She was hesitant at first but agreed to it as long as it was only temporary. I know Natalie's holding back because she's going back to Northmeadow, and she doesn't want to get too attached.

Being able to spend a few weeks together was better than I imagined. We were able to work out some of the initial kinks. My little sub did well following the rules. I only had to punish her once. Not biting her nails is going to be a challenge for her.

She took advantage of my fully stocked kitchen, making sure there was a home-cooked meal for us to sit down to together every night. It reminded me of my childhood. The aromas coming from the kitchen as my mother lovingly prepared dinner for my father, of us sitting down to meals and talking about our days. I didn't realize how important those memories are to me and how much I desire that in my life now.

Coming home after work to find her kneeling in my foyer waiting for me is something I quickly grew used to. I miss it now that she's back at her apartment and our time together is limited. She's in the middle of her final semester, juggling classes and an internship, and I've been busy at work.

Maxim is expanding his operations and is hoping I'll take on another client. It would bring in a lot of money, but it will also mean giving up a great deal of time. Natalie and I only have a few months left together. I don't want to waste a second of it.

I put my briefcase on the dining table and loosen my tie before walking over to the windows. Looking out over the water, I recall the look on Natalie's face the first time she stepped into my apartment. Her green eyes shimmered as she took in the view, something I never stopped to appreciate before that moment. I took for granted everything she saw. I miss her presence here, and I want her back. That thought stops me in my tracks. Natalie's temporary, she's leaving soon. The realization causes a stirring in my heart—I don't want her to leave. What is it about this girl that has me turned upside down?

There's something about her; maybe it's her innocence. Even though I've told her little about my personal life, she's been open about hers. Losing her brother to suicide greatly impacted her and is the driving force behind her career choice. She's also told me about her ex-boyfriend, the one who broke her heart but is also responsible for her new outlook on life. His loss is my gain. I can feel myself starting to care about her as more than just my submissive, but I have to shut those feelings off. She made it clear this was nothing more than a few months of fun before she goes back home.

NATALIE

The remainder of the semester flies by. Finals are over, and graduation is in two weeks. It's bittersweet. I'm thankful that my schooling is complete, and I'll be able to start my career. But at the same time, I feel like I've just started to allow myself to embrace life in the city, and it's all coming to an end, fast.

Then there's Alex. We've grown close over the past few months. We see each other one or two days during the week and spend weekends together. Every Friday night, he comes home from the office to find me kneeling inside his foyer. His eyes heat the second he sees me. I've learned to keep dinner on warm because we rarely make it to the table before we're naked and he's inside me.

I promised myself this was nothing more than a few months of fun, trying out something new, no strings attached. It seems that promise has backfired. I think I'm falling in love with him. Too bad he doesn't feel the same way about me. I have to remind myself his kindness and affection is all part of the contract. Part of his being my Dominant and nothing more. Our relationship, just like my time in the city, comes with a rapidly approaching expiration date.

"Nat, your phone's ringing," Lana calls from the living room.

I didn't realize I left it out there. "Who is it?"

"It's Alex," she says in a sing-song voice before she answers my phone.

I hurry down the hall and into the living room.

"Here she is," Lana says and hands me the phone. "Did you invite him to graduation?" she whispers.

I put my hand over the phone. "Of course, I did."

She nods in acknowledgment. "I'm getting my bag. Brandon will be here any minute. I'll see you at the ceremony."

"Okay, have fun," I say before walking to my bedroom. Lana's going to stay at Brandon's this week. The two of them are nearly inseparable.

"Hello?"

"Hi, baby girl," Alex says. "Did I catch you at a bad time?"

"No. I was just saying goodbye to Lana," I answer. "She's headed to Brandon's."

"He told me she's staying with him for a while," he says. "Sounds like they're getting pretty serious."

I feel a pang of unwanted jealousy. I'm happy for my best friend but sad for me.

"Are you coming over this weekend?" Alex asks.

It's our last official week together.

"Yes." It's going to be hard to say goodbye.

"Why don't you spend the week with me?" His voice holds a glimmer of hope.

"I can't. I have to pack and get everything shipped home." Although that's true, it's more of an excuse. Everything's pretty much packed. There's no way I can handle spending the whole week with him and then having to say goodbye.

"We can stay at your place," he says. "I can help you."

"Alex." I pause. "I don't think that's a good idea."

"I had to try," he says. "I'll have Viktor pick you up tomorrow?"

"I'll be ready."

I disconnect the call and already feel my heart breaking. How am I going to say goodbye to Alex? Walking away from him is going to be the hardest thing I've ever had to do.

I fight back the tears as Viktor takes my bag and walks me to the waiting car. It's a quiet drive across town, although that's not different than most days. Viktor doesn't talk much—he's all business.

We pull into the parking garage and the usual spot. "I'll bring your bags up in a few minutes. I have something I need to take care of," Viktor says.

"Take your time." I smile and get out of the car.

The elevator takes me to Alex's apartment. When the doors open, I see a trail of roses through the apartment. They lead me into the bedroom, where I find a note.

Take a hot bath with the toiletries I left for you and prepare yourself for me. You have one hour, then I expect to find you on my bed wearing only the item provided.

I pick up a red blindfold and rub my fingers over the silky material—excitement pulses through me as I try to imagine what Alex has planned for tonight.

In the bathroom, I find a bottle of lavender vanilla body wash. I turn on the hot water and squeeze some of it into the bath before stripping my clothes and allowing myself to sink into the deep tub. I don't often take the time to soak, but I should; it feels heavenly. I rest my head back and allow the hot water to relax my tense muscles. After giving myself some time to unwind, I make sure my body is ready to Alex's specifications.

Climbing out of the tub, I notice another note on top of a

white bathrobe. I slip into the robe, tying it around my waist before reading the card.

Make sure your hair is pulled back and off your shoulders.

I make my way to the mirror and run the brush through my hair before braiding it and pinning it up in a bun. Alex must have something special in store for tonight if he's instructing me to put my hair up.

Once I'm back in the bedroom, I check the time—five minutes to spare. I didn't realize I took so long in the tub. I finish drying and lay down on the bed before sliding the blindfold into place. Without my sight, my other senses are heightened. I lay still and quiet, listening for any hint that Alex is home.

I don't know how long it takes before I hear footsteps approaching from the hall. The door opens and closes, and I hear the lock click into place. The room fills with the familiar scent of citrus and sandalwood. I know it's Alex. He says nothing as he walks around the room. Drawers open and close. I feel him set things down on the bed, but I have no idea what they are.

I startle when I feel something light being run gently up my leg.

"That tickles," I giggle.

"Shh," Alex says. "No talking."

The same item, a feather perhaps, is being dragged over my arms, leaving a trail of goosebumps in its wake. Then it's gone.

"Spread your legs," Alex commands.

Without hesitation, I do as he instructs.

"Mmmm...beautiful," Alex says.

I feel him secure a cuff around one ankle then the other before attaching them to the hidden clips on his bed. He then moves to my wrists, tying them over my head to the headboard. I'm completely at his mercy, and I love it.

Following the same path the feather took, there's now what feels like a spiked wheel rolling over my skin. Although the sharp sensation is such a contrast from the feather, it feels good. Alex continues rolling it up my abdomen before rolling it across my breasts. The spikes cause my nipples to harden. The sensation stops as abruptly as it started.

I think I hear him leaving, and I call out, "Alex? Are you still here?"

"I'm not going anywhere, baby girl," he answers in a lust-filled tone.

Leaning over my body, he kisses me before placing a set of headphones over my ears. The sudden loss of hearing surprises me, and I pull on my restraints. Alex gently places his hands on my shoulders, kissing me deeper. I lose myself in the passion and allow the anxiety to dissipate. He removes his hands from my shoulders, but I can still feel the warmth of his body. I know he's close.

My back arches when something cold swirls around my belly button and down my stomach before he drags it through my slit, where it leaves a trail of burning fire. I thought it was ice, but there's also a warmth. The contrast in feeling makes me wonder what the object is. It's not until I feel him suck on my nipple that I decide it is ice, and it's been in his mouth the whole time. The thought causes wetness to pool between my legs. But just like last time, the sensation disappears instantly.

The silence from the headphones is replaced with soft music. Alex places feathered kisses down my body, bringing me back to a state of relaxation. His body is gone once again, and I'm left waiting for the next experience.

He doesn't make me wait long before I feel something warm and slick on my back entrance. I immediately tense, we've not had anal sex before, and although I'm open to the idea, I'm also nervous.

Before I have a chance to panic, Alex's fingers begin teasing my clit. My arousal intensifies as an orgasm quickly begins to build. At the same time, I feel something firm yet smooth penetrating the tight muscles. Alex increases the pressure on my clit as he gently eases the toy in and out of me until it's fully inside and I'm on the edge of an orgasm. Then he stops abruptly, causing me to moan in frustration. I try to pull my legs together to quell the overwhelming sensations, forgetting they're restrained.

The music changes. I don't recognize the song until I hear the lyrics. It's Eminem's "Lose Yourself." I hold back a giggle. This isn't our usual playlist.

As if on cue, the toy begins to vibrate a pattern in time to the music. I'm overwhelmed with the sensations. My body feels as though it's on the edge of a precipice but is unable to fall off the other side. Alex's fingers begin to tease my clit again. I raise my hips, needing more, but his other hand pushes them down. Just when I think I can't take it anymore, I feel his tongue penetrate my entrance. It's all I need to send me over the edge.

Before my orgasm ends, he's already inside me. I've never felt so full as he establishes a hard, fast rhythm. My second orgasm rockets through me, leaving me breathless. Alex doesn't stop his punishing rhythm. He takes off the headphones and pulls the blindfold from my eyes. It takes a minute for my eyes to adjust, but when they do, I find him gazing deeply into mine.

"You're changing me," he says. "You're making me a different man. A man who wants us to be more than just a contract."

As soon as the words leave his mouth, he explodes inside me. I follow right behind him. My body convulses with a climax stronger than I've ever felt.

My eyes close as blackness creeps into my vision, and I'm floating in quiet, peaceful bliss.

NATALIE

*T*he day I've been dreading since Alex and I finalized our Dom/sub agreement has finally come—the end. He asked if we could sit and talked after I shower. I close my eyes and allow the hot water to run over me while trying to imagine how our conversation will go.

When we met, we agreed that neither of us was in it for anything more than a few months of exploring the lifestyle together. I'd get some firsthand experience, and Alex would have a sub to play with—no strings attached. As hard as it was going to be, I prepared myself to say goodbye. To walk away, leaving him in my past. But then last night, he had said something that possibly changes everything. He said he wants something more than a contract.

What am I going to do? I graduate in exactly one week, and there's a one-way plane ticket back to Northmeadow, Missouri, sitting on my desk at home. No matter how much I want to continue exploring this dynamic, I'm tied to Northmeadow for the next five years. I don't have a choice—I signed that away when I accepted my scholarship.

After I finish my shower, I wrap a fluffy white towel around my body, blow dry my hair, and put on some make-up. I have so much stuff here. It's a good thing I brought a bigger bag. I'm packing it all up, knowing I plan to return to my apartment after our conversation today. I know Alex wants me to spend the week with him, but I can't. I need some time alone to figure everything out. Slipping on my pink sundress, I look in the mirror, a sad reflection stares back at me. It's time to be strong, Natalie.

Barefoot, I make my way into the kitchen, where Alex sits at his table waiting for me. He looks up, a gorgeous smile on his face; his eyes hold so much hope. When he sees me, his shoulders slump, and the smile disappears from his face.

ALEX

$\mathcal{I}$ retrieved two copies of our Dom/sub agreement from my office. Today is the expiration date, the day to reevaluate where we want to go from here. I fully anticipated saying goodbye to Natalie today. I had no intention of this arrangement ever being anything more than a few months of playtime for her and me, but then something happened.

Somewhere along the way, my feelings toward her started to change, my heart began to soften. Natalie's special; she isn't like any woman I've ever met. So much about her is pure innocence, yet she's wise. Despite having a strict, conservative upbringing, Natalie's curious and open to new experiences. Being a submissive comes naturally to her. She's genuine and beautiful, both inside and out. I've grown to care about her, and after seeing the look on her face last night when I told her I wanted more, I think she cares about me too. I can't let her leave without fighting to keep her. I have a plan, something I hope she'll agree to.

I hear her footsteps as she approaches the kitchen. Excited to share my idea with her, I turn around, but the breath is sucked from my body when I see her face. It isn't the face of a girl ready to fight for us. She's prepared to say goodbye.

Natalie takes a seat across from me. She looks down and

fidgets with her fingers. I see her inner struggle not to bite her nails. She's made so much progress, and I'm so proud of her.

"I know you're planning to leave next week, but I don't want you to go without trying to make us work; however that might look," I say.

She lifts her face. "Alex," she says, standing and walking over to the windows. It's a move she makes whenever she's struggling with something. "You live here, with all this." She motions out the window. "I'll be halfway across the country in a small farm town."

I lean forward, resting my elbows on my spread legs. Sensing she has more to say, I stay quiet, not wanting to interrupt. I need to hear her thoughts.

"I just don't see how we can be together." She rests her forehead on the glass.

I stand and walk to her, wrapping my arms around her tiny frame. "We can be anything we want to be."

Turning in my arms to face me, she asks, "How?"

"I see two options. I own my business. I can visit you whenever I want. You'll get vacation days. You can fly back here too."

She pulls away and laughs. "I won't be making a fancy New York salary. Plane tickets back and forth aren't in my future."

"Then let me buy out your contract," I blurt out and turn her to face me. "You don't have to leave. You can stay here, with me."

Natalie frees herself from my arms. "I will not have my boyfriend, my Dominant, whatever you are, buying out my contract." She crosses her arms over her chest. "I made a commitment, and I intend on keeping it."

I'm losing this argument to the very beautiful yet stubborn woman standing in front of me. But as much as I want to, I can't force her to stay, to choose me.

"I don't want to walk away from us either." Her emerald eyes fill with tears. "I'm so confused right now."

"Natalie, please," I beg. "Don't walk away from us."

She reaches out and cups my cheek in her hand. "These past few months have been the best of my life." A sad smile on her face. "Can you take me back to my apartment?"

Feeling defeated, I nod my head, reluctantly accepting her answer.

NATALIE

$\mathcal{W}$ e drive in silence; a heaviness hangs between us. I don't want to walk away from this, from Alex. There will be hundreds of miles between us though, how do we make that work? I know firsthand the betrayal that can happen when distance is involved. Alex is different. He's a man of integrity. But I don't know if I'm willing to take that chance, to put my heart on the line again.

"We're here," Alex says as he puts the car in park. For the longest moment, neither of us moves. "We're so good together, baby girl. Don't give up on us. Please, give us a chance."

The longing in his voice shatters the last slivers of my resolve. "I'll try."

He turns and looks at me. "Will you let me buy out your contract?"

"No," I answer without hesitation. "I'm going back to do my job. I'll try this long-distance. I do have some requests, though."

Alex smiles. "Can I walk you up? We can discuss them inside."

"Yes," I answer.

We get out of the car and walk together to my second-floor

apartment. I fumble in my purse for my keys when the door opens.

Alex quickly steps in front of me. "Who are you?"

"Who are *you?*" I hear a very familiar voice ask in return.

I stand on my tip-toes and peer over Alex's shoulder. "Dad? Mom? What're you guys doing here?"

"I was able to find coverage for the store. We thought we'd surprise you by coming early." Dad looks from Alex back to me. "Looks like we accomplished our goal."

"That you did." I smile, trying to hide my shock. And to be honest, my disappointment.

"Are you going to introduce us to your friend?" Dad asks.

"Mom, Dad, this is Alex."

Alex reaches out to shake my father's hand.

"Nice to meet you, Mr. Clarke."

"We thought we'd get to spend a few days with you before graduation." Mom reaches around Dad and pulls me in for a hug. "I can't wait to get you packed and home."

They definitely surprised me. My head is spinning. I can't even form a sentence.

After an awkward silence, Mom speaks again, "Why don't you two come in? I'll put some coffee on." She turns and walks toward my kitchen.

Alex looks at me, and I mouth the words I'm sorry. We were supposed to be alone to figure out how to move forward. My request was going to be to keep our relationship a secret from my parents. I know how they feel about the city and the people in it. I can't ever tell them he's my Dominant. I hoped to see if things worked out long-distance. If so, then I'd figure out a way to tell them we are a couple. If not, they'd never need to know. Tonight could very well be a disaster.

We make our way to the kitchen. My mom fumbles around in the cupboards. "Where do you keep your coffeepot, sweetie?"

I point to the Keurig on the counter. She looks at it and shakes her head disapprovingly. My parents resist anything new.

"I'll take care of it," I tell her. "Please, everyone, sit down."

While I make everyone coffee, my parents start the inquisition.

"How do you know Natalie?" Mom asks.

"I met her through her roommate," Alex answers. "I'm a friend of her family."

He's a friend of Svetlana's family? I'll have to remember to ask him about that.

"What's the nature of your relationship with my daughter?" Dad asks as he leans forward.

I nearly drop the coffee cup I'm holding. "Dad, please."

"It's okay, Natalie." Alex places his hand on mine. "We've been seeing each other for the past few months," he answers calmly.

"You do realize she has a boyfriend at home," Mom says.

"Tommy and I broke up years ago," I respond sharply. "Can we please stop this and just have a normal conversation."

"Natalie tells me you own a pharmacy?" Alex smoothly changes the subject.

Dad's face lights up. He's proud of his business.

"Alex owns a marketing firm, Dad," I say as I place a cup of coffee in front of my father. "Maybe he can give you some ideas for advertising?"

The tension between my father and Alex seems to subside, at least for the moment. Mom is a different story. She sits back, her arms crossed over her chest. She's not going to let this go easily.

I'm in awe of Alex's composure. My parents' presence does not shake him at all. Actually, he and Dad seem to have hit it off quite well. While Alex and Dad talk, Mom and I chat about what needs to be done before graduation next weekend.

"It looks like the evening's gotten away from us," Alex says. "I'd love to take you all out for dinner."

I smile at him, appreciating how accommodating he's being.

"Thank you, but we'll be eating in," Mom says. "We're not much for the chaos out there."

I roll my eyes. "You're more than welcome to stay for dinner," I say to Alex.

"I'm afraid I didn't make enough for a guest," Mom says as she stands and walks to the counter, where she turns the oven on. I hadn't noticed the covered baking pan sitting on the stove before.

"Mom," I say, embarrassed by her rude attitude.

"It's okay, Natalie," Alex says. "I'm sure your parents want to spend some time catching up with you." He stands. "It was wonderful meeting you both."

Dad stands and shakes Alex's hand. "You, too."

"I'll walk you out," I say.

We walk together back outside and over to his car. "I'm so sorry for that." I motion up to my window. "I had no idea they'd be here."

"It's okay." He pulls my body close to his. "It's clear your parents care a great deal about you."

"A bit too much," I say. "They tend to go a bit overboard. And that bit about my ex—"

"I'm not worried about it." Alex places a kiss on my lips. "I know the truth."

"I should get back upstairs before they come looking for me." I let out a sarcastic laugh.

"That's probably a good idea." Alex threads his hands in my hair as he kisses me goodbye. His kiss is passionate and purposeful. Without using words, his body is telling me he doesn't want to let me go. He pulls back, "Text me your stipulations, and we'll figure it out."

"Yes, Sir." I smile. "I'll try to call you tomorrow."

Alex gets into his car. I stand on the sidewalk and watch him pull away. Even though the air is warm, my body shivers at the loss of his presence. My fingers touch my lips as if reassuring myself that his lips just touched there, that the memory of his kiss will not fade. With a deep breath, I start the climb back up to my apartment and my waiting parents.

NATALIE

ankee Stadium is quite a sight to behold. I'm not a baseball fan but sitting on the field for our graduation ceremony is an incredible experience. Not everyone can say they've been here.

After the long ceremony, I walk through the crowd to meet up with Lana. She sees me first and runs up to me, wrapping me in a tight hug. "Can you believe it? We graduated!"

"We did it!" I squeal.

"My parents insisted your parents ride in the car with them. Alex went with Brandon. He left Viktor to bring us to our apartment so we can change," Lana says. "I told them we'd meet them at the restaurant."

"Sounds like a good plan." I hug her, suddenly feeling very emotional. "I'm going to miss you."

"You can always change your mind and stay. I know someone else who'd like that too." We start walking to the parking area to find Viktor.

"Alex told me he wants us to try a relationship. He asked me to stay." I sigh.

"And?" She stops dead in her tracks and looks at me. "What did you say?"

"I really like him, Lana. But I have to go home." I resume walking, and Lana follows. "I agreed to try something long-distance, though. That's all I can give right now."

"I get it." Lana puts her arm around me. "It's too bad. He hasn't shown an interest in anyone in a long time, neither have you. You and Alex are so good together."

"He has girls falling all over him," I say. "Every time we're at the club, they're practically drooling when he walks in. He can have anyone he wants."

Lana laughs. "Subs are always trying to turn his head, but it never works."

"There's Viktor." I point in his direction.

We walk the final steps to the car and climb in the backseat.

The drive from the stadium back to our apartment takes forever. One thing I won't miss is the constant traffic. We're quiet inside the car, neither of us wanting to continue our discussion with Viktor present.

The silence allows me to get lost in my thoughts. I can't deny the fun Alex and I have had. Not to mention he's the hottest guy I've ever met. But where can we go from here? He's not going to wait five years for a girl he only sees now and then. I learned that lesson the hard way.

We finally pull up to our apartment.

"Wait here, Viktor," Lana says. "We won't be too long."

Lana amazes me. When she's with Brandon, she's the perfect submissive. But in her day-to-day life, she's anything but submissive. I've always been envious of her ability to take charge in any situation. Since becoming Alex's submissive, I envy that even more now. I wish I could be more like that. I've never been any good at standing up for myself.

We walk into our apartment, and I let myself flop onto our sofa. "Long-distance relationships just don't work." The words slip from my mouth without even realizing it.

Lana sits down next to me and puts her arm around my shoulder. "Is there any way you would consider staying?"

"Lana, you know I can't." I rest my head on her shoulder. "If I don't go back, I have to pay back the scholarship. I don't have that kind of money." Even if my heart feels like it's torn in two.

"Alex offered to pay for it," she says. "Why don't you let him?"

"I can't do that."

We sit quietly for a few minutes, each of us lost in our thoughts. The buzz of Lana's phone breaks the silence. Lana takes it from her purse and glances at the screen.

"It's my dad," she says. "I'll let him know we're leaving in a minute."

"Give me a few minutes to get changed."

Five minutes later, we're walking out the door and getting back into the car. I'm thankful for the quiet ride. It gives me the time to clear my head before we get to the restaurant.

The Russian Tea Room comes into view, and so does Brandon, who's outside pacing back and forth.

"You're finally here." He rushes over to Lana as we step out of the car. "I was going to send out a search party to look for you." He laughs.

"Sorry. That was my fault," I tell him. "I needed a few minutes."

"Are you okay?" Brandon turns his attention to me.

"Not really, but I will be." I try to force a smile. "I'm a bit overwhelmed with graduation and all the changes about to happen."

"I'm always here if you need to talk," Brandon offers.

"Thank you."

He holds the door open. "After you, ladies."

Walking into the restaurant, I'm surprised to see that it's empty except for our families.

Brandon moves closer behind us and whispers, "Mr. Solonik rented the entire place for the evening."

Lana chuckles. "Somehow, that doesn't surprise me." She threads her arm through mine. "Let's go celebrate."

I take a deep breath, trying to clear my melancholy mood. I owe it to everyone here and myself to have a good time tonight.

Mr. Solonik stands as we approach. "Ah, our guests of honor are finally here." He stops and kisses us on both cheeks in greeting. "I am so very proud of both my girls."

"Thank you, Mr. Solonik."

"Natalie, you must call me Maxim. We are family now." He bends closer to whisper in my ear. "Especially now. Lana tells me you've entered the lifestyle."

My eyes grow wide and dart to my parents, who are standing and beginning to make their way toward us.

"Do not worry, your parents know nothing, and it will remain that way unless you say otherwise."

"Thank you." I sigh in relief.

"Alex tells me—"

Maxim's interrupted by my mother. "Sweetheart, Dad and I are so proud of you." She wraps her arms around me and squeezes tight. "The house feels empty without you. We can't wait for you to come home."

I try to hide the conflict I'm fighting inside. "Can we talk about that later? Tonight's for celebrating."

Mom steps back and crosses her arms in disapproval. Lana shoots me a concerned look from behind her.

Maxim speaks, his deep voice and strong Russian accent filling the room. "Irina and I would like to thank you all for coming to celebrate the girls' graduation. Let's sit down and begin the meal." He signals a waiter standing nearby who nods in acknowledgment before going into the kitchen. "I took the liberty of ordering the full menu for tonight's festivities."

"Isn't that wonderful," Mom says with a saccharine smile before taking my arm and leading me away. She whispers in my ear as we walk. "Is he always so loud and overbearing? Your father would never dream of acting like that."

She's right; he certainly wouldn't. My father's usually quiet and easy-going. Mom makes the decisions—whether Dad likes it or not.

The tables have been rearranged to make one long table. My parents are sitting on the end. I'm sure trying to stay as far away from the others as possible. There's an empty seat for me between Mom and Alex. When we reach the table, Alex stands and pulls my chair out for me. We take our seats, and the festivities begin.

Maxim has spared no expense. He really ordered everything from the menu, complete with a wine pairing for each. He encourages my parents to try tasting at least one of the wines, but they decline. They don't drink alcohol for any reason, something Maxim, being Russian, can't understand.

Despite the disapproving glares from my parents, I try each of the wines with the various courses. I've grown to love both Russian food and wine since living with Lana. I'm going to miss her and her food, but I'm glad she'll have Brandon.

Alex tries to engage with my parents throughout the meal. Dad seems to be enjoying their conversation, despite Mom's disapproving glances. Alex has some ideas to share with them for the pharmacy.

I turn to my mom. "Alex put together a small marketing campaign for the store," I say.

"We're doing fine on our own," she answers.

"Dad told Alex that business has been slow."

"It'll pick back up." Mom takes a drink of her water. "It always does."

"Maybe Alex's ideas will help," I say. "He's doing it pro bono."

Mom just shrugs.

From the look on Dad's face as he talks to Alex, he's excited about the idea. Hopefully, he'll get Mom on board. If only she'd relax and give him a chance, I know she'd like him too.

The celebration is set to continue late into the evening. Dessert is just now being served, a Russian Napoleon Cake. I take a bite of the flaky pastry and savor the rich flavors and the crème filling.

"The cake is delicious, isn't it?" I ask Mom.

"It's okay," she responds. "Although I'm not sure why we couldn't have a more traditional cake."

It takes all my willpower not to roll my eyes. "It's a Russian restaurant, and this is a very traditional Russian cake." I don't understand why my parents, my mother in particular, can't ever just enjoy something without being critical.

While we eat our cake, servers come out and place a shot glass in front of each of us. The glass is filled with a clear liquid that I know is going to be Russian vodka.

"Can I have everyone's attention for a moment?" Maxim asks. "I want to propose a toast to two exceptional young ladies." He rounds the table, so he's facing us. "Svetlana and Natalie, you have both worked diligently and today, we celebrate that accomplishment. I know you will both meet success in whatever ventures await you." He raises his glass, and we all follow. "k uspekhu nashikh dvukh baryshen. To the success of our two young ladies."

Cheers are called out from those around the table as we all drink our shot of Vodka.

The burn of the alcohol in my throat makes me cough. Alex laughs softly next to me. I've done Vodka shots with the Soloniks before, but I have the same reaction every time. Guess I'm a bit of a lightweight.

"Natalie, it's time we head home. We have a flight to catch tomorrow," Mom says as she stands. Dad follows her.

"You guys go ahead," I answer. "I'm going to stay awhile longer."

"Don't be late, honey," Dad says before Mom has a chance to reply.

"I won't."

Maxim and Irina get up to say goodbye to my parents.

"I'll send a car to take you to the airport tomorrow," Maxim says.

"We'll take a cab," Mom replies.

"It was a pleasure meeting you." Irina ignores my mom's icy attitude.

I watch as my parents walk out the door and breathe a sigh of relief. Tonight could've gone much worse.

ALEX

"*A*re you ready to go?" I ask Natalie. The party has wound down, and I want to spend some time alone with her before she leaves for Missouri tomorrow.

"Yes, Sir," she answers. "Can I say goodbye to Lana first?"

"Take your time." I know saying goodbye isn't going to be easy for her.

We walk across the room to where Lana and Brandon are standing. The girls embrace one another, tears flowing freely.

"I can come by in the morning to see you off," Lana says.

"That'll only make it harder to leave." Natalie wipes her face.

"Okay," Lana says. "But call me as soon as you land."

"I will," Natalie says through more tears.

Brandon leans in to hug her goodbye. Ordinarily, a Dominant wouldn't touch another Dominant's sub, but this is different. Brandon's like a brother to me.

"Keep in touch," Brandon says. "Call us if you need anything."

He slaps me on the shoulder as we make our way to Maxim and Irina. It's hard to watch her in pain, especially knowing I can change all of this if only she'd let me.

The air is cool when we exit the restaurant, Natalie shivers. I take off my suit jacket and help her slip it on.

Viktor pulls the car to the curb. We both slide in the backseat.

Natalie sits close, her head on my shoulder, as she cries softly. Putting my arm around her, I pull her tightly to me. I don't know how I'm going to say goodbye.

It's after midnight when we finally get to my place.

She takes my hand and leads me to the bedroom. This isn't about Dominance or submission. Tonight is about showing Natalie how much I care about her.

I help her out of my jacket and slowly remove her clothes before laying her down on the bed. I take my clothes off, dropping them on the floor, and climb into bed beside her. My hands caress her body, committing every curve to memory. Tears slide down her face, and I kiss them away, their salty taste lingers on my tongue.

"No more tears, baby girl," I whisper. "Just let me love you."

I make love to her slowly and gently, savoring every second I'm inside her. After we're both sated, I roll on my back and pull her close to me. She rests her head on my chest. It doesn't take long until she falls asleep.

"Alex, wake up." Natalie shakes me, panic filling her voice. "It's 9 a.m.. We must've fallen asleep."

I open my eyes and find her rushing around the room looking for her clothes.

"What are you doing? Come back to bed."

"I have to get back to my apartment," she says. "My flight is this afternoon and my parents..." She checks her phone. "Ten missed calls, all from my parents." Her fingers frantically swipe across the screen. "I'm sending them a text."

I get out of bed and pull on my pants. Then I walk over to Natalie and place my hands on her shoulders. "Look at me." She pulls her attention from her phone to my face. "Slow down and breathe. It's a short drive to your apartment. We'll get dressed, and I'll have you back to your place long before you need to leave for the airport."

She visibly relaxes as she leans into my touch. The ringing of her phone interrupts the moment. "It's my dad."

"Go ahead and take it. I'll finish getting dressed."

"Hi, Dad. I'm fine. I'm with my friends."

She looks at me for my reaction. I raise my eyebrow.

"We were up late talking. I meant to text you, but I guess I fell asleep. Yes, I know what time it is. I'm already packed. I'll be home in a little bit. Okay, bye."

I watch, impressed, as she slips back into her panties mid-conversation without missing a beat.

I hold her dress out to her. "Are they always this overprotective?"

"They're used to being in a small town where everyone knows everyone." She shrugs her shoulders. "They tend to get a bit jumpy when they're here."

I wrap my arms around her, holding her close to me. "Are you sure I can't talk you into staying?"

"Unfortunately, I'm very sure." She looks down. "I'm going to miss you, though." Her green eyes fill with tears once again.

"We'll talk, and I'll fly out to see you in a few weeks." I kiss her trembling lips.

"We can meet somewhere, right?" she asks. "Until we see if this is going to work, I don't want my parents to know I'm still seeing you."

Her words sting, but I understand. She's been hurt in the past. "I don't like it, but for now, we can do that." I'll agree to just about anything not to lose her.

She stays wrapped in my arms as we ride the elevator back to the garage. I open the car door, allowing her to slip inside before circling to the driver's side and getting in. My finger hovers over the start button knowing this ride will bring us one step closer to her leaving.

I'm at war with myself. I want to tell Natalie I've fallen in love with her, but I've never said those words to a woman before. With my breath held, I push the button and start the drive back to her apartment.

"Alex," she says quietly. "I'm sorry."

"You have nothing to be sorry for." I reach out and take her hand in mine.

"For not staying," she says.

"There's still time to change that." I glance at her.

"I can't." She turns her head to look out the window.

When we pull up outside her building, I get out first before walking around and opening her door. I offer her my hand, helping her out.

"We're going to make this work. I'm not letting you get away." I kiss her deeply, wanting to make sure she remembers the feel of my body on hers. Willing her not to forget me; forget us.

The kiss ends too soon. "Thank you for last night." With those words, she backs away until just our fingertips are touching. "I'll text you when we land."

"I'll be waiting."

She turns and walks toward her building. When she reaches the door, she looks back over her shoulder. Tears are streaming down her face. It takes every amount of discipline I possess not to go after her and carry her over my shoulder back to my apartment. Instead, I stay rooted in place until she's out of sight.

NATALIE

I nearly trip over a suitcase when I walk into my apartment. Mom and Dad are sitting at the kitchen table. I'm not used to having anyone around that I have to answer to. But the looks on their faces tell me they aren't going to let this go.

"I'm sorry about last night," I say. "We were talking, and I guess we fell asleep."

"You had us very worried, young lady." Mom narrows her eyes. "We thought you might've been killed."

I let out a sarcastic laugh. "Alex was there. He'd never let anything happen to me."

"She's here now," Dad says and pats Mom's arm. "Safe and sound."

Mom pulls her arm away and stands. "Our taxi will be here any minute. We can finally get out of this place."

"Are you ready to go?" Dad asks.

"I have to grab something from my room," I say. "I'll be back in a minute."

I hurry down the hall to the now bare bedroom. All that's left is the furniture. Everything that made it mine has been packed and shipped back to Missouri. I grab my notepad from the backpack I left on the bed and jot a quick note for Lana.

I take a minute to reminisce about how we met. I was the quiet girl from a small town, afraid I wouldn't be able to make the transition to one of the busiest cities in the world. She was a girl from another country, excited to experience a new culture. We were randomly paired together as roommates and have been best friends ever since.

Lana,

Thank you for being the best friend I could've ever asked for. You've changed my life in so many ways, and I'll be forever grateful for that. I won't say goodbye because our friendship will never end.

~Natalie

I grab my backpack and take a final look around my room. I can't believe six years of my life have gone by so quickly, and now I'm going home. *Home.* I've always considered Northmeadow home, but if that's true, why does it feel like I'm leaving my home now? All the thoughts and feelings are a jumbled mess in my head.

I slowly walk down the hall to meet my parents, who are impatiently waiting at the door.

"I'm ready," I say and try to muster a smile.

"Good," Mom says. "Let's go."

When we get outside, the cab is waiting for us. Dad puts our luggage in the trunk, and the three of us pile into the back seat. I watch out the window as we pull away from my apartment. A heavy sadness washes over me.

Mom places her hand on my shoulder. "I know it's hard to

leave, but remember you felt this way when you first left Northmeadow."

I nod my head.

"This was just one chapter, and now it's over. It's time to turn the page and move on." She pats my shoulder as if her words somehow make everything better.

I know she means well, but I'm not sure she's right.

"What if I'm not ready for it to be over?"

"Are you talking about that man, Alexander?" Mom sighs.

"Yes."

"Honey, I understand why you *think* you like him. He's successful and very handsome, but he's not like us."

"He likes me and asked to keep seeing me," I tell her.

Dad leans forward from around Mom's shoulder. "Long-distance relationships are very hard, sweetheart."

"I know, but—"

Mom interrupts. "And there is a certain young man that's been waiting for you to come home."

"Who?"

"Thomas," she says.

"Tommy Moore?" I roll my eyes. "We broke up a long time ago."

"He comes in the pharmacy every week and always asks about you. He's the one who's helping at the store while we're here." She looks to Dad for his agreement. "He's grown into a fine young man, and he can't wait to see you."

Thankfully, we pull up at JFK, and our conversation is interrupted. I never told my parents why Tommy and I broke up, and I don't plan to now. I never want to talk about that night ever again.

I sit in the back of my parents' car as dad drives the familiar windy roads through the Ozark Mountains. We pass a herd of deer grazing on the side of the road, a sight that was once familiar but one I haven't seen in a long time.

As we get closer to Northmeadow, familiar farms begin to come into view. Mr. Johnson is tending his cows in the field. When I was a little girl, I used to love it when we drove this way. Dad would slow the car down, just like he's doing now, so I could see the new calves in the fields with their moms. Dad smiles at me in the rearview mirror, and I return it with a smile of my own.

Next, we pass through the central area of town. Nothing's changed since the last time I was home. The same buildings with the same storefronts line the three blocks that comprise downtown Northmeadow. It's late Sunday afternoon, which means nothing is open, the streets are quiet and empty. It's a foreign feeling after living in NYC for so long. The streets are never quiet and empty there.

Pulling out my phone, I text Alex.

(Me) We landed a little while ago. We're almost home.
(Alex) Glad you got there safely, but I miss you already.
(Me) I miss you too.
(Alex) Will you be home at 9?
(Me) Small town, everything's closed today. LOL I'll be home.
(Alex) Good, I'll video call you then.
(Me) Can't wait. TTYL

I shoot a quick text to Lana, letting her know I arrived safely before we make the last turn for home.

Dad pulls into our driveway just as I'm sliding the phone back into my pocket. When I look up, my mouth hangs open in shock. Strung from end to end on my parent's front porch is a large, brightly colored banner that reads "Welcome Home Natalie." Bouquets of rainbow-colored balloons are tied across the rail. There, standing on the steps, is Tommy Moore. He's dressed in dark jeans and his old Northmeadow High Football T-shirt. His dirty blond hair is cut short, and he's wearing a huge grin on his face.

"Surprise!" My mother beams with pride.

I'm genuinely speechless and not in a good way.

NATALIE

J sit, frozen in shock, as Tommy confidently walks toward the car and opens my door. He reaches in and grabs my hands pulling me out and into him for a hug.

"Welcome home, Natalie," he says and leans in to kiss me.

I turn my head just in time for the kiss to land on my cheek.

"I've really missed you." He bounces back without hesitation.

"Umm. Wow. I don't know quite what to say."

Mom gets out of the car and comes right over to Tommy. "You did a great job with the decorations." She pulls him in for a big hug.

"Thanks, Mrs. C." He turns and looks at me. "I'm just so glad she's finally home."

I silently watch their interaction. It's like a bad movie playing out in front of me, except it's not a movie at all. It's really happening.

"I wouldn't miss it for the world," he says. "I know you just got home, but can I steal you for a walk?"

"I don't think—"

"Of course, you can," Mom answers for me. "It'll give you two kids a chance to catch up."

Tommy grabs my hand, but my feet are lead weights, unwilling to move. His hand holding mine feels wrong. It isn't the hand I want holding mine—it isn't Alex.

Tommy gives a tug forcing me to move.

We walk behind my parents' house to a well-worn path alongside fields that used to be farmland, although they don't look like they've been planted for many years, until we get to a wooded area.

I'm hit with an onslaught of memories, all the times Tommy and I snuck off here while we were in high school.

He was my first boyfriend, my first kiss, and the boy I lost my virginity to. Everyone expected we'd get married. Once upon a time, I expected that too, but then he shattered that dream and my heart.

Tommy stops walking and turns to face me. "Natalie, I know things ended badly between us."

"You could say that." The hurt I'd buried stabs me in the chest, reopening old wounds. "It was you and me against the world. We were supposed to get married," I yell. "Until I came home and found you in bed with my best friend. Seeing the two of you like that ripped my heart out."

He pulls my unwilling body against his. "And I'm so sorry for that. I was lonely. It'll never happen again, I swear it."

"You think saying you're sorry will magically make it go away?" I pull out of his hold.

"It was a long time ago," he says. "I thought we moved past it."

"Tommy, I—"

"You're back now. We're together again." His voice sounds desperate. "Things'll be different this time."

"What you and Ashlynn did is unforgivable. We are not *together*, and we never will be again." I start walking toward home.

"Natalie, wait."

I turn around and cross my arms in frustration. "What?"

Tommy takes a few steps before reaching into his pants pocket and pulling out a prescription bottle. Opening the lid, he takes out a tiny white pill and swallows it.

"What did you just take?"

He leans up against a nearby tree. "After we broke up, I got hurt in a game. I couldn't play anymore and lost my scholarship." He holds up the bottle giving it a little shake. "Now and then, I need a little something, so I have these guys."

My parents had mentioned something about Tommy getting hurt, but I didn't want to hear about him, so I never asked for details. "Have you seen a doctor?" I ask. "I don't think popping pills is a good long-term solution, do you?"

"I've seen a doctor, more than one doctor." He pushes himself off the tree and closes the distance between us. "There's nothing else they can do. Let it go. I'm fine."

"Whatever you say." I turn and resume walking. "I'm going home."

"I'm right behind you."

When we get back to the house, my mother's just putting dinner on the table. "I had your Aunt Delia stop by and throw a casserole in the oven for us. You two are just in time."

"I'm not very hungry," I say. "I think I'll just go and unpack."

"You'll do no such thing, young lady." My mother scolds me like I'm a child. "You have a dinner guest."

"*You* have a dinner guest," I answer, a hint of sarcasm in my voice. "Not me."

My parents looked shocked at my tone.

"Natalie, you'll not speak to your mother in that tone," Dad says. "You will apologize right now."

At this moment, I can feel myself shrinking back into the girl I was before I went away, the girl who did as she was told and would never defy her parents. "I'm sorry for being disrespectful."

With those words, I do what's expected of me and take my seat.

Dinner is excruciating. It's my turn to be the silent one, the outcast at the table. Tommy and my parents talk like they haven't missed a beat. It's like they've been talking all these years, carrying on as though we're still a couple. There's no way we'll *ever* be a couple again.

Although I didn't think Tommy would ever leave, dinner finally winds down, and he says his goodbyes, promising he'll see me soon.

After Tommy leaves, Dad retires to the living room to watch the nightly news while Mom and I clean up.

"It's so good to have you home, honey," she says as she puts the last plate in the cupboard. "And seeing you back with Tommy, well, everything is just perfect now."

"Tommy and I are not together." I put the dishrag on the counter. "We broke up a long time ago. I've moved on."

"You left him; you should be thankful he still wants you." Mom reaches behind her, untying her apron. "Most girls around here would jump at the chance to be with him."

"They can have him." I check the time on my phone. It's 8:45 p.m.. "I'm feeling a bit off. Probably jet lag. I'm going to get to bed early."

"Please be smart, Natalie. That man from the city is not right for you." She kisses my cheek. "I love you and want you to be happy. I'm sure you'll see reason after you've had a good night's rest."

"Night, Mom." I don't argue any further. She isn't ready to see things my way.

"Night, Daddy." I kiss him on the cheek as I pass through the living room on my way upstairs.

Once I'm in my room, I close the door and look around. I feel like I've entered a time warp. I haven't been in my bedroom in nearly two years, yet everything is exactly where I left it. The flowered sheets and pink ruffled bedspread from when I was younger still dress my twin bed. I pick up a pillow and smell the familiar scent of the laundry detergent my mother makes. She must've made sure the sheets were freshly washed. My stuffed animals and dolls sit neatly on my chair in the corner. I walk to my dresser and run my fingers over the pictures taped to the mirror—pictures of my youth. Carefully, I pull one off to look at it closer.

It's a picture of Tommy and me on the first day of our senior year in high school. He was so handsome, tall, and muscular from working out. I remember how lucky I felt to be dating the starting quarterback. He has his arm around me, holding me close. I'm staring up at him, a girl head over heels in love. I set the picture on my dresser and pull another down. This one's from the end of my senior year. I'm standing with a group of my friends, including Ashlynn, we're all in our caps and gowns. Each of us young and naïve. Each with very different dreams for our futures.

I'm not the same girl as I was then. None of the girls in this picture ever left Northmeadow; we've led very different lives. Will they like the person I am today? Will they accept me back into their circle? Do I even want to be accepted by them?

My phone buzzes in my pocket, bringing a smile to my face. I set the photo on my dresser and take out my phone to answer the call.

It takes a second, but the image of Alex pops up on the screen. He's sitting in front of his windows, the city light illuminates the night sky behind him.

"Hi," I say and sit down on my bed. "Nice view."

"I thought you might be missing it tonight."

"I can't believe how much I miss it already."

"Do you miss anything else?" he asks with a hopeful tone.

"Hmm—let me think," I tease. "I miss Lana. And there's this guy. I forget his name." I flash him a cheeky grin.

He puts his hand over his heart in mock surprise. "You forgot me already?"

I giggle. I could never forget Alex. That's part of the problem. If this long-distance thing doesn't work, I don't know how I'll be able to get over him.

"How was your flight home?"

"Pretty uneventful," I say. "Mom talked my ear off. She made sure I was up to date on all the Northmeadow gossip." I roll my eyes.

Alex laughs. "What are your plans for tomorrow?"

"For starters." I flip the camera so Alex can see my bedroom. "I need to make this room fit for an adult. Other than that, I don't have any plans."

Conversation has always come easy for us, but I find myself at a loss for anything to talk about right now. The divide I was afraid of is already rearing its ugly head. This is why I don't want to tell anyone about us. I don't know how we can make it work.

"Natalie, stop biting your nails," Alex reprimands.

"Sorry, I didn't even realize I was doing it." I shrug my shoulders.

"What's bothering you?" He leans forward, bringing his face closer to the camera."Nothing."

"There's something," he says. "Talk to me."

I look down, trying to figure out how to put my feelings into words. "I'm terrified of the distance between us," I say. "I don't know how it's supposed to work."

"Right now, we take it one step at a time," he says. "You need to get settled back there. Then, we'll figure out how we want us to work."

"How can I be your submissive when we don't live in the same city, the same state?" I don't mean to snap at him. "Sorry for raising my voice, Sir."

"I forgive you," he says. "We *will* make this work. I told you, we can fly to see each other whenever we want."

I remain silent, trying to process his words. He makes it sound so easy, but selfishly, I need more.

In the few months we've been together, he hasn't told me much about his personal life or family. Although I've told him a lot about my family, it isn't typically shared in a contractual relationship. I'm hoping we're at a place where he's willing to share it with me.

"May I ask you a personal question, Sir?"

"You can ask me anything." He sits back and relaxes.

"How did you get involved in the lifestyle?"

"My parents," he says before his expression changes to one of sadness. "My dad and my mom were involved in the lifestyle for many years. Until she passed away."

"I'm sorry." I didn't know he lost his mom. My heart hurts seeing the pained look on his face and knowing I'm not there to comfort him. "How old were you?"

"I was thirteen. She died from breast cancer." He shakes his head. "I knew from an early age I had dominant traits."

I'm starting to think everyone but me had been raised in this lifestyle. "I'm guessing you were able to talk to your dad about it?"

"Yes, my father supported my interest. We lived just outside Seattle. There's very active BDSM communities in the area," he tells me. "He allowed me to get to know his friends in the community. I developed a great respect for many of them, Dom and subs alike. I liked their ideals and what they stood for. But after seeing what Dad went through after losing Mom, I decided I wasn't interested in any sort of relationship—BDSM or otherwise."

"What changed your mind?"

"It was a few months after I came to New York," Alex says. "Maxim walked into my office and hired me to do a big marketing campaign for him."

"Maxim? Lana's dad?" Now I'm beginning to see the connection. Alex must've been Maxim's contact in the states. The person Lana said looked out for her.

"Yes, Lana's dad." He smiles. "After I took his account, he

flew me out to Russia to complete the deal. I stayed at his home and spent a great deal of time with him and Irina. I recognized their Dom/sub relationship immediately." He closes his eyes as if lost in the memories.

"Why me?" I don't understand what he sees in a 24-year-old girl from a small town in Missouri with no experience in BDSM. "Why do you want to do this with me? Especially now that I'm so far away."

"I'm drawn to you. There's a connection between us," he says. "Do you feel it too?"

"I do," I say softly. What scares me is I feel it too much. I fell in love with him even though he told me this wouldn't become anything more. But now, after our last night together, I think things are different.

"Do you still consent to move forward?" Alex asks. "I don't know what it'll look like, but we'll take it one step at a time."

Even though I'm still not sure how or if this will work, I can't say no; I don't want to say no. "Yes, I consent to that."

"I have some ideas for our Dom/sub dynamic," Alex says and picks up a piece of paper. "I emailed you a copy."

I reach over the side of my bed and grab my bag, pulling my laptop out. Once it's fired up, I open my email to see what he's sent. There's a list of suggested rules, a modification of our Dom/sub contract.

We read through the list and agree on a set time to call him each morning with my plans for the day. Every night, at 9 p.m., we'll have a video call. He promises to fly out one weekend a month. My schedule will determine when I can visit him in NYC.

"I think this is a good starting place," Alex says. "The rest, we can see where that goes on its own.

"I think that's a good plan." Our relationship feels a bit more stable having these rules in place. I close my laptop and yawn.

"You look tired, baby girl."

"I am. It's been a long day," I say. "I really should go. I have to work at dad's store for a few hours tomorrow."

"I have a full day too. I'll be at the office late," he says. "I'll call you tomorrow night."

"I can't wait." I smile. "Night, Alex."

"Sleep well, baby girl."

NATALIE

*I*n Missouri, August brings oppressive heat and humidity, made worse by the lack of air conditioning in my parent's house. Although I've just showered, I'm already sweating, and my curls are a frizzy mess. Come on, hair, not today. I struggle to pin up the unruly strands. In an hour, I'm meeting with Mr. Meadows, the principal of Northmeadow High and my new boss.

Finally, I get my hair secure in a loose bun, and I start putting on make-up. I'm attempting to look polished and professional; although I don't know why I'm going through the trouble, I'm only going to sweat it off.

Since my job at the school doesn't officially start for a few more weeks, I've picked up as many shifts at Dad's pharmacy as I can. Between that and the small amount of money I saved while I was away, I managed to pick up a used car. A 2002 silver Honda Civic I've nicknamed Rhonda the Honda. She's not fancy, doesn't even have power windows, but she runs and gets me where I need to go. Best of all, she's mine.

My next goal—an apartment. Living with my parents is not something I can do long-term. They're always questioning every move I make and giving me *advice* on what I should or shouldn't be doing. Suddenly, I'm a teenager again living under my parents' thumb. It's driving me crazy and putting a strain on our relationship.

I give myself a once over in the mirror before I head out the door and get into Rhonda.

Aside from the years I was gone for school; I've never lived outside of Northmeadow. As I drive down Main Street. I realize absolutely nothing has changed. The same mom and pop shops with their run-down storefronts line Main Street. There are no chain stores or restaurants; the residents fought hard to keep them out of town. It's both positive and negative. Small, local-owned businesses have kept their doors open, but just barely.

The summer months bring tourists from Finn Lake. It's that revenue most businesses rely on to get them through the rest of the year. Residents who don't own a business in town work on their farms, often struggling to make ends meet. It's a stark contrast from New York City with its booming businesses and crowds of people.

When I graduated high school, I was the only one in my class leaving the state for college. Heck, I was the only girl pursuing a college degree. Most were content to stay here, marry a local boy, and have his babies. Once upon a time, I planned to marry a local boy, but not until after I had a chance to experience life outside of Northmeadow. See how well that worked out, Natalie?

I make the turn into the parking lot of my old high school. It feels odd to pull into a spot designated for faculty. Resting my head against the seat, I close my eyes and take a few calming breaths.

This town was once my home, and this was my dream job. I wanted to serve the youth in my community. But things changed —I changed. I can't help wondering if I could have served the youth in NYC with the same satisfaction. Now I'm locked into this position for the next five years.

"Six years flew by in the city. These will go by just as fast." I say the words aloud, trying to convince myself they're true, but the excitement I once felt when I imagined this moment is absent.

Taking one final deep breath, I turn off the ignition, grab my bag, and step out of the car. I take a second to straighten my black skirt and silky white blouse. Despite everything, I want to make a favorable impression.

Instinct urges me to use the student entrance, but I continue past it and walk to the building's front instead. I've never actually stopped and looked at the historic building that houses the school. It truly is a work of art. Four sections make up the three-story stone structure. Each floor holds four sets of four windows that sit in perfect symmetry. Drawing the eye to the center of the building are four large columns that flank the sides of the main entrance. The building is typical of classical revival architecture —something I learned about during my time in the city.

One by one, I walk up the granite steps until I reach the main door and pull it open. It's a lot heavier than it looks.

Stepping inside, I'm hit with a sense of déjà vu. The familiar school smell brings me right back to my days as a student. It feels as if I've just walked these halls yesterday instead of six years ago.

The building is empty, except for a few custodians who appear to be freshening up the paint on some lockers, while a few others are cleaning up the desks. The click of my high heel shoes echoes in the hallway as I make my way to the main office.

"Excuse me, miss. Can I help you?" a male voice calls from behind me.

Startled, I turn around. An older and slightly rounder version of the Mr. Meadows I remember from my high school days stands with his hands on his hips wearing track shorts, a tank top, and a baseball cap. Guess I'm a little overdressed.

"I was just heading to your office," I say, walking back toward him.

"And you are?"

"Natalie Clarke." Do I have the wrong day for our appointment?

His forehead wrinkles, and his eyes narrow as he takes in my appearance. "I didn't recognize you."

"I guess it has been a few years."

An awkward silence lingers between us. The warm feelings I felt when I first walked in have disappeared, replaced with an icy unwelcomeness. Ms. Campbell told me she was getting a lot of pushback from adding a therapist to the faculty.

Mr. Meadows finally speaks. "Your office is this way. Follow me." Without warning, he turns and takes long strides down the hallway.

I do my best to keep up with him but fall behind. Besides being nearly a foot shorter, I also have a skirt and heels to contend with. We pass classrooms that were once a daily home for me. I try peeking into them, hoping to rekindle the feeling of belonging, but come up empty. Instead, I am left feeling like an outsider—an intruder.

"This is your office." He waves his hand at the open door. "You'll notice your window has been frosted, something about maintaining privacy."

"That's perfect, thank you." I smile.

"It wasn't my doing," he says sharply. Digging into his pocket, he pulls out a key. "This belongs to you."

I reach out to take the key, which he hesitantly hands over before taking the first step into my new office. The walls have recently been painted a crisp, clean, and oh-so-plain cream color. The smell of fresh paint lingers in the air. Scuff marks from the many shoes that have walked in and out of the room mar the tile floor. A metal desk, standard high school issue, sits in the room's center with a chair on each side. The wall behind the desk holds a large window that overlooks Main St. and offers the natural light this otherwise poorly lit space needs. Looking around, I'm surprised at how spacious the room is. With some creativity, I'll be able to transform this bare space into something special for the students.

Mr. Meadows walks past me, heading straight toward the chair behind my desk.

"Let's go over the paperwork, shall we?" he says as he lowers himself onto the padded leather chair.

Feeling a bit intimidated, I answer quietly, "Okay." I walk to the chair opposite him, a simple wooden chair the same as those found outside the principal's office. Sitting down, I immediately notice the cushion the chair once had has long since disintegrated. I add it to my mental list of things that need to be redone. Not sure where to put my bag, I hold it on my lap and fidget with the straps. It'll help keep me from biting my nails.

Mr. Meadows opens a red binder that's sitting on the desk and takes out a stack of papers. He flips through them, mumbling to himself before he glances up at me.

"Looks like your clearances have come back and are in order. Did you bring a copy of your licensure?"

I reach into my bag and pull out a folder containing my paperwork. "Here you go," I say, giving him my license.

His eyes quickly skim the paper. "This looks like it's OK. I need your signature on a few pages, and then we'll be done." He slides a stack of papers and a pen across the desk.

Seeing no other choice, I set my bag on the floor so my hands are free. I pick up the first paper and begin to read through it.

Tap. Tap. Tap. The impatient rhythm of Mr. Meadow's pen tapping on the desk urges me to move quicker.

I glance up and see Mr. Meadow's looking at his watch. Sensing his growing impatience, I try to read as fast as I can without missing anything important. Don't bite your nails. I struggle to keep my nerves in check.

"Ms. Clarke." His voice is sharp. "These are just your standard employment papers."

"I'm sure they are, but I'd feel more comfortable reading through them before I sign." I pause. "I'm sure you understand."

"As long as this doesn't take too long." He looks at his watch again. "I have another appointment in ten minutes."

I nod my head and skim the last few pages, barely reading them. The final paper restates the requirement of remaining employed by the Northmeadow School District for five years, at which time a new contract may be negotiated. Termination of employment before five years will result in immediate repayment of all scholarship money. With trembling hands, I grab the pen and sign my name.

"Very well then," Mr. Meadows says as he grabs the papers and taps them on the desk. "Your schedule and employee handbook are in here." He points to the red binder before he makes his way to the door.

I follow after him. "Am I able to redecorate the office?"

He spins around with a less than amused look on his face. "Isn't it to your liking?"

Shrugging my shoulders, I say, "It's fine, but it's kinda plain." I look around the room. "I was hoping to make it a bit more inviting. Maybe add some artwork to the walls, an area rug, some bean bag seating. To help the kids feel more comfortable in here."

He crosses his arms in front of him and tilts his head as if trying to figure me out.

Ticking from the clock, usually unheard, echoes in the absence of other noise.

"You can do as you see fit." He lowers his hands and begins to walk away, pausing to add, "But it will need to come out of your pocket. We don't supply a *decorating* budget."

"I understand. Thank you." I feel as though I've won a small victory.

He shakes his head and mutters to himself as he walks down the hall.

I close the door and lean against it. It doesn't surprise me that Mr. Meadows isn't exactly thrilled with my being added to his faculty. He made that known the day I was offered the scholarship.

It was one-week before my high school graduation. Our community was still suffering the devastating effects of both Evan and Michael's suicide the year before. The world was changing, and Northmeadow wasn't immune to those changes. Our young people were experiencing problems the older generations either didn't face or refused to acknowledge, and it was taking its toll.

After losing my brother, I decided I didn't want to work at my dad's pharmacy like we had planned. Instead, I wanted to pursue psychology with the hopes of working with young people and preventing another tragedy. My sights were set on New York University. In my opinion, it would give me the chance to experience life outside of Northmeadow while getting a solid education. After I graduated, I would come back, marry Tommy, and work with our young people.

I was eligible for financial aid, but it wasn't enough to cover the expenses. Unfortunately, my parents weren't in support of my going away to school and refused to help with the difference. I'd just about given up on my dreams until I was summoned to a meeting in the principal's office.

When I arrived, Mr. Meadows had been there along with Ms. Campbell, the district superintendent. I sat across from them, not knowing the importance this meeting would have on my future.

"How are you today, Natalie?" Ms. Campbell asked

"Today's a pretty good day," I said.

"I'm glad to hear that." She smiled. "I'm sure you're wondering why I've asked you here.

"Yes, I am."

After Evan died, Ms. Campbell stepped in as a sort of counselor. She allowed me to talk about Evan and Michael without fear of judgment for my feelings—feelings I could not express at home.

I had the best childhood filled with so many happy memories. My parents were never wealthy, but they made sure Evan and I never wanted for anything. The four of us were very close. My parents' relationship was one I always looked up to. They demonstrated such love and respect for each other, but they turned ice cold once everything happened. I was lost without my brother, yet I was forbidden to discuss anything about him at home. My parents took his pictures down and even emptied his room. It was like he never existed. I don't know how I would have gotten through that first year without Ms. Campbell's help.

Ms. Campbell told me she'd heard whispers from within the student body about other issues, including violence, recreational drug usage. That there were other young people struggling with issues related to their sexual orientation—something our conservative religious town found abhorrent.

Our conversation was raw and honest; her words have remained with me through the years.

"Natalie, as you're all too aware, our young people are struggling," Ms. Campbell said.

"Yes." I looked down, trying to hold back the tears that were threatening to fall.

"Your generation is dealing with issues most of us," she gestured between Mr. Meadows and herself, "just don't understand."

Mr. Meadows sat back in his chair and crossed his arms. I sensed a growing tension between the two adults in the room.

"Would you be willing to share with Mr. Meadows why you're so passionate about pursuing higher education?" Ms. Campbell asked.

I was a bit uneasy sharing something so personal with Mr. Meadows, but Ms. Campbell gave me an encouraging nod to ease my discomfort.

"You both know I lost my brother last year," I said and looked between them. "I saw what that did to my family. To Evan's mom. To our community. I want to study to become a therapist. I don't want anyone else to have to go through what

Evan and Michael did." I pause and swallow over the growing lump in my throat. "I don't want anyone else's family to have to lose someone they love. I don't share the beliefs of my family or community. The heart can't help who it loves."

Mr. Meadows mumbled under his breath, earning a disapproving glance from Ms. Campbell.

Ms. Campbell sat forward on her chair. "Natalie, if we don't do something, we're going to lose more youth to a senseless tragedy."

Mr. Meadows shifted, clearly uncomfortable with the conversation.

Ms. Campbell turned her attention to him. "Jacob, will you excuse us for a few minutes?"

A vein pulsed in Mr. Meadow's neck, the only outward sign of his anger, as he stood and walked out of his office, closing the door a little too forcefully.

"Natalie, I know you applied and were accepted to New York University."

"Yes, ma'am," I said.

"Have you replied to your acceptance letter yet?" she asked.

"Not yet," I said. "But I'm going to have to decline."

"The school board has talked and agreed. We're prepared to make you a generous offer." Her face lit up with excitement. "We're offering a scholarship to cover the full cost of your education in exchange for your agreement to work in the district for five years."

It took a few minutes for her words to sink in fully. "You'll pay for everything?" I asked, still not believing what I thought I heard.

"Yes," she said. "Tuition, books, room, and board." She pulled a paper from a folder I hadn't noticed lying on the desk in front of her. "It's all right here. If you agree, you just need to sign the contract." She handed me the paper.

At the time, I had every intention of living in Northmeadow and marrying Tommy. He was going to be away at school on a football scholarship, and now I'd have the opportunity to get my degree as well. It was a dream come true. Since I was eighteen, I didn't need my parents' permission. I didn't think twice; I signed the contract right then and there.

Ms. Campbell has had a significant impact on my life. We've kept in touch over the years. She's the only person, aside from Lana, who knows everything that happened with Tommy. I've told her about Alex, although I've been hesitant to tell her everything. She knows I've been seeing Alex in secret all summer, something neither Alex nor Ms. Campbell is thrilled about. They both think I need to tell my parents the truth. That's much easier said than done; they don't have to live with them.

I grab my bag off the floor and dig through it to find my cell phone. After taking a few pictures of my office, I send the images and a text to Lana.

(Me) Before pictures. Drab and boring, typical US high school office.
(Lana) Looks pretty similar to my school in Russia. Please tell me you can change it?
(Me) Amazon is calling my name, LOL. How's it going with the job hunt?
(Lana) Have another interview today. Fingers crossed I get hired soon. Guess what…
(Me) What?
(Lana) I was going to call you tonight, but I can't wait. Brandon asked me to move in, and I said yes!
(Me) OMG! I'm so happy for you!!

Although I'm happy for my friend, I'm also sad for me. If I'd been able to stay in the city, would that be Alex and me?

(Lana) How's everything there?

It's awful. My parents are smothering me. My ex-boyfriend

won't leave me alone, and the man I love is halfway across the country.

(Me) Doing good, getting used to living in a small town again. Did you guys get the invitation to the birthday party my parents are throwing for me?
(Lana) We did, but we won't be able to make it.
(Me) I knew it was a long shot. It was supposed to be a surprise party, but Dad spilled the beans.
(Lana) I wish we could've made it. Is Alex going to be there?
(Me) I didn't invite him. They don't know I'm seeing him still, remember?
(Lana) Oh yeah, that. I'll call you tonight. You can try to explain why you won't tell them. I'm about to walk into an interview.
(Me) Good luck.

I sink into the chair behind my desk, it's much more comfortable than the other chair, and set my phone down. The red binder draws my attention. I reach out and slide it in front of me. Opening the cover, I flip through the pages, beginning to familiarize myself with policy and procedure.

When I finally look at my phone, I see two hours have passed. I mark my page and close the binder. "I'll finish reading you later," I say and slide the binder into my bag. With one final look around the room, I lock up and head home to do some online shopping.

NATALIE

$\mathcal{I}$ arrive back at a quiet house. As soon as I walk in the door, I kick off my heels and throw my bag on the couch. It's moments like this, when both my parents are at work and I have the house to myself that remind me how much I miss living on my own.

Another thing I miss—coffee shops. If I want an afternoon pick-me-up, it's either the diner or homebrewed.

Opening the cupboard, I pull out a paper filter and push it into the plastic receptacle of my parents' old Mr. Coffee machine. After spooning in the grounds, I turn it on and wait. "Maybe I'll get them a Keurig for Christmas," I say aloud and laugh. "As if they'd ever use it." They prefer the older methods of doing things.

It was only right before I left for college that they stopped using the stainless-steel coffee pot that perks on the stovetop. They haven't thrown it out. It now sits on the windowsill above the kitchen sink with fresh-picked flowers in it.

While the aroma of coffee fills the kitchen, I busy myself putting away the dishes Mom left on the plastic drying rack. I always hated handwashing. It was such a treat when Lana and I got our apartment, and I finally had a dishwasher. Mental note—when apartment shopping, make sure it has a dishwasher.

Ten minutes later, the coffee pot finishes. I grab my favorite mug off the accordion rack under the cupboards and pour the liquid gold. A little sugar and creamer, and the coffee is perfect. I grab my things and go upstairs.

Setting everything down on my desk, I strip off my work clothes, exchanging them for shorts and a tank top that expose my now toned abdomen. Another benefit I came home with from the city. Lana and I used to get up early to hit the gym before class. Once I met Alex, I added running with him to my routine. The physical changes have helped me see my body differently. Since being home, I haven't exercised at all. I'm going to have to get back to it, or I won't be wearing clothes like this for long.

The unpacked boxes in the corner of the room draw my attention. I was hoping to have my own place by now, but that hasn't worked out as planned. I've saved enough money to pay for a few months' rent, but I haven't been able to find an available apartment in Northmeadow. I'm not giving up; something has to open up eventually.

Meanwhile, somewhere in this mess are books and decorations I want for my office. The goal for this afternoon is to go through the boxes and find everything. As I stare at the task ahead of me, I realize I should've done a better job when I was packing. At the time, my only thought was to get everything boxed and shipped out. Now, as I look at the pile of twenty boxes, I'm feeling a bit overwhelmed. Nothing's going to get done just standing here.

One at a time, I rummage through the boxes, making a separate pile of items for my office and another pile to be repacked. After I finish the last one, I start taping them back up when my phone chimes, alerting me to an incoming text message. Alex hasn't texted all day, and I'm anxious to talk to him, so I grab the phone quickly.

(Unknown Number) I'm picking you up at 5.

(Me) I think you have the wrong number.

(Unknown Number) Unless this isn't Natalie, I have the right number.

(Me) Who is this?

(Unknown Number) It's me.

Me? Who the heck is me?

(Me) I'm gonna need a little more to go on than "me."

(Unknown Number) Tommy

I roll my eyes. Oh my God, just go away already.

(Me) How did you get my number?

(Tommy) Your mom.

She and I are going to have a little talk about not giving out my phone number.

(Me) I'm not going out with you tonight.

(Tommy) Yes, you are. Be ready at 5.

(Me) No.

(Tommy) I've already talked to your parents. We're going out tonight.

Already talked to my parents. Is he for real?

(Me) I'm not in grade school. You can't ask my parents for a play date with me.

(Tommy) Already did. You better be ready.

(Me) I'm not going out with you.

(Tommy) See you at 5.

I drop my head in my hands. How do I get rid of him? He obviously doesn't understand that we're over.

Done.

Never getting back together.

I decide not to waste all afternoon arguing with him through texts. I have more important stuff to do. I'll deal with him if he shows up. Until then, I have money to spend and shopping to do.

The sound of gravel crunching in the driveway grabs my attention. Checking my phone, I see it's 4:55 p.m.. Wow, I didn't realize I was shopping for that long. Curious to see who it is, I pad across the worn-out carpet on my bedroom floor and pull aside the ruffled purple curtains to look outside. Tommy's beat-up red Chevy pick-up is in front of my house.

This is ending right now. I race across my room and slam the door. I take the steps two at a time, intending to stop Tommy before he makes it onto the porch. He can turn that truck right back around because I'm not going anywhere with him.

What I didn't see from my room becomes apparent when I open the front door. Tommy's helping my mom out of the passenger seat. Mom looks up. The smile fades from her face when she sees me.

"You aren't going out dressed like that?"

I look down at my outfit before answering. "I'm not going out."

"You and Tommy have a date." She smiles at him.

Tommy leans against the rusty old truck. There's a smug look on his face as he listens to our exchange.

"Tommy told you wrong." I cross my arms.

"Excuse us a minute, dear," Mom says to Tommy before she hurries up the steps and grabs my arm, forcing me to follow her into the house. "Stop acting like an ungrateful child. That young man out there is crazy about you."

Sure that I've misunderstood her, because we've already gone over this at least a hundred times, I ask, "Excuse me?"

"You don't live in the city anymore," my mother says in a raised voice. Her eyes narrow. "You need to get off whatever high horse you climbed on while you were off playing house." She uses air quotes to emphasize *playing house*. "You're back home, where you belong, and you need to start acting like it." Pointing to the steps, she says, "Now march upstairs and put something presentable on. You will not keep him waiting."

My mouth hangs open. I'm speechless. I find myself right back to the same struggle I'd gone through in my teenage years. My mom had always been strict, but after Evan died, she held on extra tight. She refused to acknowledge I was an adult and could make my own decisions.

"Now, Natalie." She crosses her arms and taps her foot on the hardwood floor.

At this moment, I wish I was more like Lana and that I had enough confidence to stand my ground, especially with my parents. It was so much easier while I was in the city and had Alex by my side. I don't have that support now. It's only my parents and me and I'm all they have left. My downfall has always been not wanting to disappoint them—to a fault. This time my upbringing wins.

Although I want to scream and yell, I quietly slip back into the role of a dutiful daughter.

As I walk up the steps and into my childhood bedroom, I feel the independence and self-confidence I'd gained while living in the city slip away, and I feel helpless to stop it.

TOMMY

J follow Charlotte Clarke's gaze to her front porch, where Natalie stands in tiny denim shorts and a cutoff shirt. Her body is smoking hot and all on display, especially when she crosses her arms, pushing her tits up higher. Even the daggers she shoots my way do nothing to dispel the arousal in my jeans. Tonight's going to be more fun than I anticipated.

Charlotte and Natalie argue while I lean back against my truck, amused by the scene. I know I have her parents on my side, which means Natalie will come around; she'll never defy her parents.

While I wait for Natalie, my hands start to shake, and sweat forms across my forehead. I grab my Oxy bottle and swallow two pills, craving the high they give me.

I saw the doctor yesterday and was able to convince him I'm still suffering. He's a pain in the ass, nagging me to try physical therapy or acupuncture. I was able to use living in Northmeadow and its lack of resources as an excuse with the promise I'd look outside of town for something. I'll spout whatever shit he wants to hear to get a new prescription.

I need to feel good tonight because I'm taking Natalie to the county fair. We used to go every year. I'm sure this will remind

Natalie how much she loves me, and if I'm right—and I know I'm right—before the night's over, I'll be buried balls deep between her legs, just like old times.

Natalie doesn't keep me waiting long. Within a few minutes, she's walking down the porch steps in the same denim shorts but with a black t-shirt tucked in. I open the door and offer my hand to help her into my truck. My little wildcat refuses my help and climbs in on her own. Smiling, I close the door behind her, walk around to the driver's side, and get in.

The fair hasn't changed. Food vendors from all over are set up, creating a virtual maze offering anything fried and on a stick. Natalie's favorite was always the stuffed pretzel stand.

"Can I have two steak and cheese stuffed pretzels?" I ask the kid behind the window. He takes my money and hands me the paper-wrapped food.

"Here ya go," I say and proudly hand one to Natalie.

"Thanks," she answers quietly and takes the food from my hand.

"Let's sit over here and eat." I lead her to an empty table.

She nibbles at the pretzel while staring off into the crowd.

"It must be nice to be home," I say, trying to get her attention. She's acting distant, and I don't know why.

"It's great," she mumbles.

"I'm glad your back," I say and place my hand on her thigh.

She pulls her leg away. "Tommy, don't."

"You never had a problem with me touching you before."

"You lost that right when you started screwing my best friend," she says and stands up, throwing away her uneaten food. "I've moved on and am seeing someone else."

"Excuse me?" I ask.

Charlotte didn't tell me this. What the hell?

"I have a boyfriend," she announces. "Someone I met in the city."

I stand up, knowing I have to plan my next move carefully. It's obvious those people have poisoned her mind, but I'll fix it. I'll fix her.

"Come on." I take her hand. "Let's go ride some rides."

She tries to resist, but I leave her no choice, and she ends up following me.

We stop at the ticket booth where I buy a few books of tickets.

"Tommy, I don't want to go on any rides," she protests.

"Loosen up," I encourage her. "It'll be fun."

Natalie is compliant, something I've always loved about her. Anything I wanted, she always did. I'm confident tonight won't end any differently.

We're riding the Ferris Wheel, and it's our turn to be stuck on top. The entire fairground, surrounded by the mountains, is in full view, but the only thing I'm looking at is the view next to me.

I put my arm around Natalie and pull her close. She tries to resist but has nowhere to go. With my other hand, I turn her face to meet mine and begin to kiss her.

"Tommy." She pushes against me. "Stop."

"Be quiet," I say. "You're going to make a scene."

"If you don't stop," she warns. "I'll scream."

"Relax," I say and drop my hand.

Patience, that's what I need. Patience and a few more pills. I pull the bottle out of my pocket and pop another pill knowing it will keep the frustration I'm feeling to a minimum.

The sun has set, and we're walking around, but Natalie's still tense. I thought by now she'd have calmed down and started to enjoy our date, but tonight isn't going as I'd planned. I should slip one of my pills in her drink. That'd calm her down.

It's not helping that her phone's been going off for the past hour. I can't see who it is, but I'm happy when she finally powers the damn thing off and sticks it in her back pocket. Now she can focus on us. I pull out my bottle and swallow another pill.

"Are you in pain?" Natalie asks. "Maybe we should go home?"

"I'm fine," I answer.

"Then why do you keep taking pills?" She stops walking and puts her hands on her hips.

"Leave it alone, Natalie," I say, a warning tone in my voice.

"But—"

I grab her arm and drag her to a dark area behind the live-stock building, caging her against the brick wall. I'm thankful there's no one around because my temper has reached boiling point. "When I say leave it alone." I get up in her face. "I mean it. Leave it alone. Got it?" She nods her head up and down quickly. There's something about the fearful look in her eyes that turns me on. I kick her legs apart and push my erection against her. "See what you do to me?"

"Please just take me home, Tommy," she whispers. "It's been a long day, and I'm tired."

"Let me kiss you," I say and press my body harder against hers.

"No." She tries to turn her head.

"Wrong answer, sweetheart." I lean in and take what I want. My tongue forces its way into her mouth, deepening the kiss. She squirms around, trying to get out of my hold. "Don't fight me. You know you want this."

I lean in to kiss her again when a light shines on us. I back up to see a security guard holding a flashlight on us.

"What's going on back here?" he asks.

"Sorry, man," I say, pulling Natalie close to me. "My girl's just come back from school, and well, I guess I got a little carried away."

"Is that true, miss?" he asks Natalie.

I squeeze her waist tight in a warning.

"Yes, sir," she says sweetly. "This is really embarrassing. We'll just get out of here. I'm sorry." She smiles at him, and I can see from the look on his face she's charmed him.

"Go on, get out of here, you two," he says, and we follow him back into the crowd of people.

I knew she wouldn't rat me out. It's the proof I needed that she's still mine. She'll soon forget the city and the people in it. I'll have her back in my bed in no time at all.

ALEX

I've spent the entire day in my office setting up the framework for Nicholai's account. I don't have all the specifics yet, but I know enough of the basics to get started. It's a complicated structure making sure that the underground aspects of Nicholai's dealings remain hidden from everyone. To my employees, it appears the same as any other ad campaign. I'm the only one with access to the encrypted data.

I check my phone and see Natalie still hasn't returned any of my texts. I know she was meeting her new boss earlier today. She was supposed to let me know how it went, but I haven't heard from her all day.

I send Viktor a text to have the car ready and slip my phone into my pocket.

When the encryption finishes, I shut my laptop off and push myself to a standing position. I'm stiff from sitting for so long.

Everyone else has already left for the night. I give the office a final once over before locking up.

When I get outside, Viktor's leaning against the side of the car. He sees me approach and moves to open the door, but I wave him off. I'm grateful for his service, but my pensive mood causes me to seek solitude.

After I slide in the car, I pull my phone from my pocket. Still nothing. This isn't like her. She usually has her phone on and responds right away. I refresh the screen like a school-boy desperate to hear from his crush.

Fifteen minutes later, the message is finally read. The three dots dance on the screen, letting me know she's typing.

(Natalie) Not a good time. I'll call you tomorrow.

Not a good time? What's that about?

(Me) Is everything okay?

Another half-hour passes, and my text isn't read. I'm pacing back and forth in my apartment. It's late, and I'm concerned. No longer willing to wait, I pull up Natalie's number and hit the call button. The phone rings and rings before going to voicemail. I leave a message:

Natalie. What's going on? Is everything okay? Call me. I need to hear your voice.

And then I wait. 9 p.m. comes and goes with no call from her.

My phone doesn't ring until the next morning. Natalie's uneasy during our conversation. Something about it doesn't sit right with me.

"My texts went unanswered all night," I say. "Where were you?"

"I was at the county fair with some friends," she says hesitantly. 'The reception was terrible."

"I see." My answer is short. I can tell from the way her voice shakes that she's not telling me the truth.

"I turned my phone off and forgot to turn it on until this morning," she says. "I'm sorry, Sir."

"I forgive you."

"Thank you."

"I'm on my way out for a run." My tone is cold. "I'll call you later."

I know she's not telling me the whole story, but right now, my hands are tied. If she's not going to tell me, I'll try Svetlana; maybe she knows something.

(Me) Have you heard from Natalie?
(Lana) Not since yesterday afternoon. Why?
(Me) She blew me off last night. We just talked, but something's off.

The message shows it's read right away, but her response takes longer than I think it should. I pace back and forth in my kitchen, waiting for a reply.

I hold off going for my run as long as I can, but Lana isn't returning my text. I need to go now so I can run off some of this frustration. Something's going on, and I want to get to the bottom of it. I turn the music app on and put my ear buds in. After securing the phone in my back pocket, I ride the elevator down and set off on my run.

After I'm a few miles in, I get a text notification. I stop running and pull my phone out.

(Lana) She told me everything was okay yesterday, but I get the feeling she's having a hard time readjusting to being home.
(Me) I have that feeling too. I wish there was something I could do to make it better.
(Lana) Any chance she changed her mind and invited you to her birthday party next weekend?

Of course, she didn't tell me, she still sees us a secret.

(Me) Birthday party?
(Lana) I'll take that as a no.

(Me) I know it's her birthday Saturday, but no, she didn't mention a party.

We've been together nearly a year. Most of that time was only a contractual relationship, but I thought she understood I'm serious about making us work. Knowing her past and the damage her ex did by cheating on her, I anticipated she'd struggle with our physical distance. Reluctantly I've agreed to her keeping quiet until she felt more secure with us.

I've flown in twice to visit her. We stayed a few hours away from where she lives. I thought things were going well, that we were making progress, but she's still holding off on telling her parents about me. I'm done being patient; I'm done being a secret.

I finish my run and take a quick shower before calling Svetlana. She gives me the information about the party and her word not to tell Natalie about my plans.

After our call, I make the necessary arrangements for a flight to Missouri on Saturday morning. My little sub will be getting a surprise visit, and we'll be discussing what the path forward will look like.

NATALIE

*B*etween what happened with Tommy at the fair and Alex's distant behavior, my nerves have been on edge all week. And now today I have this birthday party. It was supposed to be a small get together, but it turns out my mother has invited half the town.

It's already mid-morning, and I still haven't been able to reach Alex. I'm supposed to call him every morning to check-in, but all my calls are going straight to voicemail. I wonder where he is? I've been dragging my feet getting ready, hoping I'd be able to get Alex before we left, but I'm running out of time.

Going through my closet, I settle on a pale-yellow sundress, sliding it on before fixing my hair. It's going to be hot today, so I grab a hair tie and pull my hair into a ponytail.

Knowing there probably won't be cell service at the lake, I dial Alex's number one last time. The call goes straight to voice-mail again. I've already left two messages and don't want to leave a third. I hang up and set the phone down on my dresser. My body collapses onto my bed; a feeling of dread washes over me. Have I messed everything up? Does he know I lied to him? Maybe this is his way of telling me it's over between us. I knew this wouldn't work. Distance makes it too easy for people to grow apart.

"Natalie, we're ready to go," Dad calls from downstairs.

"Be right down." I close my eyes for a moment. Alex said he wants this with me, but he's used to far more than I can ever offer him.

Dragging myself up off my bed, I stand in front of the mirror. *You're nothing but a small-town girl. You'll never be anything more. You had your fun in the city, but now you're home, back where you belong.*

I don't want my parents to be right about Alex, but what if they are? Maybe today needs to be the day I stop resisting and give reacclimating myself into the town of Northmeadow an honest effort.

Grabbing my phone, I slide it into the pocket of my dress before I leave the safety of my room. I make it down the steps just in time to hear my mother call for me from the kitchen.

"Natalie, come give me a hand, dear."

I enter the kitchen and gasp. "Did you buy everything in the store?" I ask with a laugh.

"I want the party to be perfect." Mom's eyes gleam with excitement. "Everyone's so happy you're home. They can't wait to see you."

It's been a long time since I've seen her excited about anything. She may be overbearing, but she has put a lot of work into this party. For Mom's sake, I'll put my issues aside and try to share in her joy; try to become a part of the community again.

The twenty-minute drive to Finn Lake is a familiar one.

Although we weren't rich, my parents did better financially than many others in Northmeadow. They gave Evan and me a good childhood, including a few weeks each summer spent in a rental cottage at the lake. Every year I'd beg my parents to stay longer. Being by the water was magical. But each time, they'd pat me on the head and tell me we had a fine home. Then we'd pack up and go back to our house.

Just like everything else, after Evan died, we stopped going.

Before I realize it, Dad turns the car onto Lakeshore Drive, and the pavilion comes into view. It's always been a popular spot for summer parties, even though it's nothing more than a concrete pad and a few wooden posts that hold up a metal roof.

"Who did all this?" I ask when I see the decorations.

"Your mom and Delia Laurel came down early this morning," Dad says.

It doesn't surprise me that Tommy's Aunt Delia had something to do with it. She and Mom have always been close. "It looks great, Mom."

"Thank you, dear," Mom says and smiles proudly.

She's outdone herself, even if it looks more like a party for a ten-year-old. Purple streamers are draped from each post. A Happy Birthday banner with pastel flowers hangs over the entrance way and waves in the gentle breeze. Purple and pink helium balloons are anchored to each picnic table. Guests are already gathering. They smile as they greet each other, the ease of familiarity written in their actions.

"I told you we should have gotten here earlier, Stanley," Mom scolds Dad.

"Yes, dear," Dad says, patting my mom's hand, pacifying her. He silently exits the car and beings to unload the food.

I jump out of the backseat. "Let me give you a hand, Dad."

"No, you don't," Mom says as she climbs out of the car and shuts the door. "This is your party. Go, say hi to your friends," she says and gives me a gentle nudge forward.

I cautiously approach the pavilion, trying to stay hidden behind some trees as I search the sea of faces—the people I once knew and who once knew me.

"Well, look who's back," a female voice says from behind me. My stomach turns at the sound. It's a voice I'll never forget and one I'd hoped never to hear again. Slowly, I turn and take in the tall, curvy blonde standing behind me, her hands on her hips.

"Finally realized Northmeadow is where you belong?" she asks mockingly.

"Why are you here, Ashlynn?"

"Your mother invited me." She walks past me, hitting my shoulder on her way. "Didn't think we'd ever see you back again."

Growing up, Ashlynn and I were inseparable, which didn't surprise anyone since our mothers were best friends. They grew up together, got married within weeks of each other, and were pregnant together. Everyone just assumed we'd follow in their footsteps.

When we were thirteen, Ashlynn's mom died in a car accident. After that, her father struggled with depression and alcoholism. Mom stepped in and filled her best friend's shoes, helping raise Ashlynn through her teen years. My mother loves her like a daughter. I never had the heart to tell her what happened between Ashlynn, Tommy, and me.

"I guess you thought wrong." I attempt to keep a bored tone in my voice while I look over her shoulder for someone, anyone else I recognize—anything to get away from her.

"Don't worry; your *boyfriend* will be along shortly."

"My boyfriend?" She can't possibly know about Alex. We haven't talked since that night.

"Don't act so coy, Natalie." She cocks her hip to the side and places her hand on it.

Of course, she means Tommy. Seriously, is everyone in this town delusional?

"If you're referring to Tommy, he and I ended a long time ago. I'm sure you remember the circumstances." Just thinking about that night, about their betrayal, makes me feel sick.

"Somebody had to be there for him after you walked away."

"I guess if you like being sloppy seconds, he's all yours," I snap back.

Before Ashlynn can respond, Mom walks up carrying a box filled with party favors, interrupting our conversation.

"I see you found Natalie," she says.

"Yes, I did, Mrs. Clarke," Ashlynn replies in a sickeningly sweet voice.

"It's so nice to see my two girls together again. I'm sure you'll pick up right where you left off." Mom places a kiss on Ashlynn's cheek. "That's the beauty of friendship," Mom says and starts to walk away.

"Let me give you a hand with those." I move quickly to catch up with my mom.

I refuse to play Ashlynn's petty games.

Despite my initial reservations, I'm having fun getting reacquainted with old friends. The only thing that could make today better would be having Alex by my side. Would he get along with these people? Would they like him?

The lives my friends here lead are so different than the lives of my friends in the city. Even though I shouldn't be, I'm shocked to see most of my old girlfriends are married, and either already have children, are currently pregnant, or both.

While holding one of their infants, a beautiful baby girl, I can't stop my mind from wandering. If I had never left, would Tommy and I be married with a baby of our own? I look up and see Tommy watching me from across the pavilion. When his eyes meet mine, I see a flash of sadness in them. I break eye contact. Did he share the same thought, or is he finally accepting we're over? When I look up again, the sadness is gone, replaced with something dark and unfathomable; it causes the hairs on my neck to stand on end.

I pass the baby back to her mother just as Reverend Miller and his wife Hannah approach. Much to Mom's dismay, I stopped attending church when I moved to NYC. I was sick of the gossip and hypocritical attitudes I'd witnessed growing up in the church. Organized religion no longer holds any appeal to me. I don't share the same beliefs as my parents; looking back, I realize I never did. I'd gotten a pass on going to church so far, but I think my time is about to expire.

"Natalie, it's so good to have you home." Hannah reaches out and hugs me.

I've always liked her. She's a genuinely kind woman who manages to steer clear of the gossip and judgments the people in this town are so good at dishing out. I still don't understand what she sees in her uptight, fire-and-brimstone husband, though.

"Thank you," I say. "It's good to be home." That's the answer everyone expects, so that's the one I give. It's easier that way.

"We haven't seen you at Sunday service," Reverend Miller says, a look of disapproval written across his stern face.

Reverend Miller's placed me on the spot, and I'm unsure how to respond to him. My hands fidget at my sides, and I desperately struggle not to bite my nails—to follow my Dominant's rule.

Hannah puts her hand on her husband's shoulder. "Dear, she's only been home a few weeks. I'm sure she's still trying to get settled in," she says, offering me a kind smile.

"Mhm." Reverend Miller nods his head. "Tomorrow's Sunday. I take it you're settled in now and can attend service?"

"I'll do my best," I reply quietly.

The wind blows, and a familiar scent of citrus and sandalwood permeates the air. "Excuse me, please," I say and quickly walk away in search of the fragrance's source.

I look around quickly but drop my shoulders. Don't be foolish, Natalie. He's not here. I take a few tentative steps before movement outside the pavilion catches my eye. Standing up against a large River Birch Tree, hands in his pockets, is Alex. Not trusting my eyes, I slowly begin to walk toward the figure. As I get closer, my heart rate speeds up. The realization hits me. He's here. He takes his hands from his pockets and opens his arms to me. Without thinking, I run into them. My head settles on his chest as I savor the feeling of his arms wrapped tightly around me.

After a few minutes, I pull back and look at him. "How? Why?"

"Happy Birthday, baby girl." He leans in and kisses me.

"How did you know?" I ask, then answer my question at the same time as Alex.

"Lana."

We share a laugh.

Then his brows draw together, and his mouth tenses. "We have some things we need to talk about."

I drop my gaze to the ground and kick my sandaled foot in the loose dirt.

He places his finger under my chin, returning my gaze to his. "Don't avert your eyes, Natalie. Talk to me."

"Well, well. Who do we have here?"

My body stiffens at the sound of Tommy's voice. I move out of Alex's embrace and spin around, ready to tell him to get lost. But Alex is already stepping forward, his hand extended.

"I'm Alexander Montgomery, and you are?"

"Thomas Moore, her boyfriend," he replies, keeping his arms crossed tightly in front of his body.

Alex drops his hand and looks back and forth between Tommy and me. His eyes are full of hurt and unspoken questions.

I ball my hands into fists at my sides, willing myself not to explode and cause a scene.

"For the millionth time, you are *not* my boyfriend," I snap.

"Very true, sweetheart." Tommy reaches out and grabs my arm, pulling me to his side. His grip is tight and will leave a bruise. "After all this time, we're so much more than that, aren't we?"

Alex's gaze turns cold. "Take your hands off her." His voice is deep and threatening.

"Or what, city boy?" Tommy puffs up his chest.

I twist my arm from Tommy's grasp. "Tommy, knock it off." I move to Alex and place my hands on his chest. "Can we go somewhere and talk?"

"I think that would be a good idea," he says, not breaking eye contact with Tommy.

The two men stand, staring each other down for what seems like an eternity before Tommy drops his shoulders and takes a step back. "I'll be here when you get back, *sweetheart.*"

Ignoring him, I thread my fingers with Alex's and begin to lead him away from the pavilion and my guests, who've stopped what they were doing to watch this scene.

"Natalie," Mom yells from behind me. "Come back here."

I glance over my shoulder. "I'll be back in a bit."

"Let her go, Charlotte," Dad says and takes Mom by the arm, leading her away.

I'm grateful for his intervention.

I lead Alex to the path that winds its way around the lake. We walk along the graveled path in silence. Anger rolls off him in waves. When we come to a clearing with a bench that overlooks the lake, I stop.

"Want to sit here?" I ask.

"Yes." His answer is cold and clipped.

I've sat on this bench many times. It's a favorite place for me, tucked far enough away from the swimming areas and houses to give the illusion of being isolated, far from everything and everyone.

The view of the lake with the backdrop of the Ozark Mountains is breathtaking. A small breeze causes the water to lap against the rocky shore gently. The sound has always been calming for me. Right now, I hope it's equally calming for Alex.

After sitting a few minutes, both of us staring at the lake, Alex adjusts his position and leans back on the bench, but his gaze remains fixed ahead of him.

"Alex." I place my hand on his arm. "Tommy is not my

boyfriend."

He turns his head. A storm brews in his dark brown eyes. "Care to share why he seems to think otherwise?"

I sit back and throw my hands in the air. "I don't know." How am I supposed to explain something I don't even understand? "I've told him over and over that we ended a long time ago. I even told him I've moved on with you."

That statement gets Alex's attention, and he finally looks at me.

"He doesn't seem to get it, and my mother keeps encouraging him to come around." I blow out a frustrated breath.

"Were you with him when I called the other night?" Alex asks.

I can't lie to him again. It's time to come clean.

"Yes." I turn my body to face him. "I didn't want to be, but there's no arguing with my mother. Tommy was in a bad mood, and I didn't want to cause a scene when you tried calling. I didn't know what else to do." The words spill from my mouth without a breath in between.

Alex sits up and puts his hands on my shoulders. "Natalie, you have to communicate with me. Talk to me. Trust me." His voice softens. "Without communication, this relationship won't work."

"I know."

Seeing the disappointment on his face and knowing I caused it is too much for me. I try to turn away, but Alex doesn't let me.

"Do you trust me?" he asks.

"Yes, but—"

"You either trust me, or you don't." He searches my face for an answer.

"I trust you."

"Good," he says. "Now, tell me everything that's been going on."

I begin recapping the events of the past few weeks, this time telling Alex the whole story.

"Apartment hunting has been useless," I say and slump back on the bench. "There's absolutely nothing available. It looks like I'm stuck at my parents' house for the foreseeable future."

"How does Tommy factor into this?" he asks.

"My parents' are insisting I go out with him." I put my head back and look up. "When I try to refuse, they start freaking out. They say as long as I'm at home, I need to follow their rules. Which leads me back to problem number one—I can't find an apartment."

"Where did he take you the other night?"

"We were at the fair," I say. Then I tell him everything that happened that night.

"I'm going to kill him." The anger in Alex's voice startles me.

"I don't want any trouble, Alex," I say, trying to calm him down. "I just feel like no one is listening to me and what I want."

"And what is it you want?" He pulls me onto his lap.

"I want you."

He presses his lips to mine and pulls my body against his. I can feel his hardness between my legs.

"I think it's time we tell your parents about us, don't you?

I reach between us and cup his erection. "Right now, there're other things I'd rather do."

"As much as I'd love to stay hidden in the woods with you," he says, lifting me as he stands, setting me on the ground and taking a second to adjust himself, "I think we should get back to your party."

"I'd rather stay here with you." I hold onto him.

"We have the rest of the weekend," he says with a mischievous glint in his eyes. "Let's go."

We follow the path back to the party. With each step, I get more nervous knowing we have to face my parents and their questions as to why Alex is here. In a perfect world, they'd welcome him, and all would be well. But I know this world is far from perfect. I just hope they don't cause a scene in front of everyone.

NATALIE

With my hand tightly gripping Alex's, we arrive back at the pavilion. My eye is immediately drawn to a picnic table where my mother sits next to Delia, the two women deep in conversation. Tommy sits across from them, listening carefully. When he spots us, he points over Mom's shoulder. She jumps up and stalks toward us, a grimace on her face.

"Natalie, may I have a word?" Mom asks, not even attempting to hide her disapproval.

I squeeze Alex's hand tighter. "Whatever you have to say, you can say in front of Alex."

"I don't think that's a good idea."

She's infuriating. The last thing I want is a big scene in front of everyone, but she doesn't seem to care. Thankfully, Alex steps in.

"It's okay, Natalie. I see your Dad over there." He motions to where my dad stands by the lake. "If it's okay, I'll go say hi to him while you talk with your Mom." He pauses and waits for me to respond.

I nod my head, letting him know I'll be okay. He places a kiss on my forehead and, with his hands in his pockets, strolls over to where Dad and his buddies are fishing.

"What is he doing here?" Mom asks.

"He came to celebrate my birthday." I try to keep my voice quiet, hoping not to draw attention to our conversation.

"I don't know why you thought it would be okay to invite that man," she says, pointing in Alex's direction, "when you have Thomas here."

I close my eyes and draw in a deep breath. "That man has a name, it's Alex," I say, "And I didn't ask Tommy to be here." My voice grows louder.

"He has no business being here," my mother responds sharply.

"Alex is here because I want him here." I pause and readjust the volume of my voice. "I don't want to argue about this. Not here, not now."

"We will continue this discussion later, with your father and Thomas."

I nod my head and walk away before I explode on the spot.

My heart is racing, and my hands are shaking with anger. I look around, needing somewhere to go to calm down. There's a small grove of trees that will provide me shade and protection from the prying eyes and ears of my guests. Leaning up against a tree, I look up. The sun shines brightly in the vibrant blue sky. White, puffy clouds float with a freedom that I envy. The view is a necessary distraction giving me time to re-center myself.

When I feel more in control of my emotions, I push off the tree and head toward the lake, but I notice Alex isn't there anymore. I look around for him and freeze when I spot him on the other side of the pavilion. The anger I had just worked so hard to dispel is back with a vengeance.

Ashlynn is talking to *my* Alex, her hand on his shoulder and her head thrown back in laughter. Alex stands stiff, not returning her overly friendly behavior but not being outright rude either. This party has turned into a disaster of epic proportions.

No longer caring if I make a scene, I quickly race across the pavilion to where they're standing and stop behind her, my hands on my hips.

"Excuse me," I snap. The polite and quiet girl is gone, replaced with a woman on a mission—a woman who right now wants to rip out Ashlynn's eyeballs for even looking at Alex.

Ashlynn turns, a satisfied smile on her face. She knows exactly what she's doing, and I just played right into her hands.

Alex removes her hand from his shoulder and walks over to me. He wraps his arm around my waist.

"Is everything okay with your mom?" he asks.

"Yes," I say, my body rigid and my sights fixed on Ashlynn. "Why are you over here?"

"Natalie, relax," she says in a condescending tone. "I'm just introducing myself to your friend."

"Ashlynn here was telling me stories about the two of you in high school."

"Oh, I bet she was," I say. "Did she also tell you—"

"Natalie!" My father calls from across the pavilion. "Time to sing Happy Birthday."

"It was nice meeting you, Ashlynn." Alex flattens his palm on my lower back and leads me away.

"How could you talk to her?" I whisper to him.

"Relax, baby girl. I know who and what she is," he says. "She can try all she wants, but I'm all yours." He flashes me his panty-melting smile as we make our way to where my mother and father stand, a gigantic cake on the table in front of them.

Knowing she's touched Alex makes me want to throw up, but his reassurance helps me see reason and calm down.

When we near the table, Dad lights the candles, and my guests break out in the birthday song. Closing my eyes, I make a wish and blow out the candles. My wish already stands next to me with a smile so bright his eyes light up. I love this man with all my heart and want nothing more than to spend forever by his side.

Thankfully, Ashlynn leaves while I'm opening my presents. My mother sent her off with an extra piece of cake to bring to her father. But Tommy remains lurking along the outskirts of the pavilion. I do my best to ignore him as I introduce Alex to all my old friends. Together we share laughs over stories from my high school days. Alex doesn't have much in common with these people, but somehow he's able to blend seamlessly into this part of my life. Seeing him comfortable here, I'm encouraged that we can make this work.

With the afternoon winding down, the last of the guests leave, and we begin to tackle the clean-up. Despite my mother's less than welcoming attitude and Tommy's refusal to leave, Alex stays by my side and helps with everything.

"Looks like we got it all," Mom says. "Let's go, Natalie."

I look between her and Alex. "Alex is in town for the rest of the weekend. I'm going to stop by the house and grab some clothes. I'll be staying with him."

My mother's face turns red, and her nostrils flare. "You are an unmarried woman. You will not be spending the night with him." She points to Alex.

"Mom, this has to stop." My tone careful and controlled. I need to be heard, but I don't want a fight. "I'm a grown woman, not a child."

Mom stands silent. Her arms by her side, her body tense with anger. Dad walks over to us with a less-than-pleased look on his face. Behind them, Tommy sits on top of a picnic table. He shakes a few pills into his hand and swallows them, silently watching the confrontation.

Alex moves to my side. "It was a wonderful party, Mr. and Mrs. Clarke." He turns to me. "Are you ready to go?"

I nod in agreement and, leaving the stunned trio behind, walk hand in hand with Alex to his car.

"If we hurry, we can get to the house and grab some stuff before they get home," I tell him.

Once I'm in the safety of his car, I'm able to take a deep

breath. That wasn't comfortable, but it went better than I antici-pated. Alex pulls out of the parking lot, and I look out the window. My parents appear to be arguing, my mom's hands flailing in the air—Tommy is shooting daggers in our direction. Dread fills my stomach. We may have avoided a confrontation this time, but we aren't going to avoid it forever.

ALEX

I'm thankful to be driving Natalie away from that scene. It's clear her parents, especially her mother, don't want me around. Her father's friendly with me, but I have a feeling that won't last much longer.

Dealing with her parents is going to be a tricky situation. If they try to silence her in front of me, I'll step in, but I must allow Natalie to use her voice; she has enough people speaking for her already. She's a capable adult who can make her own decisions. She just needs to remember that.

There's also Tommy. If he comes near her again, so help me, he won't live long enough to regret it.

"I'm very proud of you, baby girl."

She looks at me, a sad smile on her face.

"I'm tired, Alex," she says and slumps in her seat. "I'm sick of having this same argument with them."

"We're going to figure this out." I reach for her hand. "Together."

"When I didn't hear from you," she says. "I thought the worst. I thought you were done with me."

"I don't think I could ever be done with you," I reassure her.

The words *I love you* sit on the tip of my tongue, but I hesitate too long, and the moment passes.

I pull in front of her house instead of the driveway. With our head start, we got here first. Parking on the street ensures we won't get blocked in.

"Wait here. I'm just gonna run inside and grab a bag." She gives me a quick peck on the cheek.

I watch her run up the front porch steps and disappear into the house. It's been nearly a month since I last saw her, and I miss her in more ways than one. We never run out of things to talk about, and although video chatting and playing long-distance is fun, I miss the feel of her body beneath mine.

She has a punishment coming for lying to me earlier in the week, but after seeing for myself the extreme stress she's been under, I'm going to have to change some things. The distance is hard for Natalie. I understand that. But the bottom line is she lied, and I can't let her off the hook for it.

While I wait for her, I get out and take a walk around the property. Her parents have a rather large house. At one point, I'm sure it was a beautiful home, but today it sits in a state of disrepair like they've given up on maintaining it. The paint on the white wood siding is beginning to peel, and the black shutters are faded. Their front porch is quintessential farmhouse style and wraps around the side of the house. Near the steps and door, the boards look to have been recently replaced but were left unpainted. The flower boxes that hang from the porch rails catch my attention. I recognize the flowers. They were some of my mother's favorites, petunias paired with ivy that trails down the sides.

Walking around the side of the house, I spot a rusted swing set. It must have been Natalie and her brother's. The vision of a young Natalie, her blonde pigtails flying in the air as she swung back and forth, brings a smile to my face. I imagine our little girl with Natalie's piercing green eyes and my brown hair, giggling as I push her on a swing. The thought catches me off guard.

Beyond the swing set is a large vegetable garden. Between the flower boxes and vegetables, it's clear someone is skilled at gardening. I wander back to my car, taking another look at the house. A little TLC and it could be beautiful again.

My phone buzzes with a text alert.

(Brandon) Just checking to make sure you made it in one piece.
(Me) I did.
(Brandon) How's it going?
(Me) She's not happy, man. The old boyfriend is still sniffing around, and her parents are smothering her...
(Brandon) Lana's told me a bit.
(Me) Speaking of parents, they just pulled in. Gotta go.

Natalie comes through the front door just as her parents pull into the driveway. My instincts tell me things are about to explode. I hurry to meet Natalie at the steps. Her eyes lock with mine. Just keep looking at me, baby girl; we've got this.

Her father's the first out of the car. "Alex, son." He uses his best fatherly tone. "I don't know how you do things where you come from, but around here, girls don't just run off and spend the night with strange men."

"Mr. Clarke." I meet his eyes. "With all due respect, Natalie's a grown woman. She's fully capable of making decisions for herself." I hold my hand out to her, allowing her to make the choice. She willingly threads her fingers with mine, and I pull her close to my side.

"Natalie, you're making a mistake," her mother pleads. "People will talk."

"Do you think I'm the only girl having sex with her boyfriend?" Natalie laughs.

"Watch your tone, young lady," her father corrects her.

"Mom, Dad, I love you both," she says, her grip tightening in my hand. "I'll see you in a few days."

I'm filled with pride, watching the woman at my side stand up for herself. Taking the bag from her, I lead her to my waiting car, help her in, and shut the door.

Her parents stand side by side, postures stiff.

"I'll have her home, Monday," I say as I put her bag in the trunk.

Stanley Clarke turns his back, as if unable to watch, while his wife holds her hand over her chest. This might have been the first time Natalie has ever willingly defied them. I don't want her relationship with her parents ruined, but they have to allow her the space to make her own choices, and right now, I'm her choice.

When no other words are exchanged, I get in the car, and we drive away.

After a few minutes, I reach across the console and hold onto Natalie's trembling hands. With us being apart, I miss the feel of her soft skin and the way her tiny hand fits inside my grasp. She's mine to care for—to protect.

"I know that was hard for you." I give her hand a little squeeze. "I'm so proud of you."

"That was the hardest thing I've ever done," she says with a sigh. "I wouldn't have been able to do it without you by my side."

"I'll always be by your side."

Natalie remains silent for a few minutes. I turn on the radio, the soft sounds of music fill the car.

"Where are we staying?" she asks.

"Water's Edge Bed and Breakfast."

When I googled the Northmeadow area, there were no hotels within a 50-mile radius. There were some lake houses still available, but then I found this bed and breakfast. It looked like the perfect place for a romantic weekend getaway.

"Mrs. Wilson's place." Natalie smiles.

"You're familiar with it?"

"I've seen it from the outside, but I've never stayed there."

Perfect. A first we'll share in her hometown. Hopefully, a first of many.

ALEX

*A*fter the twenty-minute ride, we pull into the small gravel parking lot. The pictures online don't do the place justice. The three-story log cabin structure is ideally situated just steps from the lake. The expansive porch houses wooden rocking chairs that sit under large ceiling fans giving the place a homey, inviting feel. Large pots holding magnificent flower displays line the natural stone steps.

I get out and grab our bags from the trunk. Together we walk inside to check-in. A desk sits inside the front door. Behind it sits an older woman. Her white hair pinned neatly on her head.

"Hello, ma'am," I say. "I called earlier in the week and reserved a room."

She stands up and peers at us over her silver-rimmed glasses that sit low on her nose. "Your name?"

"Alexander Montgomery."

There's no computer to check for the reservation. The woman has a spiral-bound notebook in front of her. She flips through a few pages. "There you are." Glancing up, she looks between us. "Two nights?"

"That's correct."

"Here's your key. Your room is on the third floor, second door on the left." She points behind us. "We don't have an elevator. The steps are over there. Enjoy your stay."

"Thank you, we will."

I smile politely and place my hand on Natalie's back as we make our way to the ornate oak staircase with a hand-carved knotty pine railing.

I can feel the woman's eyes boring into our backs as we walk away. The judgmental attitudes in this town are unbelievable. Having always lived in a bigger city, I've never experienced anything like this. I'm getting a taste of what Natalie has had to deal with these past few months.

As we climb the two flights of steps, we take our time to look at the candid photos of couples and families enjoying the bed and breakfast and the small beach. They add to the charm of the place.

We make it to the third floor and walk down the hall to the door of our suite. I place the key in the lock, and with a click, it opens. Turning the handle, I push the door open, allowing Natalie to go in first.

"I've always wondered what these rooms looked like," she says as she walks into the room. I follow closely behind her.

The woodsy feel of the outside has been carefully balanced to create a warm, country atmosphere. The long wall directly across from the entrance houses windows overlooking the lake. The balcony doors are open, allowing the evening breeze to flow through the room. The windows provide a magnificent view of the sun setting over the lake. In front of one set of windows sits a table and chairs. They have the same carvings as the handrail on the steps. Upon further inspection, I see the carvings mimic the mountains and lakes in the region. They are indeed a piece of art. The hardwood floors creak as we walk. To our right is a four-poster canopy bed with sheer curtains flowing in the breeze. A handmade quilt stretches across the bed with a variety of pillows arranged neatly at the top. Next to the sides of the bed are tall wood tables, each holding a small matching lamp. The wall to the bed's right is home to an expansive dark wood armoire allowing guests a place to unpack. The antique furniture and country décor add to the quaint and welcome feeling one expects from a bed and breakfast.

There's a sitting area with a vintage sofa arranged across from a large stone fireplace. That must be incredible on a chilly winter night. The table in front of the couch is constructed from a reclaimed crate. Sitting on top of it is a large vase of lilacs; their fragrance fills the room.

Natalie walks out of the doors and onto the balcony. I set our bags on the table and follow behind her, wrapping my arms around her waist. She lets her head fall back on my chest; her body relaxes in my arms.

"When I was growing up, we spent every summer in a rental cottage right over there." She points off to the right, where I can see the lights from a few small cottages in the tree line along the lake. "Evan and I would see couples standing on these balconies, and we'd make up stories for them. I always thought it would be romantic to stay here."

I enjoy the stories she tells me about her childhood.

Natalie sighs. "Things were so different back then." She lifts her head and moves out of my arms to lean against the rail of the balcony.

I move next to her and look out at the lake. "Are you happy here?"

"Yes. No. I don't know." She paces back and forth. "Nothing is like I remembered it. Maybe I changed too much while I was away?"

"You don't have to stay. You can come back to the city with me, get a job there."

"You know I can't do that."

I push off the rail and stand in front of her. "I can get you out of the contract."

She stops mid-step, her eyes opening wide.

"I'll pay the money for the scholarship," I say. "You can come back home with me."

In my mind, this is easy. With a quick phone call, the money will be transferred, and this can be done.

"We've already been over this. You are not paying my way out of it." She laughs and shakes her head. "That would make me feel like nothing more than your whore."

"Natalie." I reach out to her.

"No, Alex," she says and takes a step back.

How dare she refer to herself in that way? I will not permit that.

"You are not a whore." I take a second to get my anger under control. "Don't you dare talk about yourself like that."

"What else would you call it if I allow the man I'm sleeping with to use his money so I can leave town with him?

I'm taken back by her words. I'd hoped I was more to her than just the man she's sleeping with. I approach her slowly, cautiously. "I'd call it a man who's in love with you and would move heaven and earth to be with you."

I walk toward her slowly, closing the gap between us.

"A man who's in love with me?" she asks.

"Yes," I answer her. "I'm in love with you, Natalie Clarke, and I want you to come home with me."

Her shoulders relax, and her eyes soften. "Alex." She walks into my arms. "I love you too."

I wrap my arms around her, needing to feel her body next to mine to reassure me this is really happening.

"I don't mean to sound ungrateful, Sir," she says. "But I just can't accept your offer. I'm sorry."

I hate her answer, but I will respect her decision. I hold her for a few minutes longer before I take a step back, breaking our connection. "But there is the issue of your lying to me earlier this week."

She looks down. "Yes, Sir. There is that."

I walk inside the room and over to my bag. Unzipping it, I pull out a black leather riding crop. "Come here," I order.

Although hesitant, she obeys. With her eyes locked on mine, she saunters into the room and stands before me.

I point, and she lowers herself to her knees.

My cock twitches, watching her willingly submit to me. That will have to wait for later. There's a punishment to be dealt with first.

I close the balcony doors and draw the curtains closed. We don't need anyone watching what's about to happen.

Holding my palm out, I hit the crop across it, allowing the sound of the sharp crack to fill the room. Natalie gasps. The crop's painless across my palm but will cause a stinging bite when used on the delicate skin of her ass. The punishment won't be too much for her, but it will serve as a reminder of her responsibilities in this relationship.

"Natalie, this lifestyle, this commitment between you and me, requires nothing less than complete honesty." I pause, allowing her to digest my words. "If we can't trust each other, if I have to question your honesty, this..." I motioned between us. "This won't work."

She drops her gaze to the floor.

"When we entered this relationship, we discussed punishments and the reasons why they are necessary."

She nods in agreement.

"Do you understand why you're being punished?"

Another silent nod.

"You need to use your voice, baby girl."

"I wasn't honest with you." She looks up at me. "I lied to you about where I was and who I was with."

If she only knew how much I hate giving out punishments. But as her Dominant, it's my responsibility to follow through. Without that, what good are the rules? A Dominant is only as good as his word, and as difficult as this will be, I will make good on my word.

I sit on the nearest chair and hold the crop across my lap. "Stand and strip." My command is short, allowing no room for argument.

Natalie gracefully stands. Although her hands tremble, she reaches behind her and unzips her sundress before slipping the thin straps off her shoulders, allowing the dress to slide down her body, exposing her sun-kissed skin inch by inch. My sweet, innocent sub acts like a sexy minx, even though she's stripping for punishment.

Turning away from me, she looks over her shoulder, her emerald eyes smoldering with desire. She reaches behind her, unclasping her white lace bra, letting it fall to the ground by her dress. She slides her hands down her body; my eyes follow as her hands make their way to her lace thong. Shimmying her hips, the fabric glides down her legs. She bends over, her ass on full display, as she picks them up from the floor. Slowly she turns to face me again. With a mischievous smile, she tosses her panties to me. She may be facing a punishment, but she's putting on a sexy show in the process.

I catch them and bring them to my nose, inhaling her sweet scent. "These are coming home with me."

She runs her tongue along her lower lip.

I take a minute to appreciate her body before I call her to me. "Come here." My voice sure and steady, betraying none of the excitement I'm feeling. "Bend over my legs."

She obeys without hesitation and folds her body across my lap. I run my hand over the globes of her ass before dragging my finger between her legs. She's wet—aroused. The knowledge further excites me.

"You will receive ten strikes." Without warning, I raise my arm. The swoosh of the crop fills the air, followed by the sound of it cracking across first one side of her ass, then the other. The leather's sting causes her to whimper. After three more strikes, her cries begin to get louder. I don't know how thick the walls are in these rooms. "You need to remain quiet," I say. "Or I'll have to gag you. Do you understand?"

"Yes, Sir," she says through her tears.

I've disciplined my past subs, but I've never felt anything when they cried out. Hearing Natalie cry pierces my heart. Part of me wants to throw the crop down and gather her in my arms, but the Dominant in me knows my submissive needs her punishment. The depth of my feeling is as terrifying as it is thrilling.

She's obedient and doesn't make another sound as I continue, alternating sides of her ass. After the last strike, I drop the crop on the floor and inspect her red skin. It's a beautiful sight. My skill ensures there's no permanent damage, but she will remember this when she sits down tonight.

I help her up and pull her onto my lap. She curls up against my chest, crying softly.

"I'm sorry I lied to you, Sir," she whispers. "It won't happen again."

"I forgive you, baby girl." I use my thumbs to wipe the tears from her face before pulling her in for a kiss.

With her punishment over, I can concentrate on giving her pleasure. I place her gently on her feet. "Don't move." That command used to be difficult for her. She was always concerned with covering her nakedness, ashamed of her body. Now, my beautiful sub stands proudly before me, allowing me an unobstructed view of her body.

"Yes, Sir."

I stand and return to my bag. Reaching in, I pull out a wrapped gift for my birthday girl. When she sees it, her eyes light up.

"Happy Birthday," I say and hand her the gift.

"May I open it now?" she asks.

"Yes."

She wastes no time ripping the shiny paper open.

"Oh, Sir, it's beautiful," she says as she runs her fingers over the length of soft jute I had dyed purple for her.

"When we first negotiated our contract, you said you wanted to include rope play."

"Yes, Sir."

"You probably thought I forgot about it."

"I did." She laughs.

"Other than a few rudimentary ties to restrain a sub, I didn't know anything about Shibari," I confess.

I continue to explain that over the past few months, I've been taking instructional classes with Master Kiyoshi.

"Most were video lessons," I explain. "Last month, he visited Fire and Ice to teach some classes. I was able to get some hands-on learning."

"Oh," she says quietly.

"Look at me." I place my finger under her chin, raising her face. "They were private lessons. Brandon offered himself as my semi-willing rope bunny."

Natalie laughs, and it's a beautiful sound.

"That is something I would've loved to see."

"I assure you, there are no pictures," I say. "I'm not an expert, but I'd be honored if you'd allow me to show you what I've learned."

She stands on her tiptoes and kisses me. "I couldn't think of a better present, Sir. Thank you."

"What are your safe words?" I ask her, making sure they're at the forefront of her mind. An injury can happen too easily, even with simple bondage.

"Yellow and red, Sir."

I begin at the top of one arm. Using a single column, I make a diamond pattern with the rope, stopping right before her wrist. With a separate piece, I do the same on her other arm. With both arms harnessed, I stop to check-in. "Does everything feel okay?"

She closes her eyes as if doing a mental inventory. "Yes, it feels good."

I return to my bag and pull out more rope. "Give me your hands."

She raises them in front of her, and I position them palms together.

Using a double-column tie, I wrap the jute around her wrists twice and loop it through the middle. It's only a beginner's harness, but with each twist of the rope, I feel Natalie's body relaxing, submitting to my control.

This experience may be my present to her, but she's gifting me with something even more special—freedom over her willing body. Having that control over her is an incredibly intimate connection, something I've never shared with another.

When I finish tying, I check to ensure the rope is taught but not tight. One final time I ask, "Does everything feel okay?"

She tries to pull her hands apart, testing the rope. "It feels good."

Grabbing the rope, I walk her to the bed.

"Lay on your stomach."

I help her onto the bed and stretch her arms above her head. Using the rope's tail, I thread it through the thick wood spindle of the headboard and tie it off. I tug at it to ensure it won't slip.

Satisfied with my work, I walk to the bottom of the bed. Natalie wiggles, trying to turn her head, but she comes up short.

"Good try, baby girl," I say and chuckle, watching her squirm.

I'm standing just out of her line of sight while I pull my shirt over my head and toss it on the chair. It lands next to her discarded panties.

"You need to stay quiet," I remind her.

"Yes, Sir."

Moving closer to the bed, I push her up on her knees, legs spread wide. Her head and chest remain on the bed with her arms stretched out before her. I admire her positioning.

"You're wet for me, already."

"Very." Her voice is breathy and needy.

The desire dripping from her words only encourages my already throbbing dick. As much as I want to sink into her tight, wet center, I still have other plans. My dick will have to wait. Walking back to my bag, I pull out a toy and turn it on. A vibrating hum fills the air.

"What's that?" she asks as she tries to look over her shoulder.

"Have you ever used a magic wand?"

"No, Sir."

"Well, then I'm happy to introduce you."

I crawl onto the bed, kneel behind her, and place the wand directly on her clit. She gasps at the intense sensation. She's already aroused from her spanking. This is going to be quick.

"You are so fucking beautiful," I say.

The words have barely left my mouth when she throws her head back in ecstasy. Her legs collapse from under her, and I use my free arm to hold her up. I keep the wand firmly in place, not allowing her body a chance to come down from its high.

"Alex, I can't," she pants.

"Relax, baby girl, you can." I turn the wand on high and continue massaging her overly sensitive center. "I want to see you come again."

Her breathing increases as her body prepares itself for a second release.

"Come for me, Natalie." Her back arches, and her body explodes with another orgasm before going limp in my arms.

I quickly work to release her from the bed and untie her. Climbing in bed, I pull her into my arms and cover her naked body with the blankets.

"I love you, baby girl," I whisper to her while she experiences the freedom of subspace.

NATALIE

I've left my body and am floating through a sea of vibrant colors.

Weightless. Peaceful.

My worries have vanished. I feel free. Whispered words of love float through the air. I want to remain here forever, but my eyes open.

The room is dark and quiet. My head rests on Alex's chest, his arm around me holding me close.

It takes a few minutes for the fogginess to clear. When I'm able to push up on my elbow, I study Alex. Even in sleep, there's an inherent strength in his face. My fingers trace the dark stubble on his jaw from not having shaved in a few days before my gaze travels down his chest. I admire the defined muscles in his abdomen and the trail of dark hair, where his jeans sit low on his hips. I struggle between wanting to open his jeans and give him pleasure or letting him sleep.

"Welcome back, beautiful," he speaks softly.

"Hi." I lean in, kissing his lips.

"It's nice to have you back."

"That was an incredible experience."

He rewards me with a sexy smile, and I find myself aroused again. I can't believe this man is here with me, that he loves me.

As I lower my hand to unbutton his jeans, my stomach grumbles, causing us both to laugh. "I guess I'm a little hungry."

"I think we missed dinner," he says.

I continue to reach for his button. "I'd rather have you first."

He grabs my hand. "And I would love that, but first, you need to eat. I know it's late, but is there any place we can get some food?"

"What time is it?"

Alex grabs his phone off the bedside table. "It's almost 11."

"There's a pizza place down the road that should still be open."

Alex calls and places an order.

"They don't deliver," he says after he hangs up. "I'm going to have to pick it up." He throws his legs over the side of the bed and stands.

I lean on my elbows, allowing the sheets to slide down, exposing my breasts to him, and earning a throaty growl.

When he's dressed, he comes back to the bed and sits. Leaning over, he takes a nipple into his mouth, nipping and sucking before he lets go.

"I'll be back in a little bit." His mouth twitches with amusement as he stands and walks out of the room.

I let myself fall back onto the pillow and blow out a frustrated breath. How can I be so turned on after all the orgasms he already gave me? He's such a generous lover he hasn't taken any release for himself. He always places my needs first. When he gets back, I'll make sure to give him the pleasure he deserves.

While Alex is gone, I jump in the shower to clean up and then slip into one of his T-shirts.

I find a switch by the balcony doors. When I turn it on, the balcony illuminates with soft lighting. I sit on one of the wooden chairs outside, allowing the warm breeze to dry my damp hair.

TOMMY

I pull into her parent's driveway, but I'm too late. Charlotte tells me Natalie left with Alex about ten minutes ago. She isn't sure where they're staying, only that Natalie said she'll be home Monday.

Other than a lake house, the only place to stay is at old lady Wilson's, so I take a chance and drive there. Sure enough, there's a fancy rental car parked in the lot. I pull my truck into the driveway of an empty cottage next door. The trees lining the property will keep me from being seen.

I open the glove box, pull out my gun, make sure it's loaded, and set it on the seat next to my night vision binoculars. Reaching into my pocket, I pull out my pill bottle and swallow two pills. I'm craving their high more and more.

I don't have a plan yet, but I'll be damned if I'm just going to let this guy waltz into town and take Natalie away from me.

It takes a few hours before movement in the lot catches my eye. Alex gets in his car and pulls away.

Once I'm sure he's gone, I grab the binoculars and, using the strap, put them over my head, then I grab my gun and tuck it in the waistband of my pants. I walk through the trees crossing onto the property of the bed and breakfast. There are a few outbuildings that allow me to stay undetected while also being able to keep an eye out for any sign of Natalie.

I'm about to give up hope when the lights of a third-floor balcony turn on, and Natalie walks out. Looking through my lens, I see her hair's damp, and she's wearing a man's T-shirt that hangs to her mid-thigh. From the way her nipples poke through the fabric, I can tell she's not wearing anything underneath, and that makes me hard as fuck. Using the camera feature in the binoculars, I snap a few pictures. I'll be getting off to these tonight.

While I'm figuring out my next move, Alex pulls back into the parking lot. I move further behind the building to stay hidden and continue watching. A few minutes later, Alex walks out onto the balcony. Natalie stands up and wraps her arms around him, her ass peeking out from underneath the shirt. I take some more pictures before going back to my truck. I need to come up with a way to get rid of him once and for all.

ALEX

When I arrive back at the room, I see the balcony door is open. Padding across the floor, I place the pizza box and sodas on the table and stand in the balcony doorway to watch Natalie. She's sitting on a wooden chair; her legs tucked up under her. The warm breeze blows her damp blonde curls in her face. She tucks the wayward hair behind her ear as she appears to stare out across the water. My heart aches, knowing the struggle she's feeling, but she's so much stronger than she realizes. I have two days to remind her of her strength.

I decide to stop staring and announce my arrival. "Hungry?"

The sound of my voice startles her. When her eyes reach mine, she runs her tongue across her bottom lip before untucking her legs and standing. Slowly, she makes her way across the spacious balcony wearing only my T-shirt.

"Starved."

The meaning behind her answer is not lost on me as she wraps her arms around my neck and kisses me. My cock stirs, but once again, it's going to have to wait.

"Let's eat out here." I smile. "It's a beautiful night."

Natalie steps back. "Yes, Sir. I'll go make your plate."

She gives me a sexy pout as she walks past me swaying her

hips. I smack my little temptress on her ass, causing her to giggle.

While she makes my plate, I lean on the balcony rail. It's easy to see how Natalie got lost in her thoughts out here. Unlike the noisy city, the only sounds here are the chirp of crickets and the occasional croak of a toad. Replacing the artificial city lights is a beautiful night sky with thousands of twinkling stars. It's so different from my daily life, but the tranquil feeling of being by the water is something I could quickly get used to. Maybe we'll have to look at getting a place by the water?

We. That's something I never imagined I'd be saying, but I've been thinking in those terms more and more.

My mind drifts to the night I met her at Fire and Ice. I've always had experienced subs. I didn't think I'd ever be attracted to someone brand new to BDSM, but then she came along. Natalie's special. She's the perfect mix of naïve and curious. She has a playful side I adore. It's something that sets her apart from others who think being in a Dom/sub relationship has to be all rules and formality. Quite the opposite. I enjoy laughing and having fun with her, in addition to following the protocols of our lifestyle.

Unknowingly, she's challenged me not only to be a better Dominant but to be a better man. I was running from my past, from love, until her. She changed my life. Her smile, the one that lights up her emerald eyes, melted the ice that had formed a prison around my heart. I can see a future with her—a forever with her.

Natalie interrupts my thoughts. "I have your dinner, Sir."

"Thank you." I take a seat, and she gives me my plate.

She drags over a small white table with her free hand and sets my can of soda on it before going back inside the room to make her plate.

When she returns, she takes the seat next to me, tucking her legs back under her. My shirt rides up, exposing the top of her leg, and I see she's naked underneath. Natalie looks at me and bites her lower lip, my lust reflecting in her eyes. For a brief moment, I consider putting my plate aside and fucking her on the balcony, but she needs to get some nourishment before I bring her back to bed and have my way with her all night.

It isn't until I take my first bite that my little sub begins to eat.

The mood shifts from the lightheartedness we shared just a few minutes ago to something that feels much more serious. While she eats, Natalie's gaze once again drifts back to the water.

I desperately want to know every thought in her head.

"What are you thinking about?"

She sets her plate on her lap. Her brow creases with worry. "It's harder being back here than I thought it would be."

"Harder, how?"

"When I first left for school, I was an insecure young girl who had lived a very sheltered life. I blindly did as I was told. It was all I knew." She looks to me for understanding before continuing. "I did a lot of growing up while I was away. A lot of changing."

My heart aches to see the conflict on her face, but I stay quiet and let her finish.

"For the first time, I was able to live life on my terms, make my own decisions. Coming back home..." She pauses and looks down at her lap. "I feel like I'm losing myself, my voice, and I don't know how to stop it."

I can make this situation go away for her, but she won't let me. It's frustrating, but I understand why. She's an independent young woman who went to NYC with a plan for her future, but unfortunately, life had other plans for her. Now she's stuck in a situation where she's not entirely happy. It would be so easy for me to buy out her contract and bring her home with me. She could have a career there, and we could come back here to visit. It would be a win for everyone. But if I force that on her, I'll be just like everyone here. As difficult as this is, my role as her Dominant is not to take away her voice.

"What can I do to help you?"

"I don't know that there's anything you can do." She meets my eyes. "Other than being here for me."

"I'll always be here for you." I put my plate on the table and turn to face her. "As your Dominant and as the man who loves you, I'll stand beside you. I'll fight for you. I'll support your decisions and catch you if you fall."

"Alex—"

"You're my world, baby girl. My whole universe. There's nothing you could say or do that would change my feelings for you." I reach over and cup her face in my palm. "I love you, Natalie."

At this moment, I finally understand the love my parents shared and why my father didn't regret a second of loving my mom, even though she left him too soon. I want the same with Natalie, and I'm willing to risk everything to get it.

NATALIE

*L*ast night something shifted between Alex and me. Barriers we'd both erected from our pasts started to crumble. When we finally finished eating, he took me to bed and made love to me all night. We fell asleep, our bodies entwined, just before the sun rose over the horizon.

By the time we wake up, it's nearly noon. We dress in a hurry, hoping to make it in time for lunch downstairs. We walk into the dining room and take our seats, just as Mrs. Wilson puts lunch on the table. A young couple follows shortly after and joins us. As soon as the food is served, Mrs. Wilson excuses herself, leaving us to eat.

The couple tells us they're just married and are passing through Northmeadow on their way farther west. We learn they're only twenty years old—high school sweethearts who decided to throw caution to the wind. Miguel, the husband, has taken a job in California, so they're using their honeymoon to drive cross country, stopping in small, out-of-the-way-towns on their way to the West Coast. All through lunch, they're continually touching each other, their love sweet and uncomplicated.

After they finish eating, they quickly excuse themselves from the table. Even as they walk away, the young bride leans into her husband's embrace—they don't have a care in the world aside from their excitement at starting their new life together. A pang of jealousy stabs my heart, and I find it hard to swallow my next bite of food.

I had a high school sweetheart. A boy I once shared dreams with. Someone I was supposed to marry—until he betrayed me. As I watch them walk away, I wonder what my life would look like today if things had worked out as initially planned. Tommy and I would be married right now. I'd be living the life my parents planned for me. That thought makes me pause. Would I have ended up resenting my life because it wasn't mine, but one forced on me since childhood?

The night I found Tommy and Ashlynn, I lost two people who'd meant the world to me, but it was also the night I found myself. After returning to New York, I took Evan's advice and allowed myself to start really living my life rather than just going through the motions. I decided to do things that made me happy and stopped worrying about pleasing other people. For the first time, I was content with who I was. What I thought was the worse night of my life was the start of the journey that eventually led me to the man sitting next to me. As much as I wish we could have an uncomplicated relationship, be more like that young couple, I wouldn't change anything and risk not being with him.

Alex places his hand over mine. "How about we grab one of the boats and spend the day on the water?"

"You know how to row a boat?"

"Nope." He flashes me his sexy grin. "Do you?"

I return his smile with one of my own. "Of course I do."

"Well then, baby girl." He stands and pulls my chair out for me. "Why don't you show me your skills?"

We take our time walking through the yard of the bed and breakfast, stopping to admire the lush flower gardens before making our way to the beach. Families are set up on blankets, some under umbrellas that are shielding them from the hot sun. Children play and splash on the water's edge.

"Do you want children?" I ask.

"Someday, sure," he says. "What about you?"

"Yes, I'd love to be a mother."

He wraps his arm around my waist, and I imagine a time when we're here together playing with our children. The image fills me with warmth.

"Come on, baby girl." Alex takes my hand. "The boats are over here."

We walk over to the dock area, where an employee meets us. Alex makes the arrangements to take the boat out, and then we're led to a waiting rowboat.

Alex takes a tentative step down into the boat. He has to grab the dock when it rocks back and forth. Having done this before, I'm sure of my footing and step safely into the boat.

I go to sit in the rowing seat, but Alex scoots me out of the way.

"I've got this." He winks at me. "How hard can it be?"

I gladly move to the bench in front and kick my feet up. I can't wait to see my city boy in action. The employee unties us from the dock and gives a little push.

I bite my lip, holding in my laughter as Alex struggles to get us moving in the right direction. We end up going in circles for a few minutes until he gets a feel for the oars and the boat's movement.

"I'm impressed, Mr. Montgomery. You catch on quick."

"I'm a man of many talents," he says with a smirk. "Which way are we headed?"

I point out the direction to take. "There's a quiet cove with a sandy beach where we can relax."

Alex rows us into the shallow water of the cove. I slip off my sandals and hop out, pulling the boat onto the sand. Alex climbs out behind me, making sure the boat is far enough out of the water that it won't float away.

The beach is a small, secluded area surrounded by trees. It's a spot not many people know about, so I'm confident we're not likely to see any other people while we're here.

Alex sits on the sand, and I lay my head on his lap. The August sun shines warm, making the water look as if crystals are dancing off it. Small waves lap gently on the rocks. The sounds of birds chirping fill the air. For the longest time, we simply enjoy the sounds of nature.

"I've told my father about you," Alex says while he plays with my hair.

"Oh?" I'm surprised by his revelation.

I only know a little about his father. He doesn't talk about him much.

"He'd like to meet you." He stops moving his hand and looks down at me, a hopeful expression on his face.

"Does he know how we met?"

"Yes."

I forget for a moment that his father is in this lifestyle too, so he'll think nothing of his son meeting a girl at a BDSM club.

As if he's sensing my wayward thoughts, he adds. "Even though my father lives in Seattle, we're close. He knows the nature of how our relationship started." He pauses. "I've also told him you're more than just my submissive, that I'm in love with you."

I sit up. Alex only just told me he loves me. I'm still getting used to this new part of our relationship. But knowing he's already told his father about us makes everything feel like so much more.

"I'd love to meet him."

Alex lets go of the breath he was holding. "We'll arrange a trip to Seattle."

"I'd like that very much."

Alex reclines back on his hands, a carefree look on his face.

He tells me about his childhood. He's an only child.

"They'd just about given up on having children," he says. "And then surprise, I came along."

I like this youthful side of him.

"My mom had a free-spirit. She believed in letting children play and explore." He stares off as he speaks. "She encouraged me to pursue anything I was interested in. That's how I got involved in martial arts and became interested in Eastern philosophy," he says. "Many of those principles I carry with me today."

I can easily see that in the way he approaches life. He's disciplined, but I can see some of his mother's free spirit in him.

"Mom would have adored you," he says.

"I wish I could have met her."

We sit in silence for a while. Alex seems lost in his memories.

The sun is getting ready to set, casting vibrant colors over the horizon. I sit between his legs, my back against his chest as he wraps his arms around me. Inside, I feel warm and content. The doubts I once had about our relationship are fading with each day that passes.

"We should start heading back," Alex says as he stands and dusts the sand off his shorts. He offers me his hand, helping me up. "I don't want to get stuck on the lake in the dark."

"You aren't scared, are you? There hasn't been a monster sighting in—"

Alex scoops me up and tosses me over his shoulder. "Shall we get in the water and find out?"

I hit his back with my fists in mock protest. "Put me down." I barely manage to say between fits of laughter.

"As you command." He motions like he's going to toss me into the water before gently setting me on my feet in the boat. "You should've seen your face." He laughs. The sound is music to my ears.

I take my seat while Alex gives the boat a small push to get us back in the water. He climbs in, trying to be careful, but we rock back and forth anyway. Good thing we're in shallow water, or we'd both be soaked right now.

We arrive back at the dock just as the last of the sunlight falls below the horizon. The attendant, who's sitting on the dock, sees us approaching and jumps up. I toss him the rope, and he ties us to the dock.

The boat rocks back and forth again as Alex stands. I hold my breath hoping he doesn't end up in the lake. He climbs up onto the dock and with a proud smile, grabs my hand pulling me up next to him. "Let's find a place to eat and celebrate not capsizing."

"Good morning, beautiful," Alex says from the table, where he's sitting with a cup of coffee in his hand, his laptop open in front of him.

"You're up early." I sit up and rub the sleep from my eyes.

"I have a meeting with a client when I get back today." He sets his cup down and comes over to sit on the bed. "I was getting some last-minute details in place."

He bends over and kisses me. I wrap my arms around his neck. "I don't want you to go."

"My offer still stands." His face is devoid of all humor.

All it would take is one phone call, and I could be on a plane going back to New York with him today. He's just waiting for me to say yes, but I can't. When I accepted the scholarship, I also accepted the commitment that came with it. It's important to me that I honor my commitment. But it doesn't make saying goodbye any easier. I don't answer. I can't say the words, so I simply shake my head no.

"Come shower with me." He stands and pulls off his shirt as he walks to the bathroom.

I climb out of bed and follow him, appreciating the view of

his muscular back and the way his jeans sit low on his hips. A part of me still can't believe this man is mine. I'm still waiting for the bubble to burst and for him to disappear

Alex turns on the hot water; the steam quickly fills the small bathroom. Turning to face me, he grabs the hem of the shirt I'm wearing and pulls it over my head. His knuckles graze my nipples, causing them to harden. My body is always quick to respond to his touch.

He gets into the shower, and then I step in behind him. Once he closes the glass door, he wraps his arms around me. His mouth is on mine, his tongue seeking entrance. The kiss is different; desperate. He lifts me, and I wrap my legs around his waist. He walks us until my back is against the tiled wall. Without breaking the kiss, he slides his hard length into me. I run my hands through his wet hair and down his arms, committing his body to memory. He takes his time, not rushing his movements. He pours his love into me through the way he reverently holds me and worships my body. In turn, I give him every ounce of me, hoping he can feel how deeply I love him.

The familiar tingling of an orgasm begins to build in my belly. I tighten my legs around his waist, encouraging him to go deeper and faster. An all-consuming orgasm rips through my body, and I ride wave after wave of intense pleasure. Alex increases the intensity of his thrusts until he comes with a deep growl in his throat.

He lowers his forehead, resting it against mine. "Change your mind," he begs. "Come back home with me."

The desperation in his voice is almost my undoing. Instead, I loosen my legs from his waist. He guides me as I slide down his body until my feet touch the floor. Reaching around him, I grab the small bottle of body wash and pour some into my hands. I wash his body, gliding my hands over the taut muscles in his abdomen and his chest before moving lower. I leave no part of his body untouched.

After our shower, we dress and pack in silence. My heart is

heavy. Saying goodbye gets harder with each visit. Knowing what tonight holds is already making this goodbye prove the hardest.

The ride back to my house is tense. I bite my nails, worrying about all the possible outcomes of the conversation that'll happen later.

"Stop biting your nails."

"Sorry, Sir." I put my hands under my legs, trying to stop myself from doing it again.

"I can reschedule the meeting and stay with you," he says. "You don't have to do this alone."

Although a big part of me wants him by my side, I need to know I can do this. "Thank you," I say. "But I have to do this on my own."

We pull up to the house, and Alex shuts the car off. Neither of us moves, not wanting the weekend to end—not wanting to say goodbye.

Reluctantly, I turn to him. "If you don't go now, you're going to miss your flight."

"That wouldn't be such a horrible thing."

I lean over the center console and kiss him. "I love you." My voice cracks. Reaching into the backseat, I grab my bag and turn to get out of the car.

Alex reaches out and holds onto my arm. "Are you sure you won't change your mind?" His eyes plead with me.

"Call me when you land?" I open the door and step out.

"I will," he says, a sad smile on his face. He presses the button to restart the car.

I close the car door and step back. Watching Alex drive away, I feel small and alone. The minute his car is out of sight, the tears I've been holding back roll down my cheeks.

NATALIE

*I*nsecurity at not pleasing my parents has plagued me all my life. My earliest memories revolve around trying to be the perfect daughter. It was made worse after Evan died. I felt I owed it to my parents to always say and do the right thing—to do what they wanted—even if it meant I hid what I felt inside. It wasn't until the night I found out Tommy was cheating on me that I realized I wasn't living, I was merely existing, continually trying to please someone else.

I started fresh and created a new Natalie—the Natalie I wanted to be. A person loyal to herself. Except now that I'm back here, I've lost that person. I've fallen into bad habits. Once again, I pushed my wants and desires aside in exchange for my parents' approval. I love my parents, that won't change, but my behavior must. Today, I return to the woman I became in NYC. I just hope my parents will understand.

Wiping the tears from my face, I walk up the sidewalk and into the house. My parents are both at work, so I have the afternoon alone. I go upstairs to my room and sit on my bed. I need a plan to get my parents to agree to get to know Alex. If they do, I know they'll see what I see.

I grab my phone and call Lana. She'll know what to do.

"Hello?" Lana answers.

"Hey, girlie," I say. "Thanks for telling Alex about my party."

"Phew," she laughs. "When I didn't hear from you, I figured you were mad at me."

"I could never be mad at you."

"How did your parents take him being there?" she asks.

"Not well. Mom freaked out when she saw him." I sigh. "They were furious when I left with him for the weekend. I haven't seen them since. That's why I'm calling. I need your help."

"Anything," she says. "You name it."

We spend the next half hour making a plan for how to approach my parents. The goal is to focus on the positives. To show them that Alex is a wonderful, caring man. He's a hard-worker and successful. He might live in a big city, but where a person lives doesn't have any bearing on their character. That thought is ridiculous. What matters is how he treats me and how we feel about each other. I want them to see that Alex makes me happy.

"Thanks, Lan," I say. "I knew you'd be able to help."

"Call me later and let me know how it goes, ok?"

"I will. Love ya."

After I unpack, I decide to make good use of my time and cook dinner. "Maybe that'll ease things up later," I say to no one as I walk back downstairs.

Once in the kitchen, I take my phone out, press the icon for the music app, and turn the volume up. Singing along to my favorite songs, I look through the kitchen for dinner ingredients. I decide on steak, fresh potatoes, and a salad from the garden.

I have many fond memories of gardening with my mother every summer. She made sure we had fresh vegetables for dinner every night. In the early fall, we'd help her harvest what we hadn't used and preserve it, ensuring we had homegrown food all winter long.

I missed having a garden in NYC. Lana and I didn't have any

outdoor space. We managed to grow a few herbs in the kitchen window and frequented the small markets for fresh food, but it wasn't quite the same.

The afternoon has gone by quickly; it's almost time for my parents to get home. I fire up the grill and start cooking. Sitting in one of our old lawn chairs, I practice what I'll say to them. The conversation plays over and over in my head. I try to imagine the many ways it might go and prepare answers to what I think they'll ask. I have to convince them to accept we're a couple.

The food is nearly done when I hear my parents' car pull into the driveway. I walk over to the back door and listen for them to come in. When they finally reach the kitchen, I open the door and peek my head in. "Dinner'll be ready in a few minutes."

There's no response. As soon as the food is done, I put it on a tray and carry it into the house. The salad I'd left on the counter is now on the table. My father sits in his usual chair, a muscle twitching in his clenched jaw. Mom sits to his right, her mouth drawn in a tight line, her eyes narrowed. The tension in the room is thick and heavy.

My hands shake as I set the food down and take my seat. I thought I was ready for this, but suddenly I'm not feeling quite as confident.

Dad quietly makes his plate and starts eating, while Mom glares at me.

"Hope you guys like it." I try my best to sound cheerful, hoping it'll break the suffocating tension in the room.

"Do you know how you've caused people to talk this week-end?" Mom asks, disapproval dripping from every word.

I sit up straighter and pull my shoulders back, steeling myself for the conversation. "Surely I'm not the first unmarried girl who's spent a weekend with her boyfriend?"

"You're ruining your reputation in this town. You're ruining *our* reputation." She folds her hands in front of her. "And you're going to ruin your chances with Thomas. Then where will you be? Who will you marry?"

I laugh out loud. Both my parents stop and look at me.

"Ruin my chances with Tommy? Mom, do you hear your-self?" I pause, taking a calming breath. Once I regain my compo-sure, I continue. "I've tried to tell you I'm not interested in Tommy, but you won't listen to me. You aren't hearing me."

"What can you possibly say to make this okay?" Mom asks.

I look back and forth between them. This is the moment I've practiced all day. They both look back at me, disapproval evident in their eyes. My instincts try to force me to back down and cave to their demands. Why was I so stubborn when Alex asked to stay? I wish he were here now. But no, this is something I have to do for myself. I can do this.

It's now or never. I take a deep breath and plunge in. "I've been seeing Alex since I came home from school." I pause, searching their faces for a reaction.

They remain stoic.

"The trips I took. The one's I said I was meeting Lana and the one for the conference for work. I lied. I took those trips to see Alex."

Their faces are now red with anger, and their stares pierce through me.

"He's a good man. He's a hard worker, and he treats me very well. He makes me happy." I'm hoping my words soften their hearts. "I plan to continue seeing him. I love him."

"That's enough." My father slams his hands on the table, startling me. "You're not to see that man again."

"What? You can't be serious!" I raise my voice.

"Natalie." Mom's tone is patronizing. "I understand you think you love him, but he isn't right for you. Once you are away from him, you'll see that too."

It feels like I've been punched in the stomach. I struggle to take my next breath. Is this how Michael felt when he told them he loved Evan? The flicker of hope I had inside, the one that believed they would see how happy he makes me and that I'm in love with him, maybe even give me their blessing, has extinguished. I'm left sitting in the dark, scrambling for options with parents who are being completely unreasonable.

"So that's it? The conversation's over?"

"We're done talking," my father says. "Whatever you think you had with him is over." He picks up his fork and resumes eating as if nothing happened.

They expect me to do as I'm told, no questions, no arguments —it's what I was raised to do; it's what I've always done. But I can't do that anymore. I refuse to do that anymore. This is about my future—my happiness. I know they think they're doing what's best for me and trying to save me from heartache, but they can't keep dictating my life. I don't want the same things they want for me. I have my own plans. I don't know why they refuse to support me. Cheer me on. Pick me up if I fall. Celebrate with me if I succeed. Somehow I have to make them see reason.

"Mom, Dad," I say. "I love you both very much. You've always been there for me. You've guided me, taught me, and raised me well. We've been through a lot, especially losing Evan." I pause, giving them a moment to take in what I've said. "I thought being the perfect daughter would make you smile again, but it hasn't," I say. "I've learned that I'm not responsible for your happiness, but I am responsible for mine. Alex may not be your choice for me, but I'm in love with him. That doesn't mean I don't respect you or your input. I do." I pause to swallow the lump in my throat. "It also means I have to ask that you both respect my choices, even if you disagree with them. I'm asking that you give Alex a chance, get to know him. He's wonderful—"

"That's enough," Dad says in a loud, stern voice. "This is my home. As long as you live under my roof, you will obey my rules."

I can't believe this is happening. My parents have shut down the conversation. They refuse to give at all. The next thing I say takes even me by surprise.

"I think it's best for all of us if I leave." It's a move I've been planning to make, but I didn't envision it would happen like this.

My father nods his head in agreement, ending the conversation.

No one speaks through the rest of dinner. The sound of my parents' forks and knives clinking off their plates fills the room. How can they carry on as if nothing happened? Is this my punishment for not obeying? I lose my family? My appetite is gone—nausea bubbles in my stomach. Instead of eating, I just push the food around on my plate.

After he finishes eating, my father walks into the living room and sits on the couch to read the evening newspaper. Mom goes to the kitchen to clean-up. I decide to follow Mom, hoping that if it's just her and me, alone, we can talk. Maybe come to a better resolution.

"Mom."

"No, Natalie. The conversation is over," she says and turns her back on me.

It's like I'm reliving the night Evan left home, except this time, it's me that's going. I have to hold onto the counter so I don't fall to my knees. I don't want to lose my family, but I refuse to give up Alex. It shouldn't have to be a choice. Why can't I have both?

I put my dishes in the sink and quietly make my way through the living room. Dad doesn't even look up from the paper. One by one, I walk up the steps, noticing every creak and crack. I pause when I reach the top and look downstairs. My parents continue to go about their nightly routine as though nothing's happened. I shake my head sadly and go to my room to look for an apartment.

I grab my laptop and sit on my bed to start the search, but like every other time I've looked, there isn't anything available in Northmeadow. I check the listings for a house on the lake, but with Labor Day being in two weeks, everything is booked solid.

I don't know where to look next, so I call Alex. His plane

should've landed by now, but my call goes straight to voicemail. I leave a message asking him to call me as soon as he can.

My next call is to Lana.

She answers on the first ring. "How did it go?"

"Awful," I say, barely keeping my composure. "Said as long as I live in their house, I have to follow their rules. They forbid me to see Alex."

"You've got to be kidding," she says. "I'm sorry, Natalie, but they're being awful."

"Trust me, I know," I say. "I want to move out, but there are no apartments. I even checked the lake for a short-term rental, but there's nothing. I don't know what to do."

"Let me think," she says. "What about a hotel?"

"I didn't even think about that."

I do a quick search for a hotel that is in close proximity. Rhonda is old and not in good condition. She's not going to make a long commute every day.

"I found something," I say excitedly. "Lakeview Motel. They have cheap rooms, and they rent by the week."

"That sounds perfect."

"It does," I say. "Thanks, Lana."

"Anytime."

We hang up, and I make an online reservation. My savings is enough to cover the rent until school starts.

My phone ringing wakes me up. I rub my eyes; the clock reads 3 a.m..

"Hello?" I answer, my voice groggy.

"I'm sorry to wake you, baby girl."

"I'm glad you did." I sit up and stretch. "You didn't just get home, did you?"

"My flight was rerouted because of a storm." He yawns.

"Oh no, you missed your meeting?"

"I ended up having it online in a quiet corner of the airport café."

"I'm sure that wasn't ideal." A yawn interrupts my talking. "I'm glad you're home safe."

"I got your message," he says. "How did things go with your parents?"

"Not well." The hurt is still raw and rushes to the surface. "I told them everything. I asked them to give you a chance, but they refused. They forbid me from seeing you as long as I live in their house. So, I told them I'm moving out."

"I'm so sorry, Nat." He pauses before hesitantly asking. "Do you need money?"

"Thank you, but I already found a place. The rent is cheap, and they don't require a security deposit." No need to tell him it's a motel room.

"That's one positive about not living in New York, I guess." He laughs softly. "It's late. Go back to sleep. I'll call you tomorrow."

"Yes, Sir." The words fall easily from my lips. "Alex?"

"Yes?"

Silence hangs between us as I war with myself. Should I ask him to rescue me? To buy out my contract and bring me back to New York? The words dance on the tip of my tongue, but they won't come out. Instead, I simply say, "Thank you for coming this weekend. I love you."

"I love you too, baby girl. Sleep well."

NATALIE

Sleep evaded me last night. Every time I closed my eyes, the scene at the dinner table replayed like a movie on repeat. My alarm didn't have the chance to wake me since I was already out of bed, finishing packing.

Today is the day I move out. None of this is happening the way I'd imagined, but it's happening anyway.

I close my suitcase and zip it up before moving it to the floor. Then I pull the sheets and blankets up, leaving my bed neatly made. Some habits are hard to break. Most of my things will have to stay here until I find an actual apartment. Although this option isn't ideal, it allows me to move out right away. I'm hoping this space is what my parents and I need to save our relationship.

I grab my suitcase and walk down the steps, setting it by the front door. Dad's already left for work. Mom's in the kitchen, going through her weekly cleaning routine. I have to try one more time.

"Mom."

She turns around, her reply curt. "Yes?"

"I found a place to stay. I'm taking some clothes with me

today." My voice cracks when I speak. "I'm going to leave most of my stuff here for now. I hope that's okay."

For a brief moment, Mom drops her mask, and I see the sadness in her eyes, but just as quickly, she replaces it. "That'll be fine."

She doesn't ask where I'm moving, nothing.

"Thanks." I step closer, hoping to at least hug her goodbye, but she turns her back on me. "Mom, please," I beg. I don't want to leave things this way.

"I think it's best if you go now."

"Yes, ma'am," I say.

Walking away, I look around the house; a lifetime of memories washes over me. My first day of school, Mom braiding my hair, and Dad tying my saddle shoes. Christmas mornings when Evan and I would sneak down the steps quietly to peek at our presents. Although tears fill my eyes, I don't let them fall. This may not be how I planned to move out, but everything happens for a reason. I grab my suitcase and purse, and with my head held high, walk out the front door.

The mid-morning sun shines brightly as I drive the half-hour to the Lakeview Motel. My commute to work just got longer. Hopefully Rhonda makes it without any issues.

I pull into a guest parking spot and turn off the car. There are only two other vehicles in the lot; that doesn't surprise me, as the place isn't exactly a five-star establishment. The planters contain the dead remains of the summer's flowers, and cigarette butts litter the walkways. The outside looks rundown, but it's all I can afford. "It's only for a few weeks." I remind myself as I get out of the car and make my way to the main office to get my key.

When I open the glass door, I find myself standing in a dingy, smoke-filled room. Off to my right are two wooden chairs with torn vinyl seats and a small table that's littered with magazines.

In front of me, there's a tall counter with dark brown paneling. I walk up and peer over it. A man sits, his back to me, a cigarette in his hand. He's watching a Cardinals game on a flat-screen TV that hangs on the wall, the volume so loud he hasn't heard me come in.

"Excuse me," I shout to be heard over the television.

He spins around on his chair. His eyes open wide when he sees me.

"Hello, little lady. How can I help you?" He stands and takes a puff on his cigarette. The smoke blows in my direction, and I cough.

Do I want to stay here, or will I be safer sleeping in my car?

"Hi," I say, trying to sound confident. "I booked a room online last night."

He nods and starts typing on an old desktop computer that sits on a desk behind the counter.

"Natalie Clarke?"

"Yes."

"I put you in room 7," he says. "You're staying for one week?"

"Your webpage said the rooms could be rented weekly?" I struggle to find my voice.

"That's correct." He takes a final puff on his cigarette before snuffing it out in the ashtray on the counter.

"Do I pay online for additional weeks?"

"No need," he says. "Stop in here, and we can process the payment."

Keys hang on a pegboard next to his computer. I guess this place doesn't do key cards. He grabs the key that hangs under the number 7 and walks around the counter, dangling it in the air.

"Can I show you to your room?"

"I think I can find it on my own." This guy's creeping me out a bit.

"Suit yourself." He shakes his head. "If you need anything,

there's a phone in your room. My name's Marshall, press #11 to call me."

"Thanks." I take the key and walk out of the office. That was awkward.

I stop by my car, grab my suitcase, and then make my way to the red metal door with a number 7 on it. The key takes a little jiggling to get it to turn, but finally, it clicks and unlocks. I turn the handle and push the door open before taking my first steps into my new home.

As soon as I enter the room, I gag a little from the overwhelming musty smell. The heavy drapes are closed, keeping the room dark. A shiny gold floor lamp, typical cheap motel style, stands in the corner. I switch the light on and then turn to lock the door behind me. This'll stay locked at all times. When I go to lock the security chain, I notice it's missing a screw. I'll have to ask Marshall to get it fixed. In the meantime, I grab one of the chairs and wedge it under the doorknob—a little extra security.

Hesitantly, I walk farther into the room. The carpet is worn and stained, probably where most of the smell is coming from. I don't want to know what's stained it.

There's a double bed on the wall to my right. As I walk by, I run my hand over the ugly floral bedspread. On the wall over the bed hangs two pictures, each in a cheap plastic gold frame. The photos must be from the 1980s with their bright colors and geometric patterns. The amount of dust on them must be from the '80s as well. Across from the bed sits a wooden dresser holding an old tv. At the far end of the room is the bathroom. I'm almost afraid to look, but curiosity gets the better of me.

Pushing open the squeaky door, I walk into the small bathroom. The first thing I notice is there's no window, only an overhead light with one light bulb burned out. I have to close the door to get to the white pedestal sink. On the wall above it hangs a cracked mirror held together by a strip of tape. Opposite the sink is a toilet, and on the back wall a walk-in shower, no tub.

"That's okay. I can live with only having a shower," I say aloud.

Closing the door to the bathroom, I walk back into the main room and sit down on the bed. It takes a few minutes for me to get my thoughts together and come up with a plan. I decide to buy some cleaning products to make sure the room is clean, and I can buy my own set of sheets. It'll help the space feel more like home.

Standing up, I walk across the room and pull open the drapes. Dust flies everywhere, and I sneeze, but now the bright midday sun is shining in the room. It makes the place feel better already. The hand crank on the window is stuck. I struggle with it for a few minutes before it finally gives way, allowing the window to open and fresh air to flow into the room. I make a mental note to buy an air freshener. It's not my apartment in the city, but it's not that bad. I can make it work until I find a real apartment.

I pull up Alex's contact in my phone. He's not going to like this, but I know he'll at least try to respect my decision. I tap the video call button and wait for Alex to answer.

"Hello." Alex smiles. "I didn't expect you to call so soon."

"I told you I'd call when I was settled."

Alex gives me a quizzical look. "It's barely been two hours. You're all moved in already?"

"Well…" I hesitate. "I didn't find an apartment, exactly."

"Natalie, turn the camera around." His voice grows stern. "I want to see where you are."

"Yes, Sir." I take a deep breath and tap the icon to reverse the camera and pan around the room.

"Where the hell are you?" Alex yells.

His tone catches me off guard. He's never yelled at me before.

"It's a little motel right outside Northmeadow." I flip the camera back to me.

"A motel? It looks like a dump," he says. "Is it even safe?"

"Safe enough." I shrug my shoulders.

"Safe enough?" He lets out an audible sigh. "Let me get you a room somewhere better."

"Alex." I search for the right words to defuse the situation. "It's only for a few weeks. I'll be okay, I promise."

The heated discussion continues with a lot of back and forth. I know Alex has the means to get me something better, and although he begs me to see reason, he doesn't force his will on me. That's one of the things I love about him. He never uses his authority to take away my voice. He's always reasonable and fair. He understands the importance of allowing me to make this choice. He doesn't like it, but he respects it—respects me.

"It's only for a few weeks. A month tops," I say. "I'll keep looking for an apartment. I promise."

"Okay," he agrees. "Promise me you'll keep the door locked and chained."

"I will."

Neither of us wants to say goodbye, but he has to get back to work, and I have to run into the office for a few hours to do some last-minute prep before school starts.

"I have meetings the rest of the afternoon. I'm expecting them to run long," he says. "If I'm going to be late, I'll text you."

I can see the stress on his face. This new client account is taking up a lot of his time.

"It's okay." I smile, hoping to ease some of his worries. "I'll be here when you get home." I reluctantly tap the screen, making Alex's image disappear.

So much has changed over the past few days. Alex showing up at my party was the best thing that could've happened to me; to us. I don't know how I would've found the courage to tell my parents everything without it. Keeping him a secret was hard on our relationship. Looking back, I see how I was unfair to him. It makes me even more thankful that he stuck around and gave me a chance. When I left New York, I was uncertain if Alex and I could have a future together; now I can't imagine a future without him.

ALEX

J was able to keep my composure, mostly, until I hung up the phone. Now, I'm pacing around my office talking to myself like a man gone mad. A motel? There's tons of work begging for my attention, but I can't focus on any of it. My mind is in Northmeadow with a certain young lady.

I need to talk to Brandon. He'll know what I should do.

"Hello?" Brandon answers.

"What the hell is she thinking?" I yell.

"Slow down, Alex."

I sit down, my body tense.

"Natalie," I say and let out a deep breath. "She had a fight with her parents."

"Lana told me about it," he says.

"She can't find an apartment, so she's staying at some cheap motel." I rub the back of my neck.

Brandon's like a brother to me and always manages to talk me off the cliff. Right now, I need his advice because I'm teetering on the edge.

"Let me get this straight," Brandon says. "The town she lives in is so small there are no apartments for rent?"

"It's hard to imagine," I say. "I checked for myself while we were talking. There isn't anything."

"Shit. That *is* a small town."

"What do I do?" I ask. Because right now, I'm fighting my instincts to get on a plane and bring her back.

"You need to give her some space."

"Space?" I ask, raising my voice. "How do I take care of her by giving her space?"

"Relax," Brandon says calmly. "You told me her parents were smothering her, trying to dictate her life?"

"Yes." I tap my fingers on my desk.

"Now you want to go there and bulldoze her with your agenda. That makes you no different than anyone else in her life," he says. "As her Dominant, that isn't your role. I promise it'll just backfire on you."

I think about his words for a minute before answering him. As much as I hate to admit it, he's right.

"I don't know what to do then." I lower my head into my hands.

"Are you in love with her?"

Brandon knows my history. He knows I didn't want to get involved with a sub, let alone fall in love with someone. When I took Natalie as a sub, he was happy for me. I haven't told him I developed feelings for her. Do I tell him? I think about how I want to answer and decide to just go for it.

"Yes." A single word.

"I'm happy for you, brother."

"Thanks," I answer. "But what do I do? How do I fix this for her?"

I'm out of my league. I know how to be a Dominant, how to make a submissive bend to my will—and enjoy it. What I don't know is how to be a Dominant and a boyfriend at the same time. The rules are different now, and I'm struggling to keep up.

"Right now, the best thing you can do is be there for her. Listen when she needs someone to talk to," he advises. "Support her, but unless it's something you've already agreed on, you can't control her decisions."

We talk until my secretary buzzes that my next client is on the line, ready for our conference call.

"I have a meeting I need to be in." I pause. "Thanks, Brand. I appreciate your help."

NATALIE

I can't believe Labor Day weekend has come and gone, and I spent it holed up in my room. The hot, humid summer air is already changing, ushering in the crispness of autumn, which is spectacular in Northmeadow. The leaves on the trees color the mountains in shades of red, yellow, and orange. Being gone for so long, I forgot how beautiful it is.

Living at the motel isn't all that bad, either. Now that I have everything clean and smelling fresh, it feels like a home. Marshall even let me put in a small fridge and a microwave. I can't make any gourmet meals, but it beats eating out every night.

With the change of seasons also comes the start of school. My alarm goes off early, as planned, giving me enough time to shower before having to leave for work. As usual, the water is lukewarm, but I've gotten used to it and now take a very efficient shower. After I wrap myself in a towel, I grab my phone and read the messages from my friends back in the city wishing me good luck. I love that they haven't forgotten about me.

With my phone in hand, I walk over to the full-length mirror I purchased. The bathroom's cracked mirror is useless. It's the one thing Marshall hasn't fixed yet. Grabbing my comb, I run it through my hair before applying some product. I take my time applying make-up while texting Lana in between.

Dropping my towel to the floor, I slip into a lacy bra and panty set. I snap a picture and text it to Alex. He loves when I send sexy pictures of myself. I've put on the outfit that I've had picked out for weeks—a black pencil skirt and a soft blue blouse. I turn to face the mirror; the image reflecting at me is that of a professional woman—put together and confident. Now, if only my hands will stop shaking.

The time on my phone reads 7:30 a.m.. If I don't get on the road, I'm not going to make it on time. I grab my bag, slip into my black heels, and walk out the door.

The holiday weekend has brought a lot of people to the motel, although I'm not sure why. When I got home yesterday, the lot was full, and I had to park at the far end.

I begin to make my way across the parking lot when I spot Marshall leaning up against the brick wall outside his office, a cigarette in his hand.

I laugh when I think back to the day I first met him. Over the course of the past few weeks, I've gotten to know him. We've shared lunches a few times at the picnic table in the grassy area outside his office. He's in his mid-thirties and has never been married. He bought this place a few years ago, hoping to make it a place tourists want to stay in, rather than a place they settle on when everything else is booked. He wants to fix it up, but it's costing more money than he anticipated. I've offered to talk to Alex for him, see if there's anything he can do to help marketing-wise, but Marshall refuses to accept a handout. At first, he creeped me out, but I've learned he's a pretty friendly guy.

"You're all dressed up today," Marshall calls across the parking lot.

"First day of work," I say.

"Knock 'em dead, kid."

"Thank you." I smile and get into my car.

The drive into Northmeadow feels like it takes forever. I'm not used to having a long commute anywhere. I miss the convenience of hopping on a subway or being able to walk wherever I need to go. Despite continually checking the listings for an apartment in town, there's still nothing available. I've even looked into a lake house, but most of the owners are closing them up. I'm already dreading this drive when winter comes.

My phone rings just as I pull into the busy school parking lot. I smile when I see who it is.

"Alex. I didn't think I'd hear from you until tonight."

"Did you think I'd let you start a new job without wishing you good luck?" Although I can't see him, from the tone of his voice, I know he's smiling.

I let my head fall back on the headrest and close my eyes. "I'm so nervous. I hope I can do this."

For the past six years, I've studied and trained for this job. I know I have the right skills, but self-doubt has crept in once again.

"Take a deep breath and relax." His voice is deep and sexy, causing my thoughts to drift elsewhere, giving me a momentary reprieve from my nerves. "I know you, and how invested you are in this. You're going to do terrific. They're lucky to have you."

"Thank you." I look at the time. "I have to get inside before I'm late. Love you, talk to you later."

We hang up, and with one final breath, I step out of my car and walk inside my old high school, not as a student now but as a faculty member. The parking lot is buzzing with activity. Students are milling about greeting each other before filing into the side entrances of the building.

No one seems to pay me any attention as I walk past them on my way to the teacher's entrance. I climb the main steps and pause for a second before opening the heavy wooden door and trip over the threshold, falling straight into Mr. Meadows. "Oh my gosh, I'm so sorry."

"Good morning, Ms. Clarke." Mr. Meadows frowns as he gives my appearance a once over. "I guess you didn't take my advice on your style of dress. In the future, remember this is a small farm town, not the fancy city."

A few students walking by snicker, and my cheeks heat with embarrassment at his public reprimand. "Yes, sir. I'll try to keep that in mind."

I didn't think my outfit was too fancy, but as I quickly glance at what the other teachers are wearing, I realize I don't fit in at all. The male teachers, including Mr. Meadows, are wearing khaki pants or jeans with a polo type shirt. Some female teachers are wearing pants, the polyester variety, with a blouse buttoned up high. Two female teachers are wearing skirts that go to their ankles. My clothes aren't revealing by any standard but compared to my colleagues' overly conservative outfits, I certainly stand out. When I was a student, I guess I never paid attention to what my teachers were wearing. When I interned in the city, my current outfit was standard. I'll have to stop by my parents' house after work and grab some of my old clothes.

I mumble an awkward good morning to the faculty members standing nearby, watching the encounter before lowering my eyes and walking away. I hear my name whispered, but I refuse to turn around. The last thing I need is for them to think they've got to me.

Ms. Campbell tried to warn me. She suspected I might not be receiving a warm welcome. She'd heard whispers that my support of Michael and Evan wasn't forgiven or forgotten. I listened to what she said but had convinced myself that enough years had passed, and they couldn't possibly still hold that against me. Guess I was wrong. Many thoughts race through my head as I walk the long hallway, weaving my way between students. I remind myself that none of that matters. It doesn't change my reason for being here. I'm here for one reason—to help the kids who feel they don't have a voice.

When I get to my office door, I reach into my pocket and grab my key, then place it in the lock. But when I turn the key, I realize the door is already unlocked. That's odd. I'm sure I locked it when I left yesterday.

Pushing the door open, I'm met with the sweet fragrance of flowers. On my desk sits a beautiful bouquet of red roses. I reach into my bag and grab my phone before tossing it onto my chair. Snapping a picture, I send a text to Alex.

(Me) Thank you for the flowers. They're beautiful.
(Alex) They are beautiful, but they aren't from me.

If they aren't from him, then who are they from? I search the bouquet for the card.

Natalie,

Roses are beautiful, but they're nothing compared to you. Good luck on your first day. I'll see you tonight.

Love Tommy.

Furious, I rip up the card and dump the flowers into a trashcan out in the hallway.

(Alex) Was there a card?
(Me) Yes.
(Alex) And? Who are they from?
(Me) Tommy. They're in the trash. I'll call you later.

After recovering from the shock of the flowers, it's time to put my game face on and get to work. Today, and every day this week, I'll stop in several classrooms to introduce myself to the students and tell them about the new counseling programs available.

After each classroom visit, I leave pamphlets the students can take and read on their own time. It's important they know I'm here for them no matter what they want to talk about.

When I get back to my office, I leave the door open and sit at my desk. I'm very proud of how the room turned out. I still have the chair with a worn-out cushion, but now it has a brightly colored rainbow shaped pillow on it. The other side of the room is much less formal.

The old floor now has a circular rug with the yin/yang symbol on it. Placed around the rug are a few tie-dyed bean bag chairs. Against the far wall, under the windows, is a small bookshelf. My psychology-themed books are on the top two shelves. The bottom shelf has various fidgets, including Rubik's cubes, stress balls, adult coloring books, gel pens, putty, and several other sensory things. On the floor in the corner is a white noise box that plays the sound of ocean waves quietly in the background. I think I've created a relaxed and welcoming environment. I only hope my future clients feel the same way.

I have a few files for students considered to be high-risk that I'm reading over when there's a knock on my door. Looking up, I see a female student standing in the doorway. I close the file I'm reading, setting it aside, before speaking.

"Hi." I smile. "Come on in. Grab a seat wherever you're comfortable."

She closes the door behind her before taking a few tentative steps into my office. Her eyes open wide when she notices the bean bag chairs. "May I?"

"Absolutely," I answer. "I'm Natalie."

"My name's Mary," she says quietly.

Mary. She looks very familiar to me. "It's nice to meet you."

"Thanks," Mary says. "My brother said you'd be nice and that you're safe to talk to."

"Your brother? Can I ask his name?"

"Billy Simmons. He was two years behind you in high school."

Oh my goodness, this is little Mary Simmons, although she's not little anymore.

"I remember your brother," I say and smile. "How is he?"

"He's doing good, now."

"Please tell him I said hi," I say. "And thank him for the good reference." I smile and laugh a little.

"When I get to talk to him again, I will." Mary looks down at her lap and fidgets with her fingers.

It's clear she's nervous, so I get up from behind my desk and walk over to a bean bag chair. "Mind if I sit?"

She shakes her head no.

I sit easily even though I'm wearing a skirt. It's a skill I perfected while I worked at an after-school program in the city. I reach over onto the shelf and grab two plastic containers with putty in them. "Want one?"

"Sure," she says with a smile.

I toss one across the rug, and she catches it easily. We both open them and work the putty through our fingers while chatting about what grade she's in, her favorite subject—the easy stuff.

After we've gotten a little more comfortable with each other, I ask, "What's brought you in today?"

She stops playing with her putty momentarily and looks up at me. "Do you know about my brother and everything that happened with him?"

"No," I answer. "Are you comfortable telling me?"

Mary tells me that when Billy was sixteen, the year after I graduated high school, he told their parents he was gay.

"They freaked out." She stands up and begins pacing the room. "They told him he needed to be cured of his evil ways, so they sent him away to get conversion therapy."

Flashbacks of the night Evan and Michael came out play in my head. I stand up from my bean back and walk over to my desk, leaning against the edge. Mary's still pacing, her face red with anger, and she has a death grip on the putty.

"Two years," she says louder. "Billy was there for two years while they did unspeakable things to him. As soon as he turned eighteen, he signed himself out." She pauses and quickly wipes her eyes. "He wasn't the same for a long time after that."

"I'm very sorry that happened to him," I say softly.

Mary stops in front of me, pushes her shoulders back, and looks me straight in the eyes. "I was born female, but I identify as male. I have a girlfriend I'm in love with. Eventually, I want to have gender reassignment surgery. Other than Billy and my girl-friend, you're the only one who knows," she says it all without taking a breath.

"Thank you for trusting me with your story," I say and smile. "I'm happy for you, and I'm glad to hear you're ready to tell your parents. I'd like to try talking it out some before you rush into that. Would that be okay?"

She grabs the rainbow pillow from the chair before sitting down. "I guess so."

"Good." I smile and take a seat behind my desk. "Before we get too far ahead of ourselves, there's some paperwork we have to do. We have about ten minutes before lunch is over," I say. "We can start it now if you want. Then we can set up a regular time to meet. I'll let your teacher know and have you excused from class."

Mary agrees, and we start the intake paperwork. We get about halfway through it before the bell rings. We agree on a day and time to meet. "I'll get the info to your teacher, and just so you know, everything we talk about in here is confidential. The same goes for your teacher knowing about your sessions, she can't tell anyone, and your parents will not be told unless you tell them."

"Good," Mary says. "I don't want them to know I'm talking to you."

We say our goodbyes, and Mary heads back out into the hall.

I watch as she easily blends back into the matriculation students. No one seems to notice or care that she's just left my office.

My first day is busier than I ever imagined it would be. Besides Mary, three more students stopped in and signed up for counseling appointments. A few others came in and asked for more information on what services are available.

After the final bell, I pack up my stuff and make sure to lock the door.

Before I go back to the motel, I need to swing by my parents' house. Hopefully, they aren't home.

When I get to the house, I use my key and let myself in. I grab some clothes and throw them into a small suitcase before I quickly leave the house. I hate putting these back on, it feels like another step backward, but I have to choose my battles.

On the way back to the motel, I stop at a grocery store to grab a few microwave meals and some sodas. They don't make the best dinners, but it's much cheaper than eating out every night. I'm trying to save every penny I can to put toward an apartment when one opens up.

When I get back to my temporary home, I put away my groceries, and even though it's early, I'm exhausted. I change into comfy pj's before I microwave myself some dinner.

For the rest of the evening, I work on the intake paperwork for my newest clients. The district has finally gone digital, which means I can access the kids' files from home instead of having to stay late at school. Good thing I have a mobile hotspot on my phone because the motel doesn't have Wi-Fi.

I'm startled when my phone rings. I didn't realize it was already 9 p.m.. I tap accept for the video call request, a pattern that's become familiar these past few months.

"Hey, baby girl," Alex says.

"Hi, handsome," I reply and blow him a kiss.

"How was your first official day?"

"Great. I had a total of four students sign-up for counseling. Can you believe it?"

"Of course, I believe it. I told you you'd make a positive difference there." His eyes fill with pride as he speaks.

"I know, but I wasn't sure." I lean back on my pillows. "The adults in this town are so close-minded. I wasn't sure how much of that had been passed down to the kids, but I think I have an opportunity to help them."

"I'm very proud of you."

"Thank you, Sir." Knowing I've pleased him fills me with pride. "How was your day?"

"Busy." Alex takes a deep breath and rakes his hand through his hair. His face is etched with concern.

"What's wrong?" I ask, suddenly filled with worry.

"It's the new account I've been working on."

"Did something happen?" I sit up, alarmed. I know this account means a lot to him.

"No, it's all good." He pauses. "It's just that this new account comes with some travel obligations."

It isn't unusual for Alex to travel, especially for his important client accounts.

"I'm assuming a trip to Russia is in your future?"

Turmoil swirls in his brown eyes. "Yes."

"When do you leave?"

"In two days."

"How long will you be gone?" I ask quietly, afraid of his answer.

He hesitates before he says, "I'll be there until mid-December."

It feels like I've been punched in the stomach, and I can't take my next breath. *Until December? That's nearly three months.* He's never had to travel for that long.

Alex is quiet, watching and waiting for my response. I see

how much he's struggling with this, so I try to put on a brave face.

"I'm sad that you'll be gone for so long, but I know this is a huge opportunity for you." I try to find a positive in this situation. "You'll be home before Christmas."

Over the next two hours, I ask him all about his upcoming trip. He appears to relax some as he tells me more about it.

On Maxim's insistence, he'll be staying with the Soloniks. I stayed there when I visited with Lana. Their home is as grand as a hotel. The trip will be long, but this account is huge for him. It'll be the second-largest account his firm holds, Maxim's being the largest.

The more we talk, the more excitement Alex shows as he explains the company's new energy-efficient technology. I don't understand what it all means or why a Russian company wants to advertise in the U.S.. When I ask, Alex tells me there are confidential parts of the business. Proprietary stuff, I guess. No matter; listening to him talk, I can't help but share in his excitement.

"It's going to mean a lot more travel," he says. "I'm hoping you'll accompany me on some of the trips."

His eyes hold so much hope as he waits for my answer. I want to tell him yes, that I'd follow him anywhere, but my schedule isn't as fluid as his.

"As long as I can get the time off, I'd love to travel with you."

The smile he gives me melts my heart.

The hour has gotten late. This is the part I hate the most, when we have to say goodbye. Each time it gets more and more difficult. After we hang up, my brave façade falls away. Being a few states away from each other is hard enough, but at least we see each other every few weeks. Now he's going to be halfway around the world, and I won't see him for three months.

I grab Alex's T-shirt, the one I kept from our last weekend together, and hold it close to me as I fall asleep.

ALEX

*A*lthough it kills me to put more physical distance between us, I left for Russia two weeks ago. There's an eight-hour time difference, which makes keeping in touch a challenge. We have our video calls when Natalie gets home from work, about midnight my time. Every afternoon I text her a sexy challenge for our calls. It's not the same as being together in person, but we're doing our best to make it work.

"Hey, baby girl," I say when the video comes to life.

"Hello, Sir," she says.

I see she's obeyed me and is kneeling next to her bed in only panties.

"You look gorgeous."

"Thank you, Sir."

"You may get up and sit on the bed," I say. "I want to talk about some Dom/sub things tonight."

Natalie stands and readjusts her laptop before crawling across the bed. I'm treated to a fantastic view of her breasts through the camera lens. I groan, wishing I was there. Natalie giggles before she sits and gets comfortable.

"With me being in Russia, it throws a wrench into things," I say. "I'd like to add some daily tasks to keep us connected."

"I like the sound of that," Natalie replies.

"I've come up with a few tasks we can both do on our own time and then come together and talk about." I pause. "I'd also like to hear if you have anything you'd like to add."

"This is a great idea, Sir."

We spend some time sharing our ideas on things we can do. Natalie asks to add daily exercise to our tasks. It was never a rule, just something she and I used to do together. Natalie's gotten away from that since she's been home, and I'll admit, I've been lax with exercise since being over here.

Natalie's struggling emotionally and needs my support. But with our time zones being another barrier, I'm not able to be there as much as I would like to. I found a journal program online and am requiring Natalie to write an entry daily. I can access the journal from here and will write back to her.

"I'm hoping this will become an important tool in keeping us connected," I tell her.

"Alex, Sir..." she says. "I don't know how you came up with this idea, but it's perfect."

"You know what else is perfect?"

"What, Sir?" She bites her lip.

"You," I say. "Now, take off your panties and let me see you."

NATALIE

I open the journal app on my laptop and write a note to
Alex.

*I'm missing you today. Work is going pretty well. I'm not making any
friends with the staff, but that's okay. Who am I kidding? I'd like to
have just one person here to talk to, to maybe eat lunch with. I've taken
to staying in my office and eating at my desk instead. I have to keep
reminding myself that I'm here for the kids, not the staff. I think I'm
making a difference with them, especially with M. She's strong and
brave. She knows what she wants, and she's not afraid to go after it. I'm
finally getting through to her that she needs to slow down and think
things through instead of jumping without thinking.*

*You asked if things were any better with my parents. Mom calls once or
twice a week now. I think our relationship is beginning to heal, even
just a little bit. Dad and I haven't talked much, but I'm hoping he'll
come around eventually. Mom still doesn't want to hear about you, I've
tried, but at least she's stopped bringing up Tommy. Hopefully, she's
realized that's a dead end. I know they'll come around and see that what
we have is real.*

I have to get back to work. Lunch is over. I love you.

~Natalie

It was a bit rocky at first, but Alex and I have fallen into a routine uniquely our own. I love having our online journal. I can write to him whenever I need to talk to him, and I know he'll read it. It's helped make the distance just a bit easier, but I can't wait until he's home and I can feel his hands on me.

The rest of the afternoon goes by slowly. I don't have any more appointments today. I'm sitting in my office, finishing up some paperwork, waiting for 3:30 p.m., when my phone rings.

"Hi, Mom," I answer cheerfully.

"Natalie, your father isn't feeling well. We have to close the pharmacy counter early, but we don't want to close the rest of the store. Can you come in and work until closing?"

"Yes, of course. Is Dad alright?"

"I think he has the flu," she says. "He's been working himself too hard."

This is the first time since I moved out that they've asked me to work. I'm concerned my dad is sick—he never gets sick—but I'm thankful they reached out to me.

"I'm done here in a half-hour. I'll come right over."

"Mrs. Smith will stay until you get there." Mom pauses. "Thank you, Natalie."

"You don't have to thank me. Tell Dad I hope he feels better."

The phone disconnects. I hold it in my hand, savoring the brief moment where it felt like things were okay between us— like nothing bad had ever happened.

I drop Alex a quick text letting him know I won't be able to call him. I'm going to miss talking to him, but I'm also glad for something to do. It gets lonely sitting in that motel room alone.

The bell rings, ending the school day. I grab my stuff and am one of the first out of the building and to my car. The pharmacy is only a few blocks down the street, so it doesn't take me long to get there.

Dad's store is small, nothing like the two-story Duane Reade pharmacies that are all over NYC. Instead, this is more of an old-fashioned operation. My parents know all their customers by name and still offer personal lines of credit to them. Dad carries only the tried-and-true essentials. He rarely orders anything new. "The people in this town don't like to try new things. They stick to what they know works," Dad always says. While that may be true, he forgets Northmeadow sees a lot of tourists during the summer and, in my opinion, he misses a lot of sales opportunities there.

I've grown up in this store, much of my life is connected to it. My Grandpa Clarke opened it when he was about my age, and my dad followed in his footsteps. He always hoped Evan would continue the family tradition, but Evan was never interested. I was their Plan B, but I wasn't interested in becoming a pharmacist either. That's where Tommy came in. My parents focused on their future son-in-law, encouraging him to pursue a PharmD so he could take over the store for them. Tommy never finished school, and I don't know what their plan is now.

The bells on the door jingle when I pull it open and then step into the store. Mrs. Smith is in a tizzy and barely gives me time to get behind the register before rushing to gather her things.

"It's about time," she says.

"I got here as soon as I could."

I smile as I watch her hurrying about, wondering why she's in such a rush.

She stops and gives me a cross look. "You wouldn't understand, Natalie," she says as if she's reading my thoughts.

"Wouldn't understand what?"

She crosses her arms, fumbling with her huge purse. "The importance of putting your husband's needs first. Things like being home and having dinner on the table for him before he gets home from work."

The truth of her words strikes me.

Grabbing her purse, she says a quick goodbye and hurries out the door.

I lean back against the counter and let Mrs. Smith's words play over and over in my head. Alex may not be my husband, but I understand that importance. It's the heart of my relationship with him. Everything I do as a submissive is to put Alex's needs ahead of my own. Our relationship isn't that much different than so many of the relationships in this town, my parents included. I laugh out loud. Except for what we do in the bedroom, *that* is much different.

An idea pops into my head. Maybe this is how I can get my parents to accept Alex? All they've ever wanted is for me to be in a relationship that mimics theirs. This isn't how they thought it would happen, but once they see it in action, they won't have an argument against it anymore. They'll see they're wrong, and they'll finally accept us. They have to.

I'll ask Alex if he's willing to come in for a weekend after returning from Russia. We can plan to meet my parents at a neutral location. It'll give us a chance to show them that part of our relationship: the *old-fashioned* part. I'm sure when they see how we are together, they'll come around. This is how I'm going to be able to have both Alex and my family. There's no way this isn't going to work.

It's finally 9:00 p.m., time to close the store. I lock the front door and do one final walkthrough of the aisles, making sure everything is neat and organized for the morning. I take the register drawer and lock it in the safe before shutting the lights off and letting myself out of the employee back door.

TOMMY

I've been watching Natalie from a distance the past few weeks. She doesn't know I have a second car, which allows me to stay undetected. It's been easy to learn Natalie's schedule; she's so predictable. She goes to work, the grocery store, and then back to that dump of a motel where she's staying.

Speaking of the motel, I stopped by last week—uninvited. I was outside Natalie's door, about to let myself in.

"What the hell do you think you're doing?" A male voice asked from behind me.

I spun around and quickly slid the lock pick into my back pocket.

"I'm a friend of Natalie's. I just stopped by to see if she was home."

"I've seen you sitting across the street watching her," he said. "And picking a lock isn't the usual way to see if someone's home."

"I was just trying to surprise my girl," I lied. "You know, trying to be romantic."

"If I see you here again, there won't be time for a nice conversation like this one. It'll be a one-way conversation." He pulled a gun from his waistband. "Now I suggest you get the hell off my property."

I lifted my hands. "No harm done, man," I said and backed away slowly.

He screwed up my plans for her at the motel, but at least I still have her parents in my corner. Charlotte called me earlier to let me know Natalie was working at the pharmacy tonight, if I wanted to stop in and visit her.

As a matter of fact, I do want to pay her a visit.

I park across the street from the pharmacy, in the lot for the grocery store. It's almost 9 p.m., Natalie will be getting ready to lock up.

This is my chance. No one's around.

The streets are deserted as usual, but tonight that works in my favor. I'm still careful to check my surroundings before I get out of my car and cross the street. I walk around the back of the pharmacy to the employee entrance, where I'll wait for Natalie to come out.

My prescription has run out, and the damn doctor won't give me another one. He had the nerve to accuse me of being an addict, suggested I go for treatment for my *problem*. Screw him. I'll find another doctor who'll give me what I need. I've done it before, but it's going to take time to find one.

The problem is, I took my last pill earlier today, and it's worn off. The withdrawal is making my eyes water and my hands tremble. Sweat is pouring off me even though I'm not hot. I need to get some pills to hold me over for a few days. Stanley always spots me a few until I find a new doctor and get a new prescription, but he's not here tonight. Natalie will do it; she'd never tell me no.

Movement catches my eye. The door is starting to open. Quietly, I move in closer. She doesn't hear me; she's focused on locking the door.

I walk up behind her and place my hands on her shoulders. She jumps.

"Relax, it's just me," I say, trying to calm my girl down.

She spins around to face me. "You almost gave me a heart attack."

"I'm sorry." I reach out and tuck a loose curl behind her ear.

She tries to move away, but I place my arms on both sides of her head, caging her against the door. "I need to get some pills."

"Dad's not here tonight. You'll have to come back in the morning." She tries to duck under my arms, but I don't let her move.

"I can't wait, Nat. I need them tonight." I rock back and forth on my feet, fighting waves of nausea.

"I've already closed up, and I can't fill a prescription even if I wanted to." She pushes at my arms, but I don't budge. "Please let me go."

"My prescription ran out. I need a few pills to hold me over." I give her the smile she's never been able to resist.

"I can't help you, Tommy." She squirms, trying to get away from me. "Please just move out of the way and come back in the morning."

Why is she making this more complicated than it has to be? "I'm not asking, Natalie." I raise my voice. "Open the damn door and get me some pills."

I know I'm scaring her. I don't want to do that, but I need her to do this. I place my hands on her shoulders and turn her to face the door.

"Unlock it." I hold her firmly until she puts the key in the lock and pulls the door open.

With my hands on her shoulders, I force her body forward. She reaches to turn the lights back on, but I stop her. "No lights. We don't need any unnecessary attention, do we?"

She shakes her head back and forth but doesn't make a sound. I guide her to the pharmacy area.

"I don't know Dad's code for the lockbox."

Natalie must think I'm stupid. She's worked here since she

was a kid; she knows how to access everything. Hell, she could be the damn pharmacist if she wanted to.

I lean in close and whisper in her ear, "Don't play dumb, sweetheart. I know you know the code." Her body is trembling. She's afraid. Doesn't she know that I'd never hurt her? But I have to admit, her fear turns me on, and I start kissing her neck. She tries to pull away, and I snicker. "Open the lockbox and get the Oxy." She still doesn't move. "Now."

I give her a small push forward, encouraging her to comply. Slowly, she punches in the code to the lockbox where Stanley keeps the pain meds. She moves her head slightly, eyeing the silent alarm button that's only a few feet away.

"Don't even think about it, Natalie." I'm running out of patience. "Just take out a few pills and hand them to me. Then we can both go home."

Without turning around, she says, "You aren't going to get away with this. There are cameras."

"I knocked them offline, and you aren't going to say anything." I know exactly how to play her. I know her weaknesses and come up with a plan on the spot. "If you do, your parents are going to get some rather revealing pictures."

"What pictures?"

"Pictures I know you don't want your parents seeing."

"Where did you get—"

"Don't worry about where. Just know I have them, and I'll use them."

She reaches into the safe and pulls out the bottle. "Three pills, Tommy. That's all you're getting."

"Four. Or your parents get the pictures."

"Fine."

With how quickly she's complied, I know I got lucky. She's hiding something. I'm gonna have to do some digging. There's gotta be dirt on either her or that guy that's hanging around. I'll call my buddy in the police department and have him do some digging for me.

Natalie hands me the pills before replacing the bottle and closing the safe.

"I gave you what you want, now get out."

I'm not taking any chances with her pressing the alarm. "We'll leave together."

She shakes my hand off her arm and rolls her eyes. I can't wait to get her back under me in bed. I like this feisty grown-up version of her. She was always a good lay, and now she'll be even better.

We get to the door, and she holds it open. "After you," she says.

I walk past her, not letting her get too far away from me.

She locks up again and looks around. "How did you get here? I don't see your truck."

Another idea pops into my head. "I walked. You're going to drive me home." I can always get a ride back for my car tomorrow.

"I'm not driving you anywhere." She crosses her arms. "You walked here. You can walk home."

"Not a chance." I grab her hand and drag her to her car. "My place is on your way."

"Fine, but this is it." She pulls her hand away from me and moves to open the car door. "I'll drive you home, but then you need to leave me alone."

I raise my hands in mock surrender. "Whatever you say, sweetheart."

If she thinks we're through, she has another thing coming. We're just getting started.

NATALIE

y hands shake as I drive Tommy to his house and drop him off. I make it a mile down the road before I have to pull over, open my door, and vomit. There's no way that just happened.

I lean my head on the headrest and take a few breaths, trying to calm my racing heart. Alex and I have exchanged photos in texts, and we have video calls, but I don't see how Tommy could possibly have gotten ahold of them. Either way, I can't take the chance. I can't tell my parents what happened and risk Tommy showing them anything Alex and I have done. They'd never understand. I'd lose any chance I might have of getting them to accept him.

Once I'm calmer, I pull back onto the road and finish the drive to the motel. By the time I make it home, it's late, and I'm mentally and physically exhausted. I send Alex a text, knowing he'll be getting up any time now. I let him know I'm home safe and I'll talk to him tomorrow. I can't tell him what happened tonight, either. He's got a lot on his plate with work. I don't want to add to his stress.

My stomach is in knots, so I don't bother eating. I get right

into pajamas and crawl into bed, hoping to sleep off the events
of the night.

ALEX

I missed talking to Natalie last night, but I'm glad she was able to work at the pharmacy. I know how important it is for her to mend her relationship with her parents.

There's some time before I need to be in Maxim's office, so I leave Natalie a note in our journal.

baby girl,

I missed talking to you last night. This distance is killing me. I can't wait to be home and have you in my arms. The things I want to do to you... Next time I have to be gone for so long you need to come with me. Have you heard about the days you requested for Christmas? I'll book the flight as soon as you get word. My client will be here any minute, so this needs to be short.

Be naked and ready for my call. I love you.

-Sir

NATALIE

$\mathcal{W}$ ith farming being a big part of the economy in Northmeadow, school closes for two weeks over the Thanksgiving holiday, allowing the kids to be home to help prepare their family's farms for winter.

I'm thankful for the vacation because I'm exhausted. I've been plagued with nightmares since my run-in with Tommy. In every dream, he has a gun pointed at someone I can't see. I wake up right as he pulls the trigger.

Somehow I have to shake the feeling that something horrible is going to happen.

I still haven't told Alex. I don't want to waste the time we get to talk, and I can't tell my parents about it because Tommy can do no wrong in their eyes. I fear if I bring him or what happened up, it will only make things with them tenser. The ice is just starting to melt. I don't want to refreeze the situation.

Thanksgiving's in a few days, and I have no plans. Lana and Brandon invited me to spend Thanksgiving with them, but I couldn't bear the thought of going to NYC without Alex being there. I have a few days left to plan something for myself.

While I'm lying on the bed watching a rerun of *Friends*, my phone rings.

"Hi, Mom," I say. "How are you?"

"I'm doing well. Busy getting ready for the holiday," she says. "Dad and I would like to invite you home for Thanksgiving."

I sit up, shocked by the invitation. Although we've been talking, it's been mostly superficial conversations. I wasn't expecting this at all.

"Why don't you come early Wednesday. We'll bake the pies," she says. "You're welcome to spend the night."

"Thanks," I say, trying to hide the shock I'm feeling. "I think that would be nice."

After we hang up, I write a note to Alex.

Sir,

I think I'm in shock. Mom called and invited me home for Thanksgiving. I'm going to spend the night on Wednesday. Maybe this is a step in the right direction? A sign that they're beginning to accept the way things are now.

I wish you were here. Only two more weeks. I got the vacation days I requested, so I'll be able to fly out and spend Christmas with you. I can't wait!

I love you.

~Natalie

After I close my laptop, I get up and take a shower. I'm too excited to sit still.

When I was growing up, we affectionately called the day

before Thanksgiving "Pie Day." Evan, Mom, and I would make apple, pumpkin, and pecan pies. Dad would always beg Evan to go to Northmeadow High's big football game, but he wasn't into sports. He was content to spend the day making intricate designs with pie crust. Together, we made not only delicious but beautiful pies for our holiday meal. I haven't been home for Thanksgiving in years. I'm excited to have this back.

NATALIE

*A*fter another restless night's sleep, I pack an overnight bag, hop into Rhonda, and drive to my parents' house. The only thing missing is Alex. I wish he could be here to spend the holiday with us. Maybe next year.

Dad's still at the pharmacy, so there's room in the driveway, but I don't want to take his spot, so I park on the street. When I shut the car off, my nerves kick in in full force. I haven't been back home in almost four months. I decide to go into the house with no expectations, take things as they come, and hopefully, everything will go smoothly.

I knock on the door before opening it.

"Hi, Mom, it's me," I yell.

"Come on in. I'm in the kitchen."

I drop my bag by the door and head straight in. The smell of spiced pecans cooking causes my mouth to water.

"It smells delicious in here," I say and kiss Mom on the cheek.

She's standing at the stove, wearing her ruffled apron with pumpkins on it. Tomorrow she'll wear her turkey apron. The sight brings back many happy memories.

"You can start on the apples if you'd like." She points to a chair at the table. "I've made you an apron. I hope you like it."

Walking over to the chair, I spot the apron. It's made from the same fabric as Moms.

"You didn't have to do that," I say as I hold it up. Mom's a terrific seamstress; it's a replica of hers. But she *really* didn't have to do this. I'm not much for wearing aprons.

"Don't be silly," she says as she pours the cooked pecans onto the waiting wax paper. "The fabric was your grandmother's. She made my apron for me when I first got married." She wipes her hands off on a dishtowel. "I've saved it all these years waiting for you to be married. But, well, never mind that. It's time you had your own."

"Thank you. I love it." I may not love the apron, but I love the thought and time she put into it. "Can you help me tie it?"

The rest of the afternoon, we keep busy in the kitchen, making tomorrow's desserts with great care. Each pie is made from scratch, the crust decorated, and the pie baked to perfection.

In my naivety, I assumed today would be like old times, care-free and easy, but instead, I can feel tension lying just beneath the surface. Conversation is limited, interrupted by uncomfortable periods of silence. I try to ignore the awkward moments, choosing to focus on the spirit of the day.

Just like when I was a child, I sample the filling for each pie before Mom pours it into the shell. Evan and I used to fight over who got to lick the mixing bowls. He'd always tease me, saying he was the firstborn, so he was entitled to lick the bowl. I'd cross my arms and pout. Mom would get me a second spoon so Evan and I could scrape the mixing bowls clean. Days like today make Evan's death hurt all over again.

"One day, you'll be doing this with your children," Mom says, a dreamy look in her eyes.

I laugh. "I don't think that'll be happening any time soon." I'm nowhere near ready to be a mother.

"You aren't getting any younger," Mom says as she puts the last pie in the oven.

"Alex and I have talked about having children," I say.

"Alex and you?" she asks. "You're still seeing him?"

"Yes, I am." I put the bowl in the sink. "He's in Russia on business right now, but I thought that maybe when he gets home, we can all get together for dinner?"

"Let's get the kitchen cleaned up before your father gets home," Mom says, totally ignoring my question. "You know how much he hates a mess."

I won't force the issue. I put it out there, and now she can think about it. We have some time before Alex is home.

We clean the kitchen in silence, and it gets done in record time. Per family tradition, we've ordered Chinese take-out. The table is set, and we're ready to eat as soon as Dad gets home with the food.

He's talkative tonight and asks a lot of questions about my job. I'm more than happy to share how well things are going. I'm surprised by how easily the conversation flows, so I take a chance and bring up Alex.

"Alex told me he sent you his marketing plans for the store," I say. "Did you have a chance to look at them?"

"I got them," Dad says. "It's not something I'm interested in."

He looks to Mom, who nods in approval.

"Is there something you'd like changed?" I ask. "I can ask Alex—"

"I've run this store on my own for over thirty years," Dad says, his voice raised. "I don't need some young hotshot coming in thinking he knows better than I do."

"I understand," I say quietly.

That wasn't the best way to bring up Alex. Thankfully, the rest of dinner goes by without any more issues.

After we clean-up, Mom cooks popcorn on the stovetop, and we settle in for another family tradition that started when Evan and I were little and would see the Christmas decorations going up on the lampposts in town. The stores would turn on their Christmas music and start selling decorations. Then we'd beg Mom and Dad to put up our tree. Each year they'd tell us "no." We had to celebrate Thanksgiving before we could celebrate Christmas. But on the night before Thanksgiving, they'd give us just a little bit of Christmas. Mom would make popcorn and homemade hot chocolate while Evan and I spread blankets on the living room floor. Then we'd all sit down and watch *Miracle on 34th Street*. It was just a taste, enough to get Evan and me through what we thought was the boring holiday that stood between Christmas and us.

"The parade is even better in person," I tell them. "Maybe next year you guys can come to New York, and we can all go together?"

"I don't think so," Mom answers. "I've seen enough of that city for a lifetime."

"I know it isn't your favorite place," I say. "But the parade is something extraordinary. Then we can all have Thanksgiving dinner at Alex's apartment, maybe start some new traditions."

"The answer is no," Mom says. "Dad and I aren't looking for new traditions."

"What happens if Alex and I have children?" I ask. "Won't you want to come to the city and spend the holidays with us?"

Mom lets out a huff. "I see you haven't gotten over your ridiculous notion of a future with that man."

"It's not ridiculous." I go to bite my nail but correct myself quickly. "Alex and I are very much together. I was hoping that you and Dad would agree to spend some time with us," I say. "I love him and want you both to be a part of our lives."

"Please don't ruin tonight with any more of this nonsense," Mom says. "This conversation is over."

They're infuriating. But I can be just as stubborn as they are.

Even though it's still early when the movie ends, Mom and

Dad say goodnight. They'll be up before the sun to start cooking the turkey.

"I'll be up shortly," I say. "It's a beautiful evening. I'm going to sit on the porch for a little bit." It's unseasonably warm, and Alex told me to call after the movie was over, even though it's the early hours of the morning there.

"Don't be up late," Mom reminds me. "Tomorrow's going to be a busy day."

"I won't." I shake my head as I walk out the front door. Some things will never change, I guess.

Alex and I only talk for a little while. I can hear how tired he is, and he has a big day ahead of him too.

Even though Russians don't celebrate Thanksgiving, the Soloniks are having a special dinner to commemorate the day for Alex. Irina's never made a turkey before, but she bought one and is planning to cook it herself. She even has Alex's mom's recipe for the stuffing. They're such a thoughtful family.

I head up to bed, my heart heavy. I'm envious of Lana's family. I'd give anything for my parents to be even half as open as Maxim and Irina.

Is it possible to love my parents and at the same time wish I had a different family?

ALEX

$\mathcal{A}$fter I hang up with Natalie, I walk quietly through the house. It's the middle of the night, and I don't want to wake anyone. As I walk down the hallway, I notice the library's door is cracked open, and the light is on. I get closer and peek inside. Maxim's sitting in one of the brown leather wingback chairs in the center of the room. In front of him is a wooden table with an open bottle of vodka sitting on top. A shot glass is in Maxim's hand.

"Come in, Alexander," Maxim's voice seems to echo in the silence.

"I'm sorry. I didn't mean to intrude," I say, stumbling over my words.

"Grab a glass and sit down," he says.

"Yes, Sir," I answer.

Walking over to the bar in the back of the room, I grab a shot glass before returning to the chairs and sitting down.

Maxim picks up the bottle of vodka and fills our glasses, and we share a shot.

I've never seen Maxim like this. His eyes are red, not from the alcohol but tears. Something has gravely upset him, but I'm afraid to ask any questions.

"Alexander," Maxim speaks. "You don't know, but I had another daughter."

I set my shot glass on the table before responding, "No."

"I think it's time I told you a story, son."

Over the next two hours and the rest of the bottle of vodka, Maxim reveals more of his story to me.

"Fifteen years ago, today," Maxim says. "Irina and I suffered an unspeakable tragedy."

Maxim and Irina had another daughter, Jelena. She was five years older than Lana. One day Jelena and Lana were walking home from a friend's house when witnesses say a van pulled up. Two men jumped out and grabbed Jelena. No one tried to help her. When questioned later, they said they feared who the men were and what they'd do to them. Instead, they stood by and watched Jelena be dragged into the car and disappear. Maxim used his connections to identify the men. They were known kidnappers for a human trafficking ring.

"I used every contact I had to find my Jelena," Maxim says. "I went days without sleep trying to find my little girl. But Jelena was young, still a virgin, and was sold right away." His eyes fill with tears. "By the time we found the man who bought her, it was too late. She'd already been used and killed."

I'm shocked and don't know what to say. I can't imagine the heartache of not only losing a child, but the way Jelena died is unimaginable.

Maxim avenged his daughter's brutal murder by taking the lives of the men who raped and tortured her.

"You are well aware the accounts you hold for me are merely shells for their true purpose," Maxim says.

"Yes," I answer.

"And you've never asked me what I was really doing?"

I laugh. "I've wanted to many times. I've spoken to Dad about it. He told me to trust you, and if you wanted me to know, you'd eventually tell me."

"You're much like your father," Maxim says. "You've proven yourself a trustworthy partner."

"Thank you." His compliment humbles me.

"It's time you know."

Maxim continues, telling me he's made it his life's mission to fight human trafficking. He finds and hunts those who seek to steal innocents from the streets and rescues as many victims as he can.

"Some of them are in horrible condition," Maxim says. "This is the most dangerous time for a victim. They struggle with finding the will to live again." He pauses and stares off into the distance. "We lost one young woman in the very beginning. I'll never forgive myself for that."

He pours himself another shot, offering me one. I pass on it. I won't be able to get out of bed if I do any more shots.

"Irina is a doctor," Maxim tells me.

"I had no idea," I say, shocked.

"She runs the recovery center." Maxim smiles. "We've learned so much and have spared no expense hiring the best professionals to help the victims we rescue." His eyes take on a haunted look. "I will hunt the scum that prey on innocents until the day I die. It will never bring back my Jelena, but I will make sure her death was not in vain."

My respect for Maxim has grown exponentially.

"I'll always be available in any way to help you win this war."

I'm honored Maxim chose me. This is a fight for a worthy cause, one that's part of making the world a safer place for so many.

NATALIE

$\mathcal{I}$ set my alarm for 7:00 a.m.. Even though it's early, I feel well-rested. I don't know if it was the comfort and safety of my old bedroom, but I slept last night without having any nightmares.

Climbing out of bed, I throw on sweatpants and a T-shirt, my chosen outfit for the day. As soon as I open the bedroom door, my mouth waters. The smell of the baking turkey has already filled the house. I hurry downstairs to the kitchen, knowing I'll find a familiar sight.

My parents have the radio on and don't hear me arrive, so I get an extra minute to take in the scene. Dad sits at the kitchen table, cutting the stuffing ingredients while Mom buzzes about working on her famous cranberry sauce. In past years, neighbors have placed orders for it ahead of time.

"Morning," I say and head straight to the coffee pot.

"Good morning, Natalie," Mom chirps.

"Morning, Dad." I set my cup on the table and kiss his cheek.

"Morning," he grumbles. "You slept late. We've already been up for hours."

I shrug my shoulders, not intending on engaging in his grumpiness. Today is a day for being thankful, not arguing.

"There's fresh biscuits and sausage gravy keeping warm on the stove," Mom says.

"I haven't had that in years," I say and hurry over. Lifting the lid off the pan, I lean in and smell the delicious southern goodness. I make my coffee and place a generous helping of gravy over my biscuit before sitting down at the table.

Mom and dad continue with their tasks while I eat my breakfast.

"Do you think you can give me the recipe for this, Mom?"

"Sure, dear."

"I'd like to make this for Alex," I say and quickly take another bite.

Mom doesn't react to my statement.

A few minutes later, she asks, "When you're done, can you start working on setting the table?"

"Sure."

"I got everything out already." She points to the dining room. "You remember how to set up the centerpiece?"

"Of course I do."

Even though it's only us, Mom always sets an elaborate table for the holiday. The centerpiece is a wicker cornucopia she and Dad made when they were first married. When we were growing up, Mom and Dad always made a big deal of filling the empty horn. Mom would tell us the word cornucopia meant "horn of plenty." Evan and I would then get to fill it with the vegetables we had spent all summer growing in the garden. After it was full, we'd take turns saying things that we were thankful for. It's a special memory that I treasure deeply.

I clean up my breakfast dishes and make my way to the dining room. On the table sits a stack of plates, many more than just the three of us need. I peek my head into the kitchen and ask. "Don't you have too many plates here?"

"No, dear. We're having company."

"Company?" I ask as dread fills my stomach. We've never had company for Thanksgiving dinner.

"Reverend Miller and his wife, Ashlynn and her dad, and a few others who don't have a family to spend the holiday with," Mom says. "It's a tradition we started while you were away." She adds. "Oh, and you'll need to change your clothes before we eat. Put on something a bit nicer."

"Please tell me Tommy isn't coming."

"Delia and Tommy are with us every year," Mom says. "And you will be on your best behavior."

I could deal with having dinner with Ashlynn. My parents don't know anything about her involvement in my break-up with Tommy. But how could they have left out the fact that Tommy was coming? I guess it's partially my fault for not asking before I arrived, but I had no reason to believe Thanksgiving had changed so much.

Without saying a word, I return to the dining room and begin my task of setting the table. I will not let Tommy's presence ruin this holiday for me. This is my house and my family.

By the time I look at the clock, it's after noon. The day has flown by while we were busy in the kitchen. We always eat early, so it comes as no surprise when the doorbell rings, announcing the first guests have arrived. I look down and realize I haven't changed yet. While mom answers the door, I race up the steps and find a dress that should be more appropriate. I make quick work of fixing my hair and changing my clothes.

The doorbell rings again just as I'm coming down the steps.

"Can you grab that?" Mom yells from the other room.

"Sure." I open the door and freeze. Tommy and his aunt are standing in the doorway. Even though I knew they were coming, I still find myself struggling.

"Hello, Natalie, dear." Mrs. Laurel smiles and walks past me, carrying her casserole dish.

Tommy remains in the doorway. He's dressed in a shirt and tie and is holding a bouquet of fall flowers. He's smiling from ear to ear, clearly amused by the situation. I, however, am not amused.

"Aren't you going to say hi?" Tommy asks.

"Hi," I say sharply and turn to walk away.

Tommy grabs my arm. "That's not a very polite way to welcome a guest," he whispers in my ear. "These are for you." He pushes the flowers toward me. When I don't reach out to accept them, he gives me a threatening glare. "Take your flowers like a good little girl."

Grudgingly, I reach out and take the bouquet before walking into the kitchen. Tommy follows close behind.

"Look at the beautiful flowers. Are they from Tommy?" Mom asks.

"Yes," I say and drop them on the counter. I start to walk away, but Mom stops me.

"Natalie, don't be rude. Put your flowers in a vase and go set it on the buffet." She goes to Tommy and kisses him on the cheek. "That was so thoughtful of you."

Everyone's already seated at the table when I walk in and set the vase down on the buffet. They murmur appreciation for the "kind gesture." I struggle not to roll my eyes.

Dad carries in the turkey and takes his seat at the head of the table. Mom sits to his right. There's one empty chair left for me, and it's right next to Tommy. He's wearing a smug look on his face as I sit down.

"Let us join hands as we say a blessing for the meal," Reverend Miller says.

My stomach turns as I place my hand in Tommy's.

He finishes his rather lengthy prayer, and there's a chorus of "amens." I quickly pull my hand away and think we are about to start the meal when Tommy stands.

"Before we eat," he says, getting everyone's attention. "There's something I'd like to say."

This time I do roll my eyes, earning a reprimanding look from my mother.

He turns to me and continues. "Natalie, you and I have known each other for as long as I can remember, and I think I've loved you for just as long."

I look around the room and plan a quick escape, not liking where this is heading.

"I know we've had some problems. Every couple does." He glances at where Ashlynn is sitting. She crosses her arms, obviously unhappy. "We weren't together for a while, but since you've been back home, it's become clear to me what I want."

He reaches into his pocket and pulls out a small box. Looking around the table, I notice no one is surprised at the scene unfurling before us. Everyone, except Ashlynn, is smiling. Reverend Miller and Hannah are holding hands. Mom is dabbing at the tears in her eyes.

Tommy gets down on one knee. "Natalie Clarke, will you do me the honor of being my wife?" He opens the box and holds out a ring. "Marry me?"

I can't move, can't breathe. I don't know what to do. I thought Tommy understood there isn't an *us*. When I moved out, I thought my parents understood it was because I was serious about Alex. By inviting me home, I assumed they had finally accepted there would be nothing with Tommy. But looking around the table now, it's clear no one has moved on except me.

"Tommy, I—"

He grabs my hand and starts to slip the ring on my finger.

"No." I pull my hand away. "I'm not marrying you."

He stands up, anger marring his face.

"Natalie, how dare you." My mother snaps.

Finally, able to move, I stand, horrified at the situation. "How dare I? How dare you. All of you." I point around the table. "You all knew about this, didn't you?"

Our dinner guests squirm in their seats.

"I've tried telling you that Tommy and I aren't a couple, and we haven't been for years." The next sentence slips from my mouth. "We haven't been since he cheated on me." With that, the room goes eerily silent.

"Natalie, don't," Tommy whispers in my ear. "Put the ring on your finger." He grabs my hand, but I pull away.

"Don't touch me," I yell. "I'm done, I refuse to do this any longer. It's time I told everyone the truth." I look around the table before I begin to tell the story. "My first year of grad school, it was time for spring break." I look pointedly at my parents. "Remember, I was supposed to come home, but at the last minute, I told you I had to work?"

They look at me but give no reaction.

"I was here. I came home early to surprise *him*," I say. "Instead, I got the shock of my life. When I opened the door to his dorm room…" I pause. At this moment, I have a decision to make. I can tell everyone Tommy was in bed with Ashlynn. But what will that do? What good will come of it? I glance at Ashlynn, who's sitting across from me. I could be vindictive and hurt her as badly as she hurt me, but that's not who I am. "I opened his door and found him in bed with another girl." That statement earns a few surprised gasps. "I left on the next plane back to New York." I back away from the table. "All these years, I've tried to protect Tommy. I tried to hide what he did and move on." I let out a sarcastic laugh. "But instead, everyone turned on me. My parents refuse to accept I've moved on and am in love with someone who treats me well. Someone who is honest and trustworthy and would never hurt me. Someone who loves me." I look at Tommy. "Instead of any of you being happy for me. Instead of my parents supporting me." I turn to face them. "You're content to trick me, to make a fool of me."

"Natalie, you will stop this instant!" Dad raises his voice.

"I'm sorry, Dad, but this is too much. I can't do this anymore. I can't be here." I turn and nearly trip over my chair as I start to walk out of the room.

"Natalie, child." Reverend Miller stands up, blocking my path. "Let's sit down and discuss this calmly."

"Move out of my way." My voice comes out in a roar. "I'm

leaving." He must sense how angry I am because he steps aside, clearing the path to the door.

Tommy follows me and grabs my arm. His voice low, so only I can hear. "If you walk out, I'll show them the pictures."

I pull my arm free. "You know what? Do it, get it over with. I don't care anymore."

"Natalie, if you walk out that door this time, you won't be asked to come back again," Mom says in an even, calm tone.

"I wasn't planning on coming back," I say and, with hurried steps, I leave—for the very last time.

I rush out of the house, thankful that I parked my car on the street and not in the driveway. With a squeal of the tires, I pull away. I can't believe I was so stupid to think everything was okay. To think my parents had accepted my choices, even if they disagreed. By the looks on everyone's faces when Tommy stood up to make his awful proposal, they all knew what was happening. They were planning this behind my back. Did they think I was going to say yes just because they were all sitting there? That I'd cave to the pressure? "Ha. They probably did," I say aloud. Well, this time, they got the message. And, come to think of it, so did I.

I'm not that girl anymore.

ALEX

J've been calling Natalie all night, but I keep getting sent straight to voicemail. My texts are all unread. I tried Lana, but she hasn't heard from Natalie either. She was supposed to call me after her family had dinner. That was five hours ago.

Where are you, baby girl?

I traded sleep for pacing the house all night, waiting for her call. Now, a new day has dawned, and I still haven't heard from her. I'm on the other side of the world and completely helpless. It's a feeling I'm not used to.

It's only 7 a.m.. I'm on my third cup of coffee, and now I'm pacing in the dining room. The caffeine is doing nothing to help my already frayed nerves.

"Alexander, you look terrible. Did you not sleep well last night?" Maxim asks as he walks into the room.

I run my hands through my disheveled hair. "Natalie never called. Her phone's going straight to voicemail." My words come out hurried. I recheck my phone—nothing.

Maxim, never one to rush a response, pours himself a cup of coffee and then sits in his chair at the head of the table. "Have you tried calling her parents?"

"I called her father's cell, no answer, and their landline is unlisted." I don't stop moving while I speak.

"Alexander, sit down," Maxim says with authority in his voice. "You are going to wear out my floor."

Although sitting still feels like an impossibility, Maxim's command leaves no room for argument. I take a seat at the table and pour myself another cup of coffee.

The kitchen door opens, and Maxim's staff serves us breakfast. As delicious as the kasha smells, my stomach is in knots. I can't eat.

Maxim pulls his phone from a pocket inside his suit jacket and types out a message.

Setting the phone on the table, he begins eating.

"I don't know what to do." I drop my head in my hands. "I need to go to Missouri. I need to find her, but I can't leave yet."

Maxim continues eating his breakfast, seemingly unfazed by my rambling.

I dial Natalie's number, and again, no answer. Hanging up, I put the phone back on the table. "I shouldn't have come. I shouldn't have left her alone."

Maxim's phone vibrates. He lifts it and looks at the screen; his face gives nothing away. A few seconds later, my text alert sounds. I rush to check it, hoping it's finally Natalie, but instead, it's a text from Maxim.

"Her parents' phone number," he says calmly.

"How did you?"

"I have my sources, Alexander." He takes a drink of his coffee. "Call them."

Pulling up my phone keypad, I input the numbers and tap the green call button. The line connects and begins to ring.

"Hello?" A man answers.

"Mr. Clarke?"

"Who is this?"

"It's Alex Montgomery. I'm trying to find Natalie. Is she there?"

There's no response. I move the phone from my ear, ensuring the connection didn't drop.

"She's not here."

"Do you know where—"

With a click, the line goes dead.

"He hung up on me." My hands shake from a mix of fear and anger. "What do I do now?"

Maxim stands and pushes his chair in, his demeanor eerily calm. "I'm going to my office to make a few calls. We will find her."

With confident strides, he walks away, and once again, I'm left alone with my thoughts. I know Maxim's reach is long; I'm hoping it's long enough to find Natalie because as much as I want to get on the next plane back to the States, I can't. I'm meeting Nicholai in an hour.

I don't know Nicholai's story, but I assume it's similar to Maxim's, which is what makes these two men such a formidable force in their fight against trafficking. Today's meeting is to set up the framework for a second treatment center. Rescuing a victim is only the first step to safety. Yesterday, I learned there's a long and bumpy road ahead of each person saved.

After our Thanksgiving meal, Maxim and Irina brought me to their current facility, Nadezhda Yeleny, Jelena's Hope. I was given a tour and witnessed first-hand the severity of the damage. The victims are often severely injured physically, but it's the mental and emotional trauma that's the most difficult to treat. These concerns need to be addressed before they are reunited with their families. Sadly, some of the victims don't have a family. Worse yet are the ones whose families no longer accept them. Maxim and Irina ensure they're set up with a new life and a support system; they will never be unwanted again.

As we walked through the facility, I could picture Natalie here with me. Her caring nature and her professional skills would be valuable. She could work alongside Irina, helping to heal the broken.

I finish my coffee before going up to my room to take a hot shower. It's time to put on my game face. There's work to be done.

I leave my room on the second floor and walk down the grand staircase to the first floor. Maxim's office is down a hallway near the front of the house. When I arrive, his door is closed, so I knock.

"Come in," Maxim calls.

His office is impressive. The exterior wall is lined with windows that overlook the front of his property. Larch wood, native to the country, was used to build the massive desk that sits in the room's center. Behind it are built-in bookshelves filled with centuries-old books on Russian history. A pair of ornately carved, neoclassical armchairs that date back to 1820 sit opposite the desk.

"Viktor is on a plane heading to Northmeadow," Maxim assures me. "He'll call as soon as he finds her."

I lower myself into one of the armchairs and relax just a bit. Viktor's been loyal to me for years. I'm confident he'll find her and keep her safe, but it does little to stop the ache in my heart that I can't be there myself.

"Thank you." The words don't seem enough, but they're all I have.

There's a knock on the door. The butler announces Nicholai's arrival. Maxim stands and walks to the door to welcome his guest.

Nicholai's an older man; I'm guessing close to Maxim's age. He's dressed in a tailored suit and carries the same air of power Maxim does. When I first met him, he was closed off, distrusting of me. Over the past few weeks, he's opened up, and I've learned he's a kind but dangerous man—I wouldn't want to be on his hit list.

His bodyguard steps aside when Maxim approaches.

I follow, shaking Nicholai's hand. "Good to see you this morning, Mr. Federov."

"Nicholai, please," he reminds me again.

"Let's sit down and get to business," Maxim says.

Maxim nods to his butler, who pulls the office door closed. Nicholai's man stands guard inside by the door.

I put my issues aside for now and give the project my full attention. With innocent people's lives at stake, every facet of this account must be completed to perfection.

NATALIE

$\mathcal{W}$hen I leave my parents' house, it's with only one thought—getting far away. I need space and time to process what just happened. Not wanting to be found, I turn my phone off and drive with one destination in mind—Finn Lake. When I pull up, I walk down the same path to the same bench Alex and I sat on during my party.

I've spent many long afternoons on this bench trying to figure out life. The rhythmic sound of the water lapping on the shore has always helped to ground me, but today it does nothing to calm the thoughts rushing through my head. Hours pass while I sit, replaying the spectacle at dinner. What sort of alternate universe is Tommy living in to imagine that I might accept his ludicrous proposal? It seems like he's not the only one living there either. I keep replaying the situation and coming to the same conclusion. Except for Ashlynn, who looked just as shocked as me, no one else seemed surprised. They all knew what Tommy had planned. I've never felt so betrayed, so unseen.

"Evan, why did you leave me?" I ask aloud. "I wish you were here. I need you." I drop my head in my hands and cry.

I stay on the bench until the sun begins to set. I reach to the side for my jacket. That's when I realize I don't have it. In the rush to leave my parents' house, I didn't grab any of my things. The air is getting too chilly to stay outside, so I push myself to a standing position and begin the walk back to my car, shuffling my feet through the leaves that litter the path on my way.

Then I begin the long, lonely drive back to my motel room.

NATALIE

*A*lthough it's three in the afternoon, the curtains are still drawn tight. I was up all night, and I'm exhausted. My hair is in a messy bun, and I haven't even bothered to get dressed. I'm lying on my bed, hoping sleep will find me, when banging on the door startles me.

"Natalie, are you in there?" A loud voice calls from outside.

I recognize the voice immediately.

What's Viktor doing here? *Alex*. I jump off the bed; my heart pounds in my chest as I hurry to unlock the door and throw it open.

"Is Alex okay?"

Without waiting for an invitation, Viktor walks into my room. "I've got her. She's right here, sir." He hands his phone to me. "It's for you."

"Alex, are you okay?"

"Am I okay? Where've you been?"

"I've been in my room." It dawns on me that I never turned my phone back on after leaving my parents' house yesterday.

"I've been worried sick about you? Are you okay?"

"Yes. No." Fresh tears fall, and I can't speak.

"Put Viktor back on."

I nod my head, even though I know he can't see the motion, and pass the phone back.

I can't make out his words, but it's clear from the volume of his voice that he's upset. Unable to handle any more yelling, I drag my feet across the carpet, lay back on the bed, and curl myself into a ball.

"She looks unharmed." Viktor is silent for a moment. "I'll stay with her and find out." He nods while Alex continues to vent. "Sir, if I may, please calm down. I'm here, and I won't leave her." More silence. "I'll have her call you as soon as she calms down." He disconnects the call and slides the phone into his pocket.

For a minute, he stands, arms crossed over his chest, his form large and imposing in the small room. He runs his hands through his hair, looking uncertain, before grabbing a chair from the table and dragging it next to the bed. Sitting down, he leans forward. He doesn't say anything. He simply puts his hand on my arm while I continue to cry.

The sound of the microwave beeping wakes me.

"Good evening, sleepyhead," Viktor says before opening the microwave and removing what smells like chicken soup. He places a bowl on the table. "Come over here. You need to eat."

I sit up and throw my legs over the side of the bed. My head pounds from all the crying I've done over the past twenty-four hours.

"What time is it?"

"Nearly 9 p.m.," he says as he pulls out a chair before turning and heading back to the microwave to put another bowl in. "You cried yourself to sleep. By the way, you look like shit." He chuckles.

"Thanks, you're too kind." I roll my eyes at him as I stand up and walk over to the mirror. I do look like shit. The bun I had put in fell out, leaving my hair poking up in all directions. My face is blotchy, and my eyes are swollen and bloodshot. Shrugging my shoulders, I continue my trek to the table and sit. "I'm not hungry," I say and push the bowl away from me.

"You can eat on your own, or I'll feed you. Boss's orders."

I let out a soft laugh. "He's so bossy, even from halfway around the world."

The microwave beeps again. Viktor grabs his bowl, brings it to the table, and sits across from me.

My stomach betrays me by growling loudly.

"Eat." He points to the bowl of soup. "And start talking. What happened?"

Grudgingly, I pull the bowl to me and take a few spoonfuls of the warm chicken noodle soup before I gather the courage to relay the disaster that was Thanksgiving. Viktor doesn't interrupt while I talk, and although his face shows no signs of emotion, I can tell from his tightly clenched fists that he's furious.

When I finish my story, he picks up his phone.

"Who are you calling?" I ask.

"Alex."

"Let me tell him, please." As much as I don't want to tell the story again, he needs to hear it from me. Viktor hands me the phone. It's already ringing.

"Thank you," I whisper.

Viktor offers me a rare smile. "I'll be just outside."

"Hello?"

I close my eyes and take a deep breath. "Alex..."

"It's me, baby girl." Unlike earlier, his voice is now calm and gentle.

"Yesterday was awful," I say before I begin retelling the story. He's patient with me as I struggle through the still-raw emotions. "And then I left. I turned my phone off because I didn't want my mom or dad calling me, and I forgot to turn it back on." He stays quiet so long I think the line may have disconnected. "Are you still there?" The sound of his breathing is the only thing that breaks the heavy silence.

"I'm sorry doesn't feel like enough," he finally says. "I feel helpless. You need me there, and I'm stuck here."

"Please don't do that." I don't want him to take responsibility for this. It's not his burden to bear. The fault lies solely with the individuals sitting around that table yesterday.

"You're mine to protect, and I'm not there when you need me." The pain in his voice is palpable even through the phone.

"You're here now."

"No, I'm not. I'm half a world away," he says, with an edge to his words.

I close my eyes, trying to fight the tears that are threatening to spill. "I know you're not here physically, but at least we can talk." My words fail to help anything. "You'll be back soon."

"I'm assuming I can't talk you into going straight to New York?"

"You assume right," I say. "I have to work. I'll be there in three weeks, and then I'm all yours until after the new year."

He sighs deeply. "Viktor will be staying with you until then."

"That's not necessary."

"This is non-negotiable." My Dominant is back. "I can't do what I need to here while I'm constantly worried about you there. Viktor will be by your side until you get back home."

I don't miss his use of the word *home*. "Yes, Sir."

There's no use arguing with him, and honestly, I'm not sure I want to. I've been looking over my shoulder ever since that night at the store with Tommy, something I still haven't told Alex about. It might be nice to have Viktor around not only for protection but also for some company.

Glancing at the clock on the nightstand, I see it's nearly midnight, which means it's 8 a.m. in Russia.

"It's late; you've been on the phone with me all night."

"I can stay on the phone as long as you need me, baby girl."

I smile, knowing I'm the luckiest girl on earth. "I appreciate that, but it's late for both of us."

"Let me talk to Viktor. He has my card. I want him to get the room next to yours."

This isn't going to go over well at all.

"He'll have to stay in my room for the weekend." I hold my breath waiting for the explosion on the other end.

"That's not going to happen," Alex growls.

"Marshall closed the motel for the weekend and went on his own vacation. He won't be back until Monday."

With tourist season over, the motel is a ghost town. Marshall knew I had nowhere to go, so he let me stay and left me his cell number for emergencies, but I hardly consider this worth interrupting his time off.

"He'll sleep in the car."

"Don't be ridiculous." I let out a sarcastic laugh. "He'll stay in my room."

"Natalie—"

I ignore the warning in his voice and open the door. Viktor is just outside, leaning against the wall. I motion for him to come back in and put the phone on speaker. I know I'm pushing Alex on this, but I'm not letting Viktor sleep in his car.

"Alex would like you to stay in Northmeadow until I leave for vacation," I say, addressing both men.

"Not a problem, boss. I'll—"

I raise my hand, interrupting him. "The motel office is closed for the weekend. You and I'll be roomies until Monday." I sit down on the chair and cross my legs in mock victory.

Viktor's mouth hangs open, and his eyes grow wide.

"Viktor," Alex yells. "Take the phone off speaker, now." I swear the walls in the room shake.

Maybe I shouldn't have pushed him that far.

Viktor shoots me a warning look as he grabs the phone from my hand and once again steps outside the room. I've just managed to upset two powerful men. Oh well, what's done is done. While they hash it out, I decide to take a much-needed shower.

After I dry off and get dressed, I crack open the bathroom door, trying to gauge the situation. Viktor's turned the chair to face this direction. He's sitting back, legs spread, arms crossed over his chest. Cautiously, I step into the main room, shrug my shoulders, and attempt a smile.

"It's a good thing that man of yours is in another country." He shakes his head, clearly not amused. "Let's hope, for both our sakes, that he calms down before he gets home."

The past forty-eight hours hit me all at once; exhaustion permeates my entire being, and all I want to do is sleep. Knowing I'm perfectly safe with Viktor, I ask, "So, what side of the bed do you want?"

Viktor cocks his head to the side. "Neither. I'll take the floor."

"That's ridiculous."

"Maybe so, but I'd like to remain alive and keep my job."

Remain alive? He's a bit overdramatic. But I concede and am happy that he at least lets me give him a pillow and blanket.

NATALIE

irst thing Monday morning, Viktor's standing outside the office waiting for Marshall to arrive. He's now my neighbor in Room 6, which means I'm alone tonight.

Alex calls on video to ensure I'm appropriately punished for my behavior the other night.

"Undress for me, slowly," Alex instructs and leans back onto the pillows on his bed.

Climbing off my bed, I turn the laptop so Alex can watch as I strip out of my clothes. I remove each piece of clothing as slowly and seductively as possible.

"Pull a chair over and sit," he says.

While I'm getting the chair, I hear the sound of his zipper. When I turn back around, he's sliding his hand up and down his hard length. Unable to take my eyes off him, I stumble when I go to sit on the chair.

"Open your legs. I want to see you," he demands.

I do exactly as I'm told, even though I don't see how this is supposed to be a punishment.

"Touch yourself."

I drag my finger through the wetness between my legs and begin rubbing small circles on my already sensitive center. Watching Alex stroke himself only intensifies my arousal. With my free hand, I pinch my hardened nipple between two fingers and moan at the sensation.

"That's it, baby girl." Alex encourages me. "You look so hot right now."

"I'm so close."

"Keep your eyes open and look at me."

"Yes, Sir," I answer.

Alex increases his pace as he chases his release.

"Alex, I'm going to—"

"Stop," he commands.

My hand stills and I watch as he brings himself to orgasm, ribbons of cum landing on his shirt. When the last of his contractions stop, he continues, "Do not touch yourself until I give you permission."

I'm so close it's painful. My legs close involuntarily, and I squeeze my thighs together, trying to take the edge off. I'm ready to drop to my knees and beg him to let me finish, but I know he won't allow it. Denying an orgasm is my punishment.

"My little sub, you need to learn not to push me, especially in front of another man."

I lower my gaze. The knowledge that my actions disappointed him hurts more than being denied pleasure.

"I'm sorry, Sir."

"Look at me," he says.

I raise my eyes to meet his.

"I forgive you." The edge that was in his voice is gone.

Punishment within a relationship is something I've had to get used to. I don't like punishments and do my best to avoid them, but I also know they serve their purpose. Alex is an experienced Dominant. His discipline challenges me but doesn't push me past my limits. The part I find the most beautiful is the complete forgiveness Alex gives me. There are no arguments or grudges held. It's just over.

The hardest part is forgiving myself—that's still a work in progress.

TOMMY

*N*atalie's behavior on Thanksgiving has anger pulsing through my veins like red, hot lava. "What the hell was she thinking telling me no?" I pound the steering wheel. The box with her diamond ring lies like a lead weight in my pocket. She left me standing in front of everyone, looking like a fool. I haven't figured out exactly how, but she'll pay for that.

For now, I'm back to following her from a distance. I've had to watch my step since that motel guy found me outside her room and threatened me at gunpoint. I found a secluded area that I can park my truck where it won't be seen. It's about a half-mile walk through the woods until I'm across from the hotel, where I sit tucked in the tree line. I use my binoculars to keep an eye on her room. I'm gonna need a new plan soon. It's getting too cold to stay outside.

Natalie's been a naughty little girl, a thought that only makes me hard for her. While her *boyfriend* is out of town, it seems she's keeping company with another man. He follows her around like a lost puppy. They do everything together, and I've got the pictures to prove it. I'll make sure her boyfriend knows what she's up to when his back is turned. Then she'll have no one to turn to, and she'll be forced to come back to me. I pull the ring out of my pocket. "Then I'll slip this onto her pretty little finger, and she'll be mine once and for all."

It's my lucky night; the curtains are still open in her room. She and that guy are sitting at the table playing happy little family. I use the zoom lens on the built-in camera to snap a few pictures before I pack up and make the trek back to the truck. It gives me time to think about all the changes for me since Natalie's tantrum.

Her parents hired me to work full-time at the pharmacy. That puts me one step closer to our original plan. I was supposed to follow in Stanley's footsteps and become a pharmacist. Natalie was going to have my babies and work part-time at the store. When her parents were ready to retire, the store would be given to us. That was until she screwed everything up when she took off for New York.

This arrangement works in my favor, though. Stanley was concerned that his new security system went off-line a few weeks ago. I played the hero by setting up new firewalls and security codes, which means I have access to them, and her folks are none the wiser. It's a handy bit of information to have since I haven't found a doctor who'll give me another prescription.

I drove three hours to Kansas City to see a new doctor, but as soon as he accessed my records, he refused to give me meds and said I had to go for some tests and other shit.

Fuck that. Instead, I found some sellers online and got some pills, but they come at a high price. Now that I'm working at the pharmacy and have been given the code for the safe, I can grab a few pills now and then.

So far, Stanley hasn't caught on, and I plan to keep it that way.

NATALIE

*I*t took a week to get past the initial awkwardness of having Viktor around all the time, but once I broke through his tough exterior, I learned he's a lot of fun. We've fallen into a comfortable pattern. He drives me to work every morning, and even though I tried telling both him and Alex that it isn't necessary, Viktor now stands guard outside my office door. After my punishment the other night, I've learned my lesson about pushing Alex too far. Every evening, Viktor and I eat dinner together and play a highly competitive game of rummy. It's not his typical assignment, that I'm sure of.

This morning, I woke to find a voicemail on my cell phone from my father. He let me know I have one week to remove my belongings from their house, or they'll be put out for the trash. Mondays are bad enough without adding this to the mix. How am I going to get everything moved out this week? Where am I going to store everything? I try to come up with some sort of a plan while I get ready for work.

Like clockwork, I receive a text followed by a knock on my door—Viktor's right on time. Usually, I am too, but today I'm running behind. I unchain the door and let him in.

"Good morning," he says and hands me a cup of coffee.

He brings one every morning. The man is a saint. "You're going to make some woman very happy," I say as I reach out and take the cup.

His mouth twitches with amusement.

"Have a seat. I'll be ready in a few minutes."

"No problem." He lowers himself onto the chair and pulls out his phone.

While I'm finishing my makeup, I ask, "Do you think we can stop by my parents' house after work today?" I lower my mascara wand and glance at him in the mirror.

He looks up. "Why?"

"I have to get some things."

"We'll go shopping." He takes a drink of his coffee. "I have Alex's card for anything you need."

After I finish applying my lipstick, I take a seat opposite him. "There's nothing I *need*, exactly." I play with my coffee cup nervously. "My dad called to let me know I have until the end of the week to move out my stuff or else it goes in the trash."

"Well, isn't that fucking fantastic of him."

I shrug my shoulders, unsure of what else to say.

Everything I'd once thought about my parents lies in a scattered debris field. I've yet to sort through the remains to see if there is any truth to my memories or if they've been this way all along and, perhaps because I never challenged them, I just didn't see it. I'm not ready to face what I might find yet, so I've placed everything in a neat little box in the back of my mind. My main focus is on making it through the next few weeks until I leave for New York. Maybe when some time has passed, I'll be strong enough to face the hurt.

"Would you mind going with me and giving me a hand?" I ask him. "It's just some clothes, books—"

"You don't have to ask. We'll go and get everything you need." He offers me a reassuring smile.

"Thanks."

"Just doing my job," he answers.

"Well, I appreciate you just doing your job."

"Right." He stands and heads for the door. "You ready to go?"

I laugh at his reaction, knowing he's operating in uncharted territory. I know Alex has threatened Viktor within an inch of his life about being here alone with me. It's a little much, but Alex is my overprotective alpha Dominant, and I do love it.

"I'm right behind you." I slip on my winter coat, grab my bag, and follow him out the door.

Winter seems to have settled in early this year. Snow flurries are dancing in the cold breeze. I reach in my pocket for my mittens and pull them on.

"Cold?" Viktor asks, a playful tone in his voice.

"Freezing." I almost forgot how much I hate the bitterly cold Missouri winters and it's only the second week in December, not even really winter yet. "Don't tell me you aren't cold?"

"This is nothing compared to a Russian winter," Viktor says as he opens the car door for me. "I've already warmed the car for you. Can't call my boss and tell him I let his woman freeze to death, now, can I?"

I punch him lightly in the arm as I get in the car. Shaking his head, he rubs his arm and laughs before shutting my door.

I've been thinking about trying to surprise Alex for the past few days. The only thing holding me back is remembering the disaster that happened the last time I tried to surprise someone. Every time I go to ask Viktor for his help, I chicken out. Time is running out, though, and since we're in the car, where I can't back out once I start, I decide it's now or never.

"Viktor?"

"Yes?"

"Would you help me with a surprise for Alex?"

He glances my way, lifting an eyebrow. "Depends on what it is."

"I want to change our plane tickets." I shift in my seat to watch his response. "I have a few personal days I can take. I'm kinda hoping we can leave for Alex's a few days early so I can get everything ready for Christmas before he gets home. But you can't tell Alex."

Viktor's face remains stoic, his eyes focused on the road ahead. I bite my nails, nervous he's going to say no. I need him to go along with this, but his expression is giving nothing away.

"Yes," he finally says in a low, composed voice.

"Yes?" I ask excitedly. "I'm so happy I could hug you right now."

"You'll do no such thing." The edge of Viktor's mouth turns up in a small smile. "I'll change our flight this afternoon."

The adrenaline rush from the mix of excitement and nervousness makes it hard to sit still. For the rest of the drive, I make a mental list of everything I'm going to need. I'll have to call Lana and enlist her help too. I want to make this our best Christmas ever.

When we pull up at the school, there's a group of kids outside with boxes of lights and ornaments. Some are already decorating the trees that line the sidewalk. Others are taking selfies by the trees.

"What are they doing?" Viktor asks.

Memories of my last year in high school rush to the surface. "The Santa Parade is this weekend. Every year the senior class decorates the trees for the parade. Businesses up and down Main Street do the same."

He nods his head as he continues to watch the kids stringing lights and garland. It's clear they're having a terrific time, and as much as I'd love to sit here and watch them, I can't. I have to get into my office before the bell rings and I'm late. I don't need to give Mr. Meadows any ammunition to use against me.

I reach for the handle on the door, but Viktor grabs my arm.

"Wait." He motions over my shoulder.

Turning to look out the window, I see Tommy across the street leaning against his parked car.

"What's he doing here?"

"Don't know." Viktor turns off the car and unbuckles his safety belt.

My eyes stay fixed on Tommy while I wait for Viktor to walk around the car. Tommy crosses his arms over his chest, undaunted by my staring at him.

Viktor opens my door, stepping into my line of sight. I hesitate to get out.

"It's okay," he says, trying to calm my nerves. "He won't get near you."

Viktor's reassurance is somehow enough to give me the courage to leave the safety of the car, but I still grasp his hand for support. His body tenses at the contact.

"Thank you," I say softly.

I can feel Tommy's eyes boring into my back the whole walk up the steps and into the building. Viktor talks to me the entire time, reminding me to be brave and not to look back. I'm relieved when we make it to the door, and we walk inside.

Tommy's appearance this morning has me spooked. I've been jumpy and distracted all day. Since his proposal, he's becoming more and more unraveled. I've heard that now he's even working at my parents' pharmacy. After everything that's happened, I know I shouldn't care, but I do. My parents are hard workers, and I don't want them to lose everything because they refuse to see what's right in front of their faces.

But this time, it's on them. I can't—no, I won't step in and fix it.

"Miss Natalie." My student's voice cuts through my wayward thoughts.

"I'm sorry, Mary," I say, embarrassed by my lack of profes-
sionalism. "Can you repeat what you said?"

"Is everything okay?" she asks.

I school my features, hoping to relieve some of the worry I
see on her face. "I'm just getting excited for Christmas. Do you
have any plans for break?" I ask, switching the focus back to her.

She studies me for a minute before answering.

"Oh yeah, big plans." She huffs a laugh. "Billy's coming over.
He'll leave his boyfriend home because, well, you know why."
Mary rolls her eyes.

I nod, knowing exactly why Billy won't be bringing Todd
with him.

Mary continues to tell her story matter-of-factly. "Mom'll be
busy trying to make the perfect dinner, but when Dad sees Billy,
he'll flip out. They'll all start screaming at each other. I'll go to
my room, and then Billy will leave." She looks at me with grief-
filled eyes. "I miss him."

"I understand how hard that will be for you." My heart goes
out to Mary.

Even though there's a five-year age gap between the siblings,
they grew up close. Billy always looked out for Mary. He still
does his best. Billy gave her a cell phone, so he can call her
without their parents' intrusion, and he tries to visit as often as
he can. He's an essential part of her support system.

"Last session, we talked about how and when to tell your
parents," I say. "We discussed the pros and cons of telling them
now or waiting until after your birthday. Have you thought
about it at all?"

"I've thought a lot about it, can't stop thinking about it." She
looks down at her hands in her lap. "I can't go through the
things Billy had to. I think I should wait until after my birthday.
It's only a few more weeks."

"That's a very mature decision."

When Mary first started sessions with me, she was fueled by

anger and on her way toward a head-on collision with her parents. She's made a lot of progress over the past few months and is doing a great job responding rather than reacting. She accepts she can't change her parent's reaction when she tells them about her sexual identity, but it will change how she responds to them.

"I'd like to take your suggestion about inviting them to a session," Mary adds. "Can we still do that?"

"Yes, we can. You'll need to sign a few papers permitting me to talk to your parents."

"Thank you for helping me understand my options," she says, a sad smile on her face. "At least I'll be eighteen, and they won't be able to force me into therapy too."

We spend the rest of her half-hour session making a safety plan. Something she may need after she tells her parents. If they kick her out, which is highly probable, I want to make sure she has somewhere safe to stay and that she's able to finish high school.

"Did you talk to Billy?" I ask.

"I did," she says. "He's glad I'm waiting to tell them. He and Todd said I can live with them as long as I need. They're already getting a bedroom ready."

I'm relieved to know she has somewhere to go. Over the coming weeks, we'll talk more about how she wants the session to happen. My role will be to facilitate, ensure it remains productive, and be there for Mary in the aftermath.

Unfortunately, stories like Mary's are all too familiar in this community. Unlike in generations past, these kids have access to the whole world via the internet and social media. They've seen ways of life different than what Northmeadow offers. Many of them hope to take advantage of the opportunities that await them, but they know they won't have the support of their parents, who expect them to follow in their footsteps. Something I'm all too familiar with.

I see myself in so many of these kids. Unlike when I was in high school, these kids have found each other and support each other. In many ways, they've been my teachers as they model bravery and self-confidence. They still have a long road ahead of them, and I refuse to lose any of them like I lost Evan and Michael. When the dust settles, they'll need someone in their corner, and that someone will be me.

NATALIE

ith Christmas break fast approaching, the energy throughout the school grows in anticipation. The students have one more week, but today is my last day. After the bell rings, Viktor and I are heading to the airport to catch our flight to New York City.

I'm sitting at my desk, working on a file, when I hear a knock on my door.

"Come in," I call.

The door opens a crack, and Ms. Campbell peeks her head in. "Am I interrupting?"

"Not at all." I close the file and push it to the side. "Have a seat."

"I wanted to see you before the holiday break," Ms. Campbell says. "I'm very pleased with the work you're doing. I know it isn't easy around here. But you're doing great."

"Thank you." She's one of my only allies in this place, and her compliment means the world to me. I sit back in my chair and let my guard down for a minute. "It hasn't been easy. You're right about that. But the kids make it worth it."

"I hope I'm not overstepping, but with everything that's happened with your family, I was wondering if you had plans for the holiday." She pauses to clear her throat. "I'd like to extend an invitation to my home for Christmas."

"Thank you so much." Her offer genuinely touches me. "I have plans already, though."

"Do those plans involve that handsome man you keep telling me about?"

"They do," I say and smile. "I'm leaving today to spend the holidays with him."

"I'm glad you're getting away for a bit," she says. "But I'm going to miss seeing that hot man standing outside your door every day."

We both laugh.

"I can introduce you, if you'd like," I say. "I'm pretty sure Viktor's single."

Ms. Campbell blushes. "Maybe after you get back." She stands and walks to the door. "Have a safe trip and a wonderful holiday."

"Same to you."

She leaves and closes the door behind her. Who knew Ms. Campbell was interested in Viktor? I laugh.

I'm anxious for the day to be over, but I swear the clock is moving slower than usual. Having a hard time focusing on paperwork, I walk across the room to the window and look out. Snow is falling softly. It's beginning to coat the decorated trees in white, making it look like a Winter Wonderland. A few people walk down the street. It's clear from the packages in their hands they've been shopping. Tommy's appearance last week still has me shaken, but everything appears normal.

My cell phone, which is sitting on my desk, dings with a text alert. Confident that everything outside is status quo, I walk back to the desk to see who's texting.

(Viktor) I'm not in the hall. I ducked out a few minutes early to warm the car up. I'll be out front.

(Me) Thank you. I'll be out as soon as the bell rings.

(Viktor) Text me when you're on your way.

Sitting at my desk, I grab the papers I was working on and finish up my notes. I refuse to bring any work home over the holidays. When I finish, I place the files in my desk's bottom drawer, locking it securely.

After what feels like an eternity, the bell finally rings, signaling the end of the day and the start of my Christmas break. I toss my phone into my bag, take one last look around the room, then I turn off the lights and leave, locking the door behind me.

I start walking toward the side entrance, texting Viktor as I go. A few students call out goodbyes, I wave to them and keep moving. I'm on a mission to get out of the building as quickly as possible. I push the door open and slam into a solid wall of muscle. I let out a squeal as two large hands come to rest on my shoulders.

"I'm sorry I startled you," Viktor says, "Tommy's out front."

I look around Viktor's imposing frame, and there, in front of the school, is Tommy, leaning against his car, watching.

"He wasn't out there a few minutes ago," I say. "Why is he doing this?"

"He's trying to intimidate you," Viktor says, "But we aren't going to let him. We're going to walk to my car like nothing's wrong."

"Right, focus on walking to the car that's parked right behind Tommy. Got it."

This time *he* grabs *my* hand. "I'm right here. I won't let anything happen to you."

I squeeze his hand in a silent gesture of gratitude.

Viktor's calm and cool, the exact opposite of how I feel. He chats with me as though we're just out for an afternoon stroll.

"Do you have everything packed, or do we need to make any stops before we get on the highway?"

It takes a second to slow my irrational thoughts and answer. "I got everything packed last night."

"Good, then we can leave right away. We'll stop to eat once we're farther from here." My eyes train to where Tommy stands.

"Eyes on me, not him."

I keep my eyes locked on Viktor's as he opens the door.

From the corner of my eye, I notice Tommy push himself off the car. He starts walking straight to us. My heart beats so loudly I'm shocked Viktor can't hear it.

"Get in the car, Natalie," Viktor says.

I don't obey. Everything moves in slow motion as I step out from behind Viktor's protective stance to confront Tommy.

"What are you doing here?"

"I want to talk to you," Tommy says.

"You did enough talking with that ridiculous proposal. Don't you think?"

"Get in the car, now," Viktor orders.

Ignoring Viktor, I take a step closer to Tommy.

"This time, you're going to listen to me." I point my finger at him. "I'm done being a pawn in whatever game you're playing. It stops now," I say, my voice raised.

"Sweetheart, you're upset," Tommy says. "You need to calm down," He reaches out to grab my arm.

"Do not touch her." Viktor steps between us.

"Hey man, back off," Tommy sneers.

I place my hand on Viktor's arm. Our eyes lock in a silent battle before he steps aside.

"Once upon a time, you were my everything. I was in love with you," I say. "When I walked into your dorm room and saw you and Ashlynn together. God, Tommy, you broke my heart." I stop and take a second. "I hated you. I hated you both."

"I said I was sorry. I told you it was a mistake."

I put my hand up to silence him.

"I forgave you long before you apologized."

Tommy smiles and puffs up his chest.

"But I forgave you for me, not you," I say and watch the smile disappear from his face. "That night ended up being the best thing that ever happened to me. It was the night I changed how I viewed life; the night I decided to start living for me." I point to my chest. "There will never be an us again. I respect myself far too much for that." I look to Viktor, who's standing next to me, his arms crossed. "This. Whatever this is you're doing, hanging around watching me. It stops now. You're never going to win me back. You and everyone else in this town need to back off and let me live my life." I turn my back to him and move to get into the car.

"You're going to regret this, little girl," Tommy says.

I spin around to face him. "You don't scare me, Tommy. Just go away."

Without another word, I slide into the car. Viktor closes the door and circles in front of the vehicle to get to the driver's door.

Tommy stands, legs spread, arms crossed. His eyes are dark as he stares at me through the window.

Without a word, Viktor starts the car, and we drive away.

Like so many years before, I don't bother looking back.

We drive in silence until we get on the highway.

"I don't appreciate that you ignored my directive back there," Viktor says. "But the way you stood up to him. I'm proud of you."

I turn my head and look at Viktor, a smile on my face. "Thanks. Do you think he got the hint?"

"Let's hope so."

What should have been an hour-long drive to the airport takes two hours because of an accident on the highway. Since we're short on time, we decide not to make an extra stop and just grab a bite to eat at the airport. Check-in takes us over an hour. I've never seen the place so busy.

It isn't until the wheels of the plane leave the ground that I'm able to breathe a sigh of relief.

Holding up my ear pods, I ask, "Do you mind?"

Viktor looks up from whatever he's reading on his phone. "Not at all, try to relax."

It's the first time in weeks I feel like I can actually do that. I put the earbuds in and open my playlist before laying my head back and closing my eyes.

NATALIE

"Wake up, Natalie."

Viktor's shaking my arm.

"We're about to land," he says when I look at him groggily.

I thought Branson was busy, but JFK is bursting at the seams. By the time we disembark the plane and get our luggage, it's after midnight. Between the nap on the flight and the chilly New York air, I'm wide awake as we walk to Viktor's car.

"You left your car parked here the whole time you were in Northmeadow?" I shake my head in disbelief. "It's going to cost you a fortune."

He puts our suitcases in the trunk and closes it before turning to me. "It's going to cost Alex a fortune." He laughs. "He made it clear; your safety is worth more than any dollar amount."

The knowledge that Alex cares so deeply about me that he'll do whatever it takes to keep me safe makes me feel cherished.

While Viktor drives, I pull out my phone and double-check the list I made. I need to get a tree, decorate, bake, and get all my shopping done before Alex gets home on Wednesday. That only leaves me five days. I sure hope Lana's up for the task.

When I look up, I'm surprised to see we're heading in the

direction of the Queensboro Bridge. I'm about to say something, but Viktor beats me to it.

"Alex told me this is your favorite way to get into the city."

I'm amazed that Alex doesn't miss the smallest detail, even from so far away.

The skyline, with all its twinkling lights, is a breathtaking sight. I have to hold in a squeal of excitement as we cross the bridge into Manhattan; I'm almost home. That's an unexpected feeling, but not an unwelcome one. I've spent so much time focusing on settling back into Northmeadow that I haven't let myself think about returning to the city or calling it home again.

But as we drive through the brightly lit streets, I let my imagination paint a picture of me living here with Alex. Of being his submissive full-time. Of us getting married and having a family. I shake my head, the image dissolves. Alex has told me he loves me and has mentioned wanting something long-term, but he's never talked about marriage. Don't do that, Natalie. Don't imagine things that aren't going to happen. You'll just end up hurt—again.

We make our final turn into the garage under Alex's apartment building and park the car.

I look at Viktor, unable to hide the smile on my face. "Thank you. For everything."

"You aren't getting rid of me yet." He chuckles as he gets out of the car.

"What do you mean?" I open my door and follow him out. "I'll be fine here."

"If I leave you alone and word gets back to Maxim, well, I'd rather avoid that unpleasantness."

"What does Maxim have to do with anything?" I ask, confused by his statement.

He hesitates for a minute before responding. "He signs my paycheck."

With a click of a button, the trunk opens, and I reach to grab my suitcase, earning a disapproving look.

Viktor removes my hand. "I've got them."

Although his voice holds no humor, I laugh anyway and raise my hands in mock surrender. It's not a battle I choose to fight. I do manage to close the trunk for him before turning and leading the way to the elevator. Without having to wheel a suit-case, I have the advantage of speed. We step in and begin our ascent to Alex's apartment.

The elevator arrives, and almost as if on cue, my phone begins to ring. Alex is requesting a video call.

"Shit," I whisper.

Viktor laughs. "Didn't plan for this part, did ya?"

I have to think quick and come up with a story. I don't want to lie, but is it a lie if it's to keep a surprise? I decline the video request and answer as a voice call.

"Hello, Sir," I say, hoping the higher pitch of my voice doesn't betray me.

"Why isn't your camera on?"

"My phone's acting up." I hate lying to him. "The camera doesn't seem to be working."

Viktor shakes his head as he walks past me, bringing the luggage to our rooms.

"Use my card and have Viktor take you to get a new phone."

"Okay, I'll do that."

"Finally, I don't get an argument." Alex's laughter is a warm, rich sound that makes me miss him even more.

"What do you have planned for today, Sir?" I ask.

"Maxim and I are meeting with Nicholai," he says. "We're finalizing the details for his account."

"I'm glad to hear that." I'm feeling extra emotional being in his home without him. "I can't wait until you come home."

"Me either," Alex says softly. "Because of this account, I'll be able to hire a manager to handle the other accounts my firm holds. That will free me up to spend more time in Northmeadow with you."

"Really?" I nearly squeal. "You'd spend more time in Northmeadow?"

"I was thinking about buying a house for us there," he says.

"Sir, I don't even know what to say."

"Nicholai just arrived. I have to go," Alex says, cutting our conversation short.

He's thinking about buying a house in Northmeadow? I'm on cloud nine as I make my way to our bedroom. Viktor has already put my suitcase on the bed. I take a few minutes to unpack, filling the drawers and closet space Alex left empty for me.

I change into my pajamas and crawl into bed, but I can't sleep. The energy in the city is contagious. Even though it's nearly 2 a.m., I call Lana, knowing she'll be awake.

She answers on the first ring. "You're back," she squeals so loud I have to pull the phone away from my ear.

"I am," I say, almost unable to believe it myself. "Are you free for breakfast and shopping tomorrow?"

"Absolutely. I'll meet you at your place."

"Sounds like a plan. I can't wait to see you."

We chat for a few minutes until Brandon calls for her. "Gotta go. I'll see you in the morning."

NATALIE

Something—or rather someone—jumping on the bed startles me awake.

"You're home!" Lana giggles. "I missed you so much."

"Oh my God, you scared me." I laugh along with her. "What time is it?"

"It's after one o'clock." Her stomach growls. "I'm starving and couldn't wait any longer."

"I can't believe I slept so late." I jump out of bed. "Give me a few minutes to get dressed, and we'll head out."

I grab jeans and a sweater from the closet and go into the bathroom to get dressed. Lana sits cross-legged on the bed, catching me up on everything I've missed while I put on some make-up and throw my hair in a ponytail. After I slip on my black chucks, I turn to her, "Ready to go?"

Lana pulls her phone out. "I just have to let Brandon know we're headed out."

"He can come too."

Her fingers fly across the screen, sending a text to Brandon. A few seconds later, he replies. "He says no. It's a girl's day out, and he'll see you soon."

"Okay." I grab her hand. "Let's go. We have a lot to do." I'm excited to spend the day in the city with my best friend.

"We're on our way out," I yell to Viktor, who's in the office.

We begin walking to the elevator when Viktor appears behind us.

Lana spins to face him. "Girl's Day, Vik. I have my car."

"No can do, ladies."

Lana rolls her eyes. "You're kidding, right?" He opens his mouth to speak, but she holds up her hand, stopping him. "Never mind, I know you don't kid around."

Watching their interaction is comical. Lana's so bossy with him. My laugh slips out at her comment on his inability to joke around.

"Viktor knows—"

"Knows how serious your safety is." He raises his eyebrows.

I'll keep his secret. It's the least I can do for everything he's done for me the past few weeks.

Our first stop is the Christmas tree lot on the corner. We pick the perfect tree and pay the delivery fee. It'll be waiting for us at the apartment when we get back.

"I need food," Lana says. "I'm starving."

The next stop is a corner café. Viktor refuses to join us. He's back to his serious, all-business demeanor. Lana and I place our order at the counter and find a table in the corner.

"How did Leo's collaring go last night?" I ask.

"I wish you could've been there," Lana says. "It was amazing."

"I'm so happy for them both."

We stop talking when the waiter arrives at our table with our sandwiches and coffees.

"I hope we get to the club while I'm here," I say. "I miss everyone so much."

We catch up with each other while we eat lunch. After we finish eating, we walk back outside where Viktor's waiting.

"Where do you want to start?" Lana asks.

"I thought we could head over to the Holiday Shops in Bryant Park," I suggest. "We can figure out where else to go after that."

We spend two hours walking through the market, marveling at the products made by the talented artisans. I find a handmade ornament with two penguins kissing under the mistletoe that I have personalized for Alex and me. It'll look adorable on our tree.

When we leave the market, Viktor drives us downtown to do more shopping. We spend the rest of the afternoon filling the trunk with packages and bags.

As we leave the last store, Viktor asks, "Where to now, ladies?" I can tell he's holding back from rolling his eyes. He's been a great sport today.

"Can you drop me off at Fire and Ice?" Lana asks. "I told Brandon I'd meet him there." She turns to me. "Wanna come? Leo and Anthony will be there."

"I'd love to, but I need to get home. I have a lot of wrapping to do," I say and laugh, knowing I might have gone a little overboard with the presents.

When we pull up at the club, I give Lana a big hug. "I missed this. I'll call you after Alex gets home, and we'll make plans for Christmas Day."

"Something tells me you might be a little tied up." We share a laugh.

Lana grabs her bags and, with a wave, heads into the club. Viktor and I head back to the house.

ALEX

I can't wait to see Natalie's face when I show up in Northmeadow tomorrow, but before I can get on the plane, I have to finish the most important task on this trip—picking up her engagement ring.

My driver pulls the car to a stop in front of a small jewelry store. According to Maxim, Yegor is the best jeweler in St. Petersburg. Before I get out of the car, I take a minute to get my emotions under control. This ring is a symbol of both my past and my future. The conversation with my mom when she gave it to me is as clear today as it was all those years ago.

"Alex, I want you to have this." She slid her engagement ring from her finger and placed it into the palm of my hand.

I tried to give it back, tried to make her put it back on.

"You're going to beat this."

"Alexander." She placed her frail hand on my arm. "I'm tired. My body can't fight anymore. Listen to me, please." Reluctantly, I sat quiet as she spoke. "Your father gave this to me when I was a young girl—a symbol of his promise to love and care for me. We've discussed this. I want you to have it. When you find a woman you're ready to make the same promise to, put this ring on her finger. Love her the same way your Father has loved me."

I put the ring away and chose not to look at it. For so many years, it only represented what I'd lost, what Dad had lost. Mom wasn't supposed to give up; she was supposed to keep fighting. She was supposed to beat cancer. It took me a long time to accept that she didn't quit, that things happened the way they were supposed to. It took Natalie coming into my life for me to understand what my parents had shared and what the ring truly symbolized. Before I left for Russia, I took the ring out and made peace with it—made peace with my mother's death.

My parent's love story will always be represented, but I chose to redesign the ring, adding our love story to it as well.

The driver comes around and opens my door. Trying to hide my nerves, I steel my shoulders and walk into the jewelers. Yegor greets me with a kiss on both cheeks. He speaks very little English, and I speak only enough Russian to conduct a basic conversation, but we manage to communicate nonetheless. He motions for me to sit in a high wooden chair in front of the glass showcase before holding up a finger, letting me know he'll be a minute. I perch on the edge of the chair and watch him walk into the back room.

When he returns, he's holding a small black velvet box. He stands across from me and places it on the glass.

"Your ring, Mr. Montgomery," he says and motions to the box. "Do you wish to open it?"

"Yes." With shaking hands, I carefully lift the lid and pick up the ring.

Even though I drew up the design, what I see is nothing short of amazing. He has transformed my mother's solitaire round stone into a heart that's set on a platinum band twisted like a vine. One row of the vine is lined with diamond pieces that were removed from the original stone. The other is lined with black diamonds. "It's exquisite."

"I'm pleased," he says and brings his hand over his heart.

Another man joins us. "The ring is beautiful, sir."

"Yegor did an amazing job with it," I say, still in awe of the ring.

"It will look beautiful on your future wife's finger," the man responds.

I pause at his words—*my future wife*. Taking a final look at the ring, I place it back in its box. "As beautiful as this ring is, it doesn't compare to Natalie's beauty."

"I see many beautiful stones come through here, but none more beautiful than my wife," the man says. "Treasure her, and you will share many happy years."

"I plan to do exactly that."

Once the transaction is complete, I walk out of the store, feeling like the luckiest man on earth.

ALEX

*a*s much as I hate to do it, it's my turn to go MIA on my girl for a bit.

Sixteen hours after takeoff, the wheels of the plane hit the ground at JFK. I have a two-hour layover until my flight to Branson leaves. I'm exhausted from the long plane ride, so I grab a coffee and find a quiet corner to wait. When I turn my phone on, I see three missed calls from Natalie. I can't call her and risk her hearing the background noises and questioning my whereabouts, so I settle for texting her and telling her I'm caught up in a last-minute meeting. I don't want to lie to her, but it's the only way to keep my surprise. It'll be worth it when she's in my arms.

A few hours and another flight later, I'm finally in the Branson airport weaving through people to get to the rental-car counter. While I wait in line, I send a text to Viktor asking him if Natalie's at the motel. I'm expecting a return text, but instead, my phone rings.

"Hello?" I answer.

"Hey, boss." His voice is uncharacteristically nervous.

"Is Natalie in her room?"

"Why do you ask?"

"Because I want to know where she is."

He pauses before he speaks. "Not exactly."

"Viktor." My voice rumbles with a warning. "Where's Natalie?"

"She's safe, boss. She's just busy right now."

"Busy?" What's going on? He knows better than to evade my questions. "Where the hell is she?"

"Shit." He's clearly frustrated. "She wanted to surprise you. We're at your place."

I laugh out loud. People walking by do their best to avoid me, looking at me like I'm crazy.

"Alex, you okay?"

"She's in New York?" I stop to laugh again. "I'm in Missouri. I wanted to surprise her."

Viktor lets out an audible sigh of relief before joining me, laughing.

"Guess my plans are changing." Excusing myself from the rental car line, I start walking the opposite way and get in line at a ticket counter. "I'll book a flight and see you guys soon. And Viktor?"

"Yes, boss?"

"Don't tell her I'm coming."

With my new ticket in hand, I get ready to board a plane back to New York. I text my flight information to Viktor and instruct him to make sure she stays home. One way or another, I'm surprising Natalie today.

NATALIE

*I*t took all morning, but the tree is up and decorated. While the chocolate chip cookies are baking, their scent filling the apartment, I'm hanging the last wreath above the fireplace. The only thing left to do is for Alex to put the star on the tree when he gets home. Climbing off the chair, I look around at my work; everything is perfect.

I was hoping Viktor would help me with some decorating, but he's been acting standoffish since a phone call he made earlier. He made up some excuse about having work to do. He's been hiding in the office ever since.

The timer on the oven goes off, and I pull out the last tray of cookies. They look so good, my stomach growls when I see them, and I realize it's dinnertime. After baking all day, I don't feel like cooking. I walk down the hall and knock on the closed office door.

"Come in," Viktor calls.

I take a few steps into the room. "I'd like to go out and get a bite to eat."

"You can order in," he says without even looking up.

I'm confused by his cold response. "I'd like to go out."

He stops what he's doing. "No."

"No?" I cross my arms, annoyed. "Why not?"

"I have things to do," he answers. "Just order something in, okay?"

I feel like I've just been dismissed. I storm out of the room, slamming the door. I don't know what's gotten into him. Part of me wants to go out anyway, the heck with him, but I know word will get back to Alex, and that'll end badly.

I end up in the living room and flop down on the overstuffed sofa. With my phone in hand, I pull up the Postmates app and start scrolling through my options. I settle on Chinese food and order enough for Viktor and myself.

While I'm waiting for the food to arrive, I grab my book and get comfy on the couch. I'm in the middle of a page when Viktor comes into the room.

"I'm going down to my apartment," he says.

"I ordered dinner for us. It'll be here shortly."

"I'm not hungry." He turns to leave. "I'll see you in the morning."

"Whatever," I mumble and go back to reading. I don't know what's wrong with him today.

A half-hour later, I hear the elevator signal its arrival. I'm not expecting company, and the delivery person doesn't have the code to get up here. I pull up Viktor's contact on my phone just as the doors open. It takes a moment for the message to travel from my brain to my legs. I jump off the couch and hurry to the foyer.

There stands Alex holding a bag of food in one hand, his suit-case in the other.

"Did someone order take-out?" he says with a huge grin on his face.

"Alex? Is it really you?"

He sets the bag on the credenza and drops his suitcase before opening his arms. "It's me, baby girl."

I run and jump into his embrace. He wraps his arms tight

around me. "You weren't supposed to be home for two more days." I pull back and look at him.

"And you were supposed to be in Northmeadow."

He doesn't give me time to respond before his mouth lands on mine, his tongue parting my lips. He lifts me as we kiss, and I wrap my legs around his waist. Alex carries me into his bedroom and kicks the door shut behind him. "I've missed you so much," he says and lowers me until my feet touch the floor.

"Why didn't you tell me you were coming home early?"

"Why didn't *you* tell *me* you were coming home early?" he asks. The amusement that was in his eyes a moment ago quickly shifts to something dark and hungry. "We can talk later. Right now, I need to be inside you."

I don't waste a second before grabbing my shirt and tugging it over my head, letting it fall to the floor. Reaching out, I begin unbuttoning his dark blue dress shirt, feathering kisses on his chest as I move down. I let my hands explore the toned muscles of his abdomen before moving lower to undo the button and zipper on his pants.

"Natalie." My name falls from his lips like a prayer.

My hands slide his pants and boxers down, freeing his erection as I lower to my knees. When I look up, I see Alex staring at me with lust-filled eyes. I fist his hard length, earning a low growl of approval. It's a powerful feeling knowing I can cause this reaction in him.

My tongue circles his velvety soft tip teasing him. I look up and see his head thrown back and his eyes closed. Starting at the base of his cock, I flatten my tongue and drag it up his swollen length. When I reach the tip, I gently blow across it before running my tongue through his slit, tasting his salty essence.

Alex grabs my hair, tilting my head up. With our eyes locked on each other, I open my lips and slide my mouth down to the base. My hands cup his balls and massage them gently as I move up and down his shaft in a steady rhythm.

"You feel amazing." His voice is deep with barely-checked control. "I'm not going to last long."

Without warning, I take him deep into my throat. His grip on my hair tightens. I relax, allowing him to take control of the pace. Within seconds, his balls draw up, and I know he's close.

"Fuck." He loses himself, shooting waves of cum down my throat.

I greedily swallow everything he has to give before dragging my tongue up his length one final time.

He grabs my arms and lifts me, so I'm standing in front of him. I reach around my back and unhook my black lace bra, tossing it to the side. The move only intensifies his desire, and he starts to advance toward me like a predator stalking its prey. I step backward until my legs hit the bed. I fall back and lean on my elbows, watching as he grabs my leggings, pulling them off in one swift motion. His breath catches when he sees I'm bare underneath. There's hunger in his eyes as he spreads my legs. "My turn." He wastes no time as he brings his mouth directly to my wet folds, causing my back to bow off the bed. He licks and sucks like he's a starving man, and I'm the meal that will save him.

My orgasm builds quickly. "Alex!" I yell his name as waves of pleasure pulse through my body. He doesn't stop until I'm lying limp on the bed.

"I've missed you," he says before he flips me over on all fours.

He rubs himself back and forth through my wet folds, teasing me. He's rock hard again.

"Please, Sir. I need you," I say, looking over my shoulder.

He leans back and grins. "Where do you need me?"

"Inside me, please." Even though I've just had an orgasm, I'm wet and needy again, my body ready to make up for our time apart.

"As you wish."

He lines his erection up with my opening, and in one thrust, he's fully sheathed inside me. He grabs my hips, his fingers digging in deep. He's not gentle, and I don't want him to be. He takes me hard and fast. Reaching his arm around my body, he begins rubbing my clit, intensifying the pleasure. His fingers pinch hard, and my orgasm crashes into me. His thrusts become frantic until I feel him explode inside me.

"I missed you so fucking much."

Shifting our position, so he's lying on his side, he pulls me into his chest and wraps his arms around me.

I lose track of time as we lie together, touching and talking to one another.

"Now that I've satisfied my desire, for now," he says. "Let's go heat up dinner before round two."

I laugh, knowing we aren't going to get much sleep tonight.

ALEX

J wake Natalie a few times during the night. We've been apart too long, and I can't get enough of her. Between that and the jet lag, it isn't surprising that although it's nearly noon on Christmas Eve, I'm just waking up. Natalie's still asleep next to me, snoring softly. I get out of bed and throw on sweatpants and a T-shirt, careful not to wake her.

I pad down the hallway and into my gourmet kitchen. I haven't eaten at home much since she went back to North-meadow. Right now, I'm thankful Natalie got here early and restocked the kitchen because I plan to make brunch to start our day.

Bacon sizzles in the frying pan while I flip the French toast. I'm in my own little world until I feel two slender arms wrap around my waist.

"That smells delicious," she says, resting her head on my back.

"I was hoping to surprise you with brunch in bed." I put my free arm around her and pull her into my side.

"I don't think we would've gotten much eaten if we were in bed." She places her hand on my chest and looks up at me, her green eyes full of desire.

I place a kiss on her head. "Why don't you make us some coffee while I finish cooking." Seeing her in nothing but my T-shirt makes me want to go all caveman, tossing her over my shoulder and dragging her back to bed, but I have other plans for today.

Natalie's putting the coffee cups on the breakfast bar right as I plate the food. We sit down to enjoy our late breakfast. It's these simple moments together I missed the most.

"I didn't get a chance to tell you how beautiful the decorations are." She transformed the apartment into a Christmas wonderland.

"Thank you." She smiles.

"I hear there were some other elves behind all this," I say and laugh.

"Oh, that reminds me." She sets her fork down and reaches for her phone. "I told Lana I'd call her today and let her know what time they should come over tomorrow."

"I've already talked to Brandon. We're all set," I say. "As soon as we finish eating, we're heading out."

Her eyes light up. "What're we doing?"

"You're not the only one who can plan a surprise," I say and motion to her almost-empty plate. "Eat up."

We finish our last few bites, and she starts gathering the dishes. "I'll get them," I tell her. "You go start getting ready."

"Are you sure, Sir?"

"Positive," I say. "And leave your phone home. We're going off-grid."

While she heads to the bedroom, I throw the dishes in the sink. I'll deal with them later. I send Viktor a quick text asking him to have the car ready before I get dressed.

Thankfully, Natalie isn't a girl who needs hours to get ready. Ten minutes later, we're in the elevator going down to the waiting car.

"Will you tell me where we're going?"

"Nope." I laugh, knowing how impatient my little sub can be.

I'm thankful we left when we did because the traffic downtown is worse than usual. When we near our destination, I see the recognition in her eyes.

"Are we going to Radio City?" She beams with excitement. "Did you know that in all the years I lived here, I've never been to the Christmas show?"

"I know." I smirk. "A little elf told me." A little elf named Lana.

Her green eyes are wide and sparkling with pure joy as we walk into the historic building.

"There's so much to see. I don't know where to look first."

She looks from the terrazzo floor up to the majestic chandeliers that hang from the four-story-high ceiling.

"Wow," she murmurs.

I take her hand and lead her into the auditorium that's already filling with people. She looks around at the three levels of mezzanines before turning, seeing the Great Stage.

I understand her excitement. Although I've been here many times, the opulence of the building never grows old. There's always something new to discover.

For the next hour and a half, the stage comes to life with Christmas magic. Natalie's totally immersed in the show, and I'm totally immersed in watching her.

When the curtain closes, she reaches over and grabs my face, planting a kiss on my lips.

"Alex, that was incredible."

"I'm glad you liked it." I stand and offer her my hand. "Let's go. There's more to do."

"More?" she asks as she follows me out of the theater.

Our next stop is right around the corner for a selfie in front of the iconic Rockefeller Christmas Tree. I pull out my phone.

"I thought you said we're off the grid today," she says with a hand on her hip.

I show her my screen. "Airplane mode."

She laughs softly before cuddling close for our picture.

Over the next few hours, we visit all the iconic Christmas sites in NYC. We stop at the oversized Christmas ornaments before making a stop at Macy's to view their holiday window display. We pretend we're tourists and take selfies at every stop. I want to have the pictures to look back at and to one day show our children.

"I'm told you've been missing New York pizza," I say as Viktor pulls the car up to our favorite pizza place.

"You have no idea. Pizza isn't the same anywhere else."

We're seated by a window, affording us a view of the people bustling by on the sidewalk. Sitting at our table for two, we eat, taking this time to enjoy each other's company.

When we finish, I check the time on my phone. "If we don't get going, we'll be late."

"Late for what?" she asks.

"You'll see soon enough. Come on."

Hand in hand, we walk the few blocks to Central Park, where the final surprise waits. I'm filled with a mix of nervousness and excitement, knowing what lies ahead. I haven't decided exactly when to ask her. I'm counting on fate to lend a hand.

We round the corner and see a white horse standing in front of a red carriage. Natalie squeezes my hand tightly. When the driver sees us approaching, he climbs down from his seat.

"Mr. Montgomery?"

"Alex, please," I say and shake the man's hand.

"My name's Liam, and this is my horse, Storm," he says with a lilting brogue. "We're ready to go if you are."

I look at Natalie. "Are we ready?"

She returns my gaze, her eyes sparkling with excitement. "I'm so ready."

I help Natalie into the carriage first, climbing in behind her. Once we're seated, I pull the woolen blanket over her lap. With the sun setting, the air has a chilly bite.

The carriage starts moving, and almost as if it were planned, the Christmas lights in the park turn on. Natalie grabs my hand as she takes it all in.

"I've walked through here so many times." She looks at me. "But something about tonight feels different—magical."

I pull her close as we listen to the clip-clop of the horse as she prances her way through the park. Bow Bridge is up ahead. Carolers stand at one side singing. A small group of people has gathered around listening.

I lean up to the driver. "Can you stop right up there?"

He nods his approval.

When the carriage stops, I hop out first and offer Natalie a hand. Holding her mittened hand, we walk onto the bridge and listen as the carolers begin singing, "Have Yourself a Merry Little Christmas." My other hand is in my pocket, holding the ring box. Fate has done her job and provided me the perfect moment.

Without letting go of her hand, I take a step away and turn to face her. "Natalie, two years ago, I was asked to escort a young lady for a night at the club. I wasn't looking forward to it and almost didn't show up." I smile as I recall the memory. "That night changed my life; it was the night I met you." I pause, swallowing over the lump in my throat. When I pull the ring box out of my pocket, Natalie lets out a small gasp. I let go of her hand and get down on one knee. "These past few months apart have been challenging, but I learned something important—I don't ever want to be without you again. You're my world, my heart, the very breath I breathe. Would you do me the honor of being my wife? Will you marry me?"

Natalie brings her hands over her mouth. Tears are streaming down her cheeks. For the longest time, she says nothing.

Her voice is barely a whisper when she finally speaks. "Yes, I'll marry you."

She said yes. I blink back my own tears. Standing up, I take her left hand in mine and pull off her mitten. The ring, made to fit her perfectly, slides onto her finger. I pull her close and kiss her.

I don't even realize we've drawn an audience until they begin to clap, calling out their wishes of congratulations.

She looks down at the diamond on her finger. "Alex." Her voice is soft. "It's the most beautiful ring I've ever seen."

"It was my mother's diamond. I had a jeweler in St. Petersburg redesign it."

Movement catches my eye, and I look up. Watching us from a nearby tree is a Cardinal. I watch it for a moment before it takes flight. I look toward heaven, knowing my mother is watching this moment.

"I love it." She wraps her arms around me. I lift her from the ground and kiss her again. At this moment, everything is perfect. In my arms is the woman who is soon going to be my wife.

NATALIE

*a*fter the proposal, we stay and listen to a few more carols before climbing back into the carriage. We sit close, wrapped in each other's arms. It's as if the rest of the city is silent—as if there's only him and me. The reality is still sinking in.

Alex asked me to marry him.

I'm going to be his wife.

As the carriage ride comes to an end, I see Viktor standing outside the car, arms crossed over his chest. When he sees us, he gives Alex a questioning glance. Alex nods his head in response, causing Viktor to break into a big smile.

"He was in on this too?"

"I couldn't have done it without him," Alex answers proudly.

When we get to the car, Viktor pats Alex on the back. "Congratulations, sir."

"Thank you."

"Congratulations, ma'am." Viktor hugs me, and I swear I hear Alex growl.

"Ma'am? What happened to Natalie?"

Viktor doesn't answer, but his smile tells me all I need to know.

When we get back to the apartment, I take Alex's hand and lead him to the bedroom. I remove his clothes before doing the same with mine.

"Lie down," he says.

He kisses me softly and gently until he's covered all of my body.

"Tonight, I'm going to take my time with you, Natalie," he whispers.

And he does. Slowly and passionately, my Dominant, my fiancé, makes love to me.

Cutting through the most beautiful dream I've ever had is the sound of my phone ringing. I wake up momentarily confused.

Alex grumbles next to me.

I'm slightly annoyed when I roll over and reach for the phone. Who would call before dawn on Christmas morning? It's my mom's number on the screen. I sit up and hit the green button to accept the call.

"Natalie?" Mom asks before I have a chance to say anything.

"Yeah, it's me." Why is she calling me at 4 a.m.?

"There was a break-in at the store," Mom says and then bursts into tears.

"Mom?"

Alex sits up. "What's wrong?"

"I don't know." I get out of bed. "Mom, are you still there?"

"Ms. Clarke?" A male voice asks.

"Yes?"

"My name's Officer Cooper, from the Northmeadow police department."

His voice is calm and steady, unlike my heart, which is beating wildly.

"There was a break-in at your family's pharmacy."

"Oh my God." So many questions run through my head, but what comes out of my mouth is: "When?"

"It was shortly after midnight. Your father recently had a silent alarm installed. He received a notification it had been triggered."

"What did they take?'

"It appears the perpetrator was after some prescription medications."

My stomach turns. I don't need to ask who did it. I already know the answer.

"Was anyone hurt?"

"Ms. Clarke, your parents arrived before we got to the scene." He pauses. "There was an altercation, and your father was shot."

My legs threaten to collapse from under me, and I grab the bed in an attempt to hold myself up. Alex is at my side in an instant. He helps me sit and takes the phone from my shaking hand.

"This is Alexander Montgomery, Natalie's fiancé," he says calmly. "Can you tell me what's going on?"

Alex walks toward the window. He's silent, listening to whatever the officer is explaining. "What's his condition?" Another long pause. "We'll be on the next flight out. Please give this number to the hospital and ask them to contact us with any updates." He drops his head against the window.

I'm cold, and my body shakes uncontrollably. As much as I want Alex to tell me what the officer said, I'm equally afraid to hear any more.

It feels like an eternity before he turns from the window and slowly makes his way across the room to sit next to me. He takes my hands in his while he relays the officer's story.

Dad recently noticed the pill count on some of the controlled substances was off. Although he had a security system in place, he began to suspect it might be an employee, so he secretly had a silent alarm installed.

They were at church for the Christmas Eve service when Dad got a notification on his cell that the alarm had gone off. He and Mom figured it was a false alarm and left the church to shut it off. When they got there, Dad noticed the employee entrance was propped open. Instead of waiting for the police to arrive, he went inside. A few seconds later, Mom heard a gunshot. She got scared and crouched down in the car. When she heard the metal door slam off the brick building, she tried to peek out the window, but all she saw was the back of a man running away.

"The police arrived within minutes and called for an ambulance." Alex rubs my hands gently as he speaks. "Your father sustained a gunshot to his chest. All the officer could tell me was he was life-flighted to a trauma hospital near Branson."

I feel bile rising in my throat, causing me to jump up and run to the bathroom. I make it just in time to vomit in the toilet. Alex follows behind me and holds my hair. When I'm sure my stomach is empty, I lean against the wall and stare up at the ceiling. Alex wipes my face with a warm washcloth before lowering himself next to me.

"Is he alive?" I barely get the words out before sobs wrack my body.

"He's in surgery." He uses his thumbs to wipe the tears from my face. "The officer said things don't look good."

I drop my head in my hands as guilt washes over me. "This is my fault." If I had just said something weeks ago, I could've prevented this.

"Look at me, Natalie," Alex demands. "This is not your fault. You had nothing to do with this."

"But I did." It takes a minute to calm myself enough to tell Alex about the night Tommy showed up at the store. The further I get into the story, the tenser Alex gets. "I'm sorry," I cry and reach for Alex's hands. "Please tell me you forgive me."

"I wish you had told me sooner." He pulls me into his lap and wraps his arms around me, holding me tight. "I forgive you, baby girl."

I tuck my head into his chest, and he rocks me back and forth, whispering soothing words to me while I cry. We stay like this until I have no more tears to shed.

ALEX

J've never experienced pure rage before, but when Natalie tells me how Tommy put his hands on her, pushed her into the store, and forced her to give him pills, I only see red. He laid his filthy hands on what isn't his to touch. It takes every ounce of self-control I possess to remain calm while she finishes her story. Her heart's hurting enough; I don't need to add to it by acting on the rage that's pulsing through my veins.

Once her crying subsides, I help her up. "Let me make you a cup of tea." She doesn't react, just silently follows down the hall into the living room. I get her settled on the couch and cover her with her favorite blanket. Her eyes are filled with so much pain; it nearly brings me to my knees. But right now, I have to be strong for her. "I'll be right back."

I call Viktor and quietly relay the information and ask him to book three tickets to Branson on the next available flight.

"I'll be up in a minute," Viktor assures me. "Boss, is she okay?"

I know he's grown fond of Natalie after all the time they've spent together. I look to where she sits, tears silently streaming down her face. "I don't know."

"Take care of your girl. I'll take care of the details," he says and disconnects the phone. He's more than a trusted employee; he's become a friend. If he says he'll take care of it, I can be confident, knowing this is one thing I don't have to worry about.

Next, I send a text to Maxim.

(Me) We have a problem. Call me on the secure line.

While I wait for his response, I finish making Natalie's tea and bring it to her.

"Thank you," she whispers as she takes the cup from my outstretched hand.

"Viktor's making flight arrangements." I brush a curl from her face. "He'll be up as soon as he has the tickets."

I get a text and check it quickly.

(Maxim) I'll call in a minute, heading to the office.

"I have to make a call. I'll be in my office if you need me. I'll only be a few minutes." I don't want to leave Natalie's side, but I need to talk to Maxim.

The phone is already ringing when I get there. I hurry to my desk and lift the receiver.

"What's wrong?" Maxim asks, his voice cold and severe. He knows I wouldn't ask for a secure call unless there were extreme circumstances.

I relay every detail I was given by the police, as well as the information from Natalie.

"Is her father alive?"

"So far." I rub the back of my neck. "But the prognosis is grim."

"And they haven't arrested Thomas Moore yet?"

"No," I growl. The rage I thought I had tampered rushes through me once again. "The security cameras were down. The police are going through the crime scene looking for evidence."

"Send me his picture. I'll get things in motion." I can hear the clicks of his keyboard. "Irina's already packing. I will be on the first flight available."

"I wouldn't ask—"

"I know," he says. "We will find him, and he will pay."

The line goes dead.

I drop my head into my hands and grab my hair. I promised myself I'd never cross that line—that I'd never ask Maxim to step in like this. But there's also never been anyone I've loved so much that I'd want to kill another for hurting them. I'm at war inside myself.

"Alex."

I hear Natalie's soft voice and look up. She's standing in the doorway wrapped in my blanket. Her eyes puffy and red from crying. I push up from my chair and go to her.

"Viktor's here," she says.

I wrap my arms around her, pulling her against my chest. "Let's go find out when we leave."

"I didn't think you'd go back with me after the way my parents treated you."

I freeze mid-step and put my finger under her chin, forcing her to look at me. "None of that matters now. They're your parents, and they need you—they need us, and we'll be there."

Her eyes fill with tears once again as she lays her head against my chest. "Thank you, Sir."

"You don't need to thank me. That's what family does." I take her hand. "Come, let's go see what Viktor has for us."

TOMMY

I just needed a few pills, that's all.

They were supposed to be in church.

Easy in, easy out. I had the bottle in my hand. I was just about to grab the pills when Stanley came in.

"Tommy? Is that you?" he called from the door. "What are you doing, son?"

I didn't stop to think. I pulled the gun from my waistband and pointed it at him. "Don't come any closer."

His eyes moved to my other hand, where I held the bottle of Oxy. Recognition came across his face.

"You're the one taking the pills."

"Shut the fuck up," I yelled. "Move out of my way, and this can all be over with."

"Thomas, let's talk about this," he said. "Just put the gun away and—"

Everything happened so fast. Stanley took a step toward me.

I didn't realize I pulled the trigger until his body fell at my feet. A pool of red quickly formed around him.

I shot him.

I'll never forget his eyes, the way they stared at me—blank and lifeless.

And the blood…

There was so much blood.

The pill bottle fell from my hand.

All I wanted was a few pills, and now I think I've killed someone.

I ran for the door and kept running to the only person I knew would keep me safe; the one who's always kept my secrets.

NATALIE

*V*iktor got us a flight at 11 a.m.. It doesn't leave us long before we have to leave for JFK. We'll be cutting it close, but Alex is confident we'll make it on time.

On the way, he calls Brandon and lets them know what happened. Lana wants to talk to me, but I can't handle talking to anyone right now. Alex promises her I'll call her as soon as I can.

Thankfully, we get through airport security in record time. Before I know it, we're en route to Missouri.

"Try to close your eyes," Alex encourages me.

"I can't. Every time I close them, all I see is Tommy pointing a gun at my father." The nightmare I was having has come to life, and now I know who the gun was aimed at. I put my head on Alex's shoulder, tears softly fall. "He must've been so scared."

"Don't go there, Natalie," Alex says softly.

Although I nod my head in agreement, I can't stop thinking about it.

My dad's been shot.

My parents and I haven't spoken in a month.

I don't know what's going to happen when we get to the hospital. Will Mom even want me there? What will she say when she sees Alex is with me? So many questions keep going through my mind; so many unknowns. I'm thankful the flight isn't long, and I won't have to wait much longer to get the answers, one way or another.

We finally land, and the feeling is surreal. Viktor and I came through this same airport a few days ago. When everything was okay. I'm thankful both Alex and Viktor are here and are taking care of everything. All I'm able to do is smile when appropriate and nod my head when spoken to. How did things change so quickly?

Alex leads me out of the airport, where Viktor is waiting in a rental car. None of us talk as we drive to the hospital. The only sound is the dinging of Alex's phone with an incoming text. He checks it and types a quick return.

"Was that Lana and Brandon?" I ask.

"Uh-huh," Alex mumbles, distracted by another incoming message.

I turn my attention out the window. Although nature has provided a beautiful Christmas backdrop, all I see is the heavy snow load the trees' branches are forced to hold. It feels much like the weight on my shoulders right now.

"We're here," Alex says, his tone somber.

We're here—the hospital. A war rages inside me. I want to rush in, hold my father's hand, and know he's still with us. But I'm still struggling with anger and hurt. How do I reconcile my feelings? I don't have time to answer that because Alex is out of the car, giving my hand a light tug.

My body moves of its own accord, following Alex's lead. He doesn't let go of my hand as we go into the hospital and take the elevator to the ICU floor. This part of the hospital is quiet and filled with the heaviness of the lives hanging in the balance.

As we round the corner, the waiting room comes into view.

"Mom," I say softly.

She raises her head. Her eyes are swollen from crying; she looks tired and weary as she slowly rises from her seat. Tears began to roll down her cheeks, but she makes no move toward us.

"We're here," I whisper. "You aren't alone now."

As if my words give her permission to move, she walks over to us. "I'm so scared, Natalie," she says between sobs.

"I know Mom, me too." I pull her in for a hug. "How's Dad?"

"I don't know. They said they'd give me an update when he's out of surgery."

"He's still in surgery?" Panic rises in me. He's been in there almost all day. Something must be very wrong.

Mom turns to Alex. "I'm so sorry."

"No apologies necessary, Mrs. Clarke," he says and grabs her hands. "We're here now, and we'll face this together."

We wait for what feels like forever until finally, we hear the sound of footsteps on the tiled floor coming closer. I look up and see a tall man with dark skin walking in our direction. He's pulling his surgical cap off. His shoulders slump, and I prepare myself for bad news.

"Mrs. Clarke?" The doctor asks.

"Yes," she answers. "This is my daughter Natalie and her boyfriend, Alex."

"I'm Dr. Fitzgerald. I operated on your husband." We exchange handshakes before the doctor motions to the nearby chairs. "Let's sit down and discuss the injuries your husband sustained."

We each take a seat in the waiting room chairs. The doctor takes his time explaining my father's injuries to us.

Dad sustained a gunshot to his right lung; the bullet lodged itself in the lower lobe. The damage caused his uninjured lung to fill with blood, which had to drain slowly. Because the injured lung wasn't functioning, he was placed on a heart-lung bypass machine for the past twelve hours while they operated—this allowed time for the wounded lung to be repaired and begin to aerate again.

"Is he going to be okay?" Mom asks, desperation in her voice.

"He's currently on a ventilator and in a medically induced coma. We're giving his body some time to heal and repair itself. The next few hours are critical." The doctor pauses. "Tomorrow, we'll wean him off the ventilator and see if he can breathe on his own. If he does, that's a good sign."

"And if he doesn't?" Nausea bubbles in my stomach.

"If he doesn't, we'll be forced to consider a lung transplant." The doctor leans forward. "Because of his injury and the amount of blood loss, we'll only consider that as a last resort," he says. "For now, we watch and wait."

"Can we see him?" Mom asks.

The doctor looks between us. "We can only allow two people in at a time."

"Mrs. Clarke and Natalie will go in; they're family," Alex interjects before anyone has a chance to answer. "I have a few calls to make. I'll be out here if you need me."

"Thank you."

Mom and I follow the doctor to Dad's room. When I look in, I freeze. He's hooked up to so many wires and tubes I can hardly see his face.

"It's okay," Dr. Fitzgerald says and places his hand on my shoulder. "You can go closer."

I look up at the doctor, who nods his head in encouragement.

Dad's body is still and pale—he looks lifeless. The steady cadence of the monitor is a comforting sound letting me know he's still alive.

Dr. Fitzgerald checks Dad and makes a few notes in his chart.

"We'll watch him closely tonight," he explains. "Tomorrow, I'll be back to wake him up."

"Can he hear us?"

"I believe he can," he answers in a kind voice. "It's okay to talk to him. Let him know you're here."

I move closer to the bed and grab his hand; it's warm.

"Daddy, I'm here." Tears pour down my cheeks when there's

no response. What did I expect? Did I think he'd hear my voice and open his eyes?

Mom walks over and puts her arm around me. I rest my head on her and allow my tears to fall.

For the next few hours, Mom and I whisper to Dad, hoping that wherever he is, he can hear us and know he's not alone.

ALEX

While Natalie and her mom visit with Mr. Clarke, I go back outside in search of Viktor. I want an update.

He's standing a short distance from the walkway where people meander in and out of the main door. Even though his back is to me, I can see he's on the phone. When I walk up to him, he nods in acknowledgment of my presence.

"Keep me updated," he says and disconnects the call.

There's no trace of kindness left on his face when he turns to me. "Maxim's in the air. He's called some local contacts who've dispatched a team and are in Northmeadow now."

"Have they found Tommy yet?"

"They checked cameras near the pharmacy and know he got away on foot. They tracked him a few blocks but lost him when he entered the woods."

"Dammit." I pace back and forth.

"We'll find him, Alex." His voice leaves no room for question.

"Did you have any luck with the other part?"

"Yes. Ms. Campbell wasn't happy that her Christmas dinner was interrupted, but after some insistence, she relented. Everything's been taken care of."

"Good." I'm done taking chances with Natalie's safety.

"Get back up to her, boss. I'll let you know as soon as I hear something." Viktor places his hand on my shoulder. "He can't stay hidden forever."

I take a minute to gather my thoughts before returning upstairs. I check at the nurses' station to see if Natalie and her mom are still in her father's room. The nurse informs me that Mrs. Clarke is in the family room and would like to see me. She points me in the right direction, and I walk down the hall.

Although the door is cracked open, I knock.

"Come in," she calls.

I enter and close the door behind me.

"Please sit for a minute, Alex," she says. "We need to talk."

I take a seat across from the hospital bed where she's reclining.

"I was exhausted. The nurses insisted I come in here and try to rest," she says. "I don't know how they expect me to do that."

"You're going to need your strength for when Mr. Clarke wakes up," I say.

"Alex," she says and fidgets with her fingers in her lap. I see where Natalie gets that habit from. "Stanley and I were wrong about you."

"Mrs. Clarke, we don't have to do this right now."

"Yes, we do," she says and sits up. "And please call me, Charlotte."

For the next half-hour, we discuss everything that's transpired over the past few months.

"We've known Tommy since he was a baby. Tommy's mom left him when he was a toddler. She never told anyone who his father was. His Aunt Delia raised him," she says. "He and Natalie grew up together; we all assumed they'd get married." She turns her gaze out the window. "We never knew why they broke up. Tommy told us one story, and Natalie told us nothing; she just stopped coming home." She wipes the fresh tears that are falling. "Stanley and I have always lived in Northmeadow.

It's all we know. First, we lost Evan," she says, her voice catching on a sob. "Then Natalie left us and wouldn't come home. We were scared." She pauses. "We never saw this coming."

"It's okay, Charlotte." The devastation on her face is too much. She's alone and hurting. I get up and walk to the bed. "May I?" I ask.

She nods in approval.

I sit next to her and take her shaking hands in mine.

"Natalie and I are here now. You don't have to go through this alone."

"We listened to Tommy and believed his lies. We were so unfair to Natalie and so wrong about you," she says. "Can you ever forgive us?"

"Already done." Life's too short to hold onto grudges. I look Charlotte in the eyes. "I want you to know I love your daughter very much."

"I can see that now." She lowers her gaze. "I just hope it's not too late to fix things with her."

"It's never too late," I say. "And when Mr. Clarke recovers, we'll have a lot to celebrate." I'm hoping our happy news will give Charlotte something positive to hold onto. "Yesterday, I asked Natalie to marry me, and she said yes."

"My little girl is getting married." She brings her hands to her mouth in surprise.

Taking the phone from my pocket, I open the photo gallery and show her the pictures from yesterday.

"She looks so happy." Charlotte smiles through her tears.

"When Mr. Clarke wakes, I'd like to ask him for his blessing—"

She stops me mid-sentence. "You already have our blessing."

I know how important it is for Natalie to have the love and support of her family. I hate that it's taken a tragedy for this healing to happen, but I'm thankful anyway. I wrap my arms around Charlotte. Her body remains stiff for a brief moment before she relaxes and returns the hug.

"Would you mind walking me back to my husband's room?" Charlotte asks.

"I'd be glad to." I stand and offer her my arm.

We walk down the hall in companionable silence. As we near the room, my phone starts ringing.

"I have to take this," I say when I see it's Viktor. "Excuse me, please."

She nods her head, and I watch as she makes the turn into Mr. Clarke's room before I answer my phone.

"Viktor?"

"We got him, sir."

"Where is he?" I ask as I pick up my pace, heading to the elevator.

"I have the address," Viktor says. "Maxim just arrived. He and his men are waiting for us there."

"I'm on my way down."

I hang up and send Natalie a text.

(Me) I'm going to get us a hotel room. I'll be back in a little while. Text me if you need anything.

I can't tell her where I'm really going.

(Natalie) Okay. I love you.
(Me) I love you too.

When I get outside, Viktor's waiting at the main entrance in the running car.

I get in and ask. "Where was he?"

"He was with a girl, Ash something," he says. "She was hiding him in an old fishing shack."

My hand pounds the car door. "Ashlynn. Natalie's supposed best friend."

I don't know where Viktor is taking us, other than it's far

from civilization. We turn onto a gravel road and drive for a few more miles until a small wooden cabin comes into view.

"Where the hell are we?" I ask. I've allowed the anger I was suppressing for Natalie's sake to rise to the surface.

"It's a safe house," he says. "It belongs to Maxim's contacts."

I'm amazed at the lengths Maxim's reach goes.

Viktor barely has the car in park before I'm opening the door and jumping out. Maxim steps out the front door as I approach.

"Where is he?" I'm anxious to get my hands on him, to instill the same fear in him that he caused for Natalie, then to watch the life drain from his eyes.

"Alexander." Maxim places his hands on my shoulders. "First, you must calm down." He stops me from entering the building.

When I actually take a look at him, I see he's the picture of calm. He's dressed in a perfectly pressed shirt and black pants. How is he so put together right now?

"I need to see him. He needs to pay for what he's done."

"And you will," he says. "But first, we need to talk. Come with me." We walk away from the building instead of going inside.

"I'm going to kill him."

"Alexander, you've never taken a life before. It changes you." He looks straight ahead. "You don't have to worry about legal implications; I'll take care of that." He stops walking and faces me. There's a cold edge in his eyes. It's something I've never seen before. They're dark and tell the story of a man who's seen and done terrible things. "You need to worry about what happens here." He puts his hand on my heart. "That man hurt your submissive. He may have murdered her father. It's only right that I give you the choice of taking his life by your hand. But you need to understand it *will* change you. It's a decision you can never undo."

I haven't thought about what happens after or how I'll

explain to Natalie that I've killed someone. I've only considered the hate I'm feeling and the vengeance I wish to extract.

Suddenly every high and low I've experienced since yesterday bubbles up inside me. I walk a few steps away. A primal yell explodes from deep inside. I fall to my knees and drop my head into my hands.

When I look up, Maxim stands before me. His face void of all emotion.

"I want to see him."

"It's time. Let's go."

I stand, and together, we walk back to the building.

Viktor's waiting in front of the door. When he sees us approaching, he opens it and steps aside, allowing us to enter, closing the door behind us.

The inside isn't what I thought. Bright lights illuminate the room, but you'd never know it from the outside. The windows must have a privacy coating on them. There are no interior walls; it's one large open space. The only piece of furniture is an old wooden chair and tied to that chair is Tommy.

When I move closer, I see Maxim's men have already taken a turn with him. His nose is broken, and one eye is swollen shut. He raises his head and meets my stare. The man still has the nerve to snarl at me.

"Well, well," he spits out the words. "Looks like the man of the hour is finally here."

His cocky attitude pushes me past my breaking point. I pick up the pace of my strides and punch him in the gut. The air leaves him in a woosh, and he struggles to catch his breath.

This is my moment. I can snuff the life out of this bastard for what he's done. I turn my back on him but make no move to walk away. "You should die for what you've done to Natalie," I say in a deep, gravelly voice.

If I kill him, there will be consequences. Can I live with them? Long minutes pass before I speak again.

"I've decided to give you one chance. You will turn yourself into the Northmeadow police and plead guilty to all charges. You will waive your right to a hearing, and you will go to prison." I walk to one of Maxim's men. "Give me your gun." He looks to Maxim, who nods his approval before handing it to me. "Otherwise." I walk back to Tommy and point the gun at his head, my finger on the trigger poised to shoot. "You die now."

There's a long pause before realization washes over Tommy, and his shoulders slump. The only way he's walking out of here alive is if he turns himself in.

"Fine, I'll do it."

I lower the gun and pull out my phone, then dial Officer Cooper's number. When the officer answers, I put the phone on speaker.

Tommy identifies himself and makes arrangements for where and when he'll turn himself in.

I disconnect the phone and hand the gun to Maxim before walking out.

A few minutes later, I watch as Maxim's men drag Tommy from the building and push him into the back of their car.

"Come, Alexander," Maxim says. "I'll ride with you."

Viktor follows the other car to the designated location.

Tommy is pushed out of the car and left alone to wait for the police to show up.

We watch from a short distance away to make sure he keeps his agreement; otherwise, his life is over.

When the officers arrive, Tommy's handcuffed and placed into the back of a police car. Officer Cooper looks around almost as if he can sense he's being watched. When he finds no one, he returns to his car and drives away with Tommy in the backseat.

It's only then that I'm able to breathe again.

"That was a brave decision that only a man of great integrity would make." Maxim places a hand on my shoulder. "I'm proud of you, Alexander."

I don't know how to respond, so I settle for a nod of my head. "Let's get you back to the hospital."

On the long drive back, I make a phone call and reserve a hotel room.

NATALIE

*M*om and I are sitting in Dad's room when my
phone rings.

"It's Officer Cooper," I say before I answer the phone.

He proceeds to tell me Tommy agreed to turn himself in. I'm
stunned when he says that Tommy confessed to everything and
waived his right to a trial.

When Alex returns, I tell him about the odd call, but he isn't
surprised.

"Do you know something about this?" I ask.

"Be thankful he's in custody, and don't overthink it."

I'm sure Alex had something to do with it; I just can't figure
out how.

We stay until visiting hours are over. Mom refuses to leave
the hospital, opting to stay in the family room. Alex and I say
goodnight and promise to be back first thing in the morning.

The next day we're gathered in Dad's room with Dr.
Fitzgerald and his team. Dad's vitals were stable through the
night, so they're moving ahead with the plan to remove the
ventilator this afternoon.

Alex wraps his arm around me, holding me tight. The room
is silent, except for the soft murmuring between the doctor and

the staff as they adjust his IV and remove the tube from his throat. The monitor keeps a steady rhythm, but Dad's eyes do not open.

Dr. Fitzgerald assures us Dad is breathing on his own, that we've crossed a huge hurdle, and he'll be called if there's any change.

I'm glad the doctor is confident because as the hours tick by and there's no movement from Dad, my hope is beginning to wane. I put my head on Alex's shoulder and sigh softly.

"You should try talking to him, Mrs. Clarke," Alex says. "Maybe if he hears your voice it'll encourage him to wake up."

"I'll try," Mom says.

She gets up from her chair and sits on the edge of Dad's bed. "Stanley, can you hear me?" She leans in closer. "It's time to wake up."

We wait and watch, but there's no change.

"Stanley, I said it's time to wake up." Her voice a bit more forceful.

"Mom," I say. "He's not going to want to wake up if he's being yelled at." I laugh.

Mom nods in agreement. I'm surprised she didn't have something cross to say.

This time when she looks at him, Mom's features soften. She takes his hand and begins stroking it with her thumb. It's the first time in many years I've seen her show Dad any kind of affection.

"Stanley, I need you to wake up," she says quietly. "Our little girl got engaged. She's here with her fiancé, and they want to tell you all about it."

I look up at Alex, who's standing next to me. "How does she know?" I whisper.

Before he can respond, Dad begins to stir.

"It's okay, Daddy, take your time."

"I'll go let the nurses know he's awake," Alex says and hurries to the door.

A few minutes later, Alex returns with a nurse and Dr. Fitzgerald.

The room is a whirlwind of activity as they take Dad's vitals and assess his pain level.

"Do the police—" Dad tries to speak but has to stop to catch his breath.

"It's okay, Dad." I try to reassure him. "Tommy turned himself in; he's going to jail."

"I'm sorry," he says and reaches for my hand.

I swallow, trying to hold back the tears. "I know, Dad," I say and kiss his cheek. "I forgive you."

It's been three days since Dad woke up. He's doing so well he's being moved out of the ICU today. Although Dad's lung sustained significant damage, and he has a long road ahead of him, Dr. Fitzgerald is optimistic that he'll make a full recovery. Dad's starting rehab in the hospital tomorrow, and if all goes well, he'll be strong enough to come home in a few weeks.

My dad being shot has changed our relationship with my parents. Alex asked Dad's permission for my hand in marriage. Dad readily said yes. They've finally accepted that Alex and I are together. My mom even bought bridal magazines from the hospital gift shop to start planning our wedding.

Alex and Dad spend hours on the computer whispering to each other. Every time I ask what they're looking at, I'm told *nothing* and that I need to be patient. The two of them are clearly up to something.

I feel like I'm living in a dream, one I hope to never wake from.

Today, Alex and I are driving back to Northmeadow. The night of the shooting, Mom came to the hospital with nothing but the clothes she was wearing. Since Mom refused to leave Dad's side, the hospital gave her scrubs to change into. But we're going to be here for a few weeks, and she needs her own clothes.

It's a two-hour round trip, so I'm hoping we make it back to the hospital tonight. I want to spend as much time with Dad as possible before returning to work next week. Then I'll only be able to see him on the weekends until he comes home.

We arrive in Northmeadow at lunchtime. "Why don't we stop at the diner and grab something to eat?" Alex suggests.

"That sounds good. It'll be nice to eat somewhere other than the hospital café."

The diner's parking lot is packed. Apparently, everyone else in town had the same idea. Knowing how gossip travels, I prepare myself for the onslaught of questions that's about to occur when we walk inside.

Leslie, the diner's owner, spots us as soon as we walk in. She doesn't waste a second before coming over. "How's your dad, honey?"

"He's doing okay. Anxious to get home."

"I couldn't believe it when I heard Tommy Moore did it," she says. "Mrs. Smith was in yesterday. She told me she heard Tommy was after drugs."

"What happened was a tragedy," I say. "Thankfully, Dad's on the mend, and we can put this behind us." I don't respond to the comments about Tommy. I refuse to take part in town gossip.

"Well, let him know we're all pulling for him," she says and then sits us at a table. "I'll be back in a minute to take your order."

"Well done, baby girl," Alex says. "You handled that like a pro."

"I've had years of practice," I say and laugh.

Alex excuses himself to use the restroom. While I wait, I look over the menu even though I already know what I'm ordering when someone approaches the table. I look up and see Mr. Meadows is standing over me.

"May I?" He gestures to the empty chair.

"Alex will be back in a minute." I glance in the direction of the bathrooms, hoping he hurries.

Despite my warning, Mr. Meadows sits anyway. I place the menu on the table in front of me. I'm instantly on edge. Something about this doesn't feel right.

"I'm glad I ran into you today," he says. "We need to make arrangements for you to come by the school and clean out your office." He sits back, a satisfied look on his face. "Figured you wouldn't stick around here very long."

"Clean out my office?" I ask. This doesn't make any sense. "Why would I need to do that?"

His eyes narrow as he looks at me. "Your termination was accepted, and your contract has been paid in full."

"Termination?"

"We've already started the process of hiring your replacement."

I'm about to ask him what he's talking about when Alex returns.

"Excuse me," Alex says. "I believe that's my seat."

Mr. Meadows stands, chest to chest like he's ready to challenge Alex. But there's no comparison between the men. Where Alex is tall and well-built, Mr. Meadows is short and overweight. Even more noticeable is the confidence Alex exudes.

"I was just leaving." Mr. Meadows shoots me a cocky grin as he walks away.

"What did he want?"

I stare at Alex, who's now sitting across from me, looking at his menu.

"Did you buy out my contract?"

"Yes." Alex doesn't hesitate with his answer.

"How could you?" I ask. "We talked about this. That was my job."

"Natalie." Alex reaches across the table for my hands, but I pull away. "Natalie, please."

"No." I push my chair back, nearly knocking it over in my hurry to get up. "You know how much this job means to me."

"Natalie, sit down," he says in a low tone.

"You took it away from me without even asking." I put my hands on the sides of my head, which is now pounding.

"Natalie, wait," Alex calls after me.

The walls feel like they're closing in on me. "I have to get out of here." With hurried steps, I reach the door and go out. I don't know where I'm going or how I'm going to get there. I just need to leave.

Alex quickly catches up and takes my hand. "After what happened, you can't stay here any longer."

"You went behind my back and decided on my career without asking me." I pull my hand from his. "Staying here and working—we agreed on it. Those kids depend on me, and you ruined it." I turn my back on him and press my hands to my eyes, fighting back angry tears. "Just go."

"You don't mean that." Alex turns me to face him. "Let's talk about this."

"You should've thought about that first," I spit the words at him. "This is over." Slipping the engagement ring off my finger, I force it in his palm. "I want you to leave."

"Natalie, please. Let's get in the car and—"

"Red," I say the one word I hoped I'd never have to use.

Alex freezes as soon as the single syllable falls from my lips.

He says nothing. His eyes reflect the horror I'm sure he sees in mine. We're frozen in time; both of us afraid to move, fearful of what comes next. I know the moment the significance of what's just happened hits him—his shoulders fall, and he walks away.

I have to turn my back. As angry as I am, I can't watch him leave. I listen to the sound of his retreating footsteps and will myself not to call out to him. I don't move until I hear his car pull out of the lot.

Alex is gone.

It's over.

I'm able to keep my emotions in check long enough to call a cab. I can't believe I was stupid enough to think I could have a man like him or that he was different than anyone else in my life.

Thankfully, it's a short ride to my parent's house because I can't hold back the tears much longer. I pay the fare and slowly drag my feet up the sidewalk and into the house. After closing the door behind me, my body slides down the wall. The dam lets loose, and tears begin to pour down my face.

Desperate for someone to talk to, I call Lana.

"Hello?" Lana answers.

"It's me."

"What's wrong?" she asks, concern laces her voice. "Is your Dad ok?"

"Yes," I say, trying to find the right words, but there are none, so I just say it. "I called my safe word and told Alex to leave."

"What?" she asks, clearly shocked by my statement. "Why?"

"He knew I said no, and he did it anyway. He ruined my career," I say between sobs. "I don't even think he cared."

"Nat, you know that's not true," she says softly. "He was scared too. He did what he thought was necessary to protect you."

"He went too far." I thought she'd be on my side, but instead, she's defending him. "Listen, I have to go. I have to get some things and get back to the hospital. I'll talk to you later." I hang up without giving her a chance to respond. She tries to call back, but I send her call to voicemail and turn off my phone.

ALEX

*J*t takes a few minutes for what she said to sink in. *Red.* She called her safe word. I've never felt so helpless in my life. There was nothing else I could do. Even though I walked away, I left a part of my heart in that parking lot.

I haven't gone back to New York. I can't make myself buy a plane ticket. I have to stay close to her, so I drive back to Branson and get another hotel room.

Once I'm settled in the room, I call Brandon.

"Hello?" he answers.

"I messed up. She called her safe word," I say. Then something unfamiliar happens, tears start to fall. "She left me."

"What did you do?" he asks.

"I bought out her contract and told the school she was quitting."

I walk to the bed and lay down.

"Shit, Alex," Brandon says, shocked. "I thought we talked about giving her the freedom to make her own choices?"

"That was before her psycho ex almost killed her father." I cover my face with my hand. "What do I do now? I can't go after her; my hands are tied."

"Where are you?" Brandon asks.

"I came back to the hotel. I got another room," I say. "I can't leave."

"Let me talk to Lana, and I'll call you back in a little bit." He pauses. "We'll try to figure this out."

NATALIE

$\mathcal{A}$ s soon as school resumes after the holidays, I visit Ms. Campbell's office.

"Is there any way you'd reconsider and allow me to keep my job?" I ask. It's a longshot, but I have to try, at least.

"I'm sorry, but that's not possible. We've already hired your replacement." She hesitates before speaking. "May I say something personal?"

"Of course."

"I know you're disappointed at this turn of events, but I also understand why Mr. Montgomery did what he did. Only a man in love with a woman would have gone through such lengths to keep her safe."

I know her words are meant to comfort me, but I'm unable to reconcile Alex's words with his actions.

"Can I see my students to say goodbye?"

"Unfortunately, because you're no longer an employee, I can't allow that." She places her hand on my shoulder. "You can write them each a note, and I'll personally deliver them.

"Thank you." I walk to the door. "I'll go clean my office out now."

"Natalie," she says.

I turn to face her. "Yes?"

"Please use me as a reference when you look for another position." She smiles. "I'm going to miss you. But I know you're destined for greater things."

Her words and her offer of a job reference are very kind but do little to mend the fracture in my heart.

I sit at my desk for the last time and write a note to each of my students, assuring them they'll be in good hands. The letter to Mary is the hardest to write. We were supposed to meet with her parents next week. I have to believe I'm leaving her with enough tools to navigate the rough waters ahead of her successfully.

I leave the notes on the desk.

I walk out of Northmeadow High with a heavy heart, closing yet another chapter in my life.

Dad's getting stronger every day. The doctors are amazed at his progress and say that he'll be discharged next week. A physical therapist will come to the house three days a week to continue therapy from home. Mom's going to have her hands full taking care of him. I can't leave the responsibility on her, so I decide to move home. It'll be easier if I'm here to help out.

I find myself packing up my things once again, this time at the motel. Marshall's been helping me all afternoon.

"I'm gonna miss you here, kid," he says as he loads the last of my things into my car.

"I never thought I'd say this, but I'm gonna miss it here too."

"I'm sorry to hear things didn't work out with that guy," Marshall says. "If you're ever free, I'd love to take you out."

"That's a very nice offer, but I'm going to have to pass."

"Can't blame a guy for trying," he says and shrugs his shoulders.

"Thank you for everything," I say and give him a quick hug.
I get in my car, and he shuts the door.
He waves goodbye as I pull out of the parking lot.

NATALIE

$\mathcal{M}$y parents and I sit in Dad's hospital room having lunch when they ask again about what happened between Alex and me.

"Explain to me why you broke off the engagement?" Dad asks.

"He bought out my contract, even though we agreed I would work the five years. He made me lose my job." I feel like a broken record. "We agreed on this months ago."

"That was before," Mom says. "I think the circumstances are different now, don't you?"

"No." I take a bite of my sandwich.

"And you haven't heard from him at all?" Dad asks.

I can't tell them about our contractual relationship and that I safe worded. I ended it. There's no going back, no reason for him to call me.

"I think you should try to call him," Mom says. "Talk to him. Give him a second chance."

"Says the person who didn't want me with him in the first place." I laugh.

"Things are different now," she says. "We were wrong about him. That man loves you."

That might be true, but he crossed a line. I've resigned myself to the fact that I'm probably meant to be single.

With my parents coming home in a few days, I decided to go shopping to restock the kitchen. It took over an hour at the store. Most of the time was spent fielding countless questions about how my Dad is doing and how no one in town can believe Tommy could do such a thing. I couldn't wait to get out of there.

I'm driving down the street and notice an unfamiliar car parked in front of my house; it looks like there are two people sitting in it. What now? I make the turn into my driveway, hoping to just go about my business.

When I shut my car off, the people get out of theirs. I look in the rearview mirror and see who it is. I almost can't believe my eyes. I throw open my door and jump out, running over to meet Lana. She wraps me in a hug. Brandon stands to the side, watching us.

"What are you guys doing here?" I ask.

"We're here for an intervention," Lana answers. "Can we come in?"

An intervention? I hesitate before answering. "I guess so."

"Hear her out," Brandon says and places his hand on my arm. "If it doesn't change your mind, we won't say another word about it."

"Okay." I agree, confident there's nothing Lana can say that will change the situation.

Opening the trunk, I grab a few grocery bags; Brandon grabs a few, helping me carry them in. I unlock the door, stepping aside to let my guests go in first.

Brandon follows me to the kitchen. "Just put the bags on the table."

I quickly put away the perishables before I ask, "Can I get you guys something to drink?"

"Water would be great," Brandon says.

I get three glasses and fill them with ice water. Lana helps me carry them into the living room, where Brandon is already sitting on the couch. She hands one to Brandon, who sets his drink on the coffee table in front of him. Lana sits next to him. I sit across from them in a chair, hoping this will be over fast.

"Alex is miserable," Lana says. "And you aren't much better."

Dark circles stain my face under my eyes from not sleeping. Between managing the store and driving back and forth to the hospital, I'm exhausted.

"It's been a rough few weeks," I say quietly. "It'll get better, eventually." I'm hoping to convince them as much as myself.

Lana looks at Brandon, who gives her an encouraging smile before she turns to me. "I need to tell you a story." Her expression changes to one of great sorrow. "It's not something I like talking about, but it's something you need to hear."

I sit back in my chair. Whatever this is, it's very important to Lana.

"I'm not sure where to start," she says. "I guess I just say it." She takes a deep breath. "My dad is the pakhan, the boss, of a group in the Bratva."

"Maxim's in the Russian mafia?" I ask and laugh at the absurdity of the idea.

"Yes," she says without a hint of amusement on her face.

"And I thought there wasn't anything more you could tell me about Maxim that would surprise me." I smile and shake my head. "But what does that have to do with Alex?"

"I had an older sister," she says, a far-off look in her eyes. "Jelena was five years older than me. She was smart and beautiful. I wanted to be just like her." She smiles sadly and grabs Brandon's hand. "I was ten years old when she was stolen. We were walking down the street when two men jumped out of a van and grabbed her; she was right next to me. Jelena yelled at me to run and not look back," Lana says and wipes the tears from her eyes.

"Oh, Lana. I'm so sorry." I had no idea she had a sister.

"They were human traffickers. Dad searched day and night for her, but even with all his connections, he got there too late. She'd already been sold and killed. Since then, Dad's used his position in the Bratva to fight the traffickers. He wasn't able to save Jelena, but he has saved many others."

I'm stunned. I don't know what to say.

"It's made Dad very overprotective of me," Lana says. "When I approached my father and told him I wanted to come to America to study, he went crazy." She laughs. "He knew my guards wouldn't be able to come with me. He wouldn't be able to protect me here, and that was unacceptable to him."

"I'm sure he was terrified something would happen to you," I add. "But I still don't see what this has to do—"

She puts her finger up. "Hang on. I'm getting to the part about Alex."

I sit back, trying to be patient.

"Dad didn't want to hold me back, so he called an old friend in the states," she explains. "This is where Alex comes in." Lana stops and smiles. "My parents and Alex's parents have been friends for many years."

I readjust my position on the chair. This story just got more interesting.

"He told Mr. Montgomery about my coming to the states and asked him if he knew anyone in NYC, possibly someone who was in the lifestyle. Mr. Montgomery gave him Alex's information."

Although Alex was a trained Dominant, he was struggling with the loss of his mother. He was living in New York City, but at that time, he'd walked away from BDSM. Mr. Montgomery was hoping Maxim could encourage Alex to get back into the lifestyle and that maybe he and Lana would click as a couple.

"Alex had never met my father. So, it allowed Dad to get to

know him without any pretense." She pauses, taking a drink of her water. "One of Dad's strengths is assessing people's character, and he was impressed with Alex's. They spent a great deal of time together, solidifying their business relationship." Lana pauses and looks at me.

This is where the story becomes more interesting, and the pieces begin falling into place.

"Dad's accounts with Alex are a front for his mission to stop human trafficking," Lana says. "They've set up an intricate web allowing others who are working toward the same goal to contact each other. I don't know how it all works." She throws her hands up. "It just does."

Her reaction makes me laugh and breaks some of the tension in the room.

"Dad's also responsible for reintroducing Alex to the lifestyle."

Okay, now we're getting somewhere.

"Dad recognized Alex had lost him focus, his direction. After they got to know each other better, he told Alex about the connection to his parents and the lifestyle. Dad asked Alex to check out a club with him," she says. "Alex was a bit resistant initially. He wasn't looking for a sub, but he agreed to go for Dad's sake."

"That's how Alex got involved at Fire and Ice," I say.

"Yes." Lana smiles. "It gave Dad the chance to see Alex's character and abilities as a Dominant. That's when he asked Alex to collar me."

The familiar feelings of betrayal creep up. "You and Alex were a couple?"

Secrets. I hate them.

"Alex and me?" Lana makes a face. "He's a great guy, but no."

Brandon steps in to continue the story. "What Lana's trying to explain." He pats her leg. "Is that Maxim asked Alex if he'd be willing to be responsible for Lana's safety. To let her wear his collar of protection."

"Doesn't wearing a collar symbolize a relationship—owner-ship?" I'm bewildered and still not sure I like where this is going.

"In some cases, yes, but there're other kinds of collars," Brandon says. "Lana was young and would be alone in a big city —in a foreign country. She was also a submissive who would be playing at a new club. Maxim wanted to ensure Lana had someone willing to protect her in his absence."

Brandon explains that a permanent collar is given to a slave or a submissive to symbolize their relationship. That's the one I'm familiar with. A collar of protection doesn't represent a part-nership but rather a Dominant's commitment to be responsible for another's safety. It also meant any Dominants interested in Lana couldn't approach her without getting Alex's permission.

"You and Alex were never a couple?" I ask, really hoping the answer is no. I can't lose any more people I love.

She shakes her head and scrunches her nose. "Nope, never a couple. Never played together."

Reaching in her purse, she pulls out a thin silver chain with a pendant hanging from it and hands it to me.

Tentatively I accept it and examine it closely.

"That was my collar," Lana says. "On the charm, you can see Alex's initials and the lowercase p to show I was under his protection."

I remember seeing this. "You wore this when I first met you."

"I wore it for almost two years." She smiles fondly, looking at the collar. "I was so excited to come here, but after Mom and Dad went home, I was lonely. Alex showed me the city and introduced me to his friends at the club. Without him, I probably would have packed up and gone back to Russia." She pauses for a minute before continuing. "It wasn't always smooth sailing." She looks at Brandon and laughs. "Alex can be overprotective.

There were decisions he made for me that I didn't always agree with."

Brandon laughs a full belly laugh. "Alex and Lana had some *very* heated disagreements. They became famous at the club. Star had to step in on more than one occasion."

That sounds just like Lana. She and Alex still fight like they're siblings.

"The thing is, he saw things and knew things I didn't. It was hard, but I had to learn to trust him to make the right decisions for me. And in the end, he was always right."

"This isn't the same, Lana," I argue.

"It is, Nat." She comes over and sits on the arm of the chair. "You may not see the big picture." She looks over her shoulder at Brandon. "I know you don't see the big picture."

"When he lost his mother, he gave up. He didn't want to get close to anyone, care for anyone, for fear of losing them. Then you came into his life and his carefully constructed walls crumbled," Brandon says. "After your Dad got shot and you told him everything that had happened with Tommy, he made some rash decisions…"

"That's an understatement," I add sarcastically. "We had an agreement, and he broke it."

"I agree with you there," Brandon says. "He and I talked about that, and he understands that he should have approached things differently. Alex is a protector, sometimes to a fault." He pauses. "He may be a Dominant, but he's human and sometimes screws up. But he's a good man. All he was thinking was that he couldn't risk losing you. I know you disagree with his decision—"

"Disagree? I more than disagree."

"That man loves you." Brandon's expression changes, the Dominant in him comes to the surface. "Do you love him?"

"Yes," I say softly.

"Do you trust him?"

"Brandon—"

"This lifestyle revolves around trust." Brandon stands up. "Do you trust him as your future husband and, more importantly, as your Dominant?"

I look down at my hands in my lap and allow my mind to wander back to the first night we met, how I allowed him to use a flogger on me when I didn't know him at all—I had just trusted my instincts. Over the past few years, we've shared many experiences, and he's never given me a reason to distrust him. He's always been there for me, even when I didn't deserve him.

Finally, I look up and meet Brandon's intense gaze. "Yes, I trust him."

"Get your coats, girls." He claps his hands together. "We're going for a ride."

Lana doesn't hesitate; she stands and grabs her coat.

I don't move, though.

"Where are we going?"

"This time, you have to trust me." Brandon shoots me a wicked grin as he heads toward the door. "Get up; let's go."

Lana grabs my hand, and I reluctantly follow; a semi-willing participant in whatever crazy scheme they've come up with.

Once we're in the car, Brandon turns around. "One more thing." He holds out a blindfold. "You need to put this on."

"You're seriously crazy; you know that?" I say, laughing but decide to play along with their game.

I take the offered blindfold and slip it over my eyes.

"Good girl. Sit back and relax."

He and Lana share a laugh.

I'm beginning to question the sanity of my friends.

I try to pay attention to the turns we're taking, hoping to figure out where we're going, but it only takes a few minutes before I'm all turned around. We drive for what feels like forever before the car stops.

"You may remove the blindfold now," Brandon says.

It takes my eyes a few seconds to focus. We're at the lake,

sitting in the driveway of a sweet little stone cottage. Luminaires line each side of a path leading to the front door.

"It's gorgeous," I say. "But what are we doing here?"

"Go knock on the door," Brandon says.

"But I don't—"

"Stop questioning and just trust me," Brandon chastises me. "Get out and go knock on the door."

With a shrug of my shoulders, I leave the safety of the car and take a few tentative steps toward the house. I stop, unsure if I should keep going or get back in the car. I hear a car door open and turn around.

"Keep moving forward," Brandon instructs.

Turning back toward the house, I continue walking and find myself at the door.

NATALIE

*B*efore I can knock, it opens. Alex is standing with one hand on the door. He's dressed in jeans and a dark blue shirt that clings to his muscles. Despite everything, I'm still drawn to him. My gaze travels up his body until it meets his eyes. The sadness in them takes my breath away.

"What are you doing here?" My voice is barely a whisper.

"Come in before you freeze out there." He steps aside, and I walk into the house. Before he closes the door, he waves to Brandon and Lana, who drive away.

The inside looks like it was recently remodeled. The quaint country feel of the cottage is mixed with modern touches. It's stunning.

"Do you like it?" Alex asks nervously.

"It's beautiful," I answer.

"I bought this for us. It was supposed to be a surprise for Christmas."

He bought this for us? My mind struggles to wrap itself around his words.

"This was going to be our home while you finished out your contract." He moves closer but doesn't try to touch me. "Then I thought maybe we'd go back to New York and use this as our vacation home." He pauses and takes a deep breath. "Natalie, I didn't mean to hurt you or betray your trust. Between what you told me Tommy did to you and what he did to your father, I went out of my mind with worry. I couldn't take any more chances. I was terrified of losing—"

"I know," I say. Although I understand why I'm still hurt.

"Can we talk?" he asks.

"Yes."

I follow him into the living room, where we sit on a large, sectional sofa. When I look closer, I begin to notice the small, personal details like the framed pictures of us sitting on the mantle over the fireplace. My favorite blanket from his apartment in New York is folded over the back of a chair. I'm not sure what to think. I have so many questions right now, but I have to stay focused. We have some serious issues to discuss.

"I entered our Dom/sub agreement with the intention of keeping my emotions out of it. I wasn't looking for a relationship. I thought by putting an ending date on us that it would protect us both," he says. "The closer that date came, the more I realized I didn't want to let you go. Somewhere along the line, I fell in love with you and couldn't imagine my life without you in it. I still can't imagine my life without you." Alex stands up and starts pacing, his nervous habit of choice.

"I understand falling in love complicates everything," I say. "But we agreed on this. I was staying to finish my contract. After the five years were up, we'd reevaluate and go from there. You went behind my back; you crossed a line." I pause. "As your submissive, I gave you my full trust."

"I screwed up and overstepped a boundary; I can't argue with you there," Alex says. "My actions forced you to use your safe word." He comes back to the couch and sits next to me. Regret is evident in his expression. "That's a position I never wanted to put you in. I was wrong, and I'm sorry." He hesitantly reaches for my hands.

"I forgive you," I say and willingly place my hands in his. "Where do we go from here?"

"As a man and as your Dominant, the last thing I wanted to do was hurt you. I want to be the one you can always count on, always believe in," Alex says. "The only thing I can do is ask if you'd be willing to give me another chance. Let me prove to you that you're everything to me. That I'm worthy of your submission."

"I didn't think there was an option to try again," I whisper. "After I safeworded."

"I put you in that position, baby girl. That's on me, not you." An uncertainty creeps across his expression. "Whether or not we move forward is your decision."

I don't answer right away. Instead, I get up and walk to the window. "I'm sure the view of the lake is stunning from here."

"It is," he replies.

I debate how long to keep him waiting for my decision and take my time before turning to face him. "I guess we have some renegotiating to do."

He raises an eyebrow. "You have the floor, Ms. Clarke."

I return to my place on the sofa next to him. "As your submissive, I agree to place my full trust in you to make decisions in my best interest," I say. "Where my career is concerned, we will discuss everything openly. My voice will be heard. You will not make any decisions behind my back."

"And as your Dominant, I promise to be the man you're expecting me to be. I will honor the trust you place in me, and I'll work every day to prove myself to you. I promise I will never again break a boundary we've put in place together. I will always listen to you before making a decision. But when the final decision has been made, I need to know you'll trust me enough to accept it."

"I will," I say. "No more secrets?"

"No more secrets." Alex agrees.

Without warning, he slides from his spot and kneels before

me. "You make me a better man, baby girl. Will you agree to be my submissive?"

"I will," I answer.

He pulls the ring from his pocket. "Will you marry me?"

My Dominant is the strongest and most honorable man I've ever known. Is he perfect? No. But he's perfect for me.

He owns my heart.

He's my soulmate.

"Yes, Sir. I'll marry you."

He slides the ring onto my finger. "Mine," he says as he pulls me against him.

I place a kiss on his lips. "Always and forever, Yours."

THE END

Dear reader,

We hope you enjoyed reading *Submitting To Him*. Please take a moment to leave a review, even if it's a short one. Your opinion is important to us.

Discover more books by T.L. Conrad at https://www.nextchapter.pub/authors/tl-conrad

Want to know when one of our books is free or discounted? Join the newsletter at http://eepurl.com/bqqB3H

Best regards,

T.L. Conrad and the Next Chapter Team

COMING SOON.... Alex and Natalie think they've found their happily ever after, but danger lurks right around the corner. There's a traitor in Alex's company, someone is trying to gain access to his encrypted files. Alex and Maxim work tirelessly trying to uncover the person behind the cyber-attacks. Keeping Natalie safe is Alex's number one priority, but will he be able to do that when danger comes knocking on their door?

ACKNOWLEDGMENTS

There are so many people who have been an integral part of my writing this story. First, my husband, George. You believed in me long before I believed in myself. You have been my rock throughout this journey. You held me up when I was unable to stand on my own. You dried my tears (on more than one occasion) and you celebrated each success with me. You even wear the t-shirt I bought you. Alex and Natalie's story wouldn't have been possible without your support, love, and endless patience, especially as you listened to revision after revision. I love you more than words can say. I can't wait to continue this writing journey and every other journey in life with you.

To my children—you have been my cheering section through school and this whole writing process. George—graduating together, even though we didn't get to walk on stage, is the coolest thing I've ever done. Your support through school and all my writing was so important to me. Jacob—your technical skills and website help was invaluable throughout all this. If it wasn't for you, I'd still be sitting looking at a blank page. Kayla—your critics and edits are something I'll never forget. Literally will never forget—I saved the page. Thank you for always being willing to read and give me your critiques. Rebekah—your unwavering support helped make this all possible. You always saw the rainbows when all I saw where the clouds.

Max—You taught me some of my first lessons in writing. Your encouragement and support means the world to me. I'm proud to call you my teacher and friend.

Jay—You've been with me since almost day one. You've been through my successes and failures. You cheered me on and gave me pep talks when I needed them. It's your turn now, I can't wait to read your book!

Norman and Nancy—Your friendship and beta reading helped shape this book into what it is today. I value the friendship I've found in you both.

Dr. C—the inspiration and brains behind Dr. Fitzgerald's character. You literally saved Stanley Clarke's life with your rock star trauma surgeon skills.

Last, but certainly not least, Paul. As a professor you are the toughest there is, but that toughness comes from a place of wanting to see your students do their absolute best. At the beginning of my classes I thought I was giving the best, but you asked for more and forced me out of my comfort zone, allowing me to grow as a writer. I can't thank you enough for the lessons I carry with me today. Thank you for holding my hand and guiding me not only through the writing process, but also through the beginnings of getting this story published. I'm honored and privileged to now call you my friend.

ABOUT THE AUTHOR

T.L. (Tara) Conrad is a happily collared submissive and is married to her husband/Dominant, Mr. George. Living a BDSM lifestyle is not always easy, it requires constantly putting your Dominant ahead of yourself, but it is the most satisfying experience. Tara hopes to share the joy of BDSM in her romance novels, where she aims to have characters living as close to real life as possible in a fictional world.

You can keep in touch her and see what she's up to by checking out her website:
www.tlconradauthor.com

or following her on Facebook:
https://www.facebook.com/TaraLConradAuthor

Instagram:
https://www.instagram.com/t.l.conrad/

Twitter:
https://twitter.com/TLConrad1

Submitting To Him
ISBN: 978-4-86750-287-7

Published by
Next Chapter
1-60-20 Minami-Otsuka
170-0005 Toshima-Ku, Tokyo
+818035793528

4th June 2021

CPSIA information can be obtained
at www.ICGtesting.com
Printed in the USA
BVHW030707120222
628863BV00004B/104